"Who taught you to kiss like this?"

"No one." Her sultry voice glided over him in a caress. "You . . . did."

"You never kissed anyone other than me?" he asked, incredulous but also absurdly pleased. When she shook her head, a rush of masculine satisfaction coursed through him. He occupied his mouth with kissing her lips, her cheek, her delicate jaw . . . anything but reveal he wanted her for his own. But Isabel could probably see right through him, the little temptress.

"You have not sold your soul to the Devil, have you?" she whispered teasingly.

"No, but he keeps pounding on my door."

"Stilgoe escorted me to the ball tonight," she shared with him as he nibbled on her adorable earlobe.

"Does he know you came out here to see me?"

She tipped her head aside, inviting him to kiss the sensitive area beneath her ear. "Sophie and Iris . . . but they don't know about you . . . yet. They promised to explain away my absence."

The relief he felt was testimony of his black character. A scrupulous gentleman would send her back inside; he would not ignore her perfectly clear and justifiable insinuations and continue to take liberties with her person. Nevertheless, she looked so achingly beautiful in the moonlight, her delicate features expressing rapture, that he couldn't let her go just yet . . .

Books by Rona Sharon

MY WICKED PIRATE

ONCE A RAKE

Published by Kensington Publishing Corporation

ONCE
A RAKE

RONA SHARON

ZEBRA BOOKS
Kensington Publishing Corp.
www.kensingtonbooks.com

For Ari—
the adorable little lion and recent addition to our family.
I love you.

ZEBRA BOOKS are published by

Kensington Publishing Corp.
850 Third Avenue
New York, NY 10022

All Kensington titles, imprints, and distributed lines are available at special quantity discounts for bulk purchases for sales promotion, premiums, fund-raising, educational, or institutional use.

Special book excerpts or customized printings can also be created to fit specific needs. For details, write or phone the office of the Kensington Special Sales Manager: Attn. Special Sales Department. Kensington Publishing Corp., 850 Third Avenue, New York, NY 10022. Phone: 1-800-221-2647.

Zebra and the Z logo Reg. U.S. Pat. & TM Off.

ISBN-13: 978-0-8217-8058-9
ISBN-10: 0-8217-8058-1

First Printing: December 2007
10 9 8 7 6 5 4 3 2 1

Printed in the United States of America

Chapter One

Like to a hermit poor, in place obscure,
I mean to spend my days of endless doubt,
To wail such woes as time cannot recure,
Where none but Love shall ever find me out.
        —Sir Walter Raleigh

London, 1817

Isabel Aubrey drew a fortifying breath and climbed the front steps of Lancaster House. The Earl of Ashby's private residence was situated on Park Lane, the finest street address in Mayfair. For years she had passed by his home, aware he was somewhere on the Continent, risking his life fighting against Napoleon. Then two years ago, soon after Waterloo, he had come back.

Her heart beat wildly as she tapped the brass knocker against the door and waited. A rotund butler answered the door. "Good morning, miss. How may I help you?"

Isabel smiled. "Good morning. I'm here to call on his lordship."

The butler shook his bald head ruefully. "His lordship

doesn't receive callers, miss. My apologies, and a good day to you." The door closed softly in her face.

Drat. Isabel stepped back, churning with disappointment. She'd been so preoccupied with tamping her emotions upon coming to see him that it hadn't occurred to her Ashby might refuse to see her at all. Yet it was not her in particular he refused to see—it was anyone.

"Shouldn't we return home now, Miss Isabel?" her maid inquired from the sidewalk, where she dutifully kept watch for passersby. Isabel glanced back. Except for a fruit cart, the street was empty. It was yet early for the *haut ton* to crawl out of its soft beds, but she still had to watch out for the demented early risers who went riding in the park. "We'll get into a lot of trouble, should anyone spot us on the Gargoyle's doorstep," her maid added fretfully, glancing right and left.

"Please don't call him so, Lucy," Isabel berated her maid. "His lordship deserves our pity, not our ridicule." Yet Lucy had a point. If word got around that she'd paid a personal visit to the Gargoyle—when it was a very strict rule that no unmarried lady with magnificent prospects ever called on a gentleman except upon a business or a professional matter—her mother would have a fit, and her elder brother, Viscount Stilgoe, would marry her off to the first single gentleman she waltzed with at Almack's on Wednesday. She'd exhausted every possible excuse for misconduct when she had turned down five eligible beaux, declaring that none of the fellows would do.

Think! she ordered herself. There had to be a way to approach the earl. Gnawing on her lip, an idea entered her head. It was somewhat bold, but it seemed to be her only recourse. She fumbled in her reticule and took out a pencil and an elegant calling card, which in addition to her name stated her active role as Chairwoman of the Widows, Mothers & Sisters of War Society. She wrote a short message on the back of the card. Before she lost her nerve, she knocked again.

The butler was quick to respond. "Kindly give his lordship my card and ask him to read the line on the back," she instructed, before he shut the door in her face a second time.

The butler's kind eyes softened sympathetically. "You are not the first young lady who has come calling, miss. He wouldn't see any of them. I am sorry."

Isabel stiffened. "I am not one of his . . . lady friends. His lordship was my brother's friend, and his senior officer. He will see me. Please give him my card."

The butler's scrutiny shifted between her and the demure maid standing a few steps behind her. He took the card. "I shall inquire." The door closed again.

Isabel kneaded her hands. What she would never have been able to imagine, even in her worst nightmares, was the formidable Earl of Ashby—Colonel Lord Ashby, Commander of the 18th Hussars—resigned to the sad state of a recluse. That a battle wound should force him into a self-imposed isolation was . . . inconceivable. The Ashby she so well remembered was a force of nature: Sharp, charming, strong, and godlike handsome, he was also fabulously wealthy, which in and of itself was enough to entice the *ton* to forgive a facial disfigurement, severe though it may be. Yet apparently his countless virtues were not enough for Ashby to forgive it.

The butler reappeared. "Do come in, Miss Aubrey. His lordship will see you."

He remembered. Pleased with her triumph, Isabel walked inside. Lancaster House was a grand, silver-and-blue palace, with a shimmering chandelier hanging from a two-story ceiling. So this was where he lived, she gazed about excitedly, where he had been hiding from the world for the past two years. She couldn't help wondering, though, how one—particularly a man as vigorous as Ashby—occupied his time caged inside a house all by himself. She'd be scaling walls within a week, and she hadn't spent years charging on horseback beneath an open sky.

Leaving Lucy in the foyer, she followed the butler into a front sitting room. A collection of sculptures set on a glass shelf caught her attention: Little monkeys skillfully whittled of wood. One of them, she noted with amused horror, bore a frightful resemblance to Wellington. Another was the spitting image of Lord Castlereagh. "The Gargoyle is an artist." She smiled, lifting a plump ape which reminded her of Prince George. "And he has a very wicked sense of humor . . ."

"The Gargoyle doesn't appreciate strangers poking at his personal effects."

Isabel jumped. Prinny was snatched from her hand and put back on the glass shelf.

"You wished to see me?" A gangling, grim, gray-haired man stood before her. He bore no resemblance to the devil-may-care hussar Will had brought to dinner years ago.

Her heart sank. *Good God.* "What hap—?" Clamping her mouth shut, she curtsied politely. Had the war done this to him? Or had her mind glorified his image over the years? Even his rust coat was too large for his frame. Morosely, she searched his face for a scar. He had none.

The earl regarded her circumspectly. "Is there anything I may do for you, Miss . . . ?"

"Aubrey, my lord. Will's sister." *He didn't recognize her.* Then what made him open his door for her when he wouldn't do so for anyone else, not even for his lady friends?

"Aubrey . . . Major William Aubrey? Oh, yes, of course I remember him. Please accept my deepest condolences for the loss of your excellent brother, Miss Aubrey. He was a fine officer."

Isabel frowned. Something was terribly amiss. Will had been his best friend for years and this was all he had to say? "Did you . . . read my card, my lord?" she asked delicately. No one but Ashby would understand what she'd so boldly alluded to in the message on her card.

Her host, however, seemed utterly clueless. "Your card?" He blinked.

The truth hit her as a thunderbolt: *This man is an imposter*. Why else would he invent an injury which did not exist other than to justify his withdrawal from Society? It meant one thing: Ashby was dead, buried somewhere in a cold field in Belgium alongside her brother, while this villain assumed his identity and lived off his estate! She had to get out of there. Someone needed to be informed of this. "Thank you for seeing me, my lord. Alas, I've just remembered I had a previous engagement. It's been a pleasure." She hurried to the door.

The double-doors opened to reveal the butler. He read her expression and instantly stepped in, shutting the doors behind him. "Miss Aubrey, we are his lordship's servants," he said quietly.

"Oh, Phipps, you bloody idiot," the imposter ranted at the butler. "We may hang for this, you know. You and your asinine ideas."

"It would've been a brilliant idea, if you hadn't been an abject imbecile," Phipps retorted, frothing with exasperation. "All you had to do was discover what she wanted."

"How was I supposed to find *that* out? What am I—a bloody Bow Street Runner?"

Isabel's sharp gaze shifted between the pudgy butler and his lanky accomplice, her mind spinning on course again. A runner—that's whom she should speak to!

The imposter dabbed a handkerchief at his damp brow. "All she mentioned was her card."

Phipps plucked her card out of his vest pocket and read the short message. "What does it mean?" he asked her, looking vastly intrigued.

"Why don't you ask his lordship?" she replied tartly. Glancing at the doors, she called out, "Lucy! Run to Stilgoe! Tell him to return with a Bow Street Runner! This man is an imposter!"

"Yes, Miss Isabel!" Lucy's muffled reply came from the foyer.

"Do not let her get away!" Phipps ordered his accomplice and ran outside. Detained by the imposter, now manning the doorway, Isabel heard the front door open and close with a bang.

"He's blockading the front door, Miss Isabel!" Lucy cried. "What should I do now?"

"Quick, Lucy!" Isabel exclaimed. "Thrust the tip of my parasol between his ribs!"

"Ouch!" the butler yelped in the foyer. "You nasty little thing!"

"It didn't work!" Lucy announced. "What should I try next?"

Isabel glared at the imposter. He shrugged apologetically. Wishing the pox on his head, she peered beyond his shoulder. "Lucy, I see a flower vase in the corner. Smash it across his skull!"

"Dudley, shut her up, will you?" Phipps begged out loud. "I am being murdered out here!"

As Dudley glanced outside, Isabel flung her reticule, bashing his head. "Hateful villains!" she cried, dashing past him. "You'll rot in Newgate for this!" She saw Phipps cowering at the front door as Lucy took aim with the flower vase. She heard Dudley stumbling behind her. She was almost there when a terrible canine bark froze the lot of them. Lucy dropped the flower vase.

"Down, Hector," a deep, masculine voice commanded from the gallery. Isabel looked up, her breath coming in short gasps. The chandelier blocked her view, but through the sculpted bars of the banister she saw a black-coated retriever sitting vigilantly next to a pair of polished black Hessians. "Dudley, is that my coat you're wearing?" Ashby's voice resonated above them.

Dudley cringed. "Yes, my lord, but I can explain—"

"I should hope so. Phipps, stand aside. Let the women go."

Phipps hung desolate eyes on the daunting form towering over the foyer. "My lord, I—"

"Now, Phipps!" Leather creaked as Ashby turned on his heel.

Isabel shook herself. This was her chance. "Lord Ashby, may I see you privately for a moment? Merely to ascertain that no trickery is played and that you are indeed—"

He halted. Distant eyes perused her through the dappled shimmer of the chandelier. "Wait in the sitting room," he said after a long pause. "I'll be with you shortly." His boot heels pounded the hardwood as he left the gallery, receding deeper inside the house.

Phipps approached her with a contrite expression. "Miss Aubrey, I beg you, forgive me."

"Me, too." Dudley nodded briskly, the overlarge coat hanging neatly on his forearm.

"We had no intention of frightening you—" Phipps continued.

"Or your maid," Dudley inserted. "He wouldn't have seen you unless we did something . . ."

"Drastic. We sincerely apologize." They stared at her pleadingly, Dudley rubbing the bump on his head, Phipps hugging his tender ribs.

Isabel eyed the two misfits. "I expect you to apologize to Lucy as well," she bit out crossly.

"We shall do so at once," they promised in unison, bowing humbly.

Isabel returned to the front sitting room. She paced about, anticipation wreaking havoc on her nerves. Confident strides approached the doorway. She held her breath, waiting to see if . . .

He walked onto the threshold, and her heart slammed hard against her rib cage. "Ashby."

Wearing a black satin mask, the earl leaned against the doorframe, his arms folded across his broad chest. "What a relief. For a moment I feared I might end up in Newgate." Thick, glossy dark hair tumbled in uneven lengths to his powerful shoulders. A white lawn shirt revealed the pulse beating at the base of his throat and the well-formed muscles shaping his chest. Snug black breeches molded his lean thighs, accenting supple sinew developed through years in a saddle. Tall, strapping, and utterly ferocious, he exuded damn-your-eyes virility.

She curtsyed, her sky blue eyes wide with awe. Years ago they said women swooned when he walked into a ballroom, and that he was the only gentleman ever in need of a dance card. She hadn't quite understood it as a girl; she did now. Even masked, his dark allure had the effect of a magnet. This was a man who could have anything—and anyone—he wanted.

Watching her through a pair of eye-slits, his gaze traveled the length of her, from the pretty yellow bonnet framing her sun-golden curls to her matching yellow morning dress. When he met her gaze, she realized her memory had deceived her in one respect: His eyes were not blue—that must have been a trick of his blue uniform—they were, in fact, an unusual shade of light marine green. Abruptly he disengaged from the doorframe. "State your business and be off."

Isabel merely gaped at him.

"I see." His sensuous lips curved cynically beneath the mask. "Well, now that you have *ascertained* whatever it was you needed to *and* satisfied your curiosity at the same time, I bid you farewell." He crossed the room in five long strides, his black dog loping after him. With a snap of his wrist, he drew the heavy curtain over the street-facing window, throwing the room into semi-darkness. She dreaded to imagine what he faced each day in the mirror. It had to be terrible indeed, for Ashby to shut himself away from the world.

Isabel pulled herself together. "Lord Ashby, I represent the Widows, Mothers & Sisters of War Society. We are a charity organization, working in aid of destitute women who've lost their male providers in the war. Shopkeepers, blacksmiths, farmers, they've left dependent relatives, women and children, behind. Today these poor souls have no one. Our goal is to help them—"

"I don't give a damn about your goals, madam. Good day." He headed for the door.

As he sauntered past her, she gripped his arm. Steely muscles bunched beneath her fingers. "You ought to, my lord," she asserted. "They concern the families of the men you commanded, your brave soldiers who died on the battlefield."

His gaze slid along his arm and returned to her eyes. "And your point is?"

She released him. "You were responsible for these women's deceased loved ones. Don't you think your men might expect you to do something—anything—to help their kin?"

Moving closer, he pinned her in his glinting gaze. "My duty was to destroy. I'm done."

She caught a whiff of his shaving soap; the cool scent made her think of forests and glades. Refusing to back down, she sustained his glare. "Perhaps if you knew my brother's name—"

"I know who you are, Isabel."

Her heart lurched. "You do?" she asked, suddenly unable to breathe. She hoped he found her . . . somewhat attractive, if only for the sake of her female pride. She was half-mad for him as a girl, while he was known to be very wicked at the time. A notorious rake, gambler, and pursuer of women, the wags tagged him, but Will claimed that most of the heavy attention his friend attracted was due to his coming into his title so early in life. It was Isabel's personal opinion, though, that it was Ashby's unique character which set him apart from the *ton's* pack of rakish young bloods.

"You grew up," he murmured. "The last time I saw you, you wore short blue skirts and had bouncing curls."

A hot flush crept up her cheeks. "That was seven years ago." The last time she'd seen him, he sported his regimentals: white breeches, a blue dolman jacket with silver bars stretching over his chest, a similar fur-lined pelisse dangling from one shoulder. He was magnificent. She made a complete fool of herself over him then. She was fifteen years old. "You kept Hector," she said.

"I promised you I would." The black satin mask concealed most of his face, but it revealed his hard jaw, chin, and mouth—which she happened to know felt as soft as it looked.

Tearing her gaze away, she sank to the carpet and gave a soft, melodious whistle. The large dog sat up, his ears twitching. Deciding to investigate up close, he came over to sniff her hand.

"Hello, Hector. Do you remember me?" She buried her fingers in his shiny coat, rubbing and stroking. "We were excellent friends once, when you were a tiny pup." He barked, wagging his tail happily. She laughed. "My, you've grown. You're so beautiful and big and strong." She lifted her eyes, seeking Ashby's inscrutable gaze. "I see you've been well taken care of."

"I have," Ashby replied, though they both knew she had spoken to the dog. "Hector saved my life twice. We're practically brothers." He offered her his hand.

Heart thumping, she put her hand in his warm, large palm and let him help her to her feet. They stood very close to one another, surrounded by the dimness created by the heavy drapes.

"I'm sorry about Will," he said gruffly. "I promised you I would bring him back. I failed."

"I'm sorry, too," she murmured. "For what happened to you at Waterloo."

"Sorauren," he breathed. "I lost my face at Sorauren."

"That was four years ago." She had only found out when people began whispering about him, referring to Ashby as "the Gargoyle of Mayfair." "Will never mentioned—"

"That I'd become hideous? Will was a saint. He never

gossiped about his friends. He made them feel human, even when there was nothing human left in them."

Staring deep into his anguished, burning eyes, her heart welled with compassion. "Lord Ashby, you are the kindest, gentlest, most generous man I've ever known. I don't believe you could ever lose your humanity."

"You'd be surprised."

His harsh words sent an unpleasant shiver through her. "I know bleakness and despair, my lord, but I discovered that by helping others—people less fortunate than I—one heals oneself."

"I'm thrilled you've found your golden path, but not every method works for everyone."

Before he turned away, she said, "Have you ever seen a child light up with joy at the sight of a hot meal or when he is warm again or when he sees his mother smiling because you helped her in some small way? You and I, we have so much to give, it is our duty to give it."

He fell silent for a moment. "What sort of help do you require of me?"

His tone didn't guarantee his assistance, but he was curious. "Our charity board has hired a solicitor to draw up a proposal for a reform bill by which annual compensations would be paid to the aforementioned relatives, women and children, now deprived of means of sustenance."

"When you say 'our board,' I presume you mean you?"

"Lady Iris Chilton, Mrs. Sophie Fairchild, and myself, yes."

"Go on."

"We seek an influential gentleman to champion our cause and push legislation across. As a member of the House, you—"

"I haven't attended sessions in the House of Lords for a long time. Nor do I intend to begin doing so in the foreseeable future. Ergo, I am not the . . . champion you seek. Anything else?"

"With your power and influence, and with your connections in the War Office, you could contribute to our cause far more than anyone else without attending Parliament."

"You are wrong, Isabel," he said solemnly. "I have nothing to contribute to anyone."

You have something to contribute to me, she thought glumly. An image of Ashby and Will laughing together wrenched her heart. "Perhaps . . . we could help each other," she offered gently.

His jaw tightened. "I wasn't aware I needed help."

"You are not the only person in England this war has scarred, my lord."

"How would you help me?" he bit out angrily. "My life is over." He glimpsed at her lips. When his gaze touched hers, she knew with a certainty he recalled *everything* that had happened outside her house that long ago night. The intensity of his stare both frightened and thrilled her.

Isabel let out a shuddering breath. Alas, she'd learned her lesson where he was concerned. "You once told me you considered Will a brother. As his sister, I would be happy to—"

"Don't—patronize me," he growled, staring at her as though she had slapped him. "I'm not one of your bloody charity cases! If I were the man I was four years ago, you'd be thoroughly compromised by now."

Isabel flinched, taken aback by the force of his fury. "Forgive me. I never—"

"Go home, Isabel, and don't come back here ever again. The *Gargoyle* deserves neither your pity nor your ridicule." He strode out of the sitting room, dismissing her altogether.

"Did I not instruct that *no one* was to be admitted inside this house?" The enraged bellow would send rats scurrying into holes in the walls, if there were any. Furious, Ashby pounded up the stairs, cursing under his breath. *Damn that chit!* Why did she have to burst into his life again?

Hurrying after him, Phipps gasped, "She threatened me with bodily harm, my lord."

Ashby turned around so abruptly, his butler nearly tumbled down the stairs. "And another thing—didn't I specifically tell you to keep the drapes drawn at all times?"

Phipps gripped the handrail, wheezing. "You did, my lord, but I couldn't very well admit Miss Aubrey into a dark room, could I?"

"You shouldn't have admitted her in the first place, you . . . abject meddler!" His temples throbbing, Ashby reached the second floor and headed for his bedchamber. He needed to . . . smash something, anything, to get the image of Isabel Aubrey standing in a halo of sunlight out of his head. Christ, had she changed! He'd hardly recognized her. Little Izzy was a beautiful doll with shining eyes and ribbons in her hair. The full-grown woman he'd just met was . . . *heart-wrenching*. Perhaps it wasn't the nicest compliment a gentleman ever paid a lady, but that was exactly how it felt, seeing that vision of femininity brightening his parlor, her exquisite oval face framed with soft, sunny tendrils, her perfect pink lips parted in astonishment, her tall, lissome, shapely figure ripe for plucking. He couldn't believe she actually suggested he consider her a sister. She didn't think of him as a brother that long ago night, when he was young and whole. *Bloody, bloody hell*. She made him feel like a relic, a doddering old man broken beyond repair, when what he ached to do was finish that kiss she had begun seven years ago.

Ashby ripped the mask from his face and threw it over his shoulder, knowing his shadow would be there to catch it. "Is there a specific reason you're tailing me around my own house? I assure you, I am perfectly capable of finding my way around."

"I should like to clarify, if I may, that Dudley was all against impersonating you, my lord."

Ashby snorted with disgust. "Where the devil is that intrepid valet of mine?"

"Gone into hiding, my lord."

"Good. Keep him there." Entering his bedchamber, Ashby strode to his dresser and pulled out a drawer. He rummaged around it, but didn't find what he was looking for. Phipps coughed. Annoyed, Ashby glared at him. "Why are you still in my doorway, huffing and puffing?"

"I'd be in a much better form were I required to admit callers on occasion, my lord."

"You'd be in a much better form if instead of putting on charades, you ran this household proficiently." Ashby pulled out the second drawer and continued his search. Unsuccessfully.

Watching his master methodically take his dresser apart, Phipps said meekly, "Most men would be in a happier state of mind after an impromptu visit from a pretty butterfly, my lord."

"A butterfly!" Ashby smirked. "She and her maid have all but done away with you."

Phipps shrugged. "I did provide her with ample reasons to think ill of me."

"You provide me with reasons daily, and yet I don't take parasols and flower vases to your person. I am, however, seriously considering packing you off to Ashby Park."

The butler started. "I wouldn't dream of abandoning you, your lordship."

"Pity." Unable to locate what he was seeking, Ashby moved to search the closet. And the pest still hovered. "Speak your mind, Phipps, before I grow old and gray."

"It concerns Miss Aubrey, my lord. I believe her purpose in coming here was not entirely impersonal." Phipps produced a calling card out of his vest pocket.

"So you've been eavesdropping. What a shock." Ashby

pushed aside the superfine jackets hanging in the closet and bent down to search the boxes neatly stacked at the bottom. He opened one after another, crushing new cravats he would never wear and tossing them over his shoulder.

Phipps went on. "Miss Aubrey's reaction upon discovering the charade was . . . well, she was quite distraught."

"Obviously. She believed you and Dudley were a pair of criminals, Phipps."

"That's precisely my point, my lord. She should have been frightened, but instead, she was furious and—well, I couldn't help noticing—genuinely grief-stricken."

Not allowing his butler to see his expression, Ashby rationalized, "She lost her brother not too long ago. He was very dear to her. I was his closest friend, his commander."

"Then why did you send her away . . . in tears, your lordship?"

He'd been half tempted to lock her in and swallow the key, but then he would have had to spend the rest of his life behind a mask. Sweet, kindhearted Isabel who took stray puppies off the streets would drop in a dead faint if she saw him unmasked. *He was not a bloody charity case!*

Gritting his teeth, Ashby confronted his butler. "Where the devil did you put it, Phipps?"

"Which item would that be, my lord?"

Ashby fixed his butler with an exasperated glare. "You know bloody well which item!"

The butler hurried forth. "In the trunk under your bed, where you keep your regimentals and medals, but do you think it's wise, my lord? The last time you—"

"I'll decide what is and isn't wise in this house. Now bugger off!" Ashby nudged him aside and dropped to his knees before the bed. He pulled the heavy trunk and cracked the lid open. He hadn't touched it in two years and his hands shook as he did so now.

"It's wrapped in the shabraque, my lord."

Ashby lunged to his feet. He turned Phipps around, pushed him out the door, and kicked it shut. On second thought, he turned the key in the lock. The daft man thought his duties included those of a nursemaid. It was the story of his life: servants who raised him, coddled him, saw to his every need, and never knew when to leave off. Exhaling haggardly, he dropped on the bed and stared at the open trunk. His regimentals were folded inside, with his fur cap, Mameluke saber, flintlock pistol, and his medals on top. The sight brought back a range of memories, few pleasant, most of them . . . unbearable. "What precisely are you hoping to find?" he asked himself.

The last time he performed this self-destructive idiocy, he ended up smashing every mirror in the house, except for one—his mother's hand mirror. Ashby buried his arm in the folds of the shabraque, his ornate saddle cloth, and there it was. He took it out, not yet daring to look at it.

Three different surgeons had refused to operate on him, swearing it would cost him his life. Only an assistant field-surgeon, a diminutive Indian fellow Will had found in a foot battalion camp, agreed to perform the surgery. Later, Ashby was told that the foreigner had saved his life.

He shut his eyes against the old pain and self-recriminations. Will had saved his wretched life and what had he done in return? The memory of a pistol shot resonated in his heart. Ashby shuddered, anguish lacerating his soul. Perhaps this was part of the torture in seeing Will's sister again. Both in spirit and in appearance, Isabel was a replica of the only true friend he ever had.

How could he help her when he could barely help himself?

He opened his eyes and stared at the gargoyle he held in his hand. "Damn you to hell," he rasped, as the gargoyle in the hand mirror mouthed the same thing back at him.

Someone scratched the door. Ashby raised his eyes in time to see a calling card sliding in from underneath the door onto the carpet. He pushed to his feet and went to pick up the card.

It was elegantly embossed with Isabel's name and role as chairwoman of her charity.

"Look at the back side," Phipps suggested. If Ashby didn't know better, he would swear the pest had drilled eyeholes in the door. Cursing, he turned the card over and a tight fist coiled around his heart. In a neat, slightly florid hand was written, "I need your special skills."

Chapter Two

Was this the face that launched a thousand ships,
And burnt the topless towers of Ilium?
Sweet Helen, make me immortal with a kiss.
—Christopher Marlowe:
The Tragical History Of Doctor Faustus

Seven Dover Street, 7 years ago

"I wonder what's for dinner." Captain William Aubrey smacked his lips as they trotted into Dover Street. "I smell oxtail stew, pork and apple pie, and roast beef with Yorkshire pudding."

"You didn't notify them that we were coming for three days?" Ashby asked.

"Why spoil the surprise?" Will smiled. "Izzy will shriek and cry and it'll be splendid fun."

A smile tugged at Ashby's lips. "She always reacts that way when you visit."

Will eyed him sardonically. "When *I* visit?"

Ashby felt his face warm. "Stop that, Will. She mustn't know that I know."

Will burst out laughing. "The entire world knows my little sister has a *tendre* for you, Ash. It's obvious to anyone with eyes and ears."

"No, it isn't, and her knowing that I know will only embarrass her."

"The only one who seems embarrassed by this is you, Ashby." Will chuckled. "I swear, with all these madwomen throwing themselves at you in every town and garrison, not to mention those here in London, my chit of a sister is the one who makes you blush. Bloody capital."

It was true. Izzy Aubrey made him blush. Furiously. He supposed the reason for his absurd reaction to the little chit had something to do with her reasons for liking him. Women had always liked him. They liked his title, his money, some even his wicked reputation, and mostly how his body made them feel, but a fifteen-year-old chit? Now that was a mystery he was unable to solve.

"Speak of the little she-devil . . ." Will chuckled as they spotted Isabel sitting on a bench near the rose garden, a tiny black pup cuddled in her lap. "Isabel Jane Aubrey!" Will called out. "Come and kiss your bone-tired brother hello!"

"Will!" Izzy shrieked, bounding to her feet. Her gaze darted to Ashby and an adoring glow spread in her wide, sky blue irises. Ashby's heart missed a beat, then it expanded to absorb the warmth she instilled in him. Vaguely he recalled feeling this way once, a long, long time ago.

"I rest my case," Will mumbled. He swung off his horse and opened his arms in invitation. Izzy put the pup in its padded basket on the bench and flew into her brother's arms.

Enjoying the scene, Ashby swung down and tossed his and Will's reins to a waiting groom. "Don't I get a kiss?" He smiled, meeting her eyes while she rested her cheek on Will's chest.

Isabel extricated herself from her brother's embrace and timidly approached him. Her color was high; her girlish smile melted his heart. "Captain Lord Ashby." She bobbed. He bent his head, and she rose on tiptoe to softly kiss his cheek.

"Major now," Will corrected.

"Congratulations! You've made it before Will did." The glorious smile Isabel bestowed on him put Ashby in a daze. She didn't mind; she applauded him. No one but his servants ever did, and they were paid to be respectful.

"Thank you." Ashby nodded stiffly, his throat clogged.

"And he'll probably make lieutenant colonel by the time he's thirty," Will remarked. "Do I smell Eccles cake?" He sniffed the air, tripping after his nose.

"You've smelled every meal from Cuidad Rodrigo to St. James's Street." Ashby smirked.

Izzy shook herself. "Will, wait. I need you to take a look at my new puppy. He won't stand on his left foreleg, but I couldn't find anything wrong with it."

"What do I know of pups? Ask the expert." He waved his arm at Ashby. "Here's your man with the special skills." He went inside the house, announcing his presence to everyone else.

Izzy stared at Ashby. He ambled to the bench. "Let's take a look at your pup, shall we?" They sat side by side. Izzy lifted the tiny black ball from its basket and put it in Ashby's hands.

"I don't know how he got here. He seems but a few days' old. I wonder what happened to his mother and siblings. I couldn't find them anywhere within a mile of Dover Street."

The tiny thing filled the palm of his hand. Ashby caressed it, running his finger along the pup's neck and making it gurgle with pleasure. "Left foreleg, you say? Let's see." He rolled the dog gently onto its back and examined the leg. "No scrapes. No bruises. No broken bones." He tried to set the pup on its feet, but favoring its left foreleg, the pup tilted aside and fell. Ashby scooped it up tenderly. "Where did you say you found this black ball of fur?"

"He was ruining Mama's roses," Isabel replied. "She wanted to toss him in the street."

"The rose garden . . ." Ashby smiled. He took the tiny leg and carefully examined its paw. "Uh-ha." He plucked out a thin, almost invisible thorn and offered it to Isabel. "Here's your problem."

Isabel's eyes shone. "You're a great gun, Ashby . . . beg pardon, Major Lord Ashby."

"Call me P . . ." His heart began thudding. "You may call me Ashby. Everyone else does."

"Thank you, . . . Ashby." As she pressed another chaste kiss on his cheek, the pup leapt from his lap, onto the drive, and hopped up the front steps. "Dear lord! Not in the house!" She dashed after the dog, burnished locks bouncing on her shoulders, short blue skirts swelling around the pantalets concealing her slender calves, and vanished inside the house.

Ashby came to a decision; it was the most shocking one he'd ever made: He wanted a wife. He wanted this, what Will and Izzy had, a home, with children and puppies to greet his face, with mouthwatering treats cooking in the kitchen. He wanted someone other than solicitors, bankers, or estate managers to correspond with from the front line. He wanted a family. It was the only sane thing worth living for, the one thing he'd want to return to when the war was over.

Whistling with satisfaction, he walked into the familiar bedlam of Seven Dover Street and met Will at the foot of the stairway. Will's mouth was stuffed with cake. "Fixed the dog?"

"I fixed the dog."

The anarchy upstairs grew louder. "Let's find out what's so bloody interesting up there."

They padded upstairs and nearly tripped over the pup as it dashed downward. Shrieks and footfalls followed as an army charged straight at them: Teddy and Freddy, Will's eight-year-old twin sisters—miniature duplicates of Izzy—were at the lead, followed by Izzy herself, and three anxious servants cringing from Lady Hyacinth's infuriated, shrill voice. "If that dirty thing is not out the door in one minute, you'll be looking for new posts first thing tomorrow morning!"

"Welcome to Seven Dover Street." Will chuckled.

Ashby grinned. *A home, with children and puppies to greet his face.* Firmly resolved, he followed Will to the first floor drawing room to greet the dragoness.

"Oh, William! My dearest boy!" Lady Hyacinth swooped on Will, pasting a loud kiss on his cheek. "And my dear Captain Lord Ashby, how good of you to come. Oh! You must join us for dinner. I absolutely insist. I care not what elaborate dishes they are presently preparing for you at Lancaster House. You must sit with us and tell us all about Wellington."

"I would love to stay for dinner, Lady Hyacinth." Ashby smiled.

"Good. Then it's settled. Now I must send someone to fetch Stilgoe from White's. Norris!"

"Your brother lives well," Ashby remarked to Will with half a smile.

Will shrugged. "Yes, well, not everyone is like you, Ash."

"Don't judge him. He has a family to look after, as most of the aristocracy. I don't."

"Of course you do." Will slapped his back fondly. "What are we, little goats? Besides, if anything should happen to you, Izzy will never speak to me again."

Ashby cracked a smile. "You know, I just might run off with her to Gretna Green, if she keeps smiling at me like that."

"Please! Do! Go off with her! Restore our peace of mind!"

"Your mama won't like it." Ashby grinned.

"Are you serious?" Will's face wrinkled comically. "My mother would make an offering to the gods! I think she secretly does, anyway . . ." Will hushed up as Lady Hyacinth reentered.

"Oh, dear. Look at you." Scowling, she perused their dusty

regimentals. "You must wash and change before dinner. Will, show Ashby to the guest chamber, why don't you, my love?"

"Ashby knows where the guest chamber is, Mama." Will strolled out, leading the way, nonetheless. "By the bye, Ash, my sister's bedchamber is over there," he pointed at the opposite direction while they traversed the hallway, "should you ever decide to run off with her."

"Don't tempt me."

"Just a thought . . ." Will threw his hands in the air as he walked into his bedchamber.

Ashby continued down the hallway, heading for the guest chamber. The idea of running off with Isabel was both amusing and petrifying. He was thirteen years her senior. By the time the war ended and she grew up, he'd be so old, she wouldn't remember what she ever saw in him.

He bathed and changed into a clean uniform and sent a note to Lancaster House, informing Phipps that he'd be arriving much later. He and Will had already made their stop at the Horse Guards to collect Ashby's new rank, so he was free for the next three days. After that it was back to hell, but not before he paid a visit to a certain lady. Tomorrow, he determined, he would go to Ashby Park to see Olivia. His heart warmed at the prospect. Olivia had hinted on more than one occasion that were he ever to propose, she wouldn't wait till after the war to have the wedding. She'd also let him know that she wouldn't mind not waiting in other respects as well, should they agree upon a later date in which to take their vows. This was something he was not in a hurry to act upon. The last thing he cared to do was leave her with a fatherless child.

As they convened around the dinner table, Ashby noticed Isabel was missing.

"Gads, Ashby! Look at you!" Charles Aubrey, Viscount Stilgoe, gave him an appreciative once-over. "What are you—a major now? Impressive, old chap. Who'd have thought back in the merry old days at Cambridge that you'd become a war hero one day?"

Ashby nodded with a smile. "I'm still not over the shock, myself." He leaned aside and in a hushed voice asked Will, "Where's Izzy? She's not dining with us?"

Will shrugged. "Haven't a clue. She never misses dinner when you're in attendance." He looked across the table. "Theodora, Frederica, where's your older sister?"

"In high dungeon!" Little Freddy announced, grunting sternly.

"In high dud-geon, puss," Will rectified. "Where is she?"

"She's very high, up in the attic with her new puppy," Teddy informed everyone.

"No, she's not!" Freddy disputed. "She's in her bedchamber, but she said she wouldn't come down to dinner until Mama agreed to let her keep the black puppy." She turned pleading eyes onto her mother. "Can we have puppies, too, Mama?"

Lady Hyacinth sniffed. "No, you *may* not. And neither may Izzy. If she is more obstinate than hungry, she may just as well remain in her bedchamber until her condition reverses itself."

"Perhaps I shall influence her to join us." Ashby excused himself from the table and went upstairs. He wasn't certain which of the girls' chambers belonged to Izzy, so he padded quietly, listening for cooing noises. What he heard was the sound of a girl crying. He swallowed hard and knocked lightly on her door.

"Go away!" Isabel's sniffling voice called out.

"It's Ashby, Isabel. May I please come in?"

"You may not. I'm alone."

Ashby shook his head, smiling. The chit was concerned with propriety. Hell, why not? He was a man; she had every right to view herself as a young lady. "I'll leave the door open, then."

"All right." She sniffed.

He found her sitting on the floor, fiddling with the padded basket. Her large blue eyes were red; her nose puffy. Leaving the door half open, he strolled in. "Where's the little black devil?" he inquired, perusing her chamber. He'd never visited little chits' chambers before, older ones' yes, but those didn't have frilly pink drapes and dolls on the bed.

"He's hiding under the bed." Izzy blew her nose in a handkerchief, not meeting his gaze. "Everyone was chasing after him and now he's scared to death, poor thing."

"He's not scared." Ashby sat on the floor beside her, one booted foot firm on the ground to support his hand on his knee. "He's too young to know the meaning of fear. He probably thought it was all just a splendid game. He'll come out soon. You'll see."

"I tried to lure him out, but he wouldn't come. No doubt he's afraid of me, too, now."

Ashby glanced at the frilly pink bed. "Did you try tempting him with food?"

She indicated a small cup of milk put on the floor close to the bed. "He won't touch it."

One day he'd have a daughter just like her, Ashby thought with pleasure. "Don't you think you are overreacting a bit? He is a dog, Izzy."

"He's my responsibility."

"He is your responsibility because you chose to make him that."

"Yes, I did." Lifting her head, her glorious mane exploded into fiery curls as coppery and golden as the sunset; her eyes blazed with emotion; her rounded cheeks glowed with heat; her plump lips trembled with fury. "We can't all put blindfolds over our eyes and pretend we do not see the suffering out there. Or worse, rely on someone else to dispose of the problem. The little dog has no one in the entire world, Ashby. Is it at all graspable to you?"

His throat constricted. A little girl—whom was he fooling?

She was a little woman with the potential to ensnare any man's heart, mind, and soul. "Why is your mother adamantly against your adopting the little dog?"

"My mother fears he'll ruin her furniture," she drawled scathingly. "I'm to leave a bowl of milk for him outside the kitchen." Tears flooded her beautiful eyes. "Food and temporary shelter aren't remotely sufficient. If he runs out to the street, a coach will squish him. He may be just a dog, but he's also a baby and an orphan. He needs to be loved. How will he survive otherwise?"

He almost wished he were the dog. "Creatures survive without love," he stated softly.

She regarded him disdainfully, as if he were the cruelest man alive. "Thank you for coming up here, my lord, but your dinner is getting cold."

Her icy glare was more than he could bear. "If I promise to take very good care of the little pup, will you let me take him with me?"

She looked horrified. "To the frontier in Spain?"

"Many soldiers keep dogs. He'll stay with the caravan while I . . ."

"When you're off risking your life," she finished, tears rolling off her creamy cheeks. The glow was back in her eyes, though, and something else—profound concern for his safety. "I apologize for snapping at you. Please forgive me. You are the kindest, most generous man . . ."

Ashby could breathe again. He stood up. "No, I'm not. Now let's go down to dinner. We'll leave the door closed, so Hector won't escape while we're dining."

"Hector?" She smiled, standing up.

"Why not? Hector was a great warrior. I might need such a friend at my side. He'll help me look after Will." He followed her out to the hallway, shutting her bedchamber door after him.

"Suppose he refuses to come out from under the bed?" Izzy asked as they took the stairs.

"He'll come out eventually. Trust me."

She stared at his profile. "For milk?"

"For milk, for a caress, whichever he needs more." From the corner of his eye he saw that his comment pleased her. He grinned. "I'd crawl out for a caress." And he walked right into it.

"I'll be sure to remember that, Ashby." She smiled engagingly.

It was comments such as this that made him blush. *Gads*.

Everyone was pleased when they joined the table between the oxtail stew and the pork and apple pie. "I'm very happy you finally came to your senses, Izzy," Hyacinth declared.

Izzy's smile was small but triumphant. "Ashby offered to adopt my dog. He'll take Hector with him to Spain."

"Hector?" Will snickered softly. "I fear you're in danger of growing a halo, my friend."

Ashby met Isabel's smiling eyes. He had his reward right here and now.

"Do you really intend to take the whelp with you?" Stilgoe asked after dinner, when only the men remained at the table to drink whiskey and smoke cigars.

"I gave Izzy my word," Ashby replied. "I can't renege now."

"You could leave it with Phipps." Will eyed him with a raised eyebrow.

"Phipps doesn't know the first thing about dogs." Ashby tossed his entire drink back and felt his throat catching fire. He also felt like an idiot, not because he'd offered to care for the pup, but because of the reason he'd done it. "And I can't very well leave the dog with Olivia."

"Olivia, right . . ." Will murmured, his eyes frosting with disdain. "No doubt she'd boil the poor thing and feed it to the servants."

"It would hurt Izzy's feelings," Ashby clarified.

"Really? How would it hurt my sister's feelings?"

Ashby met Will's suspicious, angry gaze. "I made up my mind to ask Olivia to marry me."

"And when did this epiphany occur?"

"Today." Why the devil did he feel like he needed to apologize? Ashby swore.

Will glanced at his older brother. "Charlie, would you mind leaving us alone for a few minutes?"

"Not at all." Stilgoe stood. "I've a card game waiting for me at Boodle's." He circled the table and patted Ashby's shoulder. "Take care, old chap. I'll see you tomorrow, Will."

As soon as they were alone, Will attacked. "Olivia? Have you completely and thoroughly lost your mind? I thought the crazy heroic thing on the Bussaco Ridge was a moment of insanity, to help push for the new rank, not an advanced stage of a fully developed mental illness."

Ashby poured himself another glass of whiskey. "That's a fine thing coming from you."

"Explain."

He whirled the whiskey in his glass. "Do you know why you consider my maneuver on the Bussaco an insanity, Will? Because you have this! This home, with its laughter and mayhem and life to come back to. I have a very large, luxurious, empty manor."

"And you believe that Lady Olivia Hanson will fill it with laughter and mayhem and life? Think again, old chap. Olivia is nothing like Isabel! She's a cold, manipulative, grasping bitch!"

"I've known Olivia since childhood. I know what she's like."

Will was virtually shaking with fury and disbelief. "And?"

"She's in love with me."

Will sagged in his chair, shaking his head and groaning. "My God, Ash. I understand why Wellington singled you out immediately, why he considers you some kind of prodigy, and why he pushes your advancement, but by Jove, you can be one stupid ass sometimes!"

Ashby considered the amber liquid in his glass and decided to pass. "I should go." Pushing away from the table, he got to his feet. "You're drunk. I'm drunk. I'll see you in three days." He lifted the small, padded picnic basket Izzy had left on a chair for him and ambled out the door. Flipping the lid open, he smiled at the black ball of fur sleeping on the cushion inside. "I hope you kissed your old mistress goodbye, because you might not see her for a very long time."

His army horse was saddled and waiting for him on the front drive. "Thank you, Jimmy." He took the reins and dismissed the groom. He was about to swing onto the saddle when the front door opened and closed. He glanced beyond his shoulder and saw Izzy running toward him.

"Ashby . . ." She panted, wildness in her eyes.

He froze. "What's wrong, Isabel? Anything happened to Will?"

She shook her head, out of breath. She swallowed. "He went to bed."

He set the basket on the ground and flipped the reins around the handle. His thoughts raced in several directions. One suggested she'd overheard his argument with Will. He didn't want to hurt Izzy's feelings, but he was a twenty-eight-year-old man. She had to expect that sooner or later he'd take a wife. "Come, let's sit on the bench." He took her elbow, stirring her toward it.

They sat down quietly, an adequate distance between them. "Lord Ashby," she began, shifting sideways to face him. "I have another special favor to ask of you."

"Your wish is my command."

She gripped her hands tightly, twining and untwining her fingers. Her eyes were very large, dark, and anxious. "I know you and Will are soldiers, fighting a terrible war against a dangerous, despotic madman who wants to subjugate England and make us all eat frogs, but—"

Ashby smiled perceptively. "Your brother is like a brother to me, Isabel, and I don't have siblings to spare. You may rest assured I will protect Will with my life, if necessary, because if anything happened to him . . . Well, let's just say I'd rather die than fail. However," he exhaled deeply, "having said that, you are mature enough to understand that in war as in peace our fates are not entirely in our hands, if at all. You have to be brave. You mustn't—"

She edged closer, whispering, "I know you'll protect Will. It's you I worry about."

"Will protects me. It's a bargain."

"Will is short and scrawny." She wrinkled her pert nose.

His smile quickened for a heartbeat. "Look at me. Am I short and scrawny?"

She took him in from head to toe. "No. You are tall and strong."

He swallowed, wishing he'd had that last shot of whiskey after all. "I appreciate your concern, Izzy. I'll be fine. Go to bed."

Crystalline tears trembled in her eyes. "Promise?"

"I promise."

"Because I'd die if anything happened to you." She wrapped her dainty white hands around his neck and pressed her lips to his. His mind went numb. Isabel Aubrey had a temptress's lips—soft, pink, full, and enticingly sweet—and for a fleeting moment his mouth responded.

He gripped her shoulders and tore his mouth away. "Oh, God." His head wilted; his heart thundered in his chest. *Bloody hell*. He forced himself to meet her gaze. Isabel's wide eyes mirrored his shock. He opened his mouth to apologize, but she got up and dashed into the house.

That night, cursing himself for being every kind of villain, he rode straight to Ashby Park, with Hector sleeping in the basket across his lap, and asked Olivia to be his wife. She said yes.

Seven Dover Street, Present Time

Isabel was exhausted when she returned home from Iris's fundraising soiree. She scarcely uttered a word the whole evening, let alone helped her friends solicit donations for their charity, though she didn't think an active participation on her part would have literally tipped the scales in their favor. The English aristocracy didn't care about poor war widows and starving babes; they only cared about their little amusements. Nevertheless, Isabel fully expected Iris and Sophie to demand an explanation for her odd behavior tonight. But deuce take it, what could she tell them? That she was devastated? That the only man she ever cared for had tossed her out of his sight and mind that morning, never to return again?

She never told them about her girlish infatuation with the earl. When they embraced her as a friend during her first season, Ashby was considered a legend among his peers: an established womanizer, a celebrated cavalry commander, thirteen years her senior, socially ten times her better, and where she was concerned—wholly unattainable. He had also been away in the Peninsula at that time, a fact which spared her the humiliation of having to face the man who had scorned her kiss.

It had taken her a long time to get over the shame—and the heartache. And it had taken her two years to muster the courage to go see him after his return from the Continent.

Go home, Isabel, and don't come back here ever again. The idea of never seeing him again shredded her soul. Inevitably her thoughts drifted to happier days in which Ashby and Will rode in unexpectedly, bringing the sun with them. They were polar opposites—Will, the carefree wit; Ashby, the intense lord—and yet they complemented each other perfectly, creating a synergy that was almost enviable.

She recalled the first time she had laid eyes on him as if it were yesterday: She was twelve-years-old; Ashby was more than twice her age. Will ushered Ashby into the parlor, where she sat on the floor playing with her twin sisters while her mother leafed through the Society pages. She remembered scrambling to her feet and bobbing politely, and Ashby taking her hand and bowing over it. "You never told me you had a beautiful little doll for a sister, Will," Ashby remarked. When she looked up at him, she met the kindest, most expressive, loneliest sea-colored eyes.

Those eyes cut right through her and captured her heart for good. Without Ashby and Will, what remained in the place where her heart once beat was a great, suffocating void she found unbearable. Ashby had closed the door in her face, and there was no going back.

Lucy jumped to her feet when Isabel entered her bedchamber; the poor maid's eyes were red and bleary. "This arrived half an hour after you'd left, miss." Lucy gestured at the exquisitely carved mahogany box sitting on Isabel's bed. It was tied with a sky blue ribbon and adorned with a daisy. "Old Norris wanted to give it to Lady Aubrey, but I happened to be nearby when the footboy arrived, and when I saw his livery and heard him say the box was for you, I snatched it."

A strange thrill meandered along Isabel's spine. "Well done, Lucy. What was special about the footboy's livery?"

"It was black and gold, ma'am."

Isabel's pulse sped up. A box from Ashby? She had offended him. Why would he send her a gift? She spun around, presenting her maid with her back. "Lucy, quick. Unlace me, please."

As Lucy undid her back, Isabel met her maid's eyes in the dressing mirror. "I, eh, hope you remembered to forget our little sojourn this morning?"

"Forget what?" With an impish smile Lucy helped her out of her gown and silk shift and removed her hair clips. "Good night, miss."

"Thank you, Lucy. Good night." Isabel quickly donned her nightshift, shook out her thick mane of curls, and climbed on the bed. Her heart racing, she stared at the box. All of her dull, unimaginative beaux sent her bouquets of red roses, but a single yellow daisy seemed a message in itself. Only she had no idea what it meant. "You're a sentimental twit," she chastised herself. Yet, her hands were shaking. Carefully she pulled the blue ribbon loose, ruining the beautiful bow, and retied it around the sunny daisy's stalk. She ran her fingertips over the mahogany lid. A lion and a lioness, surrounded by their little cubs, were etched in the wood—a pride of lions. She opened the box. "Banknotes?" Then it dawned on her—a donation. She counted the money: *One hundred, two, three . . . a thousand, two thousand . . . five thousand pounds!* "Goodness gracious!"

Slack-jawed, Isabel gaped at the heap of bills scattered on her bed coverlet. "Five thousand pounds . . ." They could accomplish *anything* with such an obscene sum. They could finally pay their solicitor, Mr. Flowers, lease office space for their charity, hire runners to extend their list of bereaved families in need. Countless ideas whirled in her feverish mind. Iris and Sophie would be ecstatic! She couldn't wait to tell them, but first . . .

A small envelope lay on the bottom of the box. The mark of a lion was stamped in the cold wax—the lion etched in Ashby's signet ring. She lifted the envelope and nearly dropped it; her hands quivered like an old woman's. She drew the small card out. In a bold, foreign hand was written, *"I beg your forgiveness and wish you success in all of your endeavors. Yours, PNL."*

"*PNL.*" With every fiber of her being she knew the L stood for Lancaster, but the *P* and the *N* were a mystery. She didn't know his Christian name. Nor his middle one. She knew so little about him. She lay back and pressed the note to her lips, shutting her eyes. *Ashby*.

She would not give up on him. Not now. Not ever. Isabel smiled. He may not wish to see her, but she needed Ashby to be a part of her life again, as he had once been a part of her family, and his donation provided her with the best pretext for paying him another visit. Somehow, she would persuade the Gargoyle to come out for a caress.

Chapter Three

"I'm sorry, ladies." Mr. Flowers closed the book he'd been perusing and scuttled to another crowded bookshelf. "I've nothing new to present to you. You'll have to come back next week."

"That's what you said last week," Isabel muttered. Cramped together with Iris and Sophie on a threadbare settee, she surveyed the dusty, cobwebbed office and fought a violent urge to get up and open a window. She had a physical dislike of closed spaces, and the stale air was making her nauseous in addition to giving her a headache.

Yet despite the pitiful condition of his office, Mr. Flowers was a brilliant legal mind, who, due to an illness that caused his hands to shake, had had to leave a successful career as a public prosecutor. If anyone could draw up a winning bill proposal, it was this man.

"Mr. Flowers," Iris began, "we have provided you with all the information you'd asked for. I see no reason why this should take so long. I'm not in the habit of speaking unkindly, but you, sir, are dragging your heels on this, and we are losing our patience."

"Ugh, you two!" Sophie sniffed scornfully. She pulled a few banknotes out of her reticule and smacked them on the solicitor's table. "Would this help speed the process along, monsieur?"

Isabel shot Sophie a questioning look but then realized that her friend, who had spent her childhood barefoot and begging for coin on the streets of Paris, was probably right. She dug into her purse and extracted a thick stack of banknotes. Before Mr. Flowers noticed the interlude, she placed half the sum owed to the solicitor on the desk and stuffed Sophie's banknotes back into her bag. Keeping her voice low, she explained, "We received a substantial donation yesterday."

Iris's head swerved toward her. "What? From whom?"

"Hush. I'll explain later," Isabel murmured.

Mr. Flowers peered beyond the pages of another moldy volume. "Well now." With a broad smile he closed the book and took his chair behind the desk. "Thank you, Mrs. Fairchild. We all need to eat from time to time." He extended a shaky hand toward the stack of banknotes.

Isabel covered it with her palm. "Mr. Flowers," she smiled, "I couldn't help noticing that when Lady Chilton referred to the information we had supplied you with, you twitched, sir."

"Hmm." The solicitor eyed her critically. "You'd make a fearsome litigator, Miss Aubrey. You have an eye for detecting irregular behavior in witnesses."

"I thank you for the compliment, Mr. Flowers. Now, if you please?" She didn't appreciate being told she had a natural aptitude for cold-blooded occupations.

"That's the thing—information!" He held up a quivering finger. "Your ideas are humane, logical, and quite advanced, I must say. However, to bring them before Parliament without an estimate of the cost the new bill should entail, will ensure the bill gets tossed offhandedly."

The three ladies sagged on the settee, grimacing. "You should have told us weeks ago," Iris admonished. "What sort of additional information do you need, Mr. Flowers?"

"I need figures, lists."

"What sort of lists?" Isabel prodded.

"Army lists—names, terms of service, ranks, and salaries, of course."

"Army personnel files?" Isabel could see her goals crumbling before her very eyes. "The lists are confidential. What's more, access to them is highly restricted."

"How do you suppose we acquire the lists, Monsieur Flowers?" Sophie demanded curtly.

He laced his wobbly hands over a heap of papers. "Any way you can."

Isabel could think of only two ways to obtain classified army files: Either break into the Horse Guards and steal them or go back to Ashby. The second was both tempting and daunting, and it served in strengthening her resolve of last night to return to him.

"Assuming we get ahold of the lists," Sophie said, "how do we go about putting together an estimate? Would you be able to supply us with examples . . . ?"

"In cases such as this, I recommend employing an accountant. It'll cost more," he warned.

"I see." Isabel twisted her lips. "All we need to do is obtain the information."

"Precisely."

"Who, in your opinion, should have access to these army lists, Mr. Flowers?" Iris asked.

"The high command, the Ministry of War . . ."

"If we are to approach influential parties and ask for collaboration," Isabel mused aloud, already plotting her next visit to Ashby, "we'll need something tangible to stir their civic-minded interest. Have you put something together, Mr. Flowers? Anything at all, in writing, that is?"

"As a matter of fact, I have." He pulled out one of the drawers in his desk and produced a leather brief. "This is the body of the proposal, but as I said, without the numbers—"

"It's but a stack of good intentions equal to nonsense."

Isabel stood up, drawing Sophie and Iris up with her. "Thank you, Mr. Flowers. I hope we shall be getting somewhere very soon."

"From now on, it'll be up to you. Good day, ladies."

As they climbed into Isabel's coach, Iris asked, "What was this bit about us receiving a substantial donation? You said nothing about it last night. Indeed, you were quite—"

"Ineffective. I know, and I apologize. I was . . . out of sorts." Isabel opened a window and breathed deeply. Yet the air in the City, the bustling part of town, was as stifling as inside Mr. Flowers's office. She settled against the squabs and bit back a smile. "But later I received a box containing five thousand pounds and a note stating it was for us."

"Five thousand pounds! *Mon dieu!*" Sophie exclaimed. "That's superb!"

Iris looked equally dazzled. "Five thousand pounds . . . Do you realize what we can accomplish with five thousand pounds?"

"Bribe a secretary at the Horse Guards for the lists we need?" Sophie suggested slyly.

Iris twisted her lips. "And how will we explain stumbling upon this information when we present our bill proposal to Parliament, pray tell?"

"Really, Iris," Sophie rolled her eyes at Isabel, "sometimes you sound like my conscience."

Iris ignored her. "Izzy, who is our benefactor?"

Oh, dear. Isabel hadn't thought of an answer to that. "I wouldn't know." She puckered her lips, resembling the cat that ate the canary. She never lied to her friends. She only fibbed when her mama became intolerably pesky and interfering. She considered explaining about Ashby, but thought better of it. While Iris and Sophie were the most delightfully eccentric, trustworthy friends, they were also very protective of her and mindful of propriety's strict rules. If she told them about her visit to the Gargoyle, she would get an earful of how a lady should and should not behave and of the risks to her reputation. Furthermore, they would want to go see him together. The idea did not appeal to her in the least. He was a recluse, for pity's sake. She had no right to inflict her friends on him. "It was signed PNL. Do we know anyone by that name?"

Thankfully, her friends looked mystified; they didn't recognize the initials. "What a bizarre thing," Iris remarked. "A benefactor who wishes to remain anonymous."

"It is the very definition of charity," Sophie declared. "'He who practices charity in secret is greater than Moses.' Our generous benefactor chose to make his contribution in secret so as not to injure the pride of those in need, which proves that he or she did it in earnest, not to gain favor in the eyes of the *ton*. I deem this person remarkable."

More than they would ever know, Isabel thought. Ashby could have given her the donation in person, but he didn't want her thanks. He contented himself with the knowledge that she would put his money to good use—and he thought Will was a saint. She smiled to herself. *Show me your friends and I shall tell you who you are.* How could she not admire him?

"We still haven't found a sponsor," Iris reminded them. "Whom do we know that could help us obtain the lists and address Parliament on our behalf?"

"I could speak to Admiral Duckworth at the assembly at Almack's tomorrow evening," Sophie suggested. "When my George died, the admiral came to call and made me promise I'd come to him first whenever I needed anything. He said he owed George his very life."

"That's a start," Iris concurred. "I could speak to Chilton, but I doubt he . . ."

"Your husband won't help us," Isabel said grimly. "He would only use this to torment you further and blackmail you into doing his bidding."

"He does that anyway." Iris lowered her eyes but said nothing more on the subject.

Isabel squeezed her hand. "Come now, ladies. We are intelligent, imaginative women. We should be able to come up with a sound plan to help us accomplish our goals. I've a grand idea. Why don't we stop for luncheon at our favorite café in Piccadilly and plot this through? I am in a desperate need of fresh air and nourishment." When her friends nodded eagerly, she stuck her head out the window. "Jackson, Piccadilly if you please!"

Forty minutes later they were drinking lemonade and gobbling cucumber sandwiches while observing the fashionable world passing by on foot and in elegant vehicles.

"How is your secret project coming along?" Iris asked Isabel.

Isabel almost dropped her glass of lemonade. "Secret project?"

"The poor widow and her little boy," Iris clarified. "The ones you took out of Bishopsgate when you rescued your maid's cousin."

Wiping her lemonade-sputtered hands on a napkin, Isabel replied in low tones, "Very well. I'm teaching Molly her letters and basic arithmetic. She's an apt pupil. And little Joe is a joy."

"What will you do with them?" Sophie asked. "You can't adopt all the waifs and strays in London. Before you know it, you'll have an army on your hands."

"You might as well open your own almshouse—St. Isabel of Mayfair." Iris smiled.

"The idea is not to keep them dependent. I hope to provide Molly with enough education to help her find a good position somewhere so that she would be able to provide for her son."

"Let's find her a husband," Sophie proposed. "We'll open a matchmaking service and—"

"Dear Lord!" Iris jumped. She snatched her shawl off the

back of the chair, looking as pale as though she had seen a ghost. "I must go. I . . . promised Chilton I'd be home before one o'clock and . . . it's nearly two."

Isabel stood up and caught her hand. "Iris, take my coach and send it back for us."

"No need. I'll hail a hack." Iris ran out of the café and disappeared in the milling crowd.

Sophie cursed in French. "That awful man! I should like to strangle him and throw him in a ditch. How dare he keep Iris like a pet in a cage? She must present him with a detailed schedule every day and ask for his permission to leave the house. She cannot dance or converse with other gentlemen. She needs the ogre's consent to breathe. Why does she put up with this treatment?"

"You know as well as I do that Iris has nowhere else to go," Isabel said sadly. "A husband is not always the answer." Their friend was a prime example of the unhappy lot of women who lost their male protectors in the war. It amazed her how Iris never once lamented her situation.

"Good God! Little Izzy Aubrey!" A deep, male voice chuckled. "I don't believe it."

Isabel looked up and felt the blood draining from her head. Yet the tall, handsome, auburn-haired hussar attired in the 18th royal blue uniform was neither Will nor Ashby. A smile that was equal parts relieved, pleased, and disappointed spread on her face. "Why, if it isn't Captain Ryan Macalister! What a pleasure it is to see you here, of all places. Why don't you join us, captain?"

"Don't mind if I do." He smiled dazzlingly and sketched a handsome bow before Sophie. When he straightened, rich brown hair fell rakishly over his eye. He settled in Iris's vacant chair. "I must say it is a pleasure to see you, too, Izzy, eh, beg pardon, Miss Aubrey."

"Isabel will do," she returned warmly. "Captain, allow me

to introduce my dear friend, Mrs. Fairchild. Sophie's husband was a navy lieutenant. We deeply mourn his loss."

Ryan's expression turned grim. "You have my deepest condolences, Mrs. Fairchild. I lost a sad number of good friends in the war." He looked at Isabel. "Your brother was the hardest loss."

"You are very kind." Isabel smiled bravely.

"Thank you, captain," Sophie echoed. "I understand you served with Major Will?"

"Indeed." Ryan nodded proudly. "Major William Aubrey made our lives tolerable when it was intolerable. I dearly miss his quick wit and friendly smile."

Isabel swiped a tear off her cheek. "So tell me. What brings you to London? I was under the impression you took a commission in India."

"I did. I am stationed in India, a major now." He showed her his new rank distinction.

The déjà vu was almost too painful. "Congratulations, major. And is India to your liking?"

"Hardly. The weather is hot. Every rock is some snake's residence. The spicy food whittles away at my stomach. The company in my new regiment leaves a lot to be desired . . ."

"A new regiment?" Isabel scowled.

"Yes. They are disbanding the 18th. Didn't you know?"

"No, I didn't."

"We suffered too many losses, among them our finest officers." He held her gaze, revealing just how deeply he shared her grief. "And now that Ashby is retired . . . Well, he is a tough act to follow. Even my regimentals are becoming obsolete. I am to acquire new ones." He grimaced.

Isabel felt like crying. "Is this the reason you are here?"

The handsome major leaned forward with a conspiratorial grin. "I'm supposedly consulting a doctor regarding a foot injury, but between you and me, I'm hoping to fall upon a reason that would keep me here for good." He winked.

"A reason?"

Sustaining her gaze, he rested an elbow on the table and cupped his chin. "A fair reason."

Her cheeks bloomed with color. "Well, major, I pray your hunt shall be successful."

"I have every reason to believe it will be, Isabel. In fact—" he grinned lopsidedly "—I feel encouraged already."

Averting her gaze, Isabel caught sight of Sophie's knowing smile.

"I must say," he went on flirtatiously, "I should have anticipated you would turn out to be a beauty. Pity I didn't speak to your brother years ago. You haven't been snagged yet, have you?"

"No, major. I haven't." Isabel bit her lip to keep from smiling like a dolt. Ryan Macalister had always been a charmer, but the effect of his regimentals was almost . . . irresistible.

"Excellent news. This calls for a toast." He raised his hand, signaling for a waiter. "What are you having, ladies?"

Sophie gestured at the large, nearly empty plate. "You may have the last sandwich."

"Thanks." He snatched the sandwich and popped it into his mouth. A waiter approached. "Kindly bring us a bottle of your finest Hock and another plate of sandwiches."

"And an ice," Isabel put in. "I should like to have a cherry ice."

"A cherry ice for the lady. Lively, man!" Ryan dismissed the listless waiter. "Incidentally, I saw a third lady leaving your table. I hope I didn't scare her off."

"Lady Chilton had to leave early," Sophie replied.

Ryan's gaze dropped to the brief resting beneath his elbow. "What's this?"

"A bill proposal for Parliament," Isabel explained, gaining a raised eyebrow.

"Indeed? Tell me about it."

Sophie and Isabel discussed the charity and its goals. Ryan seemed genuinely impressed.

"The trouble is," Isabel went on, "without the lists our proposal is worthless. Do you by any chance have access to the army's personnel files?" she asked hopefully.

He shook his head. "But I know someone who does. And so do you."

Isabel prayed her expression didn't give her away. "Who?"

He filled their glasses with wine. "Ashby."

Isabel's hand shook as she lifted a spoonful of cherry ice to her mouth. "Colonel Lord Ashby hasn't been to Seven Dover Street for many years."

"Who is this Ashby, Izzy?" Sophie inquired.

Isabel swallowed the ice. "He was Will's best friend. By the end of the war he commanded the regiment. Now he is a . . . recluse."

Sophie lowered her voice. "Is he the one they call 'the Gargoyle'?"

Isabel met Ryan's dark gaze and was heartened to note he found the derogatory epithet as distasteful as she did. "Damned shame, that is," he said. "I still can't believe he has withdrawn from Society altogether."

Isabel leaned forward, endeavoring not to seem overly intrigued. "What happened to him?"

Ryan sighed. "A cannon-shell exploded in his face during a charge in Sorauren, wounded him within an inch of his life. He underwent a field surgery and was bedridden for six months."

"Did he go about in a mask afterward?" Isabel inquired quietly.

"*A mask?* Ashby?" Ryan snorted with disdain. "As soon as he was on his feet, he went on leading every charge. He used to joke about it, saying that the sight of his face would kill more Frenchmen than us good-for-nothing cowards could. Wellington awarded him the Gold Medal."

"If he didn't mind it then, why did he become a recluse upon returning to England?"

Ryan dropped his gaze. "I didn't say he didn't mind. As I recall, there was talk of a scandal involving his . . ." He clammed up.

Isabel gritted her teeth. She ached to know everything about Ashby. "Why is he a recluse?"

"I think his withdrawal from Society has something to do with the death of your brother," he hedged, "but don't take my word for it. He was my superior officer. He didn't confide in me."

"He never came to call on us after Will died."

"Don't hold it against him," Ryan asked softly. "He was devastated over Will."

A lump formed in her throat. "I believe you, and I don't hold it against him."

"Why don't you and Major Macalister call on Lord Ashby together, Izzy? He may just be the sort of sponsor we need."

Isabel stiffened. "But . . . but . . . he's a recluse."

"I called on him before I left for India," Ryan mentioned, "but the butler wouldn't allow me inside Lancaster House. One would have to be Wellington to get admitted there."

"Do you know Wellington, major?" Sophie inquired. "An introduction to the Iron Duke would greatly benefit our cause."

"I salute him when I see him. He sometimes remembers my name, but other than that . . ." He smiled sheepishly, shrugging. "Sorry."

"Do you attend Almack's tomorrow evening?" Isabel asked. Perhaps during a waltz, she might get him to reveal more about Ashby without Sophie hanging on their every word.

"Ryan," he amended. His eyes smoldered as a devilish smile formed on his lips. "I'm not sure they'll let me in with all those debutantes fluttering about, but now that I know you will be there, I shall endeavor to procure myself a voucher. Will you reward me with a waltz, Isabel?"

"With pleasure."

"I should very much like to call on you sometime, pay my respects to Lady Aubrey."

"I shall look forward to seeing you. I'm sure Mama and Stilgoe would love to chat with one of Will's old cronies."

He contemplated her eyes. "There is an excellent place on Berkley Square that sells ices. Would you go walking with me Saturday afternoon?"

"I would be delighted to, Ryan."

"Excellent." He consulted his pocket watch. "And now, ladies, I must be off." He stood, beckoning their waiter. "How much for the table?"

Isabel caught his arm. "No. I forbid you to pay for us—"

"Already done." He took her hand and lifted it to his lips. "Until Saturday. Mrs. Fairchild." He bowed handsomely.

"Major."

As he sauntered off, Sophie gripped her hand. "You like him. I must say I liked him too."

"Ryan is very charming," Isabel agreed, while her thoughts centered on Ashby. If his self-imposed seclusion had something to do with Will, why did he kick her out of his house?

"Pity he is in Queer Street."

Isabel smiled at the Frenchwoman's mastery of English cant. One would think she grew up on the streets of London. "What makes you think he's penniless?"

"When a man needs a wife to quit the army . . ." Sophie tsk-tsked. "As I said, I like him, and obviously he likes you, but I'd be on my guard, Izzy. That man is hunting for an heiress."

"He can't be all that hard for currency if he paid for our luncheon."

"A clever predator never allows a lady to pay for anything until after the wedding."

"Perhaps you're right," Isabel mused. "You have a better nose for this sort of thing than I do, but I daresay, if pushed to the altar, Ryan would make the least offending choice of groom."

Sophie's dark brown eyes twinkled naughtily. "On that, *chérie,* we are in agreement."

"Home, Jackson," Isabel told her coachman after dropping Sophie off at Lord and Lady Maitland's town house. Unlike Chilton, who terrorized poor Iris and forever brandished her lack of fortune and family over her head like the sword of Damocles, Sophie's in-laws were kind and affectionate and treated her as a queen, regardless of Sophie's checkered Parisian past. They were always happy to look after their five-year-old grandson, Jerome, and never pried into his mother's private affairs. Isabel's mother made a career of prying into her daughter's affairs.

The dappled afternoon sun danced on her cheek as the carriage trundled through Mayfair. Tapping the leather brief containing their bill proposal on her knees, Isabel wondered when and how she would call on Ashby again. With the Season at its peak and her charity taking up every spare minute of her time, she wasn't likely to do so anytime soon. Unless . . .

"Jackson," Isabel leaned out the carriage window at a busy intersection, "please take me to Lancaster House on Park Lane."

"Yes, Miss Aubrey." The coachman didn't sound perturbed in the least that a block away from Seven Dover Street they were changing direction, or that she was heading to parts unknown without her lady's maid. Their household staff was split into two camps: those in cahoots with her mother's spy, Norris, and those who despised the old tyrant and rejoiced in caballing behind his back. Since Jackson was listed in the second camp, she could count on his discretion.

She wiped her clammy hands on her pink muslin day gown

and pulled on her kid gloves. Delicious nervousness turned her stomach. What wickedness possessed her! To call on a single gentleman *twice* in one week, uninvited, unchaperoned . . . But then, Ashby had always awakened the brazen streak in her. She hoped she looked presentable. Not that she had any illusions about Ashby. He wouldn't notice her if she pranced naked before him—now where did this outrageous thought spring from? She didn't dare probe too deeply or she might lose her nerve altogether. She took a deep breath and concentrated on what she would say to him.

"Lancaster House," Jackson announced from his perch. His son, the footman, opened the door and flipped open the steps. He took her shaky hand and helped her down.

Arching her spine, Isabel made herself walk instead of run up to the imposing facade and thumped the brass knocker against the door. Phipps appeared in the threshold. "Miss Aubrey!"

"Kindly inform his lordship that he has a visitor," she said, straight-faced.

Phipps dithered for a moment before a resolute gleam etched his eyes. He stepped back to let her pass and closed the door. "Right this way, if you please." He took the lead, crossing the magnificent foyer and ushering her deeper inside the house.

She took that as a promising sign. Yesterday she'd only been permitted in the front sitting room. She was definitely moving up in the world. He stopped outside a door and bade her wait. When he reemerged, shutting the door behind him, Isabel nearly wept, but instead of showing her out, he smoothed the bulge in his breast pocket that hadn't been there before and marched on.

They arrived at a wood and iron door. He opened it to reveal a narrow flight of stone steps; it only led downward. She followed mutely, but when she became aware of steady metallic thumping that grew louder the deeper they descended, she asked. "Where are you taking me?"

"To the wine cellar."

Isabel was horrified. "Lord Ashby spends his days in the wine cellar?"

"Not as often as he used to. The first six months, it was impossible to draw him out. Now he only spends the better part of his nights there."

Poor Ashby, Isabel thought; drowning his despair in one bottle after another. Thank God she had the sense to come back despite his hostile dismissal.

They reached the bottom of the stairs, a dim little room, a wine cellar, similar to the one they had in Seven Dover Street. There was no sign of Ashby. "Miss Aubrey, I must beg you to wait again." Phipps disappeared behind one of the bottle racks. The thumping stopped.

"What?" She heard Ashby's deep, short-tempered voice reverberating inside.

"My lord, you have a visitor."

"Get rid of him." Something hard hit the floor.

"It's Miss Aubrey, my lord."

She heard a steady rasping noise. Unable to contain her curiosity, she tiptoed past the bottle rack and peeked through the arched opening. A cavernous chamber sprawled before her, aglow with candlelight in various heights and niches. Although outside the sun had yet to set, inside this chamber night ruled. The walls were stacked with wine bottles up to the vaulted ceiling. Sawdust coated the floor. Sculptures, furniture, and raw timber occupied most of the space. She stretched her neck and saw long, sinewy legs clad in glove-tight breeches braced apart at a work table.

He circled the table to stand facing her. "Did she say why she was here?"

"No, my lord, she didn't, but if I had to hazard a guess,

I would say it had something to do with the package you sent her."

Goodness. Ashby was naked from the waist up. Powerful shoulders topped thickly corded arms. His broad chest tapered to a wasp, muscle-winged waist. Hard sinew undulated in perfect symmetry across a flat abdomen. Perspiration covered the hairless skin in a fine glistening sheen.

She was highly disappointed that his overlong hair veiled his features as he forcefully filed a slab of timber smooth. Undeterred, her eyes caressed his beautiful body, entranced by the play of muscles beneath the smooth, burnished skin. She had seen sturdy stack boys shirtless, but none of them looked like *that*—a masterpiece of masculine brawn carved in marble-like flesh.

What a strange and wonderful creature he was, Isabel thought. The rich and powerful earl, who instead of hiding behind his lofty title at home had ridden against Napoleon without the slightest regard for his personal safety, was a carpenter. That was how he filled his lonely hours, by creating beautiful things—like Vulcan, the suffering, deformed god of craftsmanship.

"Did she come by herself?" Ashby demanded to know.

"Yes, my lord, I believe she did. She has a carriage waiting." Phipps reached inside his breast pocket and produced the black satin mask. He set it in front of his master.

A moment passed. "Show her in."

She jumped back, loath to be caught snooping. She wrung her hands while pretending to examine the dim antechamber. Phipps materialized. "You may go in now, Miss Aubrey."

Tension knotting her nerve-endings, she drew in a steeling breath and walked in. Her gaze fell on a shapeless stump covered with an old sheet. Carpentry tools were scattered around it.

"Don't touch anything," a voice commanded.

She spotted Ashby's tall back bending over a dresser near

the far wall. An antiquated, four-poster bed stood there, draped with a red counterpane. Water splashed in a sink. He washed his face, then plowed his fingers through his thick, dark mane, smoothing it back past his nape. He reached for a creased shirt and dried his face. The next object he reached for was the black mask. He tied it around his head and spun around to face her in all his semi-nude glory.

She snapped her jaw shut. "Lord Ashby." She curtsied, curbing the impulse to lick her lips. It galled her how instead of outgrowing it, her fascination for him had evolved into something far more disturbing and physical. "I apologize for—" Her breath caught as he swabbed his sculpted, glistening chest with the crushed shirt. She never imagined men could look so . . . delectable.

"Why are you here?" His voice summoned her gaze back to his head.

She forced herself to concentrate. "My lord, I . . . I came to—"

"Ashby," he insisted, his green eyes glittering against the black satin. "I hear enough 'my lord' to make me gag." He tossed the crumpled shirt aside and started in her direction, his boot heels pounding along the stone-flagged floor. "Didn't I specifically tell you never to return?"

She bit her lip. "I came to thank you in person for your impossibly generous donation."

"You're welcome, but you could have sent a thank-you note."

"You could have sent a smaller sum." She looked around her, awestruck by the exquisite carvings littering the chamber. He wasn't merely a carpenter; he was an artist. "I liked the box even better," she confessed in a throaty voice she hardly recognized. "Did you make it yourself?"

He halted right in front of her, his raw masculinity as compelling as it was daunting. His sweetish, musky scent instantly reminded her of their brief kiss on the bench.

Everything came back to her: his quickly drawn breath, his warm, supple lips molded to hers, and then his tongue flicking shockingly, erotically at hers, branding her with his whiskey-spiced taste forever.

A sharp tremor shot through her body. She wanted to kiss him again, and touch him, very badly, but she didn't dare risk another rejection.

His eyes darkened. "Christ, Isabel! Why won't you let sleeping dogs lie?" he growled, as though he had read her mind. "Nothing good will come of this. Believe me."

She didn't want to hear that. "I need to know—what made you change your mind?"

"I didn't change my mind. You solicited active participation. I gave you money."

"Still, you were quite adamant the—"

"The message on your card was effective," he bit out grudgingly. "You are a formidable sharpshooter, Isabel Aubrey. When you take aim, you hit your mark at its softest spot each time."

"I apologize. My intention was—"

"Don't apologize to me. *Ever*. God knows I've a lot more I ought to apologize to you for."

She flushed to the roots of her hair. He was alluding to that infernal kiss he had scorned. Damn him. "I came to convince you to join our cause." She was all businesslike from then on. "I know you said you didn't attend Parliament or move in Society anymore, but I would greatly appreciate your commentary on this." She offered him the leather brief.

"What's this?" He took the brief and quickly thumbed through it.

"Our bill proposal. I told you about it. I haven't had a chance to read it myself yet, but—"

"What makes you think I know anything about legislation?" He skimmed the pages.

"In Will's words—you are the man with the special skills." She smiled challengingly.

"My skills are many and varied, but you already have my answer." He returned the file.

Blast. "There is something else. We need the army's lists."

"Go up to my library." He shrugged nonchalantly. "I've the army lists, the navy lists . . ."

"You don't seem to understand. We need the lists of casualties, including terms of service, ranks, salaries, and other pertinent details to prepare an estimate of the cost the new bill should entail. You're the only person I know who might have access to army personnel files."

"Army personnel files? That's classified information! No one would give you those files."

She felt like stomping her foot. On his. "How in blazes is a civic-minded person expected to improve anything in this country?"

"You're not. Which is why we have Lords and Commons and a monarch."

She eyed him irately. "You won't lift a finger to help me?"

"My contribution to your cause ended with the five thousand pounds donation." When she fell silent, duly chastised, he sauntered to a side table. He uncorked a semi-full wine bottle and poured red wine into two glasses. "Look, I've had my crusade," he explained. "Now all I want is to enjoy my private existence, despite its drawbacks." He returned to put a wineglass in her hand and knocked his glass against hers. "Cheers."

They drank in silence, sustaining eye-contact. Did he find the experience as intimate and titillating as she did, she wondered as the flavorsome elixir glided down her throat. Long ago she would have sold her soul to the Devil to share such a moment with him. *Say something!* "What sort of wine is this? Not Madeira, I daresay." Delicately she licked a red drop off her lip.

Her subtle gesture riveted him. "Madeira is for debutantes and well-manicured dandies."

Intrigued, she took another sip. "You may think me silly, but this wine is . . ."

"Multifaceted? Like a person." He nodded. He whirled the remaining wine in his glass and inhaled the fumes. "It's Navarrese. Fruity, provocative, smooth, and full of hidden meaning . . . I bought dozens of cases in Spain and had them shipped home."

"Listening to you, I feel so green and uninformed," she confessed, blushing.

"Don't. It makes me feel old and jaded." He tipped his head back, emptying his glass.

The sight of a red drop gliding down his bare throat enticed her beyond reason. She shook herself. "What sort of drawbacks do you find in solitude?"

"Several."

Perhaps that was the key. If she knew what he missed most in life, she could offer to fulfill this void, get closer to him, and thus keep him in her life. "Name one."

"Celibacy."

She sputtered her wine.

A wicked glow spread in his sea green irises. "You asked."

Perhaps he might not be as unresponsive as she had assumed if she undressed before him, but there would be no victory in that. According to her knowledgeable friend, Sophie, a man who desired women and a man who desired *a* woman were two very different beasts. "I had luncheon with one of your former officers today," she mentioned casually, returning sideways to her old topic. "Ryan Macalister. He's a major now. Even he thought you'd make the best sponsor to our cause, and I haven't told him anything—"

"Is he courting you?"

His harsh tone startled her. "What if he is?"

"You don't want Macalister, Isabel. Stay away from him." He set his empty glass aside.

"My lord, I do not appreciate vague hints and arbitrary commands."

He stared at her. "You want a reason? Fine. Ryan Macalister will break your heart."

Was he serious? Didn't he have an inkling of what he had done to her heart? Of course not. Charming rakes never did, particularly when the hearts they crushed were too young to be of any import. Suppressing her old resentment, she dissembled, "I had no idea you predicted futures, my lord. How very clever of you."

He took a step toward her. "I mean it, Izzy. Stay away from Macalister. He's not for you."

He almost sounded jealous, which didn't make sense. Looking up into his eyes, she asked, "Are you warning me off because he is penniless?" All she got in return was a fierce, unreadable glower. She set her empty glass next to his. "Lord Ashby, as someone whom I once considered as dear as an older brother, I beg you to divulge any information that may prove vital to my future happiness."

"Damn it, Isabel! I am not your brother!" he growled at her.

She flinched. "No, of course not. Y-You don't owe me anything."

He let out a ragged sigh that made his magnificent chest rise and fall. "Go home. Don't be foolish. I could never take Will's place in your life."

"I know that. I'm not asking you to. I'm not a child anymore, Ashby. Nor am I foolish."

His gaze flitted over her, swift yet thorough, unlike the young bucks who conducted long discussions with her bosom. "Indeed, you are not a child, which makes it even more dangerous."

Hope leaped in her breast. She searched his brilliant eyes. "Why is it dangerous?"

He reached out and ran his rough knuckles along her cheek. "Because if anyone should see you coming in or out of my house," he breathed, "you'll have a devil of a time facing the gossip. You are a lovely young woman, Isabel. It would be a great pity if your future were to be ruined."

Her hope crumbled to dust. He still didn't want anything to do with her, even though he was injured and alone and felt compelled to wear a mask. She should have long since abandoned any hope of winning his affections. Knowing that, however, she still craved his friendship. "You are concerned for my reputation. How good of you. Just like an older brother."

This time he didn't take the bait. "Goodbye, Miss Aubrey." He marched past her, leaving her alone in the windowless cellar. Her throat constricted, and she hastened upstairs for air.

Chapter Four

The moment she entered Almack's, Isabel was ambushed by her brother. "You know my sister, don't you, Hanson?" Viscount Stilgoe spoke to the man at his side.

She could neither see the gentleman nor hear his response because Iris and Sophie were chatting energetically and blocking her view. "We had an agreement, Charlie," she hissed in her brother's ear. "I attend the marriage mart once a week and in exchange you and Mama cease your matchmaking schemes."

"What good is that when you waste the entire evening standing and gossiping with your friends?" he gritted out almost inaudibly. "Now hush and be charming."

"Good evening, Lady Chilton, Mrs. Fairchild," a cultured voice spoke. Her friends moved aside as a white-blond head approached, his black jacket enhancing his unearthly coloring. Isabel gaped. As much as she detested Stilgoe's sly matchmaking maneuvers, Lord John Hanson VI, whom the *ton* called the Golden Angel, was simply too beautiful to remain indifferent to. "Miss Aubrey, you look exquisite this evening." He bowed over her gloved hand.

"Lord John." She curtsied, smiling despite herself. "It is a pleasure to see you again."

His translucent azure eyes examined her features. "The pleasure is all mine, I assure you."

"Hanson heads several legislation committees and is crying for reform as keenly as you do, ladies," Stilgoe contributed. To Isabel, he whispered, "See how supportive I am, of your cause?"

"You're so supportive," Isabel returned in the same low voice, "you refused to support us."

"What do you suppose I'm doing right now?" her brother whispered while Iris and Sophie questioned John about his political activities. "John's grandfather is the Duke of Haworth. Some say the duke intends to skip a generation and name John as his successor instead of the father. Imagine the good you could spread in the world with such a sponsor, Izzy."

"It's difficult to concentrate with wedding bells pealing in my ears," she ribbed. Charles was neither ambitious nor greedy; he was simply an old woman, she thought, anxious for his recalcitrant sister to wed. "Now hush and go away. I want to join this conversation."

"My main focus is reducing land taxes," Lord John answered Sophie's question.

"You support landowners, then," Isabel interjected, hoping her tone didn't come out as harsh as she imagined. She had no use for an aristocrat who acted for the benefit of his peers.

"Anything that would encourage the employment of demobilized. Ex-soldiers, that is."

"Oh." Isabel met Iris and Sophie's gazes, reading their thoughts. Hanson might just be the representative they sought. "Lord John, it appears we may have a similar concern." She stepped a little closer to the blond god, ignoring Stilgoe's smug chuckle. "Do tell us more."

"I would love to, if you granted me the pleasure of escorting you onto the dance floor for this next waltz, Miss Aubrey."

"Why . . . I—" She looked over at Stilgoe, who merely shrugged. She beamed at John. "Yes, I thank you." As she took his proffered arm and let him lead her to the floor, she couldn't help noticing the number of heads turning in their direction. Never before had she been the subject of so many women's envy. What was John doing with her, anyway? She was pretty, she supposed, but they hardly exchanged more than a polite greeting now and then, and Lord John had a flock of admirers eating from the palm of his hand. What the devil was Stilgoe up to, she wondered.

"Stilgoe tells me that you and your friends founded a charity in support of war widows," John remarked as he whirled her across the floor, keeping the correct distance between them.

"We act for women and children who lost the breadwinner of their family in the war and are now facing beggary and workhouses as their sole means of survival."

"What made you decide to help this particular group?" He stepped and turned, moving in tune with the music.

"My brother died at Waterloo. Iris's father, an officer with the 95th Rifles, died in Spain. Sophie's husband, a navy lieutenant, died at sea. We felt it was our duty to help other women who shared our grief but didn't have the benefit of our economic and social stability."

"What are your goals? What efforts have you made so far?"

"We visit almshouses, workhouses. We donate food and clothing. We hold a meeting every Friday afternoon and invite bereaved women in order to build a list and to learn more regarding what needs to be done. We're also working toward submitting a bill proposal to Parliament. We believe the government should financially compensate these women for their loss."

"I'm impressed. A woman as young and as lovely as yourself taking on a task of this magnitude . . . I can't imagine it's easy, considering your personal loss. In which regiment did your brother serve?"

"The 18th Hussars, my lord."

His shoulder stiffened beneath her hand. "Call me John, I insist."

"Very well, John." She smiled. "You may call me Isabel."

"Isabel. Your name has a distinct feminine ring to it. It suits you well."

"Thank you, John." She saw Sophie dancing with the elderly Admiral Duckworth. There seemed to be a physical tug-of-war going on between these two, which her friend did not enjoy.

"Will I have the pleasure of seeing you at the Barrington ball tomorrow?" John inquired.

Isabel dithered. The Barrington garden bordered on Lancaster House. She disliked the idea of Ashby sitting alone in the dark while she danced, sipped wine, and made polite conversation a mere garden away, but since John was attending, perhaps it was in her charity's best interest to make an appearance after all. "Yes, of course." She smiled.

"Splendid. Will you save the first waltz for me? And the last one? And a cotillion?"

Why this sudden interest in her? Mystified, she met his twinkling gaze and decided to play along until she figured this—him—out. "Three dances with the same gentleman at the course of one evening is an invitation to be ruined, John."

"Or married by a special license." He grinned wolfishly. "But you're quite right, my lovely Isabel. One dance is socializing, two are a mark of genuine affection, and three are an outrage."

Isabel decided that Lord John was far too accustomed to women fawning and cooing over him while he basked in his golden glory. No doubt he was curious to see how fast and hard she would fall on her face and join his club of worshipers. Unfortunately for John, she wasn't likely to start tittering any time soon. She had a feeling that not succumbing to his charms would in fact make an even stronger impression on him—which might help in enlisting his political support. "I will grant you the first waltz of the evening and a cotillion, but you shall owe me a favor."

"Interesting." His angelic features creased in thought; he was also smiling. "I accept."

"Until tomorrow evening." She curtsied elegantly and walked off the dance floor.

By the time she reached Iris, the buzz around her was almost deafening. "What was that about?" Iris gripped her arm, her voice low. "You didn't let him escort you off the floor."

"It's a new tactic I'm testing out." Isabel smiled wickedly. Sophie materialized beside her, huffing and puffing. "What happened with Admiral Duckworth?" Isabel asked.

"Lecherous old blighter! He thought that because he was short-sighted and half deaf I'd let him maul me. He didn't know I tramped over ancient toads like him at the opera in Paris."

Iris and Isabel exchanged amused glances while endeavoring not to laugh out loud. "Does this mean we should scratch the admiral off our potential list of supporters?" Iris asked.

Sophie sniffed with disgust. "Impertinent libertine! I hope he drowns in his bathtub." She looked at Isabel. "How was your waltz with Lord John?"

Iris debriefed her, finishing with, "Isabel was about to enlighten us about her new tactic."

"I'm keeping the Golden Angel guessing." Isabel grinned. "I don't know why he let my brother foist this introduction on him or why he thereupon asked me to dance and showed an interest in our charity, but I have every intention of finding out tomorrow at the Barrington ball."

"I thought you'd begged off," Iris said.

"I changed my mind. Lord John asked for three dances in advance. I need to find out why."

"Where's the mystery?" Sophie pouted very French-like. "A friend introduced him to a beautiful young woman, who isn't a featherbrain, and he wants to further the acquaintance."

"Did you ask if he would consider sponsoring our cause in the House or if he knew anyone who could obtain the lists for us?" Iris queried.

"Not yet. I did tell him about our efforts and he seemed interested. We'll see."

"Izzy knows someone else who could help us obtain the lists," Sophie mentioned.

"Indeed?" Iris looked delighted. "Who?"

"It's no one." Isabel squirmed. "An old acquaintance of my brother's. Some recluse."

Sophie twisted her lips. "According to the dashing major, you knew this recluse quite well, Izzy. I am certain a resourceful minx such as yourself could contrive a way to approach him."

"What dashing major?" Iris inquired guardedly.

"Me," a low voice spoke behind her.

Iris whipped around, her eyes wide with terror, her complexion ashen. She and Ryan stared at each other in deafening silence. Sophie and Isabel exchanged bemused glances.

Ryan was the first to recuperate. "Lady Chilton, I believe." He took her hand. Iris snatched it back, her light blue eyes glinting murderously. Softly Ryan said, "Don't cause a scene, Iris."

"Why not?" Iris hissed. "I'm amazed our patronesses allow the likes of you in here at all."

He smiled icily. "I could say the same about you," he murmured. "At least I didn't . . . sell my assets to be here."

Her flinty gaze flitted to his nether regions and returned to his face. "You just offer them to let. I wonder, however did you procure your voucher for this evening?"

Isabel choked. She never imagined that quiet, gentle Iris had such a ruthless streak in her.

Ryan didn't blink. "You know me, I am *my own* master. As it happens, I'm shopping not selling tonight. I'm told this place offers the pick of the debutantes."

"Oh. I see." Iris's sweet smile dripped poison. "You're hunting for a fortune, then?"

Macalister's jaw tightened. "Not so much a fortune as a woman of *true* nobility."

"Interesting." Iris tilted her head aside. "Why would a woman of true nobility want you?"

"For love?" He raised a cocky eyebrow.

Isabel decided to step in before they killed each other. "Good evening, major. How nice of you to join us. Would you be a dear and fetch me a glass of lemonade? I'm parched."

A devilish smile lit his face. "Isabel, *you're* a sight for sore eyes. Your glow brightens even the dowdiest of creatures." Though he didn't spare a glance in Iris's direction, he hit the mark.

Perceiving the hurt in Iris's eyes, Isabel wished he'd leave her poor friend alone. Nor did she appreciate being wielded as a weapon. She would get to the bottom of this later. She curled her hand around his arm. "I've a better idea. Let's stroll together to the refreshments table."

"Actually, I was hoping to lure you onto the dance floor."

Isabel was about to refuse, but caught Sophie's strict, prompting glare. Isabel reconsidered. Unless she cared to wipe the blood off the floor, whatever method drew Ryan away from Iris was good enough for now. She cast Ryan a charming smile. "How could I refuse?"

Yet before she managed to drag him off, he seized Iris's dance card and signed his name next to the last waltz. "There is something to be said for vintage as well."

"I am not dancing tonight," Iris clipped sternly.

"Then you shouldn't have tied your card on." He took

Sophie's card and marked a country dance. "Tonight, no woman is safe from me. Until later, ladies." He bowed and led Isabel away.

At the edge of the dance floor they were accosted by Lady Jersey, one of the seven high and mighty patronesses of Almack's. "Ryan, darling, how lovely to see you!" Lady Jersey cooed, grasping his free sleeve and leaning into his side.

"Sally." Ryan brought Lady Jersey's hand to his lips. "What can I say—*ravissante!*"

Sally tittered with delight. "I do so adore compliments from men in uniform. They sound . . . much more sincere." She let out a brandy-spiced breath—which was shocking in itself since only the mildest drinks were served at the assembly. No doubt Sally carried a little flask in her purse, Isabel thought as she observed the cozy interlude. It certainly solved the mystery regarding how Ryan had managed to come by a voucher in the space of two days. He had his own patroness.

When Isabel felt Sally's assessing gaze on her, she bobbed. "Lady Jersey."

"Miss Aubrey." Sally returned the gesture, but not without palpable antagonism. To Ryan she murmured, "I shall see you later, darling."

"Or sooner." He winked, and swept Isabel into the country dance.

Any illusion Isabel might have entertained regarding his potential as a future spouse was dashed this evening, for more than one reason. Ashby had been right to warn her off Ryan. Only it depressed her to know he had done so out of concern rather than jealousy. Her big brother.

Thankfully the dance was too lively to engage in conversation, and Isabel was spared the unpleasantness of dealing with the fallout of Ryan and Iris's confrontation. Tonight Ryan was the enemy, but she'd still agreed to walk with him Saturday afternoon, and while she was sorely tempted to cancel their engagement, he was the only person who knew some of Ashby's secrets.

Ashby. How many nights had she lain awake, envisioning herself gliding across the dance floor in his arms? She could almost imagine that the broad chest sporting the 18th silver and blue dolman jacket and the elegant pelisse swelling off the shoulder were his, not Ryan's.

They weren't waltzing, however, and as they stepped and turned, changing partners, Isabel came up against Lord John Hanson. They exchanged brief greetings and danced on to the next partner. She turned her head, curious to see with whom he was standing up.

"Louisa Talbot?" Both her friends looked horrified when Isabel reported the observation a while later. "Are you certain?" Sophie whispered in disbelief. "That dreadful creature everyone dislikes? Why in blazes would he want to dance with her?"

Isabel glanced at the far side of the ballroom, where a twittering circle converged around a white-blond head. Once upon a time, it was Ashby who held the title "Society's most sought after bachelor." Only in Ashby's case, because he was sinfully irresistible, he was pursued not only by every ambitious mother's debutante daughter, but by the mothers, the daughters, their sisters, and every other blasted female in sight. They all fancied him. Some of them had even gotten him—temporarily. "Perhaps he lost a wager," Isabel said, shrugging. "Who knows?"

"I know," Iris put in. "Louisa Talbot is as rich as Croesus. Her American father owned the largest tobacco plantation in the world. When he died last year, Louisa's mother married her old sweetheart, Lord Larimore, who'd also been her longtime lover throughout her first marriage. Louisa got the entire inheritance. Her mother didn't see a ha'pence."

"Lord John stands to inherit his grandfather, the Duke of

Haworth," Isabel asserted. "Why would he chase an ugly, in-
sipid, unpleasant woman for her money?"

"It's difficult to ignore all that money," Iris scoffed. "Prinny
has been known to pay her a compliment or two, himself.
Nevertheless, I hear that her American uncle is arriving next
week and that he despises the English aristocracy. He's
coming to town to keep his niece from falling prey to an impoverished lord. Some say he's already hired runners to dig
up dirt on her beaux."

"Louisa has beaux?" Isabel blinked. "She has trouble be-
friending her own persuasion, a fact which I find suspicious
in itself."

"There she goes again." Sophie indicated the freckled
insect loping cheerfully on the dance floor straight into the
arms of . . . none other than Ryan Macalister.

Sophie and Iris were right, Isabel acknowledged. He was
hunting for an heiress.

"Would you mind if we left early tonight?" Iris blurted.
"Unless Izzy wants to have another tête-à-tête with Lord
John, coax him into reading our bill proposal . . . ?"

Isabel met Sophie's knowing gaze. Their friend didn't want
to wait for the last waltz Ryan had imposed on her. The gentlemen of the *ton* knew that Iris's dance card was an "ornament" and nothing more, thanks to Chilton. Ryan would
cause a scene, and they'd had one too many scenes this
evening. It didn't take a genius to realize that Iris and Ryan
knew each other well. How well and what the source of their
mutual animosity was remained to be unraveled. The one
good deed Ryan had unwittingly performed tonight was side-
tracking Iris and Sophie from questioning her about Ashby.
"We may leave whenever you wish," Isabel replied. "I already
made up my mind to speak to Lord John about our bill proposal at the Barrington ball tomorrow evening."

"It is better this way," Sophie concluded. "Let him fall in

love with you first. Then, when he is too besotted to refuse, ask for his sponsorship."

Isabel smiled. "Sophie, you are awful! How can you suggest I delude the poor man?"

"Perhaps while working your wiles on him, the Golden Angel will work his wiles on you, and instead of deluding, we'll have a happy, socially conscientious couple." Iris smiled.

Isabel narrowed her eyes. "Did Stilgoe put you two up to this?"

"No! Of course not." Sophie shuddered.

"We would never collaborate with the enemy," Iris reassured her as they headed for the doorway. "However, I fail to see why you are so averse to the concept of marriage. I know mine isn't the best example, but Sophie was very happy with her George. Weren't you, Sophie?"

"Very happy." Sophie nodded glumly. "George was my strength. He took a poor Parisian opera singer and transformed her into a queen. He gave me Jerome. And I'll tell you something else. If I'm ever so lucky as to find another man as wonderful as George, I won't hesitate to say 'yes' again. I miss being married. There are several benefits to the situation."

A dark bench and a certain heart-stealing hussar appeared before Isabel's eyes. Letting out a sigh, she banished the image from her mind. "I'm not averse to the idea of marriage," she said. "I'm simply saving myself for . . . the best candidate who comes along."

"Look at the bright side, Izzy," Iris said. "If the best candidate turns out to be Lord John Hanson, you will have the most adorable babies London has ever seen."

A glorious idea exploded in Isabel's mind. "Did you say 'babies'?"

Chapter Five

A silent suffering, and intense;
The rock, the vulture, and the chain,
All that the proud can feel of pain,
The agony they do not show,
The suffocating sense of woe,
Which speaks but in its loneliness.
—Lord Byron: *Prometheus*

"What the devil?" Ashby raised his eyes from the stack of bank statements and investment reports his man-of-affairs had brought to his inspection and glared at his office door. Chaos had taken over his foyer. In the old days, he would have marched outside and put an end to the crisis, but experience had taught him that the sight of his face would only augment whatever was going on. Gnashing his teeth, he settled for an account. "Phipps!" he growled, startling Mr. Brooks.

The broker smiled timorously, pushed his spectacles back onto the bridge of his nose, and reburied his face in his papers. Since his injury, Ashby felt that few people could look him in the eye and ignore the scars on his face. Mr. Brooks was not one of them.

Phipps came in, and Ashby's jaw fell open. "What's this?" he asked, gawking at the pretty pink bundle in his butler's arms. It couldn't be what he thought it was. During the course of his thirty-five years of life, a number of women tried to saddle him with babies, but his hired runners disproved their claims. This time what stumped him was a crystallizing realization that he would not mind learning the child was his. Only it was impossible. He hadn't been with a woman in over two years and the little girl Phipps held couldn't be much older than twelve months.

"This is Miss Danielli," Phipps announced, smiling with pleasure at the infant clinging to his neck. "She has come to call on you, my lord." The rosy bundle was busy surveying his office.

Pushing his chair back, Ashby rose to his feet. He approached them. The baby girl's wispy golden hair was tied atop her head in a pink ribbon that matched her clothing; her wide, curious eyes reminded him of a cloudless sky in Spain; her small pink lips curled up in a smile. *Oh, God.* Black depression choked him. "Who brought her here?" he asked, already knowing the answer.

"The, eh"—Phipps glanced at the broker's back hunched over the massive desk—"same individual who was here the day before yesterday and the day before that."

Ashby shut his eyes. So this was what the Greeks called "divine retribution, the vengeful judgment of the gods." Losing so many of his men, his best friend among them, and his hopes for a future was not enough; he had to walk among the living and keep paying for his sins until the day he died.

Mr. Brooks collected his belongings. "Perhaps I should leave these with you, my lord, to review in your own time, and I shall return to take down further instructions next week."

"Very well, Brooks. You may go." His head wasn't in it anyway. Ordinarily, handling his lucrative assets was a pastime he enjoyed and that also kept the mold from his brain. Isabel's visits had set him completely off kilter. As during the first six, hellish months of his self-imposed incarceration, he could scarcely sleep or eat. He spent long nights in the cellar, trying to convince himself that seeing her again had had no effect on him whatsoever. But the sad truth was he had never felt more alone than he did now. Even his nightmares were different: Instead of reenacting Waterloo and Sorauren and failing each time anew to rescue either Will or his own person, in his new recurring dream he was standing alone in the smoky-black aftermath of battle, surrounded by miles of corpses, not knowing in which direction lay England.

He had also had a very erotic dream of Isabel, but that was something he really didn't want to brood over. Suffice it to say he'd experienced a very rude awakening. Just knowing she was here, in his house, and that he was about to see her, stirred the mutinous part of his anatomy to life again. Damn the woman. *The woman* . . . Not girl. It was significant, even in his dreams.

"Good day, my lord." Mr. Brooks nodded stiffly and hastily escaped the office.

Ashby extended his hands and lifted Danielli into his arms. If Isabel trusted his butler with the infant, he safely assumed she wouldn't mind if he held Danielli a bit. A vanilla-scented cloud descended upon him. The plump bundle was light, delicate, and soft, suffusing his veins with unbidden tenderness. "My God," he murmured. "My God." *This* he would never know—holding his own child in his arms. The sensation was humbling, uplifting. "Where's Isabel?"

"Downstairs with Mrs. Nelson." Phipps tickled Danielli with his finger, making her giggle, but she quickly returned her attention to Ashby. She seemed utterly fascinated by him.

Ashby scowled. "With the housekeeper? What the devil happened?"

"Hector jumped on her when she came in through the door and covered her with drool. She went to wash it off. She mentioned something about his being a pup when she found him . . ."

"She gave him to me." Disregarding his butler's curious gaze, Ashby kept his eyes on the bubbly girl. Her blue eyes dancing with mirth, Danielli raised her hands and smacked her palms onto his cheeks. At his shocked expression, a shriek of laughter left her lips. *He didn't scare her*.

"I believe she likes you, my lord."

Amazing. Cradling her against his chest with one arm, Ashby peeled one tiny hand off his cheek and brought it to his nose. The effect nearly dissolved him altogether. He understood how men fell in love with infants at first sight. She looked so much like Isabel, his heart clenched.

Someone scratched the door. "Phipps, are you in there? May I come in?" Isabel called.

Bloody hell. Ashby wasn't prepared to expose his private hell to her. Nor was he about to dive underneath the desk. "Phipps, take the girl and go to her."

His butler reached inside his coat and produced the black mask. "I'll expect a considerable increase in wages, my lord."

Good old Phipps. "How does a ten percent increase sound?" Grabbing the mask, Ashby returned to his chair and settled Danielli in his lap. Tying the mask on proved tricky as she kept sticking her tiny fingers in the eye-holes. Nevertheless he wasn't ready to relinquish his treasure yet. "Come in," he finally called, startled by the sudden acceleration of his heartbeat.

"There you are, my darling." Isabel sashayed in and didn't stop until she reached his side. Her muslin morning gown was the color of pale lavender with a high crepe collar and a purple ribbon sewn beneath her full, pert breasts—of which he received an alluring view as she bent over to lift Danielli into her arms. His torture didn't end with that—she, too, smelled of vanilla.

Ashby went hard. He stood, wishing he were shorter, or

that his desk were taller. "Get out, Phipps." At least he was still alive, he mused morbidly, tipping his head to inhale more of her, of Isabel. Her soft, full lips were attached to Danielli's rounded ivory cheek. The sight twisted his insides. One thought possessed him: These two beautiful girls could have been his—if only he had played his cards right, if only he had waited until she grew up and spoken to Will, if only he hadn't been an abject idiot . . . "I thought I told you to stay away from me," he rasped softly.

"Did you think you could scare me off so easily?" As her head swerved to meet his gaze, a soft, loose curl brushed his lips, making his mouth water. Her bright smile was his final undoing.

He moved closer, his gaze focused on her cherry lips. Abruptly, she hoisted Danielli to a firmer embrace, shattering his lustful stupor. Christ, he felt like a lapdog being led on a leash.

"I told my charity board about your donation." She grinned at him. "You should have seen their faces. Five thousand pounds! They were eager to thank you in person. I had to lie through my teeth and claim you were an anonymous donor. Sophie insisted it was the very definition of charity—giving in secret so as not to shame the poor. She said our benefactor was remarkable."

And there it was—the adoring glow in her beautiful eyes. His chest constricted. His hoarse voice sounded foreign to his own ears. "But you know who it was from."

"Even so." She put her hand on his arm. "I have yet to meet the man whose generosity and kindness surpasses yours, Ashby."

He winced. She really was clueless regarding who he was or what he'd done in his life. His first impulse was to enlighten her, but what would that serve? Disillusionment had poisoned his soul. Why would he do that to her? "I was glad to do it, but . . ."

"Don't." She shook her head, remaining a vision of sweetness and light. "I didn't come here to plague you further. I respect your decision."

"You do?" He frowned behind the mask. "Then why did you come?" His curiosity was killing him. A new fear suddenly gnawed at him—what if she stopped coming?

Smiling, Isabel lifted the infant and—to his utter stupefaction—deposited her in his arms. "I told Danielli so much about you, she wanted to meet her uncle's best friend."

"U–cle!" Danielli piped and ran her soft, chubby palm along his hair and ear. Her delicate touch did strange things to him—it almost made him feel human again. *Extraordinary.*

Isabel's sky blue irises filled with love. "Isn't she adorable? I'll have you know she rarely pats anyone outside our family. Congratulations on being accepted to a most prestigious club."

"The Aubrey pride of golden lions?" A grin tugged at a corner of his mouth. "So . . . what did you tell her about me?"

"I told her you liked puppies, for one. The rest is between us girls."

Warmth seeped into his jaded soul as he cuddled the soft angel against him. "She's so pure, so defenseless." Gazing at the tiny face beaming at him, a sudden, inexplicable instinct to protect her overwhelmed him. "How is such a perfect little creature to survive in our ugly world?"

"That's her ammunition—she's so small and lovable, she makes you want to protect her."

His throat clogged; he glanced at Isabel. She had the same damnable effect on him. Very gently he caressed Danielli's silken head. "She's enchanting. How old is she?"

"Thirteen months."

He knew he had no right to be jealous, but he couldn't resist asking, "Who's her father?"

Isabel frowned. "Interesting question," she replied, eyeing him strangely.

The thought of Isabel belonging to another man, who made love to her every night and saw her smile every morning, gutted him. "She's yours, isn't she? You married."

She studied his eyes. "She's Stilgoe's. He married."

Heady relief broke over him. As if released from invisible chains, a faint grin attacked his lips. "Congratulations. Your brother is a fortunate man. Whom did he marry?"

"Angela Landry. Will was present at their wedding. Didn't he tell you? It took place right after Bonaparte's first abdication. Come to think of it, I believe you were invited."

"I can't recall." He had been invited, but he had chosen not to come. After their forbidden kiss, he had made a point of staying away from Seven Dover Street—at first, because he had to, because he couldn't trust himself near Isabel anymore, and later, because he didn't have a choice. He didn't want her pity; he wanted her adoring glow. He contemplated her morosely. Everything about her—her spirit, her beauty, her gestures, her voice—was incredibly lovely and feminine. No doubt he wasn't the only man who noticed what a bruising Venus she had become or knew about the hundred thousand pounds to be settled on her when she married, and the wolves were circling her at every rout. Sooner or later she would end up married to one of them, and then what would become of him? The problem was: He felt paralyzed to do anything about it.

"Who was the man who left before I came in?" Isabel inquired. She took out a handful of biscuits wrapped in a napkin from her pocket and offered one to Danielli.

"Mr. Brooks, my man of affairs. Why?"

"You let him see you without a mask."

"How would you know that?" If she had figured that out, she must have also done a quick calculation and realized he'd been wounded the year before her oldest brother's wedding.

"You made me wait outside. I imagine you weren't putting your clothes on." She flashed that engaging smile of hers that used to turn him beet red. "You didn't the last time I was here."

His mouth began falling, and he clenched his jaw against it. He couldn't believe it. Little Izzy Aubrey was actually flirting with him! His old self would have parried with a sly comment about how easily he could shed his clothes if she cared to join him in some recreational activities in the bedchamber—she was, thank God, an adult now—but his new, damaged self settled for the truth. "Mr. Brooks's sensibilities do not concern me. Yours do."

"I think my sensibilities might surprise you," she asserted quietly.

"I wouldn't recommend it." Leaning back against the edge of the desk, he returned his gaze to Danielli, who was tracing his mask with her tiny fingers.

"I promised Angie I'd take Danielli to the park. Why don't you join us? It would be fun."

He laughed huskily. "So that's where you're supposed to be, in the park."

She smiled back. "Why is it amusing?"

He caught her gaze, grinning predaciously. "It's always a good sign when a woman lies to her family to be with me." Her cheeks went up in flames, which was an even better sign. After her absurd suggestion that he consider her a sister, it felt good to have his old teeth back.

Joining the fun, Danielli stuffed her half-chewed, drool-soaked biscuit into his mouth.

"I told her we'd feed the ducks at the pond," Isabel explained with a chuckle.

Inescapably he swallowed the soggy thing. "I see. I'm a duck."

"A very"—twinkling eyes raked him from head to toe—"large one, my lord."

The muscles across his abdomen tightened. He may have lost his face, but he was not *that* far gone; his male instincts operated in full, blasted capacity. *Isabel still had a tendre for him*. The good news was she was a full-grown woman with ripe sexual needs; the bad news was she wanted the man he'd once been. Yet he couldn't resist saying, "I have a garden with a fishpond."

"You do?" She bit her lip on a timid smile while Danielli wrinkled her nose, hissing, "Fiss! Fiss!" through tiny white teeth. Isabel's bright blue eyes sparkled naughtily. "Lead the way."

"Is the guard necessary?" Ashby spoke in Isabel's ear, creating goose bumps on her skin.

Standing beside him on the lush bank of his garden fishpond, Isabel watched Danielli and Lucy playing with half a dozen dolls and wondered why he, of all men, had to have such a potent effect on her. It was an old mystery. "The guard?" She frowned. "Oh, my maid. Yes, for two reasons. Lucy dislikes your butler. I thought it prudent to separate them."

"I assure you the feeling is mutual. However," his tone sharpened, "I don't relish making an exhibition of myself for the benefit of strangers. Get rid of her."

Though she was considered tall, his great height forced Isabel to tip her head back to meet his gaze. He was impeccably groomed: A teal silk waistcoat complemented his eyes; a starched white collar framed his square jaw; his superfine jacket and trousers were gray. With his black mask, vivid green eyes, and too-long, thick dark hair brushed to a shine, he made her think of a wolf disguised as a nobleman. So he didn't make a habit of wearing a mask, and she sensed he felt awkward doing so, but he was very choosy of his confidants. She longed to remove it, to see his beautiful features again—the ones etched in a secret place in her heart. Whatever he concealed behind it, she didn't think it would make the slightest difference to her.

"You're staring," he muttered, his gaze fixed ahead.

Uh-oh. "Apologies. It's just that I haven't seen you for so long, I . . ." Her voice dropped to a whisper. "Would you consider removing your mask if I sent Lucy inside the house?"

"No."

Stifling her disappointment, she reassured herself that that too would come. She had made excellent progress so far. He'd finally invited her to prolong her visit. She was patient as well as resourceful—hadn't her disarming little niece succeeded in softening his resistance? "If you are concerned about gossip, rest your mind at ease. Lucy never carries tales, and neither do I."

"You, I trust. Your maid . . ." He cast a stern look at the compact female settling Danielli on her pink baby-blanket.

Curling her hand around his sleeve, Isabel rose on tiptoe and whispered, "Lucy's cousin, Mary, lived with her husband in Cheapside, where they ran a tailor shop. Frank took a ball in the war, and Mary was left alone. Two weeks ago, the lease on her shop terminated, and Mary was evicted to the street. She ended up in a workhouse. I brought her to Seven Dover Street and—"

"You ventured into a workhouse? *Alone?*" He glowered at her.

His tone made her feel like a little girl in short skirts—which she wasn't any longer. "I'm not a hoyden. I never venture out alone anywhere. I went with Lucy."

His lips formed a grim line. "To which workhouse did you go?"

"To Bishopsgate. We took the poor girl out of that nasty place and now—"

"Bishopsgate—in *Spitalfields?*" he growled. "Does Stilgoe know about this?"

"No, he doesn't," she hissed, indicating Lucy's back. "As I

was saying, we took Mary out of there, and now she mends our staff's livery for the time being, but I hope to find her a better position soon. So you see, Lucy would never gossip about me or my friends."

His gaze softened. "Isabel the lioness, defender of the weak, protector of the unfortunate." He leaned aside, pulling away the errant curl clinging to her lips. "What's the second reason?"

Her breath caught. She kept telling herself that all he'd ever felt or would feel for her was fondness, but adhering to her decision to just be fond of him proved to be extremely difficult.

"Lucy minds Danielli, and I . . . wanted to be free to talk with you, my lord."

His eyes turned cold. "Was there something in particular you wished to discuss with me? Your charity, perhaps?"

"No, just to chat." She smiled nervously. She was going to help him feel human again if it killed her—which was a real possibility, considering the risk to her reputation . . . and to her silly heart. Only this time she was older and wiser. No moonlit kisses, no stupid love confessions. She would offer friendship and expect nothing more than his friendship in return.

"Just to chat?" he repeated, unconvinced. "You have no special requests—some documents for my perusal or some wretched soul I should help you save?"

"No, nothing," she said in earnest.

"Very well. I'll mind Danielli. Call off your dragon."

Isabel watched him saunter to her niece and sit on the grass beside her. Danielli instantly pounced on him. Hector loped over. Ashby introduced him to the girl. They were becoming one big happy family. Fine. If he preferred being alone with her, it would only make her task that much easier. She approached Lucy. Her maid was pretending not to notice their host at all. Blind, deaf, and dumb, Lucy would make a splendid butler. "You may go inside the house now, Lucy. The sun is strong today. You'll get those terrible headaches again. I'll look after Danielli."

Her maid shot her a puzzled look—they were sitting in the mottled shade of a large elm tree—but made herself scarce nonetheless.

Ashby shrugged out of his jacket and laid it out on the grass for Isabel. "Thank you." She plunked herself down and arranged her skirts over her ankles. She saw Hector sniffing Danielli, who seemed both mesmerized by and afraid of the black retriever. Instinctively Isabel leaned forward, uncertain whether the dog could be trusted with such a young person.

A hand stayed her. "She's safe. Hector would never hurt her."

"How can you be sure?" Isabel retorted, annoyed to be held back.

"Because I trained him," Ashby said. "She isn't the first toddler he has sniffed. We passed through many villages in Spain."

Danielli tugged on Hector's ear. Isabel's heart stopped, but the dog slumped at Danielli's feet and let her assault him without so much as a twitch. Isabel let out a sigh. "Be nice to the doggy, pudding."

"Don't you trust me?"

His masked face loomed mere inches away. The tiniest tail of a scar on his right cheek escaped the pall of his mask. She curled her hands into fists to keep from tracing it with her finger. "I do trust you, but I am not her mother and therefore must be thrice as vigilant."

"Because she's your responsibility . . ."

"Correct."

". . . along with all the unfortunate strays in the city?" It was a statement, not a question.

"You're making fun of me."

"No." He reached out and looped one of the soft curls floating beside her cheek around his finger. "I still don't like the idea of you wandering through Spitalfields and its rookeries-infested environs," he murmured. "Next time, come to me first. I'll send someone with you."

"Why not come with me yourself? You'll find the experience fascinating, I assure you."

"You think I haven't seen enough misery in my life? I told you—I'm done with that."

Who was he fooling? She contemplated his expressive eyes. "Your neighbors are throwing a ball this evening," she mentioned conversationally.

"I know," he said dryly. "Believe it or not, I still get my fair share of invitations."

"You're a war hero, Ashby. Everyone wants to shake your hand. You should attend. You'll cause quite a stir. Lady Barrington will be delighted."

"I'm not Wellington," he grunted. "I don't go about with an entourage, hopping from balls to soirees, expecting standing ovations. Nor do I relish shaking the hands of those who couldn't tear themselves away from their clubs to actually make a difference in the damned war."

An idea poked at her brain. "Do you dance?"

"What?"

"Do you enjoy dancing?"

"Not recently. What does that have to do with anything?"

"Well, I would very much like to dance with you." She bit her lip, shocked at her audacity. She couldn't imagine speaking like this to anyone else, but with Ashby she had nothing to lose. It was just them, and she had already made the worst possible blunder with him.

Humor touched his eyes. "I'm beginning to think you are a hoyden. Does Stilgoe know you call on single gentlemen and ask them to dance?"

And with that he slew her good humor. Why hadn't she learned her dratted lesson and kept her mouth shut? "I will take that as a 'no,' my lord."

He put a finger beneath her chin, forcing her to look at him. "This is not an affront to you."

"Of course it isn't. Don't be silly." She deflected his hand with a composed smile.

"I mean it," he breathed. "My not going into Society has more than one drawback."

"What is it this time?" she asked, her annoyance with herself overriding her mortification.

"Not being able to dance with you."

A welter of feelings twisted her insides. If he asked her to dance, she would hum a tune for them to dance to, if necessary. "What is your Christian name?"

He drew back. "My name has expired."

"Expired?" She saw him picking up a twig from the grass and snapping it in two.

"No one used it in over thirty years. Then yes, it has expired."

"*Thirty years?* How is it possible?"

"Thirty-one years, to be exact." He shrugged dismissively. "I became 'my lord' or 'Lord Ashby' when I was four, and 'Ashby' when I attended Eton. The French had gaudier names for me." He smirked blackly. "I suppose at some point my Christian name lost its meaning."

"How awful."

His gaze shot to hers. "Why?"

"Because . . . your name is a part of who you are. It defines you."

"Good God, I sincerely hope not." He eyed her with interest. "How does your name define you, Isabel Jane?" His soft enunciation of her first and middle name drew her attention to his lips; they had a slight, natural, tempting pout to them that simply begged to be kissed. Of course that was what had gotten her in trouble with him years ago.

"I don't know how precisely, but it does. Names have meanings."

"Pity." His kissable lips twisted sardonically. "Mine is distinctly unflattering."

To keep her gaze and her thoughts from lingering on his mouth she pulled Danielli into her lap and offered her another biscuit. "Well—" she smiled "—should I try guessing it?"

His tone was brittle. "I just explained—"

"Peter? Paul? Percival?" She sent him a speculative glance. "Pierce? Philip? Peregrine?"

He grinned wryly. "Who told you it begins with a P, minx?"

"You did. You signed your card PNL. Lancaster is your family name, is it not?"

"Uh-hmm. How did your brother and his wife come up with Danielli's name?"

She stroked Danielli's fair plume. "Her name is Daniella Wilhelmina Aubrey. We also call her pudding, puppet, precious . . ."

He ignored her poorly veiled hint. "William Daniel Aubrey. You named her after Will." He playfully tugged at Danielli's biscuit, eliciting lilting laughter from the little girl.

Isabel's heart expanded at the spectacle: the big, bad, rakehell wolf gadding with a toddler. She had an insuppressible desire to gad with him too. "Colonel Ashby, don't be squeamish," she cooed sweetly, imitating that awful flirt Sally Jersey while batting her long, curling eyelashes at him. "Tell me your name."

"Squeamish?" With a pulse-quickening grin, he lunged at her. Laughter filled her throat as she put out a hand to stop him. His chest was steel swathed with fine fabrics. "Take it back."

"No. Why else would you keep mum about it? Is it a military secret?"

"It ought to have been. I can well imagine the quips I'd have gotten from my men had they known my first name."

Supposedly keeping him at bay, she kept her hand on his chest and fought the urge to slide it over his silk waistcoat in a slow caress. It was awful how she couldn't stop touching this man. "Did Will ever ask what your first name was?"

He shook his head. "Some women I knew did."

The rapt look in his eyes made her heart flip-flop. "And did you tell them?"

"No, I did not tell them."

Inadvertently she dampened her lips, a gesture that instantly drew his gaze to her mouth. She felt his heart thumping against her hand, and it was all she could do to keep from grasping his waistcoat and pulling him closer for a kiss. *Stop it,* a stern, inner voice rebuked her. She must not allow her emotions to spiral down that pit again. Nothing good would come of it. The man had said so himself, a moment before admitting to the chief drawback of his isolation.

Bored with the two of them, Danielli scrambled to the grass. She knocked Isabel's hand off Ashby's chest, putting more distance between them. "She is the sweetest thing," he observed, watching her niece try to feed one of her dolls to Hector. "Everything is good in her little world."

Tentatively, Isabel studied his masked profile, noting the wistful look in his eye. He had lost his parents when he was so young, but instead of finding a wife and making a real home for himself, he shunned the world. "Do you remember your parents?" she asked quietly.

"It's difficult to know for certain, growing up with so many portraits and stories as I have. I remember my mother's hands and eyes. She had beautiful blue eyes, full of light." He looked at her. "Like yours."

His gaze sent her heart aflutter. One moment he treated her as a child, the next he aroused her deepest emotions. "What happened to them?"

"A horse riding accident. They were dead on the spot."

"That's terrible. I'm so sorry." She covered his large hand with hers. She couldn't begin to imagine what it had been like for him to find himself alone in the world at the tender age of four. Like Danielli, she grew up in a doting, protective family that made her the center of the universe.

"So am I." He raised her hand to his lips and pressed a soft, searing kiss to her knuckles.

She felt the heat of his lips spreading in her veins. "Which relative took you in?"

"I don't have any. My mother was an only child. My father was a second son. His family was killed in the Colonies. I've been unable to trace anyone else. My title will die with me."

"That depends entirely on you, Ashby."

"Not entirely." He eyed her. "You do know it takes two to produce the required results."

Despite the gentle breeze ruffling the leaves above their heads, she was beginning to feel uncomfortably warm in her multilayered gown. "Who took care of you?"

"An army of servants, solicitors, and stewards—more care and attention than most children receive in life. I had a perfectly miserable childhood."

She was glad he hadn't lost his sense of humor. It showed strength of character, a sign that he had what it took to regain his old self. "Do you think of having a family of your own?"

Sudden, black tension vibrated from him, and belatedly Isabel realized she hit upon a nerve. He lunged forward and caught her niece around her midsection. "Danielli, sweetheart, we don't swim with the fishies," he explained. "We just look at them." He held her upright, pointing at the golden slivers winding in the water.

Isabel all but suffered an apoplexy as it dawned on her what had very nearly happened. She bolted to her knees and pulled Danielli into her arms, her heart hammering. "Thank goodness for your sharp instincts." She exhaled, chastising herself for her inattentiveness. She felt his hot gaze on her face and fought the impulse to look up. Man, woman, and child. *Charming.* If Stilgoe saw them like this, she would be married to Ashby faster than she could say, *He doesn't want me.* Yet for some inexplicable reason there was no doubt in her mind that Ashby would do the right thing by her. She focused her attention on her niece. "Precious, let's play with your dolls."

"Fissies! Fissies!" Danielli protested, fighting Isabel's hold on her.

Chuckling, Ashby rolled up his sleeves. He lay on his stomach, stretched out on the ground with his head facing the pond, and dipped his hand in the water. "Let's tickle the gold-fishies."

Danielli pealed with laughter. Isabel laid her next to Ashby and watched the little girl aping his every move. Something achingly sweet and wistful stirred in her heart. It was *not* longing. She wasn't panting after him anymore. It simply heartened her to see Will's friend playing with their niece— as Will ought to have been doing. She sat back on her heels and laughed as man and babe splashed water to every direction, petrifying the goldfish.

This was the Ashby who had rid Hector of the thorn in his paw, the one she had been hopelessly in love with. Her gaze traveled over his sprawled, large form, from his whipcord arms to his long legs. The fine material of his gray trousers stretched over his hard bottom, showing no signs of the two years he'd been buried in his house. Her brother had grown visibly flaccid since becoming domesticated, despite his regular visits to Gentleman Jackson's. Then again, Stilgoe didn't labor on slabs of timber in his cellar for months on end.

"What are you looking at?"

Startled, Isabel met Ashby's twinkling eyes, blushing profusely. "I was admiring your . . ."

"My boots, perhaps?" He pushed up to a sitting position. "Or was it the cut of my trous—"

"I was admiring your children skills," she blurted quickly, wishing she could douse her flaming face in the fishpond. "You seem quite adept at making little girls happy."

"I'm quite adept at making older girls happy, too," he drawled in his richly sensual voice.

She froze for a heartbeat. Since her coming-out, she had been flattered and flirted with and even propositioned by enough male members of the *ton* to recognize his line for what it was—*but Ashby?* The man had physically shoved her away from him when she had tried to kiss him. Of course, back in those days, she thought acidly, he wasn't living the life of a lychnobite monk.

She glanced at her niece. Danielli was fast asleep on her pink blanket in the shade, a vision of angelic sweetness.

"You did say you require my special skills, did you not?" Ashby's voice was no more than a warm whisper of air in her hair.

Her heart began to race. She dared not look at him. "It is irrelevant now."

"Why?" His breath was warm on her cheek.

Summoning her earlier resolve to be his friend and nothing more, she drew back and faced him. "I wrote the message in the hopes of persuading you to support my charity."

"I see. But why come to me? Your brother sits in the House of Lords."

"Yes, well, he is encouraging me to look for representation elsewhere in the hopes it would solve his *other* problem."

"What other problem?"

She shifted uneasily. "It is Stilgoe's—and Mama's—foremost wish that I should marry."

He went very still. "Stilgoe wants you to marry me?"

Her gaze locked with his for a sizzling moment. He seemed so serious, almost shocked, she wondered whether she ought to be offended. "I never told him I intended to ask for your help."

"Ah." He nodded grimly and with this simple gesture withdrew his magnetic hold on her; the effect was akin to dropping hard on the ground. "Why is it a problem, then?" he asked. When she refused to answer, he smiled perceptively. "There's the rub. You don't want to marry."

Her eyelashes gave an involuntary flutter. "Not at the moment. No."

"Why not? You must think me ancient, but I still recall that most chits become obsessed with the topic the instant they are launched into Society."

"I don't think of you as ancient."

"That's reassuring, but you still haven't answered my question," he said softly, undeterred.

She squirmed inwardly. She hated that question, mostly because she had trouble answering it herself. "I lost a brother two years ago. Marriage wasn't my primary concern."

"And now?"

She evaded his gaze. "That depends."

"On what?"

For goodness sake. "You're like a dog with a bone, aren't you?"

"That is one of the skills that made me a competent field commander and kept me alive." His charming, self-assured smile numbed her brain—definitely his superior talent, she thought. "You love children. Don't you want to become a mother, Isabel?"

She gritted her teeth. "You ought to ask yourself the very same question, Ashby. You are the one in need of an heir and a spare, and yet you are decidedly against marriage."

"You are wrong about me," he said quietly. "I was engaged once."

Her world shook. "You were? What happened? You didn't marry—?"

"It's a long story, and we were discussing you. I wager there are a good number of eager young bucks dancing attendance on you."

"Hordes. What of it?" she countered, straight-faced.

He leaned closer, his voice low, husky, and full of temptation. "Don't you want a man who adores you, Isabel? A man who'll introduce you to the physical aspects of love? Surely you are curious about such things."

Drat. She felt so awkward discussing this with him, mostly because the only man she had ever come close to experiencing such things with was *him.* "I suppose I am. Slightly."

"Slightly?" A ghost of a smile danced on his lips as his eyes darkened. "I recall a girl who was more than slightly curious."

She sucked in a breath. "How dare you throw *that* in my face?" She blanched, wishing she *had* drowned herself in the pond. "I should go." She started collecting Danielli's dolls.

"Wait." His hand closed on her arm. "Don't be angry. We never had a chance to discuss it, but I think it's time we did, don't you?"

"There is nothing to discuss." She couldn't look at him; she felt so mortified.

"I disagree. You were very sweet that night, and I was—"

"There's no point in rehashing the past." She tried to jerk free of his grip, but he wouldn't allow it. Damn the man. Tears stung her eyes. If he apologized for spurning her, she would turn into a watering pot. "I came as a friend," she retorted, "and I'd very much like to leave as one."

"A friend."

"Yes, a friend. For years you were a part of our family, then you stopped coming. When Will died, and you still didn't come to call, I . . . worried about you. You imprison yourself in this grand house, alone. You never go out in Society. You tell me your life is over—"

"Then you decided to rescue me." He stared at her as though he considered throttling her. "Listen here, Miss Charity," he clipped tersely. "I'm not one of your poor unfortunates. Nor am I your responsibility. I don't need your help—or your frigging pity! I never lamented not having a sister, and now I know why. So I strongly suggest you whisk your lovely bottom out of here and stay the hell away from me!"

As he pushed to his feet, panic possessed her. She fisted his shirtsleeve, staying him on the ground. "I didn't come here out of pity! I came because . . ." Lord, this was so difficult.

"Because you needed my help with your charity."

"There's that, but . . ." Her voice shook. "You also remind me of Will, whom I miss dearly."

"We mustn't forget that." He began to rise again.

She tightened her grasp on his sleeve. "Everything I said to you is true, but the reason I —" She was that wide-eyed little girl again—the one he'd scorned years ago. Her heart thundered in her ears. In a small voice, she said, "I came because . . . I missed you, Ashby. I missed you every day for the past seven years. I had to see you. I . . ." Tears streamed down her cheeks; the pain in her heart was unbearable. If he banished her forever, she didn't know what she would do.

His eyes glittered as brilliant and hard as emeralds. "You shouldn't have come to me at all." There was fury in his voice, yet something else that sounded like desperation. He wrapped a hand around her nape. "Damn you," he whispered, drawing her closer. "You make me remember things I vowed to forget." He angled his head and covered her mouth with his.

Lightning seared her spine. His lips were faintly familiar, achingly soft. They molded hers, savoring the initial contact of their mouths. Knowing what was to come next, she parted her lips against his and sighed with pleasure as he tasted her with a gentle stroke of his tongue.

Sweet heaven. This was as far as they had gotten seven years ago, before he had torn his mouth away. This time, however, she refused to let him retreat. She locked her arms around his muscled waist and returned his kiss with years-old longing.

"Ashby . . ." She sighed, tipping her head back and rising to his kiss as if her life depended on it. Her lips clung to his, seeking, needing, beckoning, helpless to resist the mystifying craving he liberally exuded. She licked his tongue and shuddered at the delicious frissions that raked her. His kiss was heavenly, better than heavenly—it was utterly sublime. And dazedly, she wondered how she could be so fortunate as to have found her way into his arms—as a woman.

"This was well overdue," he murmured, not allowing more than a sigh between their slow, sultry mouths.

"What was?" she asked, blissfully lightheaded, her eyelashes as heavy as bricks.

"This. Us." He made love to her mouth with the patience and skill of a master seducer, flooding her with a wealth of feelings and sensations. "The night we kissed," he went on in his low, mesmeric voice, feeding on her mouth as if it were a cup of Lydian elixir, "you unleashed the devil in me. Who'd have thought that a wispy innocent should kiss like Aphrodite herself? You made me ache to kiss you like this, not as one kisses a child, but as a man kisses a woman." He deepened their kiss, tangling their tongues in a hot, sensual, nerve-thrumming duel.

Never in all her girlish dreams of him did she imagine his kiss would be like this—all the passions and yearnings in the world distilled into the soft motion of his lips, into the thorough explorations of his tongue. "You pushed me away then," she admonished softly.

That night, she hadn't been thinking; she hadn't known the first thing about kissing a man. *He* was the one who had surprised *her* with her first brief lesson in what kissing should be like between a man and a woman when his tongue swept along the seam of her lips and licked inside her mouth. His assault had been shocking, electrifying, and all too fleeting. An instant later he had repelled her, as though he himself had felt repelled. If his sole concern had been her young age, he should have made that clear, instead of leaving her feeling awkward and . . . unappealing.

"What was I supposed to do? Ruin my best friend's little

sister? God knows I wanted to." He put his lips to her ear and whispered, "You've no idea what a confounded mess you made of my life when your sweet mouth opened to mine . . ."

His warm breath in her ear had a narcotic effect on her. "Really?"

"Really." He dipped his tongue in her ear, turning her brain to mush. Shivers swept over the back of her neck and snaked to her belly. "You were so young, Isabel," he murmured, as he dragged his mouth along the side of her neck, inhaling her with scalding kisses. "My reaction to you was . . . reprehensible. I felt nothing but disgust for myself afterward. If I upset or offended you, I apologize. I botched the whole thing like a cloddish schoolboy."

Her smile was unquenchable. "Thank goodness age is not a permanent condition."

He held her head and scrutinized her face closely, his eyes smoldering. "Thank goodness."

He recaptured her mouth and gently lowered her to the grass. Caught in a trance of passion, she felt his brawny torso coming down atop her, crushing her soft breasts. Her hands roamed his broad back in wide circles, embracing him close to her heart. It was an exhilarating sensation—lying beneath him, kissing him, embracing him, inhaling him—and felt as natural as breathing.

Their kiss went on and on, growing rougher and more demanding. He kissed her insatiably, soaking up her very essence and infusing her with molten heat in return. She wanted to absorb half of him into her and leave half of herself with him, so that he would feel linked to her as she felt toward him. No wonder she refused every man who showed an interest in her. Not one of them was Ashby. He had ensorcelled her girlish heart with a spell so powerful no other man could ever break. Everything became crystal clear to her at that moment: She wanted Ashby. She adored him, craved him, loved him, had never stopped loving him, no matter how hard she fought it or lied to herself about it, and she had every intention of keeping him forever.

"This mouth," he whispered, as his hand sailed up her throat in a slow caress. "I could kiss this luscious mouth . . . these cherry lips forever . . ."

"Then you'll have to keep me, too, as we are attached," she returned breathlessly.

She sensed his slow smile against her lips. "What a shame . . ." His large hand came to rest on her thigh. Slowly it cruised up to her waist, over her ribs, lingered a while beneath her breast, and swept down the way it came. "If we go on like this much longer, you will have to stay with me forever," he murmured, his voice was thick with need, his breathing growing harsher and heavier.

Yet he didn't stop. His mouth moved possessively, leisurely over hers. As did his body. Shifting his weight to his arms, he moved atop her and lodged himself between her thighs in a shockingly thrilling, intimate position. Through the thin layers of her muslin gown she felt every inch of him hardening against her boneless body. His bulky frame radiated such heat she felt she was going up in flames. She lost herself in their long-drawn-out kisses. With each foray of his tongue her belly tightened, her body tingled, her response matured and intensified. The memory of his half-nude body sleek with sweat, laboring over timber, haunted her as some natural opiate. Of their own volition her fingers pulled his cambric shirttails out of his trousers and splayed over his bare back. His skin was warm velvet, stretched taut over finely tuned sinew. She fingered the two dimples at the base of his back and sailed higher along the muscled ridges flanking his spine.

A groan reverberated in his throat. He ground his taut body over hers, drawing a soft moan from her lips. Her feeble sense of propriety gave way to the dormant wanton awakening inside of her, wanting to eat him alive—and he seemed perfectly willing to let her do it . . .

A little voice began sobbing. "Danielli!" Isabel nudged Ashby aside and scrambled to her feet. With great tenderness she scooped the drowsy infant into her arms, murmuring soothing sounds, and encouraged Danielli to put her head on her shoulder and continue napping. "I should go," Isabel whispered. "She'll wake up any minute now and want her mother."

Already on his feet, Ashby nodded grimly while tucking his shirttails into his trousers. He escorted them to the foyer in silence, but she was physically aware of his covert glances. Strange how neither one of them knew what to say when not too long ago they had conversed freely.

Phipps opened the front door. Two footmen carried Danielli's perambulator down the front steps.

Ashby gripped her fingers, staying her inside. "Isabel . . ." His emerald eyes were on fire. A battle seemed to be raging behind those eyes. She sustained his gaze expectantly, her longing for him written across her face. "Thank you for a lovely visit," he relented gruffly.

Her heart sank. He didn't ask to see her again. "Thank you." *Dash it all.* She couldn't stand there all day moon-eyed with the door open. She smiled and tugged her hand. "Goodbye."

His fingers opened stiffly, letting go of hers one by one. "Goodbye."

As the front door closed behind her, Lucy pushed the perambulator in the direction of Seven Dover Street. Isabel hummed inside. If his farewell handshake was an indication of the way he felt toward her, then she would see him again. *Soon.*

Chapter Six

Isabel lay smiling beneath her white, lacey canopy, absent-mindedly running her fingertips over her lips. Ashby had kissed her. She still couldn't believe it, even after sniffing his masculine scent on her morning gown's collar. The possibility that he merely gave in to his pent-up lust was inconceivable. He kissed her as though the world would come to an end if he didn't.

Feelings were definitely involved or he would have turned to someone more experienced—and less "proper" than herself—to . . . accommodate him. One did not grow up in a household with two older brothers and not know that there were fancy women out there on the lookout for rich benefactors. Although, in retrospect, perhaps she was not as "proper" as she'd imagined herself to be. Why, if Danielli hadn't interrupted them, who knows how far her naughtiness would have carried them? It was simply beyond her to preserve any semblance of propriety in this man's presence. She stretched out on her bed, smiling dreamily. There was only one thing left to do—*marry Ashby*. The thought sent a jolt of excitement and anticipation through her. After flouting her family's matchmaking attempts for four years, giving them nothing but excuses and grief, she was practically drooling over the notion of marriage. Marriage to Ashby.

Her bedchamber door slammed open, and her fifteen-year-old twin sisters pranced inside. "Izzy, come quick!" Freddy exclaimed. "You'll never guess—"

"What?" Isabel scrambled off the bed, her heart beating a fast tattoo. Was he here? Had he come already? She checked her image in the dressing mirror and flounced after her sisters all the way down to the downstairs hallway, where Norris huddled with the servants around a table.

"Look!" Teddy pointed at a flower vase bursting with pink roses wrapped with matching curled ribbons. "This has just arrived for you! And there's a card, but it's sealed, dash it all."

It was just like her rascally sisters to try reading her private correspondence. "That'll be all, Norris." Isabel dismissed the hive of speculating servants. She drew a steadying breath and took the card. The hand was unfamiliar. "My lovely Isabel," it read, "I look forward to dancing with you this evening. *Twice*. Fondly, JH." Oh. Her smile collapsed.

"Well?" Freddy nudged closer and read the note. "Who is it from? Who's JH?"

"Lord John Hanson." Isabel let out a sigh of disappointment. Her sisters, however, yelped with delight and leaped into song and dance. She reread the card. *Fondly.* That was interesting. "Fondly" was the term most gentlemen used. Ashby signed his "yours." She hadn't dared read too much into it before. Now, though, it seemed significant. "Mine." She closed her eyes and smiled.

"Lord John Hansome." Freddy let out a heartfelt sigh, covetously eyeing Isabel's bouquet. "Isn't he dreamy? His hair is spun gold. His eyes are as clear as blue water. His . . ."

"Water is colorless, you nitwit," Teddy mocked her twin.

Freddy paid her no heed. "I wish I were old enough to waltz with Lord John Handsome!"

Teddy sent Isabel a petulant look. "It's not fair that you, who balk at the idea of marriage, should have two dances with him in one evening while we don't even get to wear long skirts."

"You will, in three years," Isabel returned.

"But it'll be too late!" Teddy stomped her foot and snatched one of the pink roses for herself. "He'll be old and married by the time we have our debuts!"

"How old do you suppose LJ is?" Freddy asked Isabel.

"LJ?" Isabel echoed. "Who's that?"

"Lord John," Teddy clarified. "It's our pet name for the Golden Angel."

"Oh. We have a pet name for him already?" Isabel chaffed. "Well, I believe he is eight and twenty. Thirteen years your senior. By the time you are my age, he'll be five and thirty."

"Oh, no!" Teddy cried. "He'll be perfectly infirm by then!"

Blushing profusely, Isabel bit back a smile. "Not where it matters," she said, sphinx-like.

Freddy creased her brow. "Perhaps if I . . . told him how I felt, he would . . . wait for me until I was full-grown."

Isabel choked down laughter. Her sisters were as awful as she was. "Perhaps. Who knows? Stranger things have happened . . ." Indeed.

"We intend to share him," Teddy declared.

"What?" Isabel squeaked. She was wrong. Her sisters were much worse.

"He'll never be able to tell," Freddy explained with a dismissive wave of her hand.

"He will, when he knows you as well as I do," Isabel muttered. "How will you share the man you love if you can't share ribbons?" The very idea of having to share Ashby with another woman was enough to get her dander up. He was hers and hers alone. She'd waited seven years for him. She was not about to relinquish him—or any piece of him—to some grasping female.

"Izzy!" Teddy took her hand. "Which gown will you wear tonight? Not the dowdy things you've been putting on lately to discourage suitors." She wrinkled her nose in distaste. "LJ will think we all have God-awful taste in clothes. You must make a very good impression."

Isabel frowned. "I haven't given thought to what I should wear." But perhaps she should. Lancaster House shared a garden wall with the Barringtons' town house. If she could slip out of the ball and . . . "Very well. We'll head off to Madam Bonnier's right away. Perhaps the gown I ordered for the Devonshire ball will be ready. Get your wraps."

Her sisters cheered and dashed up the stairs. "And we need new ribbons!" Freddy shouted over her shoulder. "Mrs. Tiddles's shop is right around the corner from Madam Bonnier's!"

An hour later, Isabel's mind was spinning with stealth tactics for a nocturnal visit to Ashby while her sisters were methodically transforming the elegant millinery shop on Bond Street into a Turkish bazaar. Her pulse accelerated each time she shut her eyes to imagine their get-together kiss—would it be achingly sweet or hard and needful, as his last kisses had been? He certainly mastered an impressive variety of kisses. Would he be as good a lover, she wondered. Lord, she was a shameless wanton! And what if she were? Ashby didn't seem to mind. He liked her.

"Oh, dear! Where did I put the new French organdie?" Mrs. Tiddles, the elderly milliner, fussed behind the counter, pulling ribbons and filmy fichus out of boxes and drawers and piling them high in a rainbow heap. Teddy and Freddy were giving the poor woman a devil of a time.

"Do I look like a gypsy?" Freddy posed before the mirror with a rich, cobalt blue scarf.

"You look like a ninny," Teddy retorted. "Gypsies don't have blond curls and blue eyes."

As she distractedly observed her sister using the scarf as a veil over her pretty face, Isabel thought of Ashby's insistence on wearing a mask in her presence, even when he kissed her. How would he wed her if he didn't allow her a glimpse of his face? Perhaps if she unmasked him, he would see that she didn't recoil in disgust, that she wanted him despite his disfiguration. There was no doubt in her mind that she would, even if he looked like a hideous gargoyle. His wounds marked him as a hero, as one of the brave men who'd delivered the world from the clutches of Bonaparte, and she had been pining for Ashby for nearly a decade. Surely she could put up with a few scars, couldn't she? As an unpleasant feeling began gnawing at her gut, she realized that the thought of losing him altogether terrified her far more than whatever he concealed.

"I'll show you how gypsies wear scarves." Teddy snatched the blue scarf from Freddy and wrapped it around her shoulders. Freddy tried to wrest it back and a rowdy argument ensued.

Isabel stepped in and confiscated the scarf. "Stop squabbling. You're making a spectacle of us, behaving like a pair of fishwives. Choose your items and let us be off. Madam Bonnier closes her shop early, and we have yet to collect my gown. It must be ready by now."

Teddy exchanged sardonic looks with her twin. "You didn't seem to care in which gown the Golden Angel would see you before the flowers arrived."

Isabel contained herself from muttering that she still didn't care. Why would she fancy a self-enamored Adonis when she could have a strong, irresistible, generous man like Ashby? She had much better taste in men than the little monsters did when she was their age.

As her sisters occupied themselves in making their final selections, Isabel held the cobalt blue scarf over her nose and stared at her image in the mirror. With only her eyes showing, she almost looked as intriguing as Ashby did in his black mask. Perhaps she ought to call on him wearing a veil. Then they would have something to negotiate over, she mused naughtily.

Mrs. Tiddles's clock struck the hour. Isabel's stomach roiled. The nervous tightening in her chest was making it very difficult to draw a breath. Just a few more hours and she would see Ashby again. How would she survive that long? She would have to waste at least an hour on dances, commonplaces, and silly flirtations before it was safe to leave the ball. The gown Madam Bonnier had sewn for her was sure to make an impression on Ashby. Would he declare himself tonight? She hoped so. She couldn't bear the wait.

"May I see the same design in yellow?" Freddy asked the milliner.

Isabel sighed with exasperation. "You've seen enough, Freddy. Make your choice."

"It's quite all right." Mrs. Tiddles smiled sympathetically. "My girls were just as exuberant at fifteen. I'm only sorry I can't find another scarf just like that one. My assistant kept everything in order, but the ungrateful girl up and left me last week without a word of warning. Ran off with her bloke, she did, after all I've done for her—taught her a profession, given her a roof over her head." The woman heaved a sigh. "Now I'm all alone again. My girls live up north, you see."

Isabel jumped at the opening. "Mrs. Tiddles, if I may, I would like to recommend someone to you, a young war widow, quiet and gentle-like, who is looking for such a post very keenly."

"Oh!" Mrs. Tiddles clasped her hands together. "Who is this young woman?"

"She's a skilled seamstress, presently employed in our household staff. She will suit your purposes very well, I should think. If you could provide lodging, I shall send her over today."

"Oh, no! I wouldn't dream of robbing Lady Aubrey of her household seamstress."

"You mustn't worry about that," Isabel assured the woman. "She is a temporary employee. You see, I chair an organization that aids women who've lost their male providers in the war . . ." Isabel explained about her charity, offering the woman one of her calling cards. "So you see, you would be doing a great service to your country, as well. After all, this young woman's husband gave his life so that we could go on with ours without fear of a French invasion."

Mrs. Tiddles's eyes watered emotionally. "How good of you, Miss Aubrey! Indeed, I'd be delighted to employ this young widow. I shall be forever grateful to you." She smiled at Isabel. "If you could spare her today, we'll have this evening to get to know each other before we begin putting this place in order to-morrow morning. What is her name?"

"Mary Higgins. Mrs. Frank Higgins," Isabel emphasized. "She's a delightful person. She'll tidy up your shop in no time." She couldn't contain her smile; she was so pleased for poor Mary. This was indeed an auspicious day, she thought euphorically. First Ashby and now this. And if her luck persisted, she would be engaged to be married by midnight.

Chapter Seven

Isabel peered into her mother's bedchamber. "You wanted to see me?"

"Come in, Izzy. I wish to speak to you." Lounging in bed, a laccy nightcap perched atop her silvery curls, Lady Hyacinth Aubrey gave a splendid impression of royalty. Isabel closed the door and approached the bed. "Oh! You look lovely, my darling!" her mother exclaimed with pleasure. "I'm glad you came to your senses. This silly mutiny was getting us nowhere."

Which was precisely the point of the "mutiny," Isabel thought but said nothing.

Her mother carried on. "Hiding yourself beneath dowdy frocks won't fend off your beaux. Men have an eye for beautiful girls. I should know." Hyacinth winked for effect. "Indeed, I was quite the thing at your age—and happily married to your father by then."

Were it any other day, a comment such as this would send her back to her room to change, just to be difficult, but tonight she wanted to look beautiful. Her new evening gown was low-cut and glamorous, made of pure silk covered in shimmering golden gauze, meant to deceive the eye of the beholder into believing at first glance that she was naked beneath the glossy material. Lucy piled her copper-golden curls atop her head in the Grecian style to expose the full arch of her neck, with ringlets dripping over her ears and nape. Her twin sisters shrieked with awe when they saw her a moment ago. She hoped the gown would have a similar effect on Ashby. She was practically fizzing with tension. "Mama, Stilgoe is waiting downstairs."

"You are not going with your friends?" her mother inquired optimistically.

"No. I'm meeting them at the ball. Angie begged off from attending this evening, and Charlie insisted I go with him."

"Well, at least you will have a proper escort. I daresay your friends are not the sort a young woman of excellent breeding should associate with. Lady Iris is tolerable, I suppose, and prettyish in a common way." Her mother wrinkled her nose. "But everyone knows she married Chilton for his money. The man is at least thirty years her senior. Her father sold cows, did he not?"

"Sir Andrew bred Thoroughbreds, Mama," Isabel replied through clenched teeth. "It was a perfectly respectable enterprise. The Regent was one of his best customers."

"Yes, well, when one goes into trade with the Regent as one's best customer, one ought to expect losing everything to the dunners. If Chilton hadn't come along, Sir Andrew—"

"Is dead, Mama. He gave his life for England, and Iris is my dearest friend. I beg you not to speak ill of her to me or to anyone else for that matter."

Hyacinth sniffed. "Well, it's that other woman I find unacceptable. That French actress you insist on cultivating a friendship with. I'm shocked they allow her in respectable homes at all."

Isabel stifled an unladylike curse. They had conducted this conversation a hundred times. It never led anywhere. "Sophie isn't an actress, Mama. She was a famous soprano in Paris before the war, and now she is the respectable widow of an officer of the blue with a five-year-old son. Even her noble in-laws think highly of her, so why shouldn't you?"

Hyacinth gave her most doting smile. "I've nothing but your best interest at heart, my love. I want to see you shine, and adored by all. Just the other day Lady Fanny Hanson remarked what a delightful young woman you have become, so lovely and accomplished, so devoted to helping the poor. She begged Stilgoe to introduce you to her son—"

Isabel gaped. "Lord John *asked* Stilgoe to introduce us?"

"Of course he did." Her mother assumed her gossiping tone. "Lady Fanny confided in us that her son is hunting for a wife but that he's being very discreet and selective about the process, as he ought to be, a man of his station. You must do your best to impress him, Izzy," her mother instructed. "If you meet his standards, you will become the Duchess of Haworth very soon."

"I'll be sure to remember this when Lord John encounters *my standards* this evening."

"Isabel Jane Aubrey!" Her mother pushed herself up against the mountain of fluffy pillows supporting her back. "I will have none of your nonsense tonight! You shall do your very best to make Lord John Hanson fall madly in love with you!"

Isabel seethed. "I won't marry a man just because you find his mother—or grandfather, in this instance—socially acceptable! Why are you so desperate to be rid of me, Mama?"

"Desperate to be rid of you? Goodness gracious! Whatever gave you that idea?" Hyacinth fanned her face. "I merely wish for you to have a happy life, that is all. I'm well aware you care more for your war widows than you do for your poor, widowed mother, but despite your selfish behavior of late, I want you to know that I have grave concerns for your future."

"My future does not merit your concern. I have it well in hand."

"Fah! For years I turned a blind eye to your naughtiness. I allowed you to run wild because my dearest William, your devoted brother, convinced me you had a happy disposition that time will eventually cure. Well, the future is upon us, and your disposition has not improved."

Isabel jutted her chin. "Then by your own admission, I cannot possibly attract someone as lofty as Lord John Handsome . . . Hanson."

"Hmm. We shall see about that." Her mother smiled slyly.

Isabel narrowed her eyes. "What are you plotting, Mama?"

"Plotting? Dear me! I never plot. Now come and kiss me good night. And tell Stilgoe to take the key. Old Norris hates it when you rouse him in the middle of the night."

Isabel stiffly kissed her mother's cheek and fled the room. Sometimes she almost wished she were without family. Families were so meddlesome. Each member seemed to know precisely what went on with the others and thought it his duty to voice his unprecedented opinion. Privacy was a luxury few possessed in Seven Dover Street, least of all she. No wonder she told them fibs and carried on precisely as she pleased. She collected her reticule and headed downstairs.

Stilgoe waited impatiently at the front door. "Gads, Izzy! You're worse than Angie."

"Mama wanted to speak to me before I left. What was I to do? Incidentally, she asked me to remind you to take the key. Norris has been complaining again." She walked out the door and let a footman hand her into the waiting carriage.

Charlie slumped on the padded seat across from her and rapped his cane on the carriage's ceiling. "Barrington House!" As the coach trundled off the driveway, a pleased smile spread on his rotund face. "My oh my, look at you! If I had known you would abandon your silly dress mutiny for Hanson, I'd have introduced him to you weeks ago. Two dances in advance, eh?"

She stuck her tongue out at him. "Must you be so annoying?"

"Gadzooks! All I meant was that you look exceptionally lovely this evening."

"Thanks." Isabel considered his mulish expression. "I shouldn't have snapped at you."

"A simple thank you now and then wouldn't kill you, you know. You may think otherwise, but I do care for you, Izzy. I care too much to see you throw your life away on some fixation."

Her eyes narrowed. "What fixation?"

Stilgoe shifted against the squabs. "Well, your reluctance to countenance the attentions of any of your admirers does stem from something, I should think."

"Yes, from my dislike of them."

Her brother eyed her circumspectly. "You weren't always so . . . averse to . . . gentlemen."

Alarm bells went off in her head. "What are you referring to?"

"I'm referring to the time you were the twins' age."

She gritted her teeth. "And which admirer's attentions did I countenance when I was still in short skirts, pray tell?"

His blond eyebrows snapped together. "You are joking, aren't you?"

"Just answer the question, if you please."

"Fine. I'm game. You gamboled around Ashby as if he were God's gift to little chits."

She feigned complete astonishment. "Ashby? Will's friend?"

"No, the Russian Tsar. Yes, Will's friend. That tall, handsome fellow in regimentals, the one you stalked and pestered relentlessly—remember him?"

She bit back a curse. She wondered who else was privy to her secret feelings. Grudgingly she asked, "Did Will know?"

"What do you think? You weren't very subtle about it. Ashby this, Ashby that . . . You gave us all a splitting headache."

"Did Ashby know?" She held her breath. The possibility that the man himself had known she had been mad for him was . . . so far beyond embarrassing, it might even put the morning's episode in a different light, an unfavorable light.

"Possibly . . . probably . . . I would have to say yes. As I said, you were tenacious. Remember saddling him with the black pup?" Laughter bubbled in his chest. "Poor Ashby, he didn't wish to disappoint you, so instead of giving it away, he hauled that picnic basket all over the Continent."

Isabel groaned inwardly. Ashby knew. The night she kissed him, it didn't occur to her he was aware of her pathetic feelings for him. And they were pathetic—a besotted fifteen-year-old twit panting after Society's favorite rake. Well, she wasn't pathetic anymore. She was a woman, and she had made him yearn for her that morning as she yearned for him. After tonight, she would make Stilgoe eat his words. Fixation, indeed. "Charlie, whom was Ashby engaged to?"

Her brother nearly jumped off the seat. "Devil take it, Izzy! How should I know?" He eyed her with concern. "Who told you he had been engaged?"

"A friend."

"I see. Well, the last communication I had from him was when Will died."

Her ears prickled. "What communication?"

"He sent a note, conveying how deeply sorry he was, etc., etc. The usual things."

"It wasn't personal?"

"No." Charles scratched his chin. "It did strike me as odd, come to think of it. He and Will were as thick as thieves. He was practically an inmate at Seven Dover Street." He paused. "You do know his face was destroyed beyond recognition?"

She nodded solemnly, feeling a pang of pity in her heart. "Did you see him after . . . ?"

"No, but people talk." His eyes narrowed into slits. "I hope you're not considering falling on the man. They say he's lost his mind and lives in his wine cellar."

"Humbug. I don't believe that for a second," she returned, remembering full well what Ashby's butler had conveyed, "and neither should you!"

"We're here." He exhaled with relief when the carriage stopped. "Be nice to Hanson, and for God's sake, don't speak to him about Ashby."

"Are you playing favorites, Miss Aubrey?" Baron de Grey grumbled unsportsmanlike. His cronies had mobbed her dance card and she refused to grant de Grey the last free space left.

"Of course not. I'm merely, er, that is . . ." Isabel looked around her, bemused by the sudden popularity she had gained overnight—since the Golden Angel singled her out at Almack's and reserved two dances in advance for this evening's affair. The moment she set foot in the crowded ballroom, she was set upon by a pack of new admirers and was not permitted to quit their sphere. No doubt they gathered to appraise her firsthand and discover what the rage was all about. She held on to the last spot on her dance card, nonetheless, hoping against all odds that the man she fantasized of waltzing with would walk in through the door. Her brother had long since vanished into one of the gaming rooms. Considering his wife was not present to scold or importune him for his attention, Isabel knew he wouldn't be emerging from it anytime soon. Still, it didn't seem she would be sneaking out to visit Ashby this evening after all. *Blast*.

Young Lord Ashton lifted a glass of Madeira off a passing tray and offered it to her. "Who is this lucky devil you are saving the last spot for?"

Isabel accepted the glass with a grateful smile. After chatting for over an hour with a score of gentlemen, all vying for her attention, she was parched. "To Prinny, should he decide to put in an appearance tonight. One should never snub a country's future monarch." As the men tittered, she caught sight of Sophie and Iris standing at the refreshments table. Smiling, her friends raised their wineglasses, toasting her social success. She sent them a pointed look, praying they would get the message and join her. These gentlemen hailed from the finest families in England, some of them having come to their titles and taken their ancestral seats in the House of Lords. Soon they would determine the fate of her reform bill. She needed Iris and Sophie's support to help her broach the subject, because so far each time she stirred the conversation to reform bills, some idiot cut her off with trite flirtation. Alas, her friends seemed to attach more importance to her finding a prospective spouse than to their making advantageous political connections.

She wondered how Iris and Sophie would react to the news that she had set her cap at the gargoyle earl. She could benefit from their savoir faire. She was maneuvering in the dark: Since Ashby was a recluse—and a masked one, at that—she had to take the initiative and become the pursuer. It was a state she felt neither comfortable with nor was skilled at.

Abruptly the cluster of males parted before her as the Red Sea had split before Moses to let a white blond head approach her. "My dear Isabel." Lord John took her hand, looking as superior as a peacock, and kissed her gloved knuckles. "I believe our dance is about to begin."

Suppressing the impulse to inform him that she was not *his* anything, Isabel took John's proffered arm and let him lead her to the floor. En route she glimpsed Lancaster House through an open window. His house was shrouded in darkness. She wondered what Ashby was presently doing and whether he might be thinking of her. He was all she thought about: Should she drop in on him tomorrow? The day after that? Wait for his summons? Because the more she mulled over the situation, the more she began to doubt that he would ever venture out of his cave to seek her.

"I see you have garnered an entourage," John remarked, as he swept her into the dance.

Was he congratulating himself? Isabel wouldn't be surprised to learn it happened to every woman he danced with—tipped to success, she believed the term for this phenomenon was. She wasn't even sure she liked it. She never lacked for male attention, and this new status was bound to put ideas in Stilgoe's head. She wasn't looking forward to his foisting new suitors on her. "They are interested in me today because they think you are," she commented impassively.

"Think? I am interested in you, Isabel. You are a remarkable, enchanting young woman, and you glow like Venus recently born." His gaze swept over her shimmering gown. "However, you give me too much credit. The reason they are buzzing around you this evening is not because I asked you to dance, *twice,*" he smiled, "but because you consented. When was the last time you granted a specific gentleman more than one dance at the course of one evening?"

He had a point, Isabel mused. After narrowly eschewing five official and seven unofficial marriage proposals, she'd become adept at discouraging new suitors. It had been a near thing last week, when the Marquis of Ailesbury's son tried to steal a kiss in Covent Gardens. If Stilgoe had come upon them before she freed herself from the scoundrel's grip . . . The very next day she had made up her mind to call on Ashby—and now she knew why.

John drew nearer. "I'm flattered you chose me over them. You mesmerize me."

His flattery left her cold. Were it Ashby speaking such words to her, they would have had to scrape her off the floor. She decided to torment John a little, see what he was really made of. "I'm certain you whisper sweet nonsense to all your dance partners," she commented blithely.

"Hardly." He went on in a confident, seductive tone. "I've been unable to think of anything but you since we danced last night. Have you spared a thought for me?"

"The flowers you sent me were beautiful. I've been looking forward to thanking you."

A glint of skepticism leaped into his eyes. "You don't sound overly convincing."

Well, gads, what did he expect, she thought with a touch of annoyance. They barely knew each other. She wasn't about to gush over him as the rest of his flock did. Yes, he was courteous and handsome, but he stirred nothing in her. She purposefully upheld her silence as they danced. Let him wonder about it. It would do Lord Handsome considerable good to learn humility.

"I seem to recall I owe you a favor. Have you given thought to what it might be?"

She smiled prettily. "Would it interest you to involve yourself in our cause?"

He blinded her with his teeth. "Anything that involves you interests me, Isabel."

She circled his lean frame, her glistening skirts swishing. She sensed dozens of female eyes envisioning her tripping and breaking her neck. No wonder he thought the sun rose and set with him. "I may have an assignment . . . though I don't expect it to be easy."

"Why don't you let me gauge its difficulty level?"

"Very well. Do you by any chance know someone with access to army personnel files?"

"Does the entire cabinet count?" He grinned superciliously. Despite his cloying smugness, she couldn't hide her delight upon hearing this. She immediately explained why she needed the lists. "Consider it done," he said. "Anything else I may do for you, my lovely Venus?"

"You could read our bill proposal and tell me what you think." She batted her eyelashes.

"I would love to. I might even try to tempt you into regaling me with its pertinent ideas during our waltz this evening. I believe it comes next."

She would applaud herself if she only knew how she had accomplished that. Perhaps he wasn't as vain and self-absorbed as she had initially assumed. "I don't know what to say, John."

"Say you'll take a drive with me through Hyde Park tomorrow afternoon."

"I'm afraid I'm otherwise engaged. As I believe I mentioned last night, every Friday we hold a charity meeting to which we invite the women we act for."

"Of course." His lips thinned in a frosty smile. Dear LJ wasn't accustomed to being put off, Isabel noted. "Are you otherwise engaged Saturday afternoon?"

She smiled ruefully. "Regrettably, yes." She was to have an ice with Major Ryan Saturday afternoon. She intended to glean more information about Ashby from him.

Incredulity flashed in his eyes. "I'm almost afraid to ask—would Sunday suit you?"

She smiled. "Sunday would be lovely, John."

His expression sobered dramatically. "No, Isabel. You are lovely."

Chapter Eight

Her lips suck forth my soul: see, where it flies!
Come, Helen, come, give me my soul again!
Here will I dwell, for heaven is in these lips,
And all is dross that is not Helena.
—Christopher Marlowe:
The Tragical History Of Doctor Faustus

Ashby shut his cavalry telescope and turned away from the third floor window. He sagged against the shadowy wall, eyes closed, and thumped his head back. *Hard.* He was in hell again, thanks to the self-destructive urge that had driven him to kiss Isabel one more time.

Just a little taste, he'd thought, to purge himself of the haunting memory of those lush lips clinging to his on a dark bench, of the brief taste of heaven he'd glimpsed then. He was a fool, a glutton for misery. There was no future in it, only frustration—and regret, decades of regret. He wasn't for her; she deserved better than a man who couldn't stand his own reflection in a mirror.

He slid to the floor and reached for a half-empty whiskey bottle. Perhaps he shouldn't have worn the damned mask. She would have taken one look at him and run off in sheer terror. If he'd leashed his blasted libido, he wouldn't be sitting on the floor in the dark licking his old wounds like some pitiful, love-starved savage. He had known beforehand that he hadn't just imagined the staggering impact her kiss had had on him seven years ago. At fifteen Isabel had set him ablaze. Why the bloody hell had he assumed her adult kiss would be like any other woman's?

Because you let your Mr. Jones do the thinking for you, idiot! He shut his eyes and cursed.

Familiar footsteps entered the shadowy room and halted at the window. His old nursemaid. Phipps trained the telescope on the neighboring ballroom and shot his master a startled look.

"Don't," Ashby clipped. "I know whom she's dancing with." He downed another swig of whiskey, wincing as the fire liquid scalded his throat, and waited for the image of Isabel batting her long, curling eyelashes at Hanson to dim in his mind's eye. He was saturated with jealousy, knowing she would most likely end up marrying the pointed neckcloth, and if not Hanson, then some other fop. "Wolves, predators, the lot of them." He swore viciously. If it were not for his curst face, he would be there now, trouncing the simpering competition. "Bastards."

Over the years he'd had countless mistresses and casual lovers, some more skilled than others; none of them had affected him as strongly as Isabel did. Oh, no. Isabel the Lioness went straight for his kidneys every time, with her glowing eyes and honeyed voice. He was growing bone-hard just remembering how she had responded to his kisses. Her warmth and eagerness, her open, passionate nature, combined with her lethal erotic flair had left him painfully aroused and throbbing for more. He had taken extreme liberties with her, yet instead of slapping his masked face, as he'd well deserved, she had buried her hands up his shirt, making him long for the sweet pain of her nails raking the skin on his back as he brought her to the point of ecstasy.

Oh, they would fit perfectly together. There was no doubt in his mind. Those soft, feminine curves had melted beneath him with artless abandon, as though she'd been made for him . . .

Hell and damnation. She *was* made for him. He had known it then; he knew it now. Yet the cruel Fates had conspired against him. No, not fate. He had done it to himself.

His eccentric butler slouched down next to him, saying, "I'm told that in foreign cultures a servant's head should never tower above his master's."

Ashby passed him the bottle. "You're welcome to relocate to a foreign culture any day, Martin. I'll even pay for your passage." Actually, he should be the one buying a passage to some remote corner of the globe. In London he was a beast in a cage. Anywhere else he would be free. Except that anywhere else was not home. He'd spent almost a decade fighting on foreign lands. The experience had cleansed his blood of the taste for adventure. Unlike those bored-to-tears clowns clamoring about town in search of artificial excitement, he cherished his peace and quiet, not rousing to the sound of cannons roaring on the horizon, not being ordered to devise attacks that would result in bloodbaths, not suffering of constant sleep deprivation and raw physical pain, not watching young men who had barely begun their lives die in rivers of gore . . . No, he preferred to sit on a barren floor in the dark and bewail his misfortune, thank you very much.

After knocking back a healthy dose of whiskey, Phipps's voice sounded hoarse when he asked, "How long have you known Major Aubrey's sister, my lord?"

"Roughly ten years, but the last time I set eyes on her she was fifteen."

"Oh," his butler said.

"'Oh,' what?" With an irritated glower Ashby pried the bottle from Phipps's hands.

"A bit young to, eh, form an attachment—"

"Put a lid on it, Phipps! And keep your foul thoughts—"

"Beg your pardon, my lord. I was referring to the young lady. I believe she's . . . quite taken with you."

Ashby slid his butler a snide look. Phipps had always been a poor prevaricator. What the interfering old bugger meant was that *Ashby* was taken with the chit. Which he was, of course. No man in the prime of his life could remain immune to such quintessence of femininity. And it wasn't just her body he desired. During her visit that morning he had been pleasantly reminded of and dazzled by the extent of her charms. Isabel possessed sparkling wit, fortitude, and—in complete contrast to Olivia—not a drop of artifice. She even made him laugh. "Phipps, imagine gazing at a rose garden of swanlike whites, blushing pinks, and fiery red roses, and one daisy stuck among them. Which flower would catch your fancy?"

"Hmm. I would have to say the daisy, my lord."

That's what had happened to him. "Why?"

"The yellow petals would stand out."

Wrong. The sunny daisy would make one smile, whereas roses . . . *Splendid*. He was spying on a chit *and* waxing poetic? What's next? Serenading beneath a certain window at Seven Dover Street? This damnable abstinence was turning his brains into semen aspic. He really ought to send for one of his old birds to take the edge off this alarmingly mounting frustration.

Damn Isabel for stirring his hunger for life again. He had been perfectly content to wallow in his quiet misery until she had shown up on his doorstep, looking like the sun incarnate.

Phipps cleared his throat. "I've been thinking, my lord. If we continue to sit on our rears and wait for a certain daisy to pay us another visit . . ."

"Us?" Ashby muttered at the mouth of the whiskey bottle before fastening his lips around the rim and swinging his head back. *Ugh. Fire.* Much better. He wiped his lips on his shirtsleeve.

Phipps eyed him closely. "Should I send Polly with fresh bed linen to the cellar, my lord?"

"What? Oh, bugger off!" Ashby growled. He was not in the mood to be treated as a child. "I'm not relapsing, if that's what you're worried about," he spat with disgust. "Now piss off!"

Alone in the dark yet again, Ashby rested his head against the wall and prayed for serenity. The orchestra at Barrington House struck up a waltz. *I would very much like to dance with you.*

Damnation. He bolted to his feet. If she could kiss him in the morning and then flounce off to flirt with every swag in London in the evening, he could bloody well take his relief where he could get it, and right now he wanted it from her. He strode out, heading for his bedchamber.

"Phipps! Dudley!" he growled on the stairs, already pulling his shirt over his head. He heard someone skid to a halt in the foyer, heard someone else in a different section of the house crash into a wall. He was running a bloody circus. "My chambers—now!"

"He did? That's excellent progress, Izzy!" Iris exclaimed.

"He said he was acquainted with the entire cabinet," Isabel concluded her account of her productive conversation with Lord John. "I hope we'll have the lists very soon."

"You found Mary a position *and* enlisted Lord John's help . . . You mighty queen!" Sophie clapped her gloved hands. "He must be falling in love with you already. Do you like him?"

"I don't know." Isabel gnawed on her lip. "He says all the

right things, but I get the distinct impression . . . Oh, faddle. I'm probably imagining things." She was about to say that Lord John's compliments and murmurings didn't seem to come from his heart but rather from his head. Yet that wasn't entirely true, because at some point during their dance conversation his interest had taken on a more personal note. Whatever she was or *wasn't* doing seemed to be working on him.

Isabel sighed. Acting in favor of her charity this evening had a serious downside, though; it foiled her plan to pay Ashby a nocturnal visit. The hour she had allotted to dancing and chatting had turned into three and now it was too late.

"Sophie and I have been quite busy ourselves today," Iris put in. "We arranged everything for tomorrow's meeting." She described the parcels they would distribute among the women they were acquainted with, those who needed immediate support. "We also attended Lady Penrose's luncheon in the hopes of enlisting new members on our board, but no one volunteered."

Isabel ruminated aloud, "Now that we can afford it, I think we should rent office space—"

"Don't move," Sophie hissed. She grabbed Isabel's elbow and ducked behind her. "Marcus the Fetus is heading this way."

Iris made a choking sound. "Who's Marcus the Fetus?" Isabel asked, smiling at Iris.

"Poor Sir Marcus is in love with our dear soprano," Iris explained, "but she will have none of him." She lobbed a chaffing look at the flushed face cringing behind Isabel's back.

"He is at least five years my junior!" Sophie muttered in indignation.

"Eight, but who's counting?" Iris winked at Isabel.

"Last night you complained about being mauled by an ancient toad," Isabel recapped with a grin. "You should post a notice at White's, specifying the age you require in a suitor."

"This is no laughing matter," Sophie returned crossly. "I seem to be attracting the attention of either infirm blighters who want to bounce me on their knees in turn with their grandchildren or unripe toddlers who drool over my Parisian past. Where are all the attractive *men,* I wonder?"

"Having a better time at the opera in Paris?" Isabel offered, and got her derrière pinched.

"He's gone." Iris smiled at the hunched figure. Sophie straightened up with a sigh.

"Are you seriously contemplating marriage again, Sophie?" Isabel asked.

"I'm lonely," Sophie admitted. "Englishmen are so stodgy. The ones I may be interested in would never consider someone of my checkered past marriage-worthy."

"George did," Isabel reminded her affectionately, taking her arm. "You're special, Sophie. Be patient. One day soon you'll meet someone who'll appreciate your uniqueness, not scorn it."

Nodding, Iris entwined her arm with Sophie's free one. "Someone worthy of you."

Sophie sighed. "I must say I had more fun as a 'game pullet' than as an 'ace of spades.'"

"What's an ace of spades?" Iris asked.

"It's cant for 'widow.'" Isabel patted Sophie's hand. "Dearest, you can always return to the opera to be a disreputable soprano," she ribbed. "We promise to attend every performance."

"I might just do that," Sophie threatened morosely.

A footman approached. "Miss Aubrey, I was asked to deliver this to you. The footboy said it was urgent." He offered her a sealed missive resting on a lustrous salver.

"For me? Not Stilgoe?" Isabel asked with concern. The first thought that crossed her mind was Danielli. The poor darling had been coughing all afternoon, which was why Angie stayed at home. Isabel prayed Danielli hadn't contracted something while splashing in Ashby's fishpond.

"No, ma'am. The footboy explicitly named you."

"Thank you." She accepted the missive and flipped it over. Excitement shot through her. Stamped in the wax was a lion. Mindful of her friends' concerned gazes, she broke the seal. She recognized Ashby's hand at once. The note read, *It has been a while since I danced, but if your challenge stands, I shall wait for you at the far left corner of the garden. P.* Her pulse jumped in a frenzied dance, her hands shook, and she had to bite hard on her lip to keep from smiling like a clot. Not only had they progressed to a first name's initial basis— Ashby wanted to see her. *Now.*

"Is something the matter?" Iris's voice was laced with concern. "You look flushed."

"I'm fine. It's nothing to worry about." Isabel stuffed the note inside her reticule. "But I do need your help." She lowered her voice. "I have to . . . leave for a few minutes. If Stilgoe comes looking for me, will you please tell him I . . ." She raked her brain for a proper excuse.

Iris's eyes narrowed. "Whom are you meeting in secret, Izzy?" As Isabel's color rose, Iris looked positively livid. "It's that obnoxious major, isn't it?"

"No, of course not!" Isabel replied hastily. Iris seemed more than angry—she was jealous! Well, well, this was a discussion best conducted at another time and place, and right now Isabel was too agitated and thrilled to give Iris the attention she deserved. Ashby was waiting . . .

"I will not help you ruin yourself!" Iris admonished. "Whom are you rendezvousing with?"

Sophie laid a hand on Iris's arm. "That's none of our concern, Iris. Izzy is a grown woman. She knows perfectly well what she is about. Don't you, Isabel?" She gave Isabel a gimlet eye.

"I hope so." Isabel smiled, releasing a shaky breath. "Will you cover for me?"

When her reluctant friends nodded, she snuck out of the

ballroom and took the backstairs to the kitchen. Her heart thumped vigorously as she hurried outside, following the gravel path to the garden. She edged along the garden wall, taking shelter behind cultivated hedges. Her gown provided little warmth against the chill of the night, but it was the state of her nerves that created the gooseflesh on her arms and the shivers skittering along her spine. She was so . . . eager to see Ashby again, she refused to consider the consequences of her reckless behavior.

A white, moonlit gazebo occupied the far left corner of the garden. Inside, a supremely tall, broad-shouldered shape clad in black eveningwear restlessly paced the floorboards. His white gloves and neckcloth gleamed in the moonlight. His dark hair was tamed in a short queue at his nape, but thick strands escaped to fall over his eyes. He kept smoothing them back, and they kept spilling over his masked brow. She smiled. She could stand there all night looking at him.

Abruptly he halted and turned his head in her direction. Glittering eyes studded his black satin mask. *My goodness*. Her heart kicked. This was what the French cavalry had encountered on the battlefield. Her reaction was quite the opposite—she gravitated to him.

"Good evening." Ashby bowed formally, his blood thickening. "You look . . . radiant."

Her iridescent gown clung to her statuesque, goddess-like figure, delectably exhibiting her physical feminine charms. Soft curls floated against her cheeks and throat. Damned if he knew what made her leave a roomful of fawning suitors—not to mention risk her reputation—to be with him. Yet he felt too charitable with the world to press his luck by questioning her wisdom.

He extended his hand in invitation, and she swished up the steps to grab it. Her eyes were bright and hopeful; her small hand shook in his. She curtsied gracefully. "You look quite dashing yourself." She was trembling, and it was all he could do to keep from pulling her into his arms.

The first notes of the last waltz of the evening drifted from the bright ballroom windows. "Am I being too presumptuous in thinking you might not have promised this dance to someone else?" he inquired, realizing he was not as calm as he appeared to be. He couldn't remember ever wanting to dance with a woman as much as he desired to dance with this one right now.

She laughed nervously. "Indeed you are not. But . . . won't you come inside and dance with me where . . . ?" She trailed off, biting her plump bottom lip, as he was tempted to do.

He shook his head, swallowing the lump in his throat. "We dance here. Just us. Privately." He placed his hand on her trim waist and swayed her into the waltz. Six inches of night separated them, the proper distance etiquette required, but as they twirled in the snug confinement of the gazebo, they drew closer and closer, until their hips brushed. He bent his head and breathed in her hair. "Vanilla," he murmured. Like a drug, her scent clouded his senses, drained his strength.

"I'm glad you ventured out here to see me," she whispered close to his ear.

"I wasn't sure you would come. Why did you?" He shut his eyes, intoxicated by the feel of her warm, lissom body swaying against him. "You're not armed with that bill proposal, are you? Waiting to spring it on me when I'm too weak to put up a resistance . . ."

He heard soft laughter in her voice. "As it happens, I think I've found a sponsor. Lord John Hanson. Do you know him? He promised to read the proposal and obtain the lists for us. Now all I need do is find an able accountant to do the figuring."

Ashby gnashed his teeth. He knew it shouldn't irk him that she'd succeeded in bludgeoning some other poor fellow into doing her bidding, but it did. "Why come out here when you have someone of Lord John Hanson's ilk ready to move heaven and earth for you?"

Smiling, she tilted her head back to meet his gaze. "Do you really need to ask?"

Looking into her eyes, he encountered someone he hadn't for a very long time—himself. The man he was when Will was alive, when he came to dinners at Seven Dover Street, when he felt human. This was not some woman he lusted after. This was Isabel—*his Isabel*.

"No, I don't." He lowered his head and tasted her lips, those sweet, tempting cherries. She went startlingly limp. Instinctively his arm circled her waist, pulling her up against him.

Isabel wrapped her arms around his neck, her body lithe, curvy, sweetly scented. "Ashby."

"Yes, sweetness?" He nibbled on her full lips, teased her pink tongue with his, and savored her luscious taste while his hands delineated her waist, molding her soft curves to his hard body.

"I . . . cannot believe I am here with you . . ."

Though he marveled at it himself, he wanted to know. "Why can't you believe it?"

He sensed slight tension in her body. Her eyelashes fluttered like butterflies, but still she held his gaze. Her voice was a Siren's whisper. "I love you, Ashby . . . I always have . . ."

Her confession dissolved him. "Paris," he whispered against her lips, "my name is Paris." He swallowed her gasp of surprise with a burning kiss. Slanting his mouth across hers, he thrust his tongue between her lips and kissed her with all the thundering need in his blood. Her mouth was as tender and delicious as a peach. He wanted to feast on it until her desire burned rampantly and hotly, as he did. *She's an innocent, tread carefully, for God's sake*, his conscience bellowed, but he shut it up. He danced her aside and flattened her against the gazebo's wall, kissing her to oblivion. Sighing, she threw herself into his kisses with equal ardor. Her tongue sparred with his in an erotic duel. His hands slid over her shapely bottom and squeezed, melding their bodies together. *Sweet Lucifer*. She didn't wear drawers, only a shift—a silk one, by the feel of it—and though he knew from experience that the reason for the tantalizing lack of undergarments was the gown and not him, Mr. Jones snapped to attention and saluted like an overeager cornet.

The teasing minx moved her hips against his. Her fingers caressed his nape, wringing a groan from deep inside his chest. "Ashby . . ."

"Paris," he insisted. "You wrested the name out of me. Now you have to make it real."

"Paris," she echoed in a breathy little whisper, forming a smile. "You are real. So real . . ."

"I know, I know. It's an idiotic name." He smiled wryly. "God knows what possessed my parents to name me after Homer's most pathetic male character."

"Paris wasn't pathetic. He was in love. But perhaps your parents named you after the city."

"Napoleon's city?" he choked, appalled.

"Napoleon wasn't in power when you were born, silly. Nor is he now, thanks to you."

"Yes, I vanquished him single-handedly, and thanks for pointing out my advanced age."

Lilting laughter filled her throat. She perched up on tiptoe, capturing his gaze at eye level. "Paris . . . I love your name." She smiled seductively, her beautiful eyes sparkling in the shadows. "It's dark, glittery, enigmatic . . . just like you."

"You're imagining the city, I think." He glimpsed at the creamy mounds pushed up against his chest and fought an overwhelming desire to bury his face in them. It had taken him twenty nine seconds to get here; it would take him even less to carry her back to his bedchamber. "You are forgetting you've known me for almost a decade. I'm no mystery." But she was—this child Aphrodite, who'd blossomed overnight into the most desirable, most feminine creature on earth. He would explode if he didn't have her. Then Stilgoe would come after him with a pistol, and he wouldn't even try to defend himself. He'd always known there was a ball out there with his name emblazoned on it; it was a miracle—or a bloody curse—he had dodged it till now.

Isabel caressed his lips. "I know so very little about you. What is your middle name?"

His mind was fogged with desire. He had to blink to clear his vision. "Nicholas."

"Paris Nicholas Lancaster." She replaced her fingertips with her lips, caressing him, teasing him, turning his brains to pulp. "Did you like Napoleon's imperial city?"

He was having a devil of a time keeping up with her line of questioning. "I suppose. I was not exactly . . . in an objective frame of mind when . . . we marched on it. I can't say I . . . viewed its attractions with touristy enthusiasm. This, however"—he kissed her vanilla-scented neck—"I'd love to tour." She had the softest skin imaginable. When she purred softly, he wanted to sling her over his shoulder and leap over the wall into his garden. Who needed a bed, anyway? He'd never been this aroused in his entire life, but he couldn't, he knew he couldn't . . . could he?

Unable to stop himself, he sailed his hand up her ribs and cupped her soft breast. Isabel closed her eyes and let out a soft sigh. He kneaded her gently, luxuriating in the wealth he held in his hand. Watching her enjoy this—his fondling her breast—sent lust roaring through his veins.

"No one makes me feel as you do, Paris."

His heart constricted. She had the uncanny ability to pronounce the exact emotion he was struggling to formulate. He felt like a bumbling ape. "Isabel, you make me feel like a besotted schoolboy." He captured her mouth with a plundering kiss, making her moan. He burned to peel her gown off and taste her everywhere, not just her mouth, though at the moment, he couldn't stop doing so. Isabel Aubrey possessed the talent to bring a man to his knees with a kiss. And he wanted to be the only one worshiping at his goddess's feet. "Who taught you to kiss like this?"

"No one." Her sultry voice glided over him in a caress. "You . . . did."

"You never kissed anyone other than me?" he asked, incredulous but also absurdly pleased. When she shook her head, a rush of masculine satisfaction coursed through him. It withered with the pang of guilt he suddenly felt. He didn't deserve her, and yet it didn't stop him from wanting her more than he ever wanted anything else in his life. "'Thou art fairer than the evening air clad in the beauty of a thousand stars,'" someone who sounded alarmingly like him murmured. *Good God*. Will must be laughing his head off on a cloud somewhere, seeing his old chap reduced to citing poetry—and to his little chit of a sister, no less. *I might run off with her to Gretna Green.* Now there was a thought. A week in his carriage, alone with Isabel, on the way to making her his wife, his companion, his countess . . . Then again, what would he do with her once she saw how scarred his face was? He would have a hysterical female on his hands in the middle of nowhere.

Her eyes closed, a dreamy expression floated on her face, her lips curled up in a smile that drove away his morbid thoughts. "You are a fan of Kit Marlowe, I take it."

"Not exactly, but this part from *Doctor Faustus* always reminds me of you."

"Always?" Her fan-like eyelashes swept up to reveal her passion-misted eyes. "Why?"

"For reasons known solely to me." He occupied his mouth with kissing her lips, her cheek, her delicate jaw . . . anything but reveal he wanted her for his own as desperately as Homer's Paris wanted his Helena. Isabel could probably see right through him, the little temptress.

"You have not sold your soul to the Devil, have you?" she whispered teasingly.

"No, but he keeps pounding on my door." *And in other places, as well.*

"Stilgoe escorted me to the ball tonight," she shared with him as he nibbled on her adorable earlobe. The hopeful note in her voice caused another pang in his chest, but he chose to ignore it.

He had a startling thought. "Does he know you came out here to see me?"

She tipped her head aside, inviting him to kiss the sensitive area beneath her ear. "Sophie and Iris . . . but they don't know about you . . . yet. They promised to explain away my absence."

The relief he felt was testimony of his black character. A scrupulous gentleman would send her back inside; he would not ignore her perfectly clear and justifiable insinuations and continue to take liberties with her person. Nevertheless she looked so achingly beautiful in the moonlight, her delicate features expressing rapture, that he couldn't let her go just yet.

Nor could he stop kissing and touching her. He dipped a finger inside her low bodice and teased her nipple. He paused for a heartbeat, but when no fast palm met his cheek, he continued teasing it into a firm, jutting bead. A sound that was equal parts a sigh and a moan left her lips.

Fire leaped in his loins. He tugged her bodice to bare her nipple, and her breast popped out, a ripe pear. If a drop of moisture rolled down this perfect breast, the nipple would serve it up to him at its tip. *She was shaped for lovemaking.* His eyes gulped the sight of her, committing her to memory, wishing he could persuade her to pose for him. He would sculpt her in real dimensions, anything less would be a crime. Imagining her sprawled in the nude on the ruby coverlet of the fifteenth century bed in his cellar stoked his desire to dangerous levels. With a low growl, he took her breast into his mouth, suckling, licking, biting the enticingly taut bud. She gasped, clutching his shoulders. If she were half as aroused as he was, he would find honey between her thighs.

Realizing his control was paper thin, he pulled her gown up, covering her breast, and let his forehead wilt against the wall beyond her shoulder. He was the adult here. It was his duty to keep them from straying too far, but how the devil was he supposed to do that? He craved her.

She stroked his hair, holding him close. "Paris, what's wrong? Speak to me."

He lifted his head. Her eyes looked soft and luminous as she smiled up at him. God, how he wanted her—in his bed, in his house, in his life. "I want you, Isabel. Does that shock you?"

She shook her head, her smile unwavering. She kissed his jaw, moving lower to the pulse pounding at the side of his neck. "I want you, too," she whispered.

"Don't say that." He groaned. How could he fight this—both himself *and* her?

"Why not?" Her hands found their way inside his coat and were moving over him in slow circles. The problem was they wanted the same things. Or rather, she thought she did.

"Did you come out here to torment me?" His voice was stark with need. Perhaps if he startled her with the intensity of his desire, she would flee. It would be a far better solution than unmasking his face and seeing the disgust in her eyes. He took her hand and guided it to the thick bulge in his breeches. Her eyes widened in shock. "Still want me?" he breathed, rubbing the palm of her hand over his impossibly stiff erection, up and down, slowly, agonizingly, sustaining her gaze. Damn, that felt good. "You've no idea what you're doing to me, do you?" He groaned.

The shock left her features, and she regarded him with rapt curiosity. "Is it always this . . . firm and . . . sizeable?" she inquired throatily, her hand moving of its own accord.

"Around you it is." He couldn't breathe with her hand cupping him, lock, stock and barrel. He gritted his teeth to keep from pumping his hips against her hand. He was torturing himself, yet the pleasure was so exquisite, he was too weak to stop. He watched her ravenously, his chest rising and falling in a powerful rhythm, his eyesight blurring, and was dangerously tempted to slide her hand inside his breeches and close it around his erect shaft. *"Christ, Isabel,"* he hissed, nearly doubling over, he was this close to erupting. "Enough." He let go of her hand, drawing a lungful of air, trying to catch his breath. Spots swam before his eyes.

Isabel raised her hand and traced his mask with her fingertips. "Why did you stop coming to Seven Dover Street? Was it because of me?" she whispered.

He forced himself to suck in air, too taut to move. "Mostly. I told you, you were too young for me . . ."

"Not anymore." She clung to him, kissed him feather light, and ran her fingertips along his jaw. "Why didn't you come when Will died? I needed you. We all did."

That was the last thing he would ever tell her. He steeled himself. He had to explain that there was no future for them. He owed her that, at the very least. "Isabel, I think . . . I know . . ."

She smiled. "You have so many secrets. I want to see you," she whispered. Before her plea registered in his foggy brain, she clasped his mask and began lifting it.

Panic blinded him. "No!" He knocked her hand aside and turned his back to her, adjusting his mask back to place. "What a mistake!" he growled, still burning for her.

"A mistake? W-What do you mean?" Isabel's soft voice penetrated the turmoil in his mind. When he refused to answer, a light hand touched his shoulder. "Paris—"

"Go back inside and don't come to see me ever again." What a blasted idiot he was, to take it this far. He'd been on top of it this morning. What in damnation propelled him to act so rashly? He knew the answer: Isabel did, with her beguiling promise of laughter and mayhem and life—and passion.

"What? *Why?*" The misery in her voice twisted his insides. "You said you wanted me . . ."

It was his cross to bear. "Leave me," he begged. *Please*. If she knew how Will died, or if she caught a glimpse of his face . . . he didn't want to imagine what she would think of him.

"I don't care what you look like," she spoke behind him. "I know who you are inside—"

She was wrong; he was much worse on the inside. He spun around. "Leave!"

His bellow startled her, but she remained rooted to the spot, watching him with those large, soulful eyes of hers. "I'm not a child anymore. I can handle this. I've seen soldiers who returned wounded from the war. I've seen little children deformed by illness . . ." Huge, diamond-like tears swam in her eyes. Her anguish clawed at his conscience. "You can't scare me off."

He couldn't stand seeing the compassion she offered, the pity. He swallowed hard. "I don't care to see you anymore," he articulated emphatically. "Is this clear enough?"

Her lower lip trembled. Her eyelashes fluttered while she tried to make sense of his insane behavior. "How can you say this after everything that transpired between us today?"

"We just kissed! It meant nothing. Men say and promise all sorts of drivel to women when they're randy. Let it be a lesson in life to you," he spat out callously, needing to drive her away while at the same time aching to pull her into his arms and banish the pain he was causing her.

Her eyes grew round and wild as understanding dawned. Yes, he'd used her, because he'd wanted to touch her, although he'd known beforehand that there would be no future for them. "No." She shook her head, tears rolling down her cheeks. "You can't do this to me, not again . . ."

He had to. There was no other choice. He shut his eyes momentarily, mustering every bit of self-control he possessed, then gave her a long, final look. "You have your whole life ahead of you. Spend it with someone you love." He strode out of the gazebo, turned left, and with a leap planted his hands on the flat surface at the top of the garden wall. He hoisted himself up, setting one booted foot firmly on the narrow ridge, and jumped over to the other side.

A heartbreaking sob came from the other side of the wall. "Damn you, Ashby!" Isabel cried. "How could you do this to me again? I hate you, do you hear me? I hate and despise you—you knave . . . you rake! I will never, ever forgive you for this! *Never!*"

Ashby stormed into his bedchamber, his temples pounding, and tossed the mask into the flames dancing in the fireplace. He was burning up, his veins flowing with desire, his conscience in shreds, his soul howling for the woman who was no longer forbidden to him and yet was still out of his reach. He couldn't breathe; he wanted her—needed her—so badly.

Cursing himself for being far worse than what she had accused him of, he fell back on his bed and lay there, staring sightlessly at the dark canopy. All these feelings, these raging emotions Isabel stirred to life again, what was he supposed to do with them now? Bury them in the cellar? For how long— a decade, a lifetime? A growl of anguish tore from his chest, and he covered his face with both hands, clawing at the slashed skin, wanting to rip it off. An abyss of hell and loneliness yawned at him, and he knew he deserved every bit of it. And then some.

Her friends found her sobbing in the gazebo.

"Iris, summon your carriage and find Stilgoe," Sophie said.

"Tell him Isabel is unwell and that we are taking her home."
She sat down, draping an arm around Isabel's quaking shoulders. "Hush, *chérie*. All will be well . . ."

Isabel turned sideways and buried her damp face in
Sophie's shoulder. "He used me," she whimpered as Sophie
stroked her back. "He never cared for me . . ."

"Who did?" Sophie inquired in a gentle voice that didn't
disguise her fury.

Isabel raised a tear-stricken face and jabbed a finger at
the gazebo's open window. "Him!"

All Sophie saw was a tall, mossy garden wall.

Chapter Nine

The only thing worse than a battle lost is a battle won.
—Arthur Wellesley, the Duke of Wellington:
on the aftermath of the Battle of Waterloo, 1815

*Hotel de l'Imperatrice, Brussels, 15 June 1815—two
years ago*

Someone knocked on his hotel suite door.

"The door is open," Ashby grunted, dragging a rumpled sheet to cover his naked loins. Sprawled on his back, his vacant gaze fixed at nothing, he recognized Will's gait in the vestibule. They had arrived from London a month ago. Most of his men were miserable, having left wives and babes at Ramsgate. Wellington was on tenterhooks. Napoleon was on the move. And Ashby felt numb inside. What did he have to return to but his responsibilities to his ancestral holdings? No wife, no babes, very slim chances of ever having any . . .

Blood and glory.

He was sick of them both.

Will walked in, whistling. "Damn me! The lads made me so fuddled that I fell off my horse coming . . . here . . . Hello."

He halted and gaped at the woman in the gossamer negligee brushing her raven locks at the vanity table. "You are La Furia, aren't you? Saw you performing at the opera last night."

The Italian opera singer gave a shrug but said nothing.

"Speak French," Ashby suggested. "Why are you here? I thought you had an appointment with Lady Drusberry."

"Change of plans. I come from the Duchess of Richmond's ball. Wellington wants you."

Ashby didn't attend balls anymore, especially ones with the entire *beau monde* of Europe in attendance. He leaned aside and lifted a golden cup full of brandy from the bedside console. "Tell him you couldn't find me. That I rode out to check on the troops at Ninove."

Smiling lopsidely, Ashby pulled on his boots. "How quick can you be?"

Will stepped closer, chuckling. "What, are there no snifters in this luxurious hotel suite that you're compelled to drink from your trophy?" He looked past his shoulder at La Furia "Did you attend the Cavalry Races?" he asked in French. "I won the silver cup."

Ashby snorted at his blatant lie. Macalister took the silver cup.

La Furia gave Will a sweeping glance. "I prefer gold to silver."

"Ouch!" Will cringed, grinning. He beat his hand against his chest. "I have gold inside."

Unimpressed, she ambled to the bed and reclined beside Ashby, snuggling into his armpit and splaying her fingers over his bare chest. He removed her hand. "He's right. My gold may run out, but his never will. Besides . . ." He whispered in her ear, "He has steel where it counts."

"Oh?" Already she was intrigued. "You are Major Will Aubrey?"

Will sketched a sweeping bow. "At your service, my lady."

She sent Ashby a sidelong smirk. "He has better manners than you do."

"He has better everything." Ashby acknowledged with a lopsided grin. "Any news?"

Tearing his gaze from La Furia's alluring figure, Will came over to whisper in Ashby's ear, "Outposts report that Napoleon reached Quatre Bras. The Cavalry is ordered forward."

Ashby lunged for his breeches. "Wait downstairs. I'll pack her off and join you."

Will cast another covetous glance at the half-naked opera singer. "I don't suppose you'll let me pack her off while you wait downstairs, eh? I doubt I have time for Lady Drusberry."

Smiling lopsidedly, Ashby pulled on his boots. "How quick can you be?"

"With this one, the last thing I want to be is quick. I'll see you downstairs."

When Ashby arrived with Wellington and his staff at Quatre Bras just after ten o'clock the next morning, their Prussian allies were already deployed against the French to the south, and more troops were coming to join the enemy forces. "Napoleon has humbugged me!" Wellington grumbled. "If the Prussians fight there, they will be damnably mauled!"

The afternoon saw heavy rain and heavier fighting in the woods and fields around Quatre Bras. As usual the French attack opened with a cannonade which, as Wellington had predicted, wrought havoc among the exposed Prussian infantry. The British foot, weary and disorganized as a result of orders and counter-orders, luckily kept arriving, and by the time the French cuirassiers swooped down on Ashby's brigade, their ever-expanding forces fiercely threw the French back.

When they reached the nearby town that evening, it was

full of wounded English soldiers. Ashby found Will hunched over a sheet of paper, writing by the light of the moon.

He crouched, offering Will his flask of whiskey. "Let me guess—dashing off a letter to Isabel?" The mere sound of her name on his lips sent lightning down his spine.

Will took a swig of whiskey, offering his pencil. "Care to jot down a line? She'd like that."

"No," Ashby replied adamantly.

"You're evil."

"Why am I evil?" he asked, wary and curious. Isabel hadn't told her brother about their improper kiss, or Will would have said something, would have killed Ashby by now.

"You know why." Will returned to hunching over the letter.

Ashby downed a healthy nip of whiskey. His right arm hurt like the devil, and he suspected the bone was fractured. Of course that was nothing compared with the wounds some of his men were suffering of. By the third gulp, he heard himself inquiring, "How is she?"

Will's head came up. "That's the first time you've asked me about her in five years, Ash."

"Not for lack of caring." Ashby scowled at his flask, wondering what she looked like as a young woman. He would never find out, because he had no intention of ever letting her see what remained of his face. If things were different—if Sorauren hadn't happened—he knew precisely what he would write to her; and his heart constricted at the thought: *Wait for me.*

At dawn Ashby was summoned to the high command together with General Vivian. They heard about the Prussian defeat even before reaching Wellington.

"General Blücher has had a damned good licking!" Wellington groused. "The Prussians have gone back. So we must go too. I suppose in England they will say we've been licked, but I can't help it. As we are agreed to fight together, we go with them."

That was depressing, but it wasn't over yet. Napoleon and Wellington had been at war for years without meeting in battle. Ashby knew that neither commander would allow the matter of their generalship go without being put to the ultimate test.

As the Allies retreated, the skies opened, drenching the fields and flooding the roads. Loud claps of thunder echoed the roar of artillery. In an instant the French attacked, falling on them on all sides, shouting their usual chants. The British cavalry covering the rear flew about, forming columns and deploying everywhere. His arm numb, Ashby couldn't see a bloody thing. Nor did he recall ever fighting during a rainstorm as hard as this. Bombshells shrieked heavily among them. Darkness fell. The French were hell bent on entangling them to force Wellington to return to their aid. With his last remaining force, Ashby rallied his hussars and drove the bastards back.

News came that the Prussians were regrouping. Orders went out for the allied troops to fall back toward a village called Waterloo. Soaked to the skin, exhausted, and out of food, the 18th Hussars bivouacked in the hedges behind the Mont-St. Jean ridge, while a mile to the south Napoleon found shelter for the night at the inn beside the road called La Belle Alliance.

Dawn gave promise of a thoroughly miserable day. It had rained all night and the troops mustering for battle were sopping wet, plastered with mud, hungry, dirty, and suffering from lack of sleep. Wellington and Napoleon's armies faced each other across a steep, rutted valley. Not the best ground for cavalry operations, Ashby noted grimly, but their army transformed the Mont-St. Jean ridge into a formidable defensive position, well suited to Wellington's battlefield tactics.

Ashby received orders to stand on the extreme left, with detachments to the east. But before the third day's battle had even begun, he was summoned to Wellington.

"Take a look." His commander passed him a telescope. "See the movement in their lines, all those officers milling 'round one particular place, the swarm of cavalry. . . . That's our friend's precious Imperial Guard, the flower of his army, the most beautiful regiments in the world . . ."

"Boney in person," Ashby said, awe-struck by the spectacular sheet of blue tipped with silver.

"Today you and I will demolish his Guard, Ashby."

Ashby met Wellington's gaze squarely. He knew the answer to what he was about to ask but wanted to hear it to his face. "Why me?"

Wellington indicated their troops. "Each man out there is imagining his dear ones at home, who rely on his safe return. You don't have anyone dependent on your return. Do you?"

"I'm expendable," Ashby scoffed. He preferred this reason to being lauded as a "butcher."

"You're fearless and focused," Wellington amended. "Your mind is on the pending battle, not on your ailing mother or on some chit you can't wait to see again. Is it?"

"No such chit." Ashby smiled. It was the first blatant lie he ever told his mentor.

"In the words of your loyal hussars, 'Fly like lightning and strike like a thunderbolt!' Or in my words, do your damnedest, Ashby. I'll spring my surprise at the last possible moment."

"When you say that, my knees begin to quake." He scowled to disguise his embarrassment. That Wellington should know how his hussars cheered him was . . . distinctly flattering.

"One last thing. General Ponsonby lost a senior cavalry officer and his ranks are slim. He needs you to send him your best man to lead the charges."

Waldie and Macalister were his best, but they were captains, and while Ashby disliked the very idea of sending Will out of his sight and into Wellington's center, he knew Will would take offense if Ashby skipped him in favor of someone else. This was a tough call. Ashby had a bad feeling about this. But Will could be just as easily hurt under his command. Wellington knew how to post his troops, and his center was famous for its unshakable stubbornness. Who was he to play at being God? "I'll send Major Aubrey," he said reluctantly, and went in search of Will.

Napoleon's cannon opened the battle with heavy fire. Concurrently he launched an assault against Wellington's left-center. The battle raged for six hours. As his hussars took punishment from hell, falling all around, Ashby was relieved he'd sent Will to Ponsonby. The Belgians, who fought under Napoleon before the abdication and were now attached to him, started to defect in droves. Ashby laid his saber across their commander's shoulder, growling, "If you don't go back, I swear to God I'll run you through!" It had the desired effect, for they all stood.

Aides de camp flitted in all directions, carrying orders and announcing that the Prussians were on their way. It was the best news Ashby had heard all day.

At noon Napoleon opened his major assault on their center with a massive bombardment from eighty guns. Ashby saw Wellington's line vanishing under a haze of flying earth and metal. The French came in four phalanx containing eight battalions each, and an avalanche of British cavalry came cascading down the slope, charging into the thick of the French columns. Ponsonby was killed, and his brigade was all but wiped out. Detained to the left, Ashby felt his heart stop.

"Will!" he bellowed, charging blindly into the fray, unwittingly leading his hussars into the enemy lines, sabring and thrashing, their exhausted horses foundering in the boggy ground. With the rain and smoke, visibility was terrible. The

King's German Legion barely held the center as fresh enemy troops kept pouring in. Going deeper was unfeasible. The battle raged on all fronts. Wellington pushed forward his infantry, using up his cavalry reserves. The carnage was frightful. And still they persevered, fighting for king and country, for the faces awaiting them at home.

Caked with mud and gore, his throat raw, his muscles burning, his eyes defying the falling darkness, the stench of smoke and metal, horse and human sweat thickening the air, submerged in the most grueling fighting of his life, Ashby feared that Wellington's surprise was not coming.

Seeing his attacks repeatedly repulsed and the English line remaining weak but unbroken, Napoleon delivered his last blow. The prestigious battalions of the Imperial Guard marched into the fray, drums throbbing out the daunting *pas de charge*. The battered French regiments greeted them with cheers and hats on bayonets. The British cannonades couldn't stop their advance. The Guard captured two British artillery battories while the guns were firing straight into their ranks.

Everything seemed lost . . .

Wellington gave the command, "Up Guards!"

From the reverse slope of the ridge, out of cannon-range, a wall of red-coated little fellows sprang to the front, firing a smashing volley into the indestructible Imperial Guard and carpeting the ground with its dead columns. Ashby beheld the sight with tears in his eyes.

Napoleon's finest, who had never before faltered in the attack, suddenly stopped.

A thundering buzz of horror swept the French, *"La Garde recule! The Guard retreats!"* The whole French army gave way that very moment. A great "Hurrah!" rose among the English.

Wellington rode up onto the ridge into plain sight of his troops, waved his hat above his head, and pointed south—the signal for a general advance. Ashby rallied his hussars and charged ahead with impetuosity and regularity as if they were at a field day exercise on Hounslow Heath. Every remaining man and gun flooded down the slope, falling like a torrent on Napoleon's army.

Napoleon was well forward when he saw his front collapse. The French began shouting, *"Sauve qui peut! Save yourselves!"* and a mass retreat ensued, a mob of men and horses fleeing across the fields, their English cavalry and foot pursuers shooting, stabbing, bayoneting . . .

It was well past midnight when Hector, followed by Ashby's groom, Ellis, found Ashby wandering among the bodies carpeting the battlefield. "My lord!" Ellis cried, rushing to his side. "You're alive! We were so worried. Luckily we fell upon Curtis who assured us—"

"Will! William Aubrey!" Ashby growled; his voice was hoarse after yelling for hours, his eyes blurry from smoke and fatigue. Many of his regiment's rank and file were dead or wounded. Those capable of movement were either sleeping like logs in the bivouac or on their way to the hospital in Brussels. Filthy and aching, supporting his broken right arm, dragging his left leg, he meandered among the dead and the wounded, choking with despair. *Will, where are you?*

Tomblike silence gripped the field. Dark shapes crawled on the ground, scavengers looting the dead and the mortally injured. "Major William Aubrey!" Ashby bellowed into the darkness. He sensed Hector's wet, rasping tongue licking his hand and instinctively patted his dog's head. "Find Will, Hector," he ordered brokenly. "Find Will."

"My lord, you must come with me. Everyone will return with carts at first light to collect the wounded and bury the dead." Ellis tried draping Ashby's strong arm across his shoulders, but Ashby pulled free. "The Prussians have gone after the French fugitives. Lord Wellington says we march into France tomorrow. You need your sleep, my lord. You are exhausted."

"You go, Ellis. I have to find Will." He limped onward, deaf to his groom's pleas.

"My lord." Ellis touched his shoulder. "Look for him tomorrow. What's in a few hours?"

"He may be dead in a few hours!" Ashby glared murderously at his groom, daring him to utter the unspeakable—that Will was already dead. All because of him, because he had sent his best friend, his brother, to be slaughtered at the center. His charger followed him like a shadow, nudging his shoulder. He would have sent the starved mare with Ellis, except that he had a ball lodged in his left thigh and a broken arm; he would need her to carry Will.

Upon Hector's bark, Ashby's head shot up. He stumbled forward as fast as he could and collapsed on the ground. A man moaned in pain. Ashby edged closer. "Who are you?" he asked.

"Dunkin, with the 13th Light Dragoons. I-I lost my . . . leg." The man whimpered.

"Ellis"—Ashby beckoned his groom forth—"help me lift this man up. I want you to take him to the camp and find someone to drive him to the hospital in Brussels."

"Aye, my lord, but what of you?" Ellis supported the limping wounded soldier.

"I'll be fine. Take him." Finding the soldier instilled Ashby with hope. He stumbled toward Hector, his heart pounding rapidly. When he reached his dog, he saw what appeared to be a sad carcass of a horse. He shoved the wretched animal's mane aside, and a pale face emerged in the moonlight. "Dear Lord. Will." His throat constricted with emotion. He put a gentle hand beneath his friend's head and touched his cheek. "Will, can you hear me? Speak to me, brother. *Please.*"

Will moaned.

Ashby gave a shout of relief, thanking God. "William, open your eyes. Look at me."

Will's eyelids lifted, and the faintest smile surfaced on his lips. "You look like hell, Ash. I gather we're still alive."

Ashby didn't know himself from joy. "Yes, we're alive! Boney goes back to improving his island of Elba, for the game on the Continent is up with him."

"Thank God." Will smiled. "We did it. We're heroes."

"I wager they'd give the entire army medals for this victory. We demolished Napoleon's Imperial Guard, and old Boney fled. The Prussians went after him to Paris."

"Splendid news, Ash. Help me sit." Will tried lifting himself up, but fell back with a cry of pain. "I can't move my arms and legs! And my stomach—oh, God!"

"Lie still." Ashby removed his jacket, pulled a flask out of its inner pocket, and stuffed the garment beneath Will's head. "Here. Drink some whiskey. It'll revive you and dull the pain." He held Will's head as he sipped, his gaze traveling along Will's torso. It was soaked with blood.

Will exhaled. "Thanks." He lay back, his breathing ragged, his eyes stark with pain.

Ashby whistled to his mare. "I'm taking you to the hospital in Brussels. I know you're in great pain, but as soon as we reach camp, I'll lay you down in a padded cart." He put one booted foot firmly on the ground and bent down to hoist Will over his shoulder.

Will let out a bloodcurdling scream of pain. "*Stop!* Stop! I'm too torn and broken up." Will vomited blood; his eyes rolled. Ashby lay him on the ground, cursing his own incompetence.

"Don't faint! Here, have another sip of whiskey. Just a trickle . . ."

When Will's breathing improved, he said, "I'm done for. I won't make it to the hospital."

"We're not giving up," Ashby informed him. "Dying is not an option. I'll go back to camp on my own and bring a cart and a surgeon with me. He'll fix you up a little and keep an eye on you while I drive us to Brussels. So you have to make an effort and stay awake for me. Will you do that? Promise me to stay awake until my return."

"If I live, they'll amputate my arms and legs." Will moaned fitfully. "I will become a freak of nature, like those poor soldiers we saw after Salamanca . . ."

"You won't die," Ashby vowed, "and you will be a well-loved freak. Think of home, Will. Think of Izzy, of . . . of Seven Dover Street . . . of Hyacinth the Dragon Lady fussing over you with her bobbing curls . . ."

Will made a choking sound. "Don't make me laugh, damn you! I'm dying. We should take this business seriously." He spat blood, and Ashby gently wiped Will's mouth clean. "Damn. I should have been quick with your opera singer."

"If you let me bring a cart and a surgeon, I promise to fetch a different opera singer to your bed every night."

"No! No! Don't leave me!" Will's pupils widened in terror, and one of his fingers dug into Ashby's thigh. "Please . . . The damned Belgians will loot me in the dark . . ."

Ashby had to clamp down on his own panic. "Christ, Will. If I don't go now, you will die!"

Will moaned heartbreakingly, blood spilling from his lips. "I'm dying, Ash. I'm dead."

Ashby took Will's face in both hands and stared into his petrified eyes. "How can you ask me to sit and watch you die? *You have to want to live!*"

"I'm not like you, Ash . . . I don't have the strength . . . My body is all broken up . . ."

The plea in Will's eyes wrenched Ashby's heart. "I'll go find Ellis and tell him to bring the cart and the surgeon. I'll be back in minutes." He got up and grabbed his mare's pommel.

Will was whimpering and moaning. "Stay . . . Stay with me . . . I beg you . . ."

Ashby closed his eyes. It was the hardest decision of his life: if he didn't go for help, his best friend in the world would die, but if he came back and found Will lifeless, he would never forgive himself for leaving Will begging him to stay and whimpering alone in the darkness. He'd been a fool to send Ellis away. He should have ordered him to come back. He crouched beside Hector, patting his head. "Listen old boy, I want you to find Ellis. Get Ellis, Hector. Now!"

As his dog lopped away, he returned to Will's side and downed a shot of whiskey.

"Thank you." Will managed a soulful smile, resembling a frightened little boy.

That was the difference between them, Ashby thought. Will was a sweetheart. No wonder everyone loved him. Ashby, on the other hand, was a selfish beast, who had fought and clawed his way since his early years at Eton, when he was the youngest boy there, because no one cared enough about him to discipline him. And the sad irony was, Will was much more deserving of life than Ashby. Then why didn't Will want to fight for it? "Want some more whiskey?"

"Do you think God will approve when I arrive at the pearly gates dead drunk?" He started laughing and coughing blood. "Dead drunk, get it?"

Ashby helped him take another sip. "You're one chatty bugger, for a dead man."

After that Will could barely talk. His continuous moans shredded Ashby's heart. "I'd trade places with you if I could," he murmured. He shifted closer to Will and gently lifted him under the armpits to embrace Will's back to his chest. "All will be well," he hummed, rocking Will in his arms. "I'll find you that Indian fellow who patched me up. He's a great and powerful wizard, who performs miracles. He has studied ancient medical techniques taught by the old wise men of India. I'll offer him my kingdom, and he will take a piece from here, patch it there . . ."

"When I die," Will murmured faintly, "I want you to go through my things. There's a small box containing Izzy's letters to me. Read them. I'm not matchmaking, but should you ever find yourself alone and . . . in need of family . . . go to her, Ash. Isabel cares for you, as I do . . . like family . . . Don't spend your life alone. Not all women are cold bitches like Olivia. . . A good woman will understand. . . . She will see past . . ." He shuddered, emitting a low, poignant moan. "I'm cold. Your Ellis is not coming."

Ashby was thinking the same thing. Hector had been gone for over an hour. Perhaps Ellis couldn't find anyone and had taken it upon himself to drive the injured soldier to Brussels. Warm tears streamed down his cheeks. This could take hours. Black, hollow despair possessed him. He rocked Will back and forth, humming a soft tune. He shouldn't have sent Ellis away with that soldier. He should have been selfish, for Will's sake. *Damn. Damn. Damn.*

"It's good to die for England, Ash, among my brave brethren . . ."

"I wish you'd let me carry you to the hospital myself." Ashby shut his eyes against the flow of tears blurring his vision. "I wish you weren't so stubborn."

"The pain . . . I can't stand the pain . . ." Will's continuous moans were low and aching.

Ashby felt them in his heart. "You're losing too much blood. If we don't go now—"

"No . . . No hospital . . . *Please* . . ."

Ashby pressed his cheek to Will's mud-crusted blond hair. "You want to rot and bleed to death? What shall I tell Izzy? What shall I tell your poor mother? I promised I'd bring you back. I can't bear to see you give up," he whispered. "You are my brother . . ."

"Do . . . something for me," Will moaned. "Stop . . . my pain . . ."

Black chill spread through Ashby's body. "No," he rasped. "Never."

"You'd do it for a bloody Frenchman, but you won't . . . do it . . . for your . . . brother?"

If he did what Will asked, then he would surely be damned. "Dawn breaks in a few hours. The men will come—"

"Too . . . long . . . Do it . . . now . . . Please . . . Can't . . . myself . . . my hands . . . broken . . ."

Ashby kept rocking Will, but it was himself he was soothing. His best friend was dying. Which was worse—putting a ball through Will's brains or letting him hurt for two, perhaps three more hours? How could he let Will bleed until the last drop of life left his battered body? It was inhuman. And yet . . . "If the pain is so great, I might as well take you to the hospital anyway. There's always a chance . . ." *Tomorrow you will despise yourself for not having cut short his torment by even a mere second,* his conscience spoke. "All right." Ashby withdrew his pistol and fisted two balls—one for Will, one for himself. He bent his head and kissed Will's cold temple. "Thank you for being my friend. I love you more than I love myself, my brother."

Almost soundlessly, Will replied, "I love you too, my brother."

Crying like a babe, Ashby put the pistol to the spot where he'd kissed Will's temple and shut his eyes. "Rest in peace." He pulled the trigger. The shot reverberated through his heart.

He sat there frozen, dead inside. What a mad and senseless world he lived in, he thought, gazing around him at the thousands of lifeless men sprawled across the field. It almost exceeded credibility that so immense a carnage should have been made in hours. *Now you.*

Still holding Will, he reloaded the pistol and pressed the muzzle to his own temple. *Do it!* He commanded himself. But the beast inside him refused to squeeze the trigger.

Chapter Ten

Iris and Sophie were extremely displeased with her. Isabel could read it in their pursed lips and in the judgmental gleam in their eyes. "Now you know everything." Finishing her story, she reached for her teacup. The tears that had overwhelmed her for three straight days had left her eyes swollen and her face pale, but she was finally able to conduct herself in a civilized fashion.

The upstairs drawing room at Seven Dover Street was garlanded with multicolored flower bouquets, courtesy of Lord John, Major Macalister, and several of her old and recent admirers, all vying to express their concern over her "illness" and their desire to enjoy her company as soon as she recovered. The bouquets' effect was a glaring reminder of Ashby's ill treatment of her.

"I don't think he was—how shall I put it?—briefly entertaining himself at your expense," Iris expressed delicately. "I've reason to believe he had a more nefarious scheme in mind."

"I agree with Iris that he wasn't after anything 'brief,'" Sophie asserted between sips of tea. "However, I don't second that it was something nefarious. As a matter of fact, I suspect—"

"The man is a recluse!" Iris interrupted. "Some say he's

barking mad and lives in his wine cellar, for pity's sake! What do you suppose he was after? He's given her five thousand pounds!"

"The money was intended for our charity," Isabel pointed out. "And I've been to his cellar. It's a workshop, not a gothic dungeon complete with a torture chamber. Ashby is sane."

"My dear Izzy"—Iris leaned forward to set her teacup on the table—"a sane individual who also happens to be wealthy and titled doesn't take to his cellar and wear a mask. He may seem to be in command of his faculties, but I'm positive he suffers of some deep . . . dark . . ."

"Depression?" Sophie offered, with a touch of anger—at Iris.

"All the more reasons for Izzy to avoid him!" Iris maintained. "Clearly he is after a poor female victim to keep him company and ease his . . . solitude." Iris folded her hands in her lap.

"But he didn't want to keep me," Isabel mumbled. If he did, they wouldn't be conducting this conversation—which was beginning to pall. She decided to change topics. "What happened between you and Macalister, Iris? And don't tell me nothing happened, because I know better."

Iris contemplated her laced hands. "All right. I will tell you the truth, for two reasons. First, because my story has a moral that Izzy may benefit from. Secondly, I've been carrying its weight for too long, and it would be a relief to unburden myself with the only two people I trust." She smiled at Isabel and Sophie. She drew a deep breath. "I've known Ryan all my life. His family lived in close proximity to my father's cottage. We grew up, fell in love, and on my eighteenth birthday, Ryan proposed to me. By that time Lord Chilton, who was one of my father's frequent customers, had taken a fancy to me. My father was deep in debt, and Lord Chilton offered to rescue him from ending up in debtors' prison, providing—"

"Your father agreed to sell you to Chilton," Sophie deduced.

"Precisely." Iris nodded grimly, every line in her body rigid. "Ryan was . . . impoverished. He couldn't have possibly made an offer equal to Chilton's. I went to him and . . . tried to impress upon him the hopelessness of our situation. If we did not elope, I would become Chilton's bride. Ryan agreed. We left that very day, taking the road to Scotland. We couldn't afford to spend our meager funds at an inn, so we spent the night in a deserted game-keeper's hut in the woods, where we were convinced Chilton and my father would not be able to find us."

"But they did, didn't they?" Isabel asked anxiously, afraid to hear the sad outcome.

"No, they didn't." Iris's expression epitomized cynicism. "I wish they had, because then I . . . But it doesn't matter now. When I awoke the next morning, Ryan was gone. I stayed at the hut for a week. I fed on berries and stale bread. There was water aplenty because it rained . . . and when Ryan didn't return, I had no choice but to go back to my father and accept Chilton's suit. If I hadn't taken off with Ryan, I might have been able to persuade my father to refuse Chilton and ulti-mately settled on someone else, someone . . . kinder. Unfor-tunately, due to my recklessness, I managed to render myself utterly ruined and gain my father's ire. I was married to the baron by a special license and the entire affair was hushed up." She stared at Isabel. "The moral of my story, dear friend, is never put your honor, your future, your life in any man's hands, even if it is someone you think you can trust, because you may end up paying a very heavy toll for your naiveté. My life is a prison. My jailer is my husband, a distinctly unpleas-ant man, whom I could have avoided had I acted less . . . friv-olously in trusting my heart. From what you've told us, the Gargoyle has all the ammunition he needs to own you, if he merely wishes it. You know very well that Stilgoe would do anything to prevent your public ruination, even if it means marrying you off to a dubious recluse earl."

Isabel opened her mouth to say that Ashby would never

conceive of threatening to ruin her publicly, that he didn't want her in the first place, and that therefore Iris's point was a moot one.

"I'm not finished." Iris's voice was terse. "You may think you admire and are fond of this man, Izzy, but how well do you really know him? Can you be absolutely certain you would love everything you might come to learn about him? Or is it possible—just possible, mind you—that you might discover things you wouldn't like, when it would be much too late?" She sent Isabel a pointed look. "Do not ever put yourself in a position to become some man's possession, unless you are absolutely satisfied with his character, honor, and virtue. That is my moral."

Isabel felt tears welling in her eyes and blinked them back. Iris had hit the nail on its head: What if Isabel discovered she couldn't stomach the sight of Ashby's scarred face? What if she learned unpleasant things about him? Ashby weltered in secrets. He wouldn't say why he hadn't come to console them when Will died. He wouldn't say whom he had been engaged to and why the nuptials hadn't taken place. Though Will loved and admired him, she knew Ashby's past was tainted with horrific stories of debauchery. Perhaps she had escaped by the skin of her teeth.

Then why did it hurt so much?

"Was your chance meeting at the assembly at Almack's last Wednesday the first time you have seen Ryan after his disappearance?" Sophie asked Iris.

"I saw him at the café after our meeting with Flowers. That's why I left. I have no desire to run into that man ever again," she spat out with vehement disgust.

"You seem to know quite a bit about his present situation," Sophie prodded.

"After I married Chilton, I heard that Ryan bought a cavalry commission and that he was fighting on the Continent."

"I find it strange," Sophie mused, "that a man, who loved

you well enough to ask for your hand in marriage, would choose to risk his life in battle over marrying the woman he loved."

"I supposed he sought to make his fortune in the army." Iris shrugged.

"Cavalry commissions are costly," Isabel said, "especially when one seeks advancement in rank. And while there are opportunities aplenty to get rich in India, Ryan told me explicitly that he wished to remain in England."

"Also, I find it peculiar that he would choose to pay advances to a woman whom he knows is a close friend of yours." Sophie gestured at Isabel. "Which makes me wonder—"

"Don't say it!" Iris glared at Sophie. "He knows I despise him, and he knows I'm a married woman. If anything, he wishes to cause trouble. He thrives on mischief."

"He seemed rather cross with you, too," Isabel ruminated aloud. "Which makes me wonder if you told us the entire story." She gave Iris an affectionate smile.

"You practically called him a cicisbeo to his face." Sophie raised an amused eyebrow. "If he thought you might have forgiven him, you certainly set him straight on that score."

"As far as I am concerned, Ryan ceased to exist the morning he left me in that hut. Now as for Izzy"—Iris exhaled—"you shall do well to stay away from Lancaster House from now on."

"That won't be too difficult," Isabel said. "We've been invited to spend a week at Haworth Castle. John's grandfather, the duke, is celebrating his seventieth birthday. Stilgoe accepted."

"Indeed!" Sophie's dark eyebrows rose. "That means . . ."

"John asked my brother's permission to court me, and Stilgoe gave it."

"Don't look so glum, Izzy. Lord John is an excellent gentleman. He is handsome, socially conscientious, intelligent, amiable, courteous . . . He hails from one of the finest families in the land. You'd do very well to encourage his affections. He is a much better choice than the . . ."

"This is why I didn't contest Stilgoe's decision to accept the invitation." Isabel shrugged, feeling a little numb inside. Ashby was not an option, she kept reminding herself. It was time she gave up her mythological fixation and concentrated on someone else. She had no desire to end up a childless spinster. If she continued to dwell on Ashby, that's precisely what would happen to her. *Men say and promise all sorts of drivel to women when they're randy*. How could he say such a crude and humiliating thing to her? All she'd ever done was admire and respect him, care for him . . . Before she drowned herself in tears again, she said, "I must beg your permission to do something. It's selfish of me to ask, but I feel it would help me . . ."

After she explained her request, her friends said in unison, "Don't think twice."

Chapter Eleven

A gown of grief my body shall attire;
My staff of broken hope whereon I'll stay;
Of late repentance linked with long desire
The couch is framed whereon my limbs I'll lay.
—Sir Walter Raleigh

"My lord . . ." Phipps took a precarious step into the master bedchamber. Daylight spilled on mahogany furniture and blue draperies and was reflected by the white walls. Phipps was pleased to note that the room was in perfect order, as was his master. Fully attired, including a jacket and a polished pair of Hessians, the earl lay sprawled on his back, staring at the canopy. Phipps prided himself on having taught his young master that nothing—not even the blackest moments in a man's life—absolved one from tackling the day properly groomed.

"My lord, a package has arrived for you."

"Go away, Martin. Leave me be."

This was worse than Phipps had thought. Unbidden, the memory of that sad morning more than thirty-one years ago, when Phipps had had to tell the new, four-year-old Earl of Ashby that his parents had gone to heaven, came back to haunt him: Innocent blue-green eyes, full of tears, yet too proud to shed them in front of a servant, looked up at him for comfort. Since the task of actually caring for the young earl had fallen on Phipps's shoulders—the boy's young valet at the time—he followed his intuition, encouraging the boy to devote his time and considerable energy to a hobby. Horses became the boy's passion—almost a religion—and by the time Lord Ashby was old enough to be sent to school, he knew almost everything there was to know about the feisty beasts. Upon his master's return from France two years ago, Phipps expected Lord Ashby to retire for a while to Ashby Park and his horses, but the earl chose to bury himself in the cellar, where for six months he slaved over timber, a hobby the earl had picked up during his years in Spain. Phipps had comforted himself with the thought that, at the least, his master had continued to be productive. Unfortunately, it wasn't the case this time.

A week had passed since Lord Ashby had slipped out to encounter Miss Aubrey at the ball. During this week the earl had not risen from his bed, except to bathe and dress and let the maids tidy up his quarters. It seemed the fight had gone out of his master altogether.

"My lord," he tried for the third time, "the package came from—"

Ashby turned hollow eyes toward the intruder at the door. "Don't you ever give up?"

Phipps stepped closer. "On you, my lord? Never."

Ashby turned his gaze away from Phipps and looked out the window at the blooming tops of the trees lining Park Lane. If he stared long enough at the rustling green leaves, the heaviness in his chest would lift and his mind would clear of thought. Until some chatty people took a stroll beneath his window and the bleakness would choke him again. Sound traveled upward in his street; whether he wanted to or not, he could eavesdrop on the quietest conversations.

"The package came from Seven Dover Street."

Ashby heard a soft click as the door closed. He glimpsed at the large hat box placed on the bed beside him. He sat up, his heart drumming the French *pas de charge,* and dragged the box to his lap. Why would Isabel send him anything after he had deliberately crushed her feelings?

He knew the answer. Warm, caring, bighearted Isabel had seen through his act and knew it for what it was. Her forgiveness, her generosity of spirit humbled him. He would do anything for her: He would see her bill proposal passed in the House, he would purchase a whole building for her charity operation, he would go to her, cap in hand, drop to his knees, and beg her to take him as he was, damaged and weary and not worth a damn . . . and if she accepted him out of pity, he would sing praises to the Lord and grasp with both hands whatever she offered him.

He had trouble keeping his hands steady as he lifted the top and bared the contents of the box. His heart froze. Inside he found the wooden box he had fashioned for her, with the blue ribbon and the dried daisy, the two notes he had sent her, and the five thousand pounds he had donated to her charity. The hammerblows at his temples blurred his vision. He couldn't breathe.

A folded piece of paper caught his eye. He didn't want to read it; the note all but scorched him when he touched it. Yet he'd always been a glutton for punishment.

Lord Ashby,

Enclosed you will find certain items I no longer wish to have among my possessions. As regards to your donation, I have obtained the consent of the WMSW's board of trustees to return its entirety to your lordship, as we have no use for it. Rest assured I shall not impose upon your lordship henceforth.

Respectfully,
Isabel Aubrey

A tear plopped and spread on the milky sheet of paper trembling in his hands. *Damnation!* His arm lashed out and sent the hat box tumbling to the floor. He fell back, pressing the heels of his hands to his eyes. *God damn him.* She'd returned *everything,* even the money she desperately needed to help her unfortunates—that in itself was an insult so acute, he felt as though he'd been kicked in the gut. The blackness closed in on him as never before. He was nothing to her, worse than nothing—a leper. Even his blunt was not good enough anymore. But he couldn't fault her. He'd done it all to himself. He'd dug his own grave, and now he had to wither away in it.

Only, suicide was not an option. He was neither brave enough, like Will, nor weak enough, like his father, even though all he had to anticipate were hours of dark pain. He had nothing . . . *Will's letters from Isabel.* He had forgotten his promise to read them. He sat up. "Phipps!"

His butler burst into his bedchamber, as though he had been lurking outside all this time. Phipps took one look at the items scattered on the floor and bent down to collect them.

"Leave it. Where did you store Major Aubrey's trunk?" Ashby demanded to know.

Phipps frowned in thought. "In the attic. I'll have it brought to your chamber promptly."

Ashby put the discarded items back inside the box and placed it on the dresser. Several minutes later two footmen brought Will's trunk. Thanking and dismissing them, Ashby dragged the trunk over to the bed and sat before it. *Dear Will.* Some day he would return the trunk to the Aubreys, but not yet. He cracked it open and gazed inside for a long moment. He was the one who'd put everything neatly in it. He had buried Will in his ruined Waterloo uniforms—as Will would have wanted him to—and put the rest of Will's belongings, everything Ashby had found, including Will's last letter to Isabel, in the trunk. What was he looking for? A box of letters.

He found the tin box at the bottom of the trunk. He took a deep breath and opened the lid. Dozens of stained, wrinkled letters filled the box. Will must have read them dozens of times.

Settling back against the pillows, he began with the one at the bottom and worked his way up. Isabel's prose was lively and affectionate, full of funny anecdotes of everyday life in Seven Dover Street, full of Izzy. He found himself laughing and wincing at her account of their butler's mishap on the stairs, a result of her twin sisters' experiment with frogs. He gulped her narration of her presentation at court and wished he could have seen her gliding up to Prinny in her finery, a young woman at last. His eyes stuck on her next lines:

> *That night I dreamt I was waltzing in the arms of a dashing hussar. Not you, Will; stop grimacing! My hussar was tall and suave, with dark hair, sea-colored eyes, and no face. I knew him in my dream, though he revealed neither his name nor his visage. A mystery hussar.*
> > *Your fanciful, loving sister,*
> > *Isabel*

Five hours and one bottle of wine later, Ashby closed the tin box and rested his head on the pillows at his back. Will had given him a very precious gift, one of hope and life. Isabel did love him; it was expressed in every letter to her brother, in an undertone style. Will had kept her well informed, for at some point, circa four years ago, just after Sorauren, her questions had become insistent. He reread the letter he'd set aside.

> *My dearest Will,*
> *Sylvia Curtis told me in confidence that she is traveling to Spain to care for her brother. The 18th charge at Sorauren, Sylvia maintains, was a field of atrocities, and*

you said not a word. Must I beg you for news of Ashby?
I am anxious and you keep mum. Is he hurt? Please,
dear brother, send word, for I do not know myself from
worrying. If he needs care, I must travel to Spain with
Sylvia. He should not be alone in his suffering. He may
need someone to hold his hand.

Whatever Will had written in response had kept her from
making the journey. *Thank God.*

He was never the same after that charge—but nor was he
now. Not after she exploded into his life like a blazing sun,
with all the subtlety of a cannonball, and made him want to
live again. How could he give her up, when he could no
longer deny his latent craving for her, and when he needed
her warmth—as every living thing needed the power of the
sun—to subsist? He would do anything to get her back. Unfortunately, his new resolution didn't change the fact that his
face was a far cry from "pretty" and that it was a ball from his
pistol that had terminated Will's life.

He put the tin box in Will's trunk, then strode back and forth
across his spacious chamber, wondering if it was necessary for
a man to sink to the bottom of a mental pit before realizing he
didn't care to dwell there. If he didn't have it in him to off himself, he had better start living, because he had no tolerance for
pain left in him anymore. *No more pain,* he repeated decisively,
plowing the carpet and replaying his first encounter with Isabel
in his mind. *You are the kindest, gentlest, most generous man*
I've ever known. I don't believe you could ever lose your hu-
manity.

Perhaps the way to feel human again was to become the
man Isabel believed he was. *You were responsible for these*
women's deceased loved ones. Don't you think your men might
expect you to do something—anything—to help their kin? You
and I, we have so much to give, it is our duty to give it. Isabel
was doubly right. While selfishly abusing his power and

wealth as a young rake, he only brought misery on himself. Donating the five thousand pounds had felt profoundly rewarding, which was why Isabel's refusal to accept it stung so much. He did want to help these unfortunate females, he realized, and if not directly, then with Isabel's help. His soldiers had followed him into hell. Wasn't it his duty to pull their families out of hell?

Invigorated by his decision, he rang for his butler.

"My lord?" Phipps stuck his head in the door.

"You may return the trunk to the attic and inform Cook that I'll have pheasant and apple pie for luncheon." Though the time was closer to supper, his household staff was used to the odd hours he kept. "On second thought, I'll have a steak and an assortment of tapas. I'm famished."

"You are?" At Ashby's cocked eyebrow, Phipps drew himself up, pleased. "Aye, my lord."

"There is one other thing. I have a mission for you." He barely contained a sardonic smile when his butler snapped to attention. "I know Mayfair is crawling with your spies. Find out what you can about Miss Aubrey. You know what *I* want to know," he added pointedly.

"Very good, my lord!" His nursemaid smiled.

Ashby rolled his eyes.

Chapter Twelve

Isabel and Lucy were packing for the forthcoming country house party at Haworth Castle when Norris appeared in the doorway. "Miss Isabel, you have a caller."

Isabel ignored the sudden leap of her heart. "Who is it?"

"Lord John Hanson."

She let out the breath she'd been holding. "Please show him into the morning room."

It was the fourth time John called on her since the Barrington ball. He took her on a drive through Hyde Park, accompanied her to a music recital, and attended one of her Friday meetings. He also made a point of dancing with her at every rout they both happened to attend. All in all, she had to admit she was growing fond of the Golden Angel. He may not have the power to melt her insides with a look, or send her untrustworthy heart aflutter, but, as Iris indicated, he was courteous, intelligent, amiable, socially conscientious—he graciously sat down to read her bill proposal and declared it "a smashing piece of genius"—and he was undeniably handsome.

"Good day, John." She breezed inside the morning room to accept his hand in greeting.

"You take my breath away, my lovely Isabel," he murmured, and tried to kiss her cheek.

Isabel pulled back before he succeeded. "Norris, would you kindly ask my mother to join us and send for some tea?"

"Very good, Miss Aubrey." Norris left the door open.

Isabel sat down on the chair opposite the sofa, dashing John's hope that she would sit next to him. Courtships didn't require contact. Privately she was vexed with herself for becoming such a stickler with a gentleman of John's repute after flagrantly flouting the rules with Ashby, but she could no more make herself crave John's touch than she could have restrained her cravings where Ashby was concerned. She was hoping and praying her feelings would change in time. Her entire family seemed to delight in the possible match, and she knew that Stilgoe would not let her off the hook this time. If John proposed, she would have to accept, no escape possible. *Think of social achievements and blond babies,* she told herself and smiled.

"I have less than an hour before Parliament assembles, but I came to assure you that I"—John glanced at the open doorway and dropped his voice to a whisper—"am hard at work trying to obtain the lists for you. And . . ." He smoothed his hand over the seat beside him.

Isabel read the invitation quite plainly, and since she was almost falling out of her chair in an effort to hear his next words, she started to rise . . .

"Miss Aubrey." Norris's voice jumped her. "You have another caller."

"Who is it, Norris?" she inquired composedly, sitting upright again.

"Major Macalister. He insists on having a word with you."

After Iris's confession, Isabel had sent Ryan away three times without seeing him. Had it been Paris Nicholas Lancaster sitting across from her, she might consider asking the major to join them, if only to incite the earl's jealousy, but John was being very straightforward in his pursuit of her. Even if she were in love with John—which she wasn't—there was no need to put the pressure on him with the presence of a potential rival. "Please inform Major Macalister—"

"That he may go to the Devil," a deep voice finished, and an instant later, Ryan's tall frame materialized beside Norris. His eyes found hers. "Go ahead. Tell me to my face."

John shot to his feet. "Now see here, soldier. Miss Aubrey has explicitly said—"

Circumventing the appalled butler, Ryan strolled into the room, looking utterly fearsome in his hussar regimentals, and stopped a step away from LJ. Isabel jumped to her feet and hurried to stand between them. "No brawling," she warned, "or I shall take myself elsewhere."

Ryan's cool gaze traveled over John's lean frame and returned to John's shorter eye level. He smiled. "I never brawl with lordlings half my size."

It was an overstatement, of course, but it worked. John looked positively apoplectic.

"Major Macalister!" Isabel glared at him. "I insist you leave at once."

Ryan looked at her, his light blue eyes expressing deep regret. "Five minutes of your time. Then I'll leave peacefully and never bother you again."

John's fists were drawn in a boxing pose he and Stilgoe practiced at Gentleman Jackson's; his voice was full of rancor. "You will leave at once!"

Isabel placed her hand on one of John's balled fists and in a placating voice said, "Thank you for standing up for me, John, but the session at Parliament begins any moment, and I see no harm in giving a Waterloo hero five minutes of my time."

John pursed his lips. "I can skip the session—"

"Please, John." Isabel smiled. "For my sake."

"Very well." John drew himself up. "I shall have you all to myself this upcoming week."

Isabel saw him out, thanking him again for his noteworthy forbearance, and this time she didn't evade his quick peck on the cheek. Ryan had also followed her downstairs.

"Walk with me, why don't you?" he asked cordially. Isabel summoned Lucy with her wrap and bonnet and followed Ryan onto the sidewalk, with Lucy trailing a few steps behind.

"You don't much like me anymore, do you?" Ryan smiled grimly, offering his arm. "I know the reason, which is why I needed five minutes of your time."

For the sake of decorum, Isabel took his arm and fell into step beside him. "I don't think it is I you should be importuning, major," Isabel returned pointedly.

Ryan let out a heartfelt sigh. "You think I haven't tried? Iris won't see me, she returns my letters unopened . . . I'm surprised she doesn't burn them."

Isabel wasn't at all certain it was on Iris's authority that Ryan's calls were refused and his letters sent back unopened, but she kept her assumptions to herself. "You want me to take a message to Iris from you."

Ryan halted and faced her. "I must see her. I need to—" He raked a hand through his thick mane of auburn locks. "I need to apologize to Iris. She needs me to apologize to her."

Isabel raised a questioning eyebrow. "Is that why you insulted her at Almack's?"

"She goaded me. She always does." He cursed under his breath. "She always did."

Isabel gave him a gimlet eye. "You still love her, don't you?" Upon his loud silence, she went on, "May I ask you a question, Ryan?"

"You may ask me anything you wish, Isabel."

His answer gave her pause. She contemplated asking him why he had left Iris in that hut. On second thought, she decided not to meddle. It was Iris's question to ask. "Was our little flirtation at the café a prelude to this conversation?" She looked at him askance.

"Yes and no." A lopsided grin formed on his handsome face. "Yes, I spotted you sitting with Iris and hoped to gain access to apologizing to her through you. No, I invited you to have an ice with me because you are exceedingly attractive, because I am determined to terminate my single status, and because, as we both know, Iris is married. Does this answer your question?"

They resumed walking down the block. "I'll be frank with you, Ryan," Isabel said.

"Please."

"This is strictly between you and me."

"You are expecting an offer of marriage from the blond pugilist."

She laughed, and then frowned. "This is not the case, I'm afraid. If John proposes, I shall be forced to accept his suit. My family won't brook any more refusals from me."

"But you don't love him," he assumed correctly.

"Not yet, I don't."

He looked at her sideways. "Have you given your heart to someone else?" When she didn't answer, he shook his head at both their follies, she thought. "This puts us in the same boat. We are both hoping to fall miraculously in love with someone . . . new." They continued in silence for half a block, then turned around and started back toward the house. "I don't suppose you'll allow me to court you a little? Give the swell some competition?" He gazed at her with interest.

Isabel smiled up at him. "You are making it very hard for me to say no, Ryan, but I must. Iris is my dearest friend. I won't hurt her for anything. Besides, I think it would take a miracle for us to fall in love with each other, knowing how we truly feel. At least with someone else we may enjoy the illusion that the other party involved is not pining for a certain other individual."

"Your point is well taken. Still, I would like us to remain friends."

"All right, but do not expect my loyalty when it comes to matters concerning you and Iris."

"Fair enough." He nodded. They arrived at the front entrance of Seven Dover Street. "My five minutes are up, I think." Ryan smiled. "Will you kindly tender my apology to Iris?"

"No, but I will pass her a letter from you, if you like."

"Thank you. For everything." He raised her hand to his lips. A moment later he swung onto his horse and rode off.

Phipps was most informative. Ashby was not surprised to discover that Isabel was the *ton's* darling, well liked and respected for her tastes and opinions. He was not terribly pleased to learn that she was pursued by the sons of the highest echelons of Society. Why would she want a dog-eared earl, thirteen years her senior, who had done nothing with his life but wreak havoc first on himself and then on others and resembled a grotesque creature carved in the stone of a cathedral?

Needing to clear his head and devise a strategy for winning Isabel all over again, he pulled on a pair of old boots and left his chamber. Usually he went riding after midnight when London was quieter, but if he remained in his house another moment, he would surely go mad. He pounded down the stairs, nicked a pair of apples from the kitchen, and went out to the stables. Hector lopped beside him, excited by the prospect of an early run. Ashby patted his dog's head. "Quiet, old boy. We wouldn't want to attract unwelcome attention, would we?"

A single lamp lit the stables. Apollo gave an impatient snort when they entered his domain. "What are you complaining about?" Ashby fed the stallion an apple and bit into another. "Soon you're off to Ashby Park to play with the pretty mares. My fun is reduced to a good run and an apple."

Apollo shook his head, baring his teeth. "You don't have to gloat," Ashby muttered.

One of the grooms came running in. "Milord, I was sent to saddle Apollo."

"I'll do it, Billy. You may return to your supper."

"Aye, milord. Thank you." The groom bowed and vanished as quickly as he'd appeared.

Ashby touched Apollo's shiny neck. "Ready?" The big black turned aside and didn't move a muscle until Ashby tightened the girth. That done, he swung up and bent his head as the three of them walked onto the front drive. *Ah, freedom.* He unbound his hair and it whipped against his face in the night wind. At the shift of his knee, Apollo turned left and trotted north, exiting the city's boundaries. Only when they were out in the open did Ashby lean forward, loosening his grip on the reins, and they went flying over the dew-coated meadow, Hector at their heels.

Ashby shut his eyes, trying to conjure up a pleasant, battle-free day in Spain, in which the sun beat mercilessly on his face. He failed. Another image settled before his eyes: A shimmering goddess materializing out of the night, her eyes starry bright, her lips begging love . . .

Hours later, perspiring and spent, Ashby found himself gazing wistfully at a lovely little house he hadn't seen in a long time. The blooming rose garden was still there, and the bench. If he could rewind time, he would return to the moment Isabel had pressed her cherry lips to his. He would kiss her all over again—*that* he would never change—but he would change everything that came afterward, make other choices, do everything differently . . .

A carriage drew up and stopped. Ashby pulled Apollo deeper into the shade of the tree. He saw a tiger jump to the ground and pull the door open. Isabel stepped out, pulling her shawl over her low neckline, but not before Ashby glimpsed the rounded, moonlit slopes of her breasts.

"Have fun in the country!" female voices chirped from inside the carriage.

"I'll see you next week," Isabel replied cheerfully. She glanced across the street, and for an instant Ashby was positive she'd made him out in the shadows. But as the tiger stood by, waiting to escort her to the front door, she concentrated on fumbling in her reticule, humming a waltz.

He relaxed in the saddle and continued to moon at her. She had an aura of feminine vitality like no other woman. An intense feeling of possessiveness struck him. A fellow officer confessed to him once after several drinks that his wife was his beacon of light. For Ashby, a man who lived in darkness for too long, Isabel was a bright, burning sun, and he was so tired of the cold.

"Drat. I forgot to take the key," she mumbled. "I'll have to awake Norris. You go on now. I'll be fine." She waved the tiger back to the carriage. Her friends took off.

Ashby could have strangled them for leaving her standing alone at night. Even Mayfair had its fair share of cutpurses and troublemakers. She looked so sweet and vulnerable standing in the moonlight, he wanted to sweep in and shield her from the evils lurking in the darkness.

Without warning she looked up and fixed her gaze straight at him. He froze in the saddle. Though she could make out his and Apollo's shapes, he doubted she identified him. Did she?

If she walked up to him, all would be lost—she would see his face, and he would lose his chance at dazzling her, with his mask on—and yet, he almost wished she would approach . . .

A good woman will understand . . . She will see past . . .

Isabel turned her back on him and stomped up to the front door. A slow smile surfaced on his face as he watched her produce a key and shove it in the lock. The little vixen had spotted and recognized him the moment she had stepped out of the carriage. She was sending him a clear message: She was furious and wasn't likely to forgive him—without some clever maneuverings on his part, he filled in the blank. Perversely her attitude pleased him. Fury was good, better than indifference, and he was up to the challenge. He waited until light sparked to life in the third window to the left on the second floor, and then trotted off, feeling optimistic.

From what Phipps had managed to glean from the milkmaids, the footboys, and several other prattlers in Mayfair, it appeared that Isabel had finally given in to her family's plight and allowed someone—other than himself—to court her. Though he couldn't fault her, it stuck in his craw that it should be John Hanson. The man was a menace to young females of fortune and good breeding. Not that Ashby was ever a paragon of selflessness and restraint, but he had rules for himself where women were concerned, and one of them was not to deflower innocents. In Hanson's case, Ashby wasn't too certain. The man was desperate. Who knew what he would do if matters did not progress fast enough to suit his needs? All Hanson had to do was arrange for him and Isabel to be caught in a compromising situation, and she would be a married woman. Ashby wished he could alert her without sounding hypocritical. But he knew damned well that if anyone had come upon *them* in the gazebo, she would have been married to him now. She would also be ruined. Ashby didn't want an unwilling bride; he wanted Isabel to come to his bed with her eyes aglow. Therefore, he would have to become the better choice of suitor—in every way.

"What do you mean she's left today? You said the house party wasn't until next week!"

Phipps had no excuses to offer. "Hang me, flog me, I plead guilty as charged, my lord. The information I had collected was inaccurate."

Ashby paced in front of his office desk, pushing his hair

back and cursing himself for not paying attention. While Isabel had been saying goodbye to her friends last night, he had been admiring her bosom. *Idiot.* Now he'd never accomplish all that he'd set out to do. Wellington was not due back in England for the next three days. *Damn. Damn. Damn.* He would have to use his own name and hope it carried sufficient weight at the War Office. "All right," he muttered. "Send Halifax and Tompkins to me, and have the coach brought around."

"Aye, my lord." Phipps straightened up with a grin.

Ashby halted. "Don't look so smug, damn you. You remind me of an old aunt."

"You don't have an old aunt, my lord."

He glanced at the closed doors. "Martin, do you—" *Damnation.* He couldn't formulate the question, let alone voice it, though it plagued him relentlessly, trammeling his psyche with fears and doubts. His lioness seemed determined to unmask him at every turn. He needed an honest opinion. Since Will was gone, all he had was Martin Phipps, the closest thing he'd ever had for a father or an uncle or an old aunt. He swallowed, beleaguered by the hammering in his chest. "Look at me, Martin," he commanded hoarsely. "If you were a beautiful, impressionable young woman, with a pack of pups gamboling about you and spouting marriage proposals, would you choose to spend your life looking at this—this hideous excuse for a man's face? Be honest. I can tell when you sugarcoat the truth."

Phipps pinched his chin—a good sign. "I must say, my lord. I do not find it at all wanting. Perhaps I have grown accustomed to it over the past four years."

"But when you first saw me, did I shock you, strike you with horror, turn your stomach?"

Phipps scowled—a bad sign. "It wasn't horror that I felt . . . but—"

"What? What was your very first impression?"

"Sadness, my lord, for the pain you've suffered."

Ashby eyed him skeptically. "Sadness, not revulsion?"

"Revulsion?" Phipps looked genuinely at a loss. He went on wistfully, "A fine-looking lad you were, endowed with Lady Ashby's likeness, a great beauty if there ever was one. God rest her soul. Now you are a fine-looking man, who wears the marks of great courage."

Christ. Ashby rolled his eyes, gnashing his teeth. He needed a woman's opinion, and not that of the experienced sort, who liked the gifts his money purchased and other things Isabel was not yet acquainted with. "I'm ready for Halifax and Tompkins now, Phipps. Tell them to report to me in their old regimentals. I trust their baggage has been kept in mint condition?"

"Of course. I'll send the boys in straight away." Phipps turned and left the room.

Ashby took his seat behind his desk. He placed a sheet of paper before him and dipped the quill in the ink bottle. While composing an urgent note to Wellington's secretary, his mind kept spinning with misgiving: What if he succeeded? They would be back to where they had started. Isabel would still want to see his face and know how Will had died. Sooner or later Ashby would have to reveal everything to her. He only hoped it would be later rather than sooner.

Halifax and Tompkins reported for duty looking spick and span, a pair of hussars about to charge into combat. "Excellent." Ashby sanded and folded the note, then stamped his signet ring in the soft wax he'd applied. "Take this letter to the Duke of Wellington's secretary at the War Office. Then wait for him to give you something to deliver back to me. It may take a while, but under no circumstances are you to return empty handed. Understood?"

Halifax stepped forward to accept the note. "Aye, milord."

"Drop my name, should anyone decide to question you or give you trouble. Remember, you're carrying out orders and are not allowed to discuss them with anyone, except with the duke's secretary." Since Wellington had refused to formally discharge him from service in the hopes that Ashby would some day resume his command, he didn't foresee any trouble, but he believed in thinking ahead and always being prepared. "Take the carriage. On the way back, sit inside and don't take your eyes off the parchment you'd be bringing to me. Return here straight away. Is everything clear?"

"Aye, milord."

"Good. Now repeat everything I said." When he was satisfied that his orders would be carried out to the letter, he called for one of his footboys. "Hardy, go to Mr. Brooks. Tell him I require his immediate services. Be sure to mention that I said I'd make it worth his while. Wait." He took out a few shillings from a box. "Here. Take a hack and fetch him with you. Now go."

As soon as Hardy left his office, Ashby resumed pacing. He hoped the note to Wellington's secretary would suffice and that he wouldn't have to visit the War Office in person. The idea of going out in broad daylight unnerved him beyond reason. He studied his unsteady hands. What a pathetic excuse for a man he'd become—a richly deserved comeuppance for the horrors he'd committed. He closed his eyes against the gory sights and the screams of pain that were never far from his thoughts. The images haunting his dreams were for the most part those of dead British and French soldiers. Sometimes he imagined the weeping faces of French mothers cursing his soul to damnation. Strange how he never once dreamed of English women accusing him of leading their men to their deaths—and those were the ones to whom he owed the most.

Penitence. The word reverberated in his head unremittingly. He dreaded to imagine what his future would have been like if Isabel hadn't awakened his conscience, among other things. Whether he'd been matchmaking or not, Will had known precisely what he was doing when he asked Ashby to read her letters. It was comforting, in a way, to know he'd always had the cure to his torments within his grasp. He'd been a fool to refuse reading her bill proposal. It would have afforded him a better understanding of what was required to push the bill across. But he'd been damned annoyed, believing she'd come to him because she needed something *from* him. That wasn't the case, though. She came to him because she missed him, because she fancied herself in love with him. Would she feel the same when she ultimately saw the real him, the Gargoyle?

Chapter Thirteen

"I had the pleasure of meeting your *late* brother once." Keeping her voice low, Lady Olivia joined Isabel on the settee in the drawing room, where they all gathered before luncheon.

Since their arrival at Haworth Castle three days ago, Isabel had come to form a distinctly unfavorable opinion of John's sister, but the unkind *late* brother bit really got Isabel's dander up. Olivia could have referred to Will as Major Aubrey, as everyone else did, but Olivia never said anything unless it incorporated abuse. The soulless ice queen was as beautiful as her brother, with his white blond hair and lucid blue eyes. She was also vain, dull, and vicious. Isabel hoped the iceberg would go chill someone else. Just sitting with her made Isabel's teeth chatter.

"A mutual friend introduced us." The iceberg smiled. "Another officer in his regiment."

"Indeed." Isabel glanced at the mantel clock, wondering how much longer the household staff intended to starve them. Freddy and Teddy looked ready to begin chewing furniture.

With the timing of a playwright, Tobias the butler materialized in the doorway. "Your Grace, luncheon is served."

"Thank you, Tobias. Shall we?" The silver-haired Duke of Haworth offered Lady Hyacinth his arm, and everyone tailed them in pairs: John's parents, Lord and Lady Hanson; Stilgoe and Angie; Olivia and her husband, Viscount Bradford; John and Isabel; Teddy and Freddy; and last but not least, Danielli and her nursemaid. The duke led the way outside, where the servants had spread several blankets on the grass and erected a table with chairs for the elderly people.

"Since the season is at its peak," the duke said, "I decided my younger guests mustn't feel deprived and so I asked Tobias to set up a picnic for us. I trust we shall enjoy it."

"What a delightful idea!" Isabel's mother exclaimed. "A picnic in one's own park. Really, Oscar, you outdid yourself."

"Thank you, madam. Coming from you, it is a compliment to savor."

As soon as everyone was seated, liveried footmen milled about, serving wine, lemonade, chicken sandwiches, an assortment of viands and cheeses, and sweet tarts.

"Quite a park you have here, Your Grace," Stilgoe commented, accepting a glass of Hock.

Indeed, the park was spectacular, Isabel thought. It had rained the first three days, forcing them to suffer indoors, but now with the sun shining over a sprawling green lawn, embellished with cultivated flowerbeds, oak trees, artistic hedges, and a majestic blue lake, she could truly appreciate the property. The house was somewhat of a disappointment; although sizeable, it was neither grand nor well-kept, its interiors falling far beneath par. John had explained beforehand that his eccentric grandfather despised change. But she could have done without the dust and the ants parading on the walls. Taking in the efforts invested in the grounds, her suspicions regarding the family's financial situation were satisfactorily dashed, though.

Danielli crawled her way toward Isabel and her twin sisters, who thereupon set their plates aside to frolic with the little darling. Isabel glanced at John, wondering what sort of father he'd make. Ashby would make a splendid father . . . to some other woman's children. She let out a sigh of the heart. She really ought to stop thinking about Ashby. She found it equally perturbing and vexing how in little over a fortnight the unpleasant memories had almost faded while her mind doggedly clung to the electrifying moments they shared in the gazebo. She never imagined a man could arouse such raging sensations in a woman, or that she would countenance such intimacies before proper marriage vows were exchanged. But in her heart, mind, and soul, Isabel had given herself to Ashby a long time ago. For that reason, when he had summoned her to the gazebo and told her he wanted her, she had foolishly believed he felt as she did.

"Join us for bird shooting after luncheon," Bradford, Olivia's husband, told Stilgoe. "Good game all 'round the park." Bradford was John's friend. He was only good for so many hours of the day, before he dropped into a bottle—or rather several bottles—and didn't emerge until noon the following day. Olivia didn't seem to mind, though. Isabel had yet to see them acknowledging the other's presence, much less talking to one another. Not the sort of marriage Isabel dreamt of.

Stilgoe gave a rueful smile. "Thanks for the invitation. However, I'm afraid I must decline. Izzy would shoot me if I dared point a gun at a helpless creature."

"In that case, I give up the sport myself," John declared, and received an approving smile from Isabel. She liked how he endeavored to please her. He didn't shower her with expensive fans, chocolates, or other fripperies, but he paid attention to the little things.

"I'd still like to tour the grounds," her brother added as an afterthought. "Do you cultivate wool or barley? In Stilgoe Abbey we've been experimenting on . . ." While Stilgoe regaled them with his enthusiasm for agricultural projects, neither the old duke nor John contributed anything to her brother's one-sided conversation. As if they cared not about their properties. Odd, that.

"Not much fun in walking about aimlessly," Bradford put in petulantly, grabbing a wine bottle from one of the footmen. "No other sports available. The horseflesh isn't worth a d—"

"We could play skittles!" Freddy announced, infecting her twin with her enthusiasm.

Teddy leaped to her feet, short pink skirts swirling. "Oh, yes! We'll set it up right there!" She gestured at an even patch of ground on the extensive lawn, and the earth began to shake.

"What the devil . . ." Stilgoe stood up as his wife hastened to retrieve Danielli.

"Oh, dear!" Hyacinth cried, clutching her chest. "An earthquake! In East Sussex!"

"Not an earthquake . . ." the duke began, as horse and rider came tearing across the lawn not far from where they sat. Hunched over the glistening neck of a great black Thoroughbred, white shirt billowing, dark mane whipping as wildly as the horse's, the rider looked so much a part of the beast, they seemed to soar rather than gallop, hooves scarcely touching the ground. Isabel had never seen such a superb demonstration of horsemanship before, though she'd grown up among swaggering cavalry officers. "That's a known devil around here," Haworth said, "or so he used to be." He cast his granddaughter a withering glance, muttering under his breath, "Silly chit."

Isabel was too entranced by the outstanding rider to care about the iceberg stiffening with an affronted gasp. There was something awfully familiar about him, but she couldn't pinpoint exactly what made her pulse begin to race.

"I've seen this horsemanship before," Stilgoe echoed her thoughts, "just can't recall . . ."

The duke supplied the answer. "That's Ashby, our next-door neighbor. Nobody sits a horse as he does. At ten years of age that boy could ride like the wind. A remarkable fellow, that one."

Isabel's breath was knocked out of her. "Ashby?" she gasped and got stern looks from both her mother and her brother. She ignored them, focusing instead on the rider approaching the edge of their vision. He didn't wear a mask, but it was impossible to make out his face at the speed he was flying. Her heart beat so hard and fast that it nearly burst out of her chest. *Ashby was here.*

"Grew up to be very wild and wicked after his parents' accident, he did," the duke went on. "A rough-and-tumble, ne'er-do-well scoundrel, he squandered half his inheritance, moved in the fastest circles, and tarnished his father's good name. Got himself into a tight spot or two, but with my guidance and his intelligence, he survived his misspent youth and acquitted himself well eventually. He bought a commission when Boney invaded Portugal and became the youngest, most distinguished colonel ever to command His Majesty's 18th Hussars." The duke puffed up proudly. "He took the golden cup of every cavalry race during the war years on the Continent. He'd make some *sensible* woman a fine husband one day." He lobbed a glower at Olivia.

"What is he about?" Lady Fanny Hanson screeched as Olivia stood up sniffling and dashed toward the house. "How dare he show his dreadful face around here after what he'd done?"

"He has every right, madam!" the duke blustered. "If your daughter had any sense—"

John leaned to whisper something to the duke that made his grandfather grunt and followed his sister in an angry stride. "Liv, wait!" he called out, before disappearing inside the house.

"I hope you are satisfied, sir!" Lady Fanny sputtered and flounced to the house, dragging her innocuous husband along. Bored with the scene, Bradford took his bottle and ambled off.

The elderly Duke of Haworth looked as flustered as a general deserted by his troops. Izzy's mother took his arm and encouraged him to his feet. "Come, Oscar dear. We've enjoyed enough sun for one day. Why don't you show me the stamp collection you've been raving about?"

Angie's sweet voice broke the ensuing silence. "I'll take Danielli in. My darling cannot abide senseless shouting. And she needs her nap. Are you coming, Charles?"

"Yes, my love." Stilgoe lifted his daughter into his arms, then freed one hand to splay it on the small of his wife's back. Together, their small family of three wandered toward the house.

Isabel was left alone with her twin sisters. She stood up, gripping their hands. "Let's go."

"But we want to play skittles!" Teddy protested, dragging her heels.

"Never mind that," Isabel snapped, and in a lower voice added, "We're going skulking."

Chapter Fourteen

They stood at the edge of the mile-long, tree-lined road and gawked at the white mansion.

"He must be a thousand times wealthier than the old duck of Haworth," Teddy murmured in awe, pronouncing Isabel's opinion. Ashby's manor house was enormous, its classical grandeur stretching to the sides with Corinthian columns and tall Palladian windows.

"Is he very old, Izzy?" Freddy asked.

"He is five and thirty," Isabel imparted, seized by tension now that they were so close.

Teddy's shoulders collapsed with a *woosh*. "Dash it, he's as ancient as Methuselah!"

Isabel's amused gaze bounced between her twin sisters. "Don't you remember him? He used to visit us quite a lot," she added reminiscently. "He was kind and amusing . . ."

"And dashed handsome in his blue regimentals," Freddy mimicked Isabel's nostalgic tone. "You keep him, then. He is too old for us and we can't waste him on some anonymous chit."

"Then, you do remember him." Isabel smiled. It was important, for some nebulous reason.

"Of course." Teddy rolled her eyes in her Izzy-can-be-so-daft-sometimes expression. "You always labored under the misconception that Ashby belonged solely to you, Izzy."

"I never labored under any such misconception," Isabel retorted peevishly, her face red.

"Not that we blame you," Freddy mused aloud. "Ashby was even better looking than LJ, in a dark sort of way, and a lot more fun. How terrible for him to have become a gargoyle . . ."

"*What*?" Isabel squeaked. "How would you know anything about that?"

"We hear gossip as well as anyone else does. We just don't bandy it about because we are clever and discreet." Teddy tossed back her head of curls in an imitation of their mama's huffs.

Isabel sighed glumly. Indeed, John didn't hold a candle to Ashby. A flood of memories inundated her: Ashby at dinner in Seven Dover Street; Ashby shirtless in his cellar, rasping slabs of timber; Ashby waltzing her in the moonlight, calling her "sweetness," kissing her breast . . .

Oh, God. There she went, daydreaming of him again. Yet how could she forget the possessive, hungry gleam in his eyes that swore he wanted her? *Blast it all.* This fixation of hers was really beginning to pall. She had a perfectly nice gentleman in pursuit of her. What could she possibly hope to gain from nursing this inane obsession except spinsterhood and heartache?

"Well, are we going skulking or not?" Teddy elbowed her. "I want to see his face."

So did Isabel, even though common sense screamed at her to quit this idiocy and return to Haworth Castle. Her dratted curiosity to see him unmasked pushed her feet onward. "Remember we are here to snoop, so we'll stay in the shrubbery and be very quiet. Understood?" Her sisters nodded compliantly. "You must promise to do exactly as I say and give me no trouble."

"Yes, yes, no trouble, just a bit of healthy snooping," Freddy promised breathlessly.

"We have to locate the stables." Isabel ushered them off the road.

Hiding in the shrubbery, they skulked around the house, which actually formed a perfect square with four identical facades and entrances, until finally they spotted the stables' yard.

A few moments later, Ashby came galloping on his horse, jumped over a fence, and reined in at the yard. He *was* unmasked, but his long hair, now damp with sweat, stuck to his face. With fluid momentum he jumped to the ground and shook out his hair at the same time as his glossy black Thoroughbred shook out his mane. The fine cambric material of his shirt was plastered to his perspiring broad back. *Drat*, Isabel thought, why did he have to stand with his back to them?

"Gavet!" Ashby called out, and a groom came rushing out of the stables, carrying a bowl on a stool. Gavet set the stool beside the stallion and offered him a handful of carrots. Then he grabbed a brush and began rubbing the shiny coat. "You have this?" Ashby asked the groom.

"Aye, m'lord. I'll see to it that Apollo gets a fine rub and a finer meal afterwards. He'll be in sterling form tomorrow morning, when we introduce him to the mares."

Ashby chuckled and, to Isabel's astonishment, peeled his damp shirt off his back and over his head. Teddy and Freddy gasped in unison. Isabel covered their mouths with her hands.

"I'll just go inside for a moment and then return to help you," Ashby said aloud.

Gavet's head jerked up. "Help me, m'lord? I assure you—"

"Yes, I'm certain you'll pamper Apollo exquisitely, but I would still like to . . . supervise."

Flinging his shirt on one shoulder, Ashby strode to the house. His strapping body was even more striking in daylight, not a dram of fat in sight but muscle and smooth skin stretching from broad shoulders to a fine, firm bottom. Isabel tingled, recalling how this gloriously sculpted back felt beneath her caressing hands. The trouble was that her feelings for him had matured to desire.

Phipps came out of the house, walking purposefully into the yard. He didn't stop, but kept marching straight toward the hedge Isabel and the twins hid behind. "Miss Aubrey!" he called, before she had time to gather her wits about her and attempt a mad dash toward the road. "Miss Aubrey"—he circled the hedge and stopped before them, wheezing—"his lordship kindly invites you to have a cup of hot chocolate and cookies with him in the drawing room."

More than mortified at being caught red-handed, skulking in the bushes, Isabel was livid. How dare he presume she would care for his company, civil or not! Bristling, she said, "We—"

"Would love to!" the twins piped up and dashed in the direction of the house.

"Frederica! Theodora! Come back here at once!" Isabel called out, vacillating between fury and panic. She was *not* going in there to collect them. *She was not*!

Ashby shoved open the door to his private rooms so hard that it banged against the wall. He shucked his boots, breeches, and drawers, leaving a trail behind him on his way to the bathing chamber. He knew she would come the instant he glimpsed the Hansons and the Aubreys sitting together as cozy as bedbugs on the lawn in front of Haworth Castle. His timing, planning, and execution were perfect, if he did say so himself. Good old Phipps made a splendid spy; and *he* deserved another medal. She even came sooner than he'd anticipated. The nosy cat was unable to resist an opportunity to catch him with his mask off. He'd hoped she would come after dark. But that could be arranged as well. If he didn't hold Isabel in his arms today, he would explode.

Dudley, his valet, came charging in. "My lord, I've drawn you a bath, but—"

Ashby glanced over his shoulder. "Good." He stepped into the copper tub and leaped out, his toes on fire. "Christ! Are you attempting to flay me alive? Get me pails of cold water. Now!"

As he waited for the valet to return, he dipped a bar of soap in the boiling water and began scrubbing his chest, armpits, and back, a smile playing on his lips. He would see her again. *Soon*.

Dudley returned with Jim, a footboy, both carrying pails of cold water. Before they spotted his embarrassing physical excitement, Ashby grabbed one bucket and dumped it over his head.

"Damnation!" He burred at the shock of ice water, but at least it succeeded in drowning his lust. He poured liquid soap on his hair and stepped into the now tepid tub, scrubbing his head. The thrill coursing through his veins reminded him of moments before battle. Only this was infinitely better—with a prize at the end. "A clean set of clothes, Dudley!" he muttered to his valet before diving beneath the water surface to rinse the soap. When he reemerged, Jim handed him a linen towel. He snatched it and swabbed his dripping body in a time-saving motion he'd perfected in Spain, then sauntered into his bedchamber, toweling his wet hair.

Dudley had laid out a hunter green jacket, a chocolate silk waistcoat, and buff breeches on the bed, and now set about to dressing his master. Ashby felt like a lad again. As he pulled on his drawers and breeches, Dudley was buttoning his shirt and waistcoat. Jim helped him into his jacket while Dudley tied a starched cravat in the Oriental style around his neck.

"Thanks. That'll be all." He shoved on a new pair of Hobys, then stomped into them on the way to the mirror hanging above a chest of drawers. He combed his fingers through his wet hair, contemplating the creature in the mirror. *With or without*? That was the question. His heart began thudding. *With*. Inside a drawer he found the masks he'd brought from London, all similar to the one he'd burned. "Don't muck it up!" he told the Gargoyle in the mirror. He chose a green mask and left the room. He marched down the hallway, fumbling with the ribbons flowing out of the sides of the mask. Lacing the mask on, he came to a sudden halt at the top of the banister.

An identical pair of pretty young faces, framed with gold-and-copper ringlets, gazed up at him from the foot of the stairwell with sheer curiosity in their sky blue eyes. Freddy and Teddy. *Damnation*. They'd seen him; he was certain of it. He should have bloody well tied the mask on in his room. To his relief, they didn't look shocked, or appalled, or horrified. Merely intrigued.

Ashby put a finger to his lips as he came downstairs. "Where is your older sister?"

The fifteen-year-old doll in the green dress replied, "Outside."

He smiled, recalling how sweet and lively and *young* Isabel was when they kissed for the first time on the bench. Christ, he *had* behaved as a pervert. Only Isabel hadn't seemed as young to him then as her sisters did now. Naturally, back then, he was much younger and less hardened than he was now; in that respect he'd aged in centuries. He leaned forward, bracing his hands on his knees. "Which one of you is Theodora and which one is Frederica?"

"I am," they both replied, grinning at his silliness.

Feeling rather daft, he rephrased and learned that the one in the pink dress was Teddy and the one in green was Freddy. "Do you know who I am?"

"You're Ashby." Freddy bit her lip on a smile while looping a curl around her forefinger.

"We remember you," Teddy added with a blush. "You were Will's friend."

"That's right. Can you keep a secret?" He straightened, cracking a grin when they sent him another sardonic look. "I'll strike a bargain with you. If you promise not to describe what you just saw to Izzy, there's a special gift to each of you in it."

"What gift?" Freddy demanded coquettishly, practicing her budding female wiles on him.

"It's a surprise, but to whet your appetites, I promise it's something your mother will never purchase you and will undoubtedly disapprove of."

"It's a bargain." Teddy extended her small hand for a handshake. He shook both the twins' hands, and together they walked outside to where Isabel stood, tight-lipped and agitated.

Ashby felt the kick to his gut the moment their gazes clashed. God, she was beautiful and desirable—and utterly furious with him. He sketched a bow, unable to take his eyes off her.

Her eyes shot to her sisters. "Freddy, Teddy, we're leaving!"

"You promised us something," Freddy reminded him sweetly, dimpling as she spoke.

"Or we might become very chatty," Teddy added, the little blackmailer.

"Stables." He indicated the outside building and followed their skipping steps. On the way he halted beside Isabel. The color of her muslin gown matched her pouting lips. "I've something for you, too." He swallowed, catching a whiff of her vanilla scent. "A peace offering."

"What are you doing here? I thought you were a recluse, who never left his home."

"Ashby Park *is* my home." *And it will be yours too, if you'll have me.*

She wouldn't look at him. "What a coincidence that you should be visiting your country estate while I happen to be spending the week on the neighboring property."

"There is nothing coincidental about my visit. I followed you, Isabel."

Her gaze flew to his, vividly blue. "Didn't you order me in

no uncertain terms to stay away from you?" she bit out. "You barked and insulted me, all because I wanted to see your face."

"And yet here we are. I could no more stay away from you than you could stay away from me," he whispered. "We belong together. I've been to hell for the past two weeks."

"As you well deserved!" She started after her sisters.

He caught her arm. "I was an idiot and reacted very badly," he murmured. "I apologize for the way I behaved, for the things I said. I didn't mean any of it. I swear it." As his eyes caressed her delicate profile, he got distracted by the sight of a tendril escaping her coiffure to float over the vulnerable slope of her nape. He had to clamp down hard on the urge to press his lips there.

Isabel looked up at him and scowled. She wrenched free from his grip and marched toward the stables. *Damnation*. If he didn't keep his physical enthusiasm under control and offered his apology with decorum, he would never gain her forgiveness. Tearing his lascivious gaze from her nicely-rounded bottom swaying in front of him, he followed the ladies inside the stables.

Daylight poured in through wide windows, warming the clean stalls and the straw-chewing happy mugs of the finest horseflesh in England. "Your gifts are in the tack room at the back," he said, anticipating shrieks of delight.

He was not to be disappointed. As soon as the three Aubrey dolls entered the small room, *ohhs* and *ahhs* poured from their lips. Smiling, Ashby followed them inside. "Hello, Buttercup." He bent to caress the new mother lying contently on a blanket, surrounded by five bouncy pups.

Teddy and Freddy dropped to their knees, consumed with tenderness. "May we pet them?"

"Please, do, and the mother, too. She's had a rough labor."

While Isabel sat down to pat the canine mother, each twin scooped up a pup and cradled it close to her face. "How come Buttercup is golden and her puppies are black?" Freddy asked.

Ashby gazed at Isabel. "Care to answer that?"

"Their sire is black," she explained. Evading his gaze, she inquired, "Where is Hector?"

"Hector?" Freddy's eyes rounded happily. "Isn't he the pup you gave Ashby years ago?"

"Yes," Ashby answered, squatting behind Isabel and feeling her back stiffening. "Hector is the pup Isabel gave me, when she still liked me. He is outside somewhere, sulking."

"Why is he sulking?" the twins asked in unison.

"My grooms gave him a bath this morning. He loathed the experience. He'll come 'round, though, for a caress." When Isabel shot him a glare over her shoulder, he grinned and stood up to open a window. He whistled and returned to crouch behind her. He knew what he was doing. Until now she had been directing this play, and he couldn't help deriving some satisfaction from feeling in control again, being in pursuit of *her*, even if he had to go about it unconventionally.

Hector came barking into the tack room. His pups jumped with joy, wagging their tiny tails. He wriggled his way between the dogs and the girls, sniffing, licking, receiving pats, and enjoying himself tremendously. Finally, he slumped beside Buttercup to slurp her possessively.

"See that? They're a family." Freddy sighed with pleasure.

Unable to resist the temptation, Ashby ran a discreet hand along Isabel's spine, conveying a silent message. She edged away from him, scooping up a sixth, blond pup that had been hiding behind his mother until then. "This one looks just like its mama." Rubbing the curled up, golden retriever beneath her chin, she cooed, "Don't be frightened, my little darling."

Ashby could well picture Isabel mothering a child of her own—*his child*. He ran his finger beneath the blond pup's neck, making it purr, and almost purred himself when Isabel cast him a surreptitious smile. He let his finger accidentally brush her soft cheek. "She's yours to name."

"My mother will never let us keep them," she said regretfully. "As you well know."

"I'll think of a solution," he promised with a wink. "Trust me. I'm a resourceful fellow."

Hector leaped to his feet and led the six pups to the yard. Laughing, the twins followed at a run, and Ashby was left alone with Isabel.

The moment she tried to stand up, he caught her about the waist, leaned over her shoulder, and kissed her. She gasped but didn't pull away. He was in heaven again, but he wanted so much more from her—a lifetime of laughter and mayhem and life, what the Aubreys had in abundance.

She twisted sideways, allowing him access to the lush secrets of her mouth, and gripped his shoulders. Instead of pulling him closer, though, she shoved him back. "D-Don't you ever do th-that again!" She glowered at him, her chest heaving, a pulse throbbing at the base of her neck.

His breath came hot and heavy as he murmured to her cheek, "Why not?"

"You know very well why not!" she muttered stringently. She made another effort to rise, but he stayed her with his arms closing firmly around her. She squirmed, straining her head back.

"Don't shy away from me," he whispered. "I know you love me. You told me so yourself."

Her blue eyes turned to icicles. Derisively she spat, "Love alters when it alteration finds."

"You can't mean that." He swallowed, as a sensation very like panic rose to choke him.

"Can't I?" She lifted a fine, golden eyebrow. "Women say and promise all sorts of drivel to men when they're in the throes of passion. Let it be a lesson in life to you."

The little temptress actually smirked at him. He let go of

her, clenching his jaw. Contrary to what she thought of him, he had learned this particular lesson a few years ago, but Isabel was not Olivia. "Your response a moment ago expressed otherwise."

"We just kissed. It meant nothing." She shrugged dismissively, barely containing a smile.

If she kept throwing his own words back in his face, he was going to kiss her senseless and prove her wrong. "An interesting turn of phrase you used, 'Love alters when it alteration finds.' Shakespeare must be wincing in his grave." Or smirking at him. "Might I ask which alteration has brought on this sudden and phenomenal change of heart?" he gritted out.

"Your behavior mostly, but also my new suitor."

"Golden Angel the 6th?" he bit out with contempt, consumed with jealousy and despair.

"And it wasn't sudden, or phenomenal. You were perfectly despicable, and John—"

"It's been only two weeks, Isabel!" A knot of hurt coiled tightly inside of him, keeping him from breathing. He hated how she enunciated the bastard's name so sweetly, so familiarly.

"A lot can happen in two weeks, Ashby," she articulated his title—not his Christian name, which he had never disclosed to any woman or man but her—frostily. "John has been the soul of gentlemanly behavior. He has even taken it upon himself to sponsor our cause in Parliament."

"You informed me of that two weeks ago. Has he made any actual progress since?"

"Substantial progress. He attended one of our charity meetings. He read our bill proposal and approved of it. He—"

"Thumbed through it, no doubt," he interrupted out of spite and resentment. He wanted to kick himself for having let that blond shark make headway while he had been procrastinating.

"He is making use of all his clout with the cabinet members to obtain us the lists—"

He pounced on that. "So he hasn't obtained them yet. Well,

let me share a little secret with you. There is no protocol on how to obtain classified army personnel files. What you do is get someone to unlock them, you peruse them, and you quickly return them. That's the procedure."

Her brow furrowed. "He must be making discreet inquiries among his peers, searching for that particular someone who'd unlock the files for us without asking questions," she replied with poise, but he could tell that he had succeeded in fracturing her confidence in Lord Handsome.

If her heart had indeed turned to John, Ashby would be making an abject fool of himself, confessing how he and Brooks had poured over the army files for two straight days, preparing an estimate for her bill proposal, how he'd ridden through the night, in the rain, because he couldn't wait another second to see her, to put the glow back in her eyes as he showed her the valuation.

Not telling her, however, would be the death of his last hope for a real, full life with her. He'd let Olivia go without a fight; he couldn't do that with Isabel. "What would you say if I told you I've put together something ten times better than the lists for you?"

She worried her bottom lip, gauging his sincerity. "What did you put together for me?"

"A complete valuation, signed and approved by a certified accountant, a one Mr. Brooks."

Shock and delight spread on her face. "You really did that, for me?"

"I would do anything for you, Isabel," he said quietly. "Don't you know that by now?"

She retained her disdainful airs. "I don't know anything, when it comes to you."

"What does your heart tell you about me?" he asked softly.

She gazed up at him with the eyes of a woman who'd tasted passion and had been burned by it. "My heart tells me I should forsake you, Paris. That you are not to be trusted."

He fingered one of her golden curls. "But you haven't yet, forsaken me." It was a question.

She straightened up. "I think it would be appropriate on my part to inform you at this point that John has gained Stilgoe's permission to court me."

An old wound began bleeding inside of him again. "Do you expect a proposal from him?"

"I like John. He is gentle and kind, not erratic or volatile. He doesn't break his promises or encourage me to sneak about with him. When he proposes, I shall be persuaded to accept."

His years of being a feckless gambler and womanizer had taught him to read nuances, in men as well as in women. If his instincts weren't mistaken, she'd just delivered him a message. She would be persuaded to say yes—which meant she wasn't yet, and she used a passive form. Would Stilgoe be persuading her? Ashby needed time with her, to regain her trust and conquer her heart all over again, so that when she ultimately did see his face, she wouldn't balk or scream in horror or vomit with disgust. She would care for him enough to understand, to see past . . .

"Before I hand over the estimate, I should like to read the bill proposal. Do you have it?"

"At the castle, but I hardly see why you need bother with it. John has gone over the entire thing and approved every word. He said he would be proud to promote it in the House."

Bloody wonderful. Now Hanson was her hero. "Humor me. I'd hate for the valuation to be immaterial or incorrect." It was a legitimate, logical argument, one he knew she would concede.

"All right, but how shall I send it to you?"

"Bring it yourself. Tonight." He studied her eyes, waiting to see if the idea of being alone with him deterred her. Even if he couldn't have her tonight, he just wanted to hold her.

"You're asking me to sneak about with you again!" she admonished distrustfully.

He immediately got insulted. "Fine. Don't come," he assumed a flat tone of umbrage. "I'll mail the valuation to you when I return to London. Then, you can figure it out by yourself."

Her fine eyebrows drew closer in a frown, and for a moment he feared she would call his bluff. "A fortnight ago you said you didn't want to have anything to do with me."

"And you believed me?" He caressed her creamy cheek, drawing her closer for a kiss.

"Stop that!" She pushed at his chest, looking over his shoulder. "Someone might come in."

"No one will come in. Your sisters are having splendid fun chasing the dogs outside." And Phipps was under strict orders to dole out cookies and keep them occupied. Ashby had no desire to be caught in a compromising situation with her. Not until he was assured of her feelings.

"I don't know what game you're playing, but—"

"This is no game," he said in all honesty. "I want you. *Desperately*."

His confession only succeeded in sparking her ire. "My friends warned me against you! They said you were up to no good!"

He froze. "You told your friends about me?"

She raised an eyebrow. "Are you a secret?" He had no good answer to that. "As a rule, if one needs hide something of a pernicious influence or nature from those who love him best, then he should either quit it or reveal it. I'm neither a fool nor a gossip, but you hurt me, Paris."

"I apologize for my conduct the other night. I would never, ever do anything to harm you." It sickened him that he'd become someone she considered to be a threat to her well-being. "I do not repeat my errors, Isabel. I'll do everything within my power to regain your trust, your love."

She stood up. "I don't understand you. I don't know what you want from me, and I doubt I could ever trust you again."

He pushed to his feet and grabbed her. "Listen to me," he

whispered harshly, cradling her coiffed curls. "You've haunted and bedeviled me for seven years, Isabel Jane Aubrey. I am not about to let you walk out of my life. So although I may be two weeks late, I'm putting myself back in the running and John Hanson be damned." He locked their mouths in a deep, thorough kiss until the fight went out of her. With a moan she yielded and started kissing him back.

By the time he lifted his head to draw in a breath, Isabel's eyes were heavy with passion, and he was ready to carry her to his bedchamber through the back door and let Phipps deal with her sisters.

"Are you saying you're courting me?" she asked breathily, staring at his mouth.

Not wanting to put himself in a position where he would have to unmask himself and ruin everything too soon, he dissembled, "I'm saying that I've been an idiot, that I deeply regret hurting you, and that I have every intention of making you mine."

"Your . . . what precisely—friend, lover, or . . . ?"

"Both." *And more*.

"Friends cannot be lovers." She sidestepped him and left the tack room.

He fell into step beside her as she walked past the horses' stalls. "You're wrong. Becoming friends and lovers at the same time is the best thing that can happen to a man and a woman."

She halted before his youngest hunter to stroke the mare's head. "It sounds like something my friend Sophie would say. I should introduce the two of you. You'd make a fine couple."

Her trick to annoy the hell out of him and thus bully him into declaring himself was—to some extent—working. But he had been playing this game long before she'd begun to and knew that two could play at it. "What makes you think we would suit each other, Sophie and I?"

Her smile faltered—she absolutely did not want him to

pursue her friend—but her eyes glinted with determination. "Well, first of all, she's older and more experienced than I am."

"That is certainly a point in her favor. What else?"

He could hear her gritting her teeth. "I won't reveal all of Sophie's secrets and attractions. You'll simply have to meet her in person and discover how suitable you two are."

He frowned. "Why? What's wrong with her?" Damn. He'd come off sounding wretchedly insecure. He quickly amended. "Why would she need help in finding beaux? Is she ugly?"

"No! She's beautiful, and there is nothing wrong with her!"

Because and in spite of her emphatic defense of her friend, he would wager that Sophie did possess a certain flaw if Isabel thought them well-matched. He was not so dense that he failed to realize that her attempts at glimpsing his face stemmed from more than curiosity. She was afraid of what she might unmask. He drew her into his arms, unable to hide his grin. "It's a good thing I haven't met her, then, or I might be tempted to further our acquaintance."

"I'd be happy to perform the introduction." She looked adorable when she was cross.

He couldn't help smiling. Gently he asked, "You would play matchmaker between me and your friend when we've just begun exploring this extraordinary thing we've always had between us?" He flattened her against him. "Me thinks the fair lady has need of another kiss—"

"That's another thing!" She stepped out of his embrace. "You shouldn't be kissing me at all! If you want to regain my trust, you should begin by behaving as a proper gentleman."

He followed her to the door. "Very well. From now on, I'll become a paragon of decorum. And the next time we kiss," he added softly, "*you* will be the one kissing *me*. That is a promise."

"Then you may rest assured that our lips shall never meet again!" she announced archly.

"I would hesitate to contradict you, except that I have it on good authority that you, Miss Isabel, are prone to pouncing on gentlemen with kisses."

"You've been misinformed." Her chin came up a notch higher.

He burst out laughing. "Care to wager on that? I'll even put a time limit—a week."

"Hold for that long a trig?" She cast him a taunting smile. "What do I win?"

"Confident, aren't we? I think we should discuss what *I* win, other than the kiss, naturally."

"If I win," she began tentatively, "you remove the mask in *my* presence."

He stopped breathing. "All right," he said slowly. "If I win . . . you spend a night with me."

"That will n—" She paused, a defiant glint sparking her eyes. "I accept the challenge. But if you break your word and try to kiss me, you lose the wager."

"Agreed." Things were definitely looking up. Thank God.

Isabel was in high spirits on the walk back. "What might you have become chatty about?"

"We saw Lord Ashby without a mask on," Freddy replied guilelessly.

"*You saw his face?*" Isabel exclaimed, coming to an abrupt halt. "What did he look like?"

Teddy set her mouth stubbornly. "We don't betray a confidence."

"We're not going anywhere until you tell me precisely what you saw," Isabel insisted.

"Then we'll get drattedly soaked, since it's about to rain," Freddy remarked.

A drop fell on Isabel's nose. "Until you portray him to me in detail, I'm not friends with you anymore." She strode on, irritated. Two things were certain: He absolutely did not want *her* to see his face, and he absolutely wanted her. Her silly heart bounced with joy, and a sly grin replaced her pout. Prone to pouncing—ha! She would best Colonel Lord Ashby at his own daft game. The wager afforded her a certain degree of control: By the end of this week she would see his face, and she had a feeling their relationship would progress dramatically after that.

Something had unquestionably changed in her favor if he'd tracked her down as far as East Sussex. But she would never fully trust him so long as he concealed his face from her. Therefore, she would have to keep her lips off him and win the wager. How difficult could that be?

Olivia watched the three Aubrey chits prancing down the road with increasing antagonism. Ashby and the dead brother had been the best of good friends, but that did not explain why Isabel felt the need to run to Ashby the moment she became aware of his presence in the area. As if he would ever look at that unremarkable female twice. Olivia smirked. Perhaps the scavenging chit thought she stood a chance with the pathetic gargoyle he'd become, but she didn't, not if Olivia had anything to say—*or do*—about it. And as a matter of fact, Olivia did.

Chapter Fifteen

Ashby knew someone was in his bedchamber the instant he opened the door. A familiar perfume scented the air. The room was dark, but he heard rustling of bed sheets. His mouth went dry. Thinking he must be delirious, he approached the bed, the eager part of his body pointing the way, his mind not fully registering the fact that Isabel awaited him there . . .

The bedside lamp flared. "Hello, Ashby."

He stilled, agape. "Olivia."

She sat upright, letting the sheet spill to her waist. Her breasts peeked through her straight, white blond hair. "You look stunned." She smiled.

"What are you doing here?" he demanded to know.

A husky laugh filled her throat. "What does it look like I'm doing? I'm waiting for you to join me." Invitingly, she folded the corner of the blanket, showing a patch of white thigh.

"You're married." It dawned on him that the scent he'd recognized was roses, not vanilla.

"Which means we can do whatever we want to, and no one will ever know . . ."

"Why now? Why after so long?"

"I called on you at Lancaster House last year, but Phipps wouldn't let me in."

On his orders. "Get dressed." Although he couldn't quell his starved body's reaction to the sight of a beautiful woman lying naked in his bed—no wonder, after Isabel had been torturing it of late—he had no desire to find relief from his frustration elsewhere, certainly not with Olivia.

As he turned his back to her and shrugged out of his jacket, he heard rustling again, and a moment later, a pair of white hands crept along his thighs. "Can't you put the past behind you, as I have?" she cooed. "We loved each other once, but we never consummated our love."

"You loved my money, Olivia. I loved a dream. Find some other cock-bawd to keep you satisfied. I'm not interested."

"You were always proud," she uttered bitterly. She softened her tone. "I still want you, even more than I did then." Her hands slid toward his stiff nether regions. "I'm so wet for you."

He leaped rather than stepped out of her claws. She'd certainly learned a trick or two over the past four years, though not from Bradford, he would wager. "You want me more than you did then . . . Then when? Before or after my injury? You'll have to be more specific."

She didn't mind standing before him without a stitch of clothing on. "I must say, your face has improved considerably since I last saw you." She glided forward. "I've always desired you. No one has ever made me feel as you did, Ashby. As you still do."

Something Isabel had said to him earlier that day tinkled in his head, and he couldn't help but feel that just by standing close to a naked Olivia he was somehow being untrue to the woman he intended to wed. He looked down at her coolly. "It's too late. I don't want you. I don't think I ever did. Get dressed." He crossed the room, putting as much distance between them as possible.

"Would it help if I told you I've been miserable ever since I cried off our engagement?"

"That's your problem, not mine."

"You say that now, but I *know* you were devastated when I left you four years ago."

"Perhaps, but I know what I felt, or rather didn't feel. And you are incapable of the sort of emotion I desire in a woman." Isabel emitted more warmth from the tip of her finger than Olivia would if he set her on fire. "For the last time, get dressed, before I summon a footman to assist you." It was his subtle way of letting her know he was about to kick her out.

Casting him a steamy look, she breathed, "Why don't you take your clothes off, and I shall demonstrate what sort of emotions I am capable of kindling in you."

Knowing precisely what she was really after, he felt sudden and acute disgust at the whole scene. "Are things really that desperate that you would prostitute yourself for your family?"

Her expression turned malevolent and hard. She grabbed her chemise off a chair and pulled it on. "Why did you stage that spectacle today if you didn't want me to come to you?"

He cocked an eyebrow. "I went riding in *my* park."

"It's that Aubrey chit!" she cried, appalled. "It's her you signaled—that . . . that sheep!"

"What if I did?" His smile quickened for a second, then died. "If you spread vicious gossip about Miss Aubrey and myself, if Viscount Stilgoe gets a whiff of scandal, he'll marry her to me in a heartbeat. That wouldn't serve your brother's cause, would it?" He strode to the door. "You have five minutes. After that I'm sending someone to escort you out, clothed or otherwise."

"Wake up, John! We have to talk." The firm command punctured his dream. Light flooded his eyelids. Grumbling a protest, John flipped onto his stomach and buried his face in his pillow. A hand shook his shoulder. "Your plump sheep is having an affair with Ashby!"

"What?" Recognizing his sister's voice, he turned his head and squinted up at her. "Liv, for God's sake, it's the middle of the night! What the deuce has gotten into you?"

Olivia looked livid. "I went to Ashby this evening and saw Isabel leaving his house."

John sat up, running his hands through his tousled hair. "You went to him? Why?"

"Never mind that. I told you she was unsuitable. You should have stayed with that Talbot chit. She is five times wealthier than Miss Aubrey and far less troublesome."

"Louisa Talbot," he spat with disgust, "is an insufferable, indigestible bug, with a great big American spider for an uncle. You know very well that his runners have already begun making inquiries into our affairs. If I resume my pursuit of her, he'll have no qualms about smearing our name in the papers. Besides, I like Isabel. She's digestible."

"I'm telling you she's just been devoured by the Gargoyle, you blockhead!"

He scrutinized her quizzically. "I thought the very sight of him repulsed you."

She wouldn't meet his eyes. "I thought that if I could make him care for me again—"

"He'd solve our money woes? Liv, I told you I'd take care of everything."

"As you did the last time?" she reproached him.

"I'm sorry about Bradford." He exhaled. "I should have investigated his financial situation more thoroughly instead of believing his outlandish tales."

She got up and started pacing the room. "I can't believe I was such an idiot! He looks . . . he looks so much better now, almost like his old self. I—"

"No sense in berating yourself now for what you felt

back then. At least Bradford's face is tolerable around the dinner table."

"Tolerable?" She glared at him. "Mother said that he was so sloshed he nearly drowned in his soup this evening. Even his smell offends me."

"Tell me about your visit to Ashby. Did he see you? Did you speak to him?"

"Yes! He spurned me, but now I know why." She mimicked Isabel, "It's that oh-so-lovable creature you're courting. Somehow, she got to him too." She resumed her seat on the bed. "John, you must begin hunting someone new. This one is too dim-witted to appreciate her good fortune. Any number of debutantes would pounce at the chance of snagging the Golden Angel. Imogen Blakely, for one. Her father would sell his soul for a titled son-in-law."

He screwed up his face in aversion. "Leonard Blakely is in trade, Liv."

"How about Miss Miles? Her grandfather was a viscount."

He reached for the near-empty glass of brandy he'd left on the bed stand. "Isabel couldn't possibly prefer the Gargoyle to me. I'm certain her visit to him was completely innocent."

"Then why would she sneak off without letting her family know where she went?"

It mustn't bother him, he told himself. He wasn't in it for love; he was in it for the money. Still, the idea that *any woman* should choose a defaced hermit over him was unacceptable.

"When I confronted him about her," Olivia went on, "he warned me not to spread rumors, or her brother would marry her to him in a heartbeat."

White hot rage surged through him. "He's right. If we aren't careful, this could blow up in our faces. And then neither one of us will get what he or *she* wants, Liv."

"What do you think I want, other than the life I deserve, that is?" she demanded crossly.

He yawned. "Knowing you, I'd wager my last tuppence that you want Ashby back."

"You're wrong!" She shot to her feet and stalked to the door. "He could rot, for all I care!"

"Consider this, if I marry Isabel, he'll remain free for the picking . . ."

That stopped her. She faced him. "You really want her that much?" she asked, dismayed.

He slid deeper beneath the covers. Isabel wasn't half as striking as Olivia or as some of his female admirers, but there was something about her that kept him on his toes. She saw past his handsome face, past his popularity, and what she unearthed didn't seem to impress her at all.

"I wonder why he took the trouble of warning you against linking his name with Isabel's," John pondered aloud. "The only logical conclusion I can come up with is that Ashby has nothing permanent in mind and that he doesn't care to find himself leg-shackled to the chit once he's finished playing with her." It bothered him, John realized, that Ashby might be her first, but he forced himself to think in a cold, rational manner. No sense in losing his head now, certainly not over a chit he had no intention of developing real affection for. "This may be good for us, Liv."

"Oh, really? How?"

"When Ashby tires of her, to whom will she run to for consolation? A ruined female with her heart in tatters is ripe game and very amenable. I say we look the other way, for now. I might even give her a subtle nudge in his direction."

"How would you do that, considering you're not supposed to know anything about it?"

"Leave that to me. Your task is to stay away from him. And don't give me that look, Liv! I know you. You want him, and you will have him. I promise. You've planted the seed in his head. Now you sit and wait. The moment he's through with his new toy, he'll come looking for you."

A smile turned up the corners of her mouth. "Sometimes, Johnny, I forget how devious you are. No doubt Stilgoe would double her dowry once he learns she's become damaged goods."

"I'm glad you finally see it as I do. Good night."

"Good night." She left his bedchamber.

John contemplated the threadbare canopy. Olivia's story hadn't come as a complete shock to him. To some extent, it helped mend his damaged pride. Isabel didn't give a pin about him. He had known that for days. At least now he knew why. It wasn't because he was losing his appeal, but because someone else had preceded him to the game. He would have preferred being the one to make her pay for making him doubt himself, but he would, in due course. Convincing her to wed him wasn't enough anymore. She would have to suffer, and she would have to love him, because she had committed the cardinal sin of making him desire her—and no one else.

Chapter Sixteen

Paris Nicholas Lancaster was arrogant, devious, incomprehensible, and drattedly irresistible. For a man who repeatedly claimed he didn't care to see her, he certainly went about it the wrong way. Her feelings were so tangled. When she was alone with him, her resolve became muddled, the world seemed right; and when he kissed her, she wanted to melt into him. She should despise him, or at the least be angry with him for thinking a few kisses and a peace offering she couldn't keep would erase his callous treatment of her, but she was deeply moved by his efforts on behalf of her charity. What John bragged of accomplishing, Ashby performed quietly and effectively.

Yet he wasn't the only one capable of subterfuge. Isabel dispatched the bill proposal with one of the Aubrey grooms and for the remainder of her stay in East Sussex refrained from calling on Ashby. Iris's story was still fresh enough in her mind to deter her from committing this folly. Not even to herself would she admit that she might not be able to keep from pouncing on him.

The last three days at Haworth Castle dragged on wretchedly. With the inclement weather raging outside—and inside among the Hansons—a pall had fallen on their party.

By the end of the week, every member of the Aubrey clan was happy to return to Seven Dover Street.

"I don't understand you, Izzy," her mother attacked when they sat down for a late luncheon upon their return. "John was about to declare himself this week, and you discouraged him!"

Isabel had her retort down pat. "How does one encourage a man who spends most of his time with his sister?"

"Of course he would spend time with his sister. You scarcely paid attention to him."

"Leave her be, Mama," Charles implored. "You know how Izzy gets after traveling in a closed carriage for several hours and after remaining indoors for days on end."

"She becomes a grouch," Freddy clarified.

Isabel's foul mood had little to do with the drive and the rain and everything to do with Ashby. Three days she had ignored his existence, and he hadn't even sent her a note!

"I would simply like to point out that John is a charming young man and that Izzy mustn't jeopardize this," Hyacinth put in huffily.

"How am I jeopardizing this—by not joining his simpering gaggle and turning into a twit?" Isabel demanded, making her siblings groan. "You would make me marry a man I don't love or want regardless of my conversational skills, so what's the point?"

"The point is that the one you do want is no longer attainable, Isabel Jane Aubrey, so you might as well accept it!" her mother clipped vehemently.

Isabel stood, raging inside. "Excuse me. I have lost my appetite." She dashed upstairs to her bedchamber, wishing Will were there to poke fun at her and promise that all would be well, but Will was gone. She flung herself on the bed, tears welling in her eyes. There was only one other man who could make her feel better, and he had forsaken her.

Someone scratched her door. "Go away!" she snapped.

"Miss Isabel," Norris spoke beyond the door. "Mary Higgins is in the kitchen. She wishes to have a word with you. I tried to get rid of her, but the impudent—"

Isabel opened the door, and Norris nearly fell in. "She is in the kitchen?"

"Yes, Miss Isabel."

"I will see her." If Mary was here, she must have lost her position with Mrs. Tiddles. Isabel hurried downstairs and was relieved to find Lucy and Mary laughing together.

"Miss Aubrey!" Mary stood, bobbing, as she spotted Isabel in the doorway.

"Hello, Mary." Isabel breezed into the kitchen. "My, you look so pretty and elegant!"

Mary beamed. "Thank you, ma'am! 'Tis your kindness that brought on this change."

A smile crept onto Isabel's face. "You enjoy working for Mrs. Tiddles, I gather."

"Indeed, I do. She is a grand mistress, and we're getting on famously together."

"I'm delighted to hear this." Isabel's gaze shifted to Lucy, who looked just as pleased.

"Mrs. Tiddles has been telling all her customers about your charity work," Mary declared, "and some of the ladies were asking if you might know of other women in need of employment."

"Yes, I do!" Isabel cried delightedly. "Please thank Mrs. Tiddles on my behalf and tell her that I will come by. . . . What's this?" she asked, as Mary handed her a folded piece of paper.

"The list of Mrs. Tiddles's customers needin' hard-working war widows like me."

"There's a list?" Isabel repeated, amazed. She unfolded the note and gasped at its length. "Mary, this is wonderful! I know most of these ladies. I will write to them at once . . ." All she had to do was crisscross between the ladies on Mary's list and the ones on her charity list and change a few lives for the better. Pocketing the list, she smiled at Mary. "Thank you for coming here, and thank Mrs. Tiddles for her thoughtfulness."

Isabel headed upstairs to Stilgoe's office to dash off notes to Iris and Sophie, as well as to the ladies on Mrs. Tiddles's list. She found a letter from Ryan in the week's pile of invitations and correspondences, no doubt the one he wanted her to forward to Iris, and several letters from various gentlemen addressed to her. Norris appeared in the doorway. "Yes, Norris?"

The butler walked up to her, holding out a letter. "This has just arrived for you, miss."

"Thank you." Isabel's heart jolted upon glimpsing the lion stamped in the wax. She waited for Norris to depart and quickly broke the seal. The familiar, bold scrawl all but growled at her. *Where are you?* It was signed with a *P* and an address, *Park Lane*. A huge smile broke on her lips. The Gargoyle was back, and he was angry. With a glance at the open doorway, she lifted the letter to her lips and kissed it. So long as Paris didn't know, she hadn't lost the wager. Yet.

"You are a cheat and a coward." Ashby slammed his office door shut and clasped Isabel's hand. He dragged her across his spacious office, slumped on the sofa, and pulled her onto his lap. "The wager is off! Now kiss me, Helen. Give me my soul again."

Chuckling, she searched his hungry eyes and almost did kiss him. Her entire being yearned to sink into his heady embrace, but then she would end up ruined, without seeing his face. So she draped her arms around his broad shoulders and let her smile express what she felt in her heart. Goodness, how she had missed him! "The wager is not off, you beast. There was no specification as to the amount of time we are required to spend in each other's company during the week."

His blue mask—matching the conservative color of his jacket—transformed his eyes into a tropical light blue. They regarded her glumly. "Didn't you miss me at all?"

So much that it hurt the heart, but she wasn't about to arm him with the knowledge. Her remaining in his lap was an answer in itself. "You have changing eyes. Did you know that?"

"Yes," he muttered sullenly.

"Sometimes they're green, sometimes they're blue. Rather extraordinary," she mused.

"Isabel, tell me you've forgiven me, my ang—"

"I've forgiven you." She smiled softly. How could she not, after his jaunt to East Sussex? He confessed to wanting her desperately and was becoming involved in her operation. She was still in awe over the fact that he desired her—Ashby, the man she had always pined for!

He let out a sigh and stared at her lips. "I wish we never made the damned wager."

"You could end it right now," she murmured. "All you have to do is kiss me, Paris."

"Your tactics are low and I shan't kiss you," he breathed back.

"You trust me so little that you won't show me your face?"

His eyes turned serious. "Does it matter this much to you? I thought you didn't care what I looked like, that you knew who I was inside."

She outlined his mask with her fingertips. "This thing is standing between us as a barrier. Can't you see that?"

"You are afraid that what you'd find behind it might change what we have between us."

"What do we have between us?" she asked softly.

His Adam's apple bulged against his cravat. "Whatever it is, I don't want to lose it, Isabel."

"Neither do I." Sighing, she rested her head on his shoulder.

The week at Haworth Castle had proven that no matter how hard she tried, she didn't want another man. She wanted Paris.

"I read your bill proposal."

She raised her head. "And?"

"I'll be honest with you, I don't . . ." He paused, reconsidering what he was about to say.

"Tell me! Don't keep me in suspense," she pleaded.

"I have two things to say about it, so please hear me out before you jump. First of all, it is very well written and to the point. Your solicitor certainly knows what he is about. However, the country is bankrupt. Having gone over the figures with Brooks, I seriously doubt the proposal's feasibility to pass scrutiny at all. You are asking Parliament to pay millions it does not have in its coffers. Perhaps in a few years, when the country bounces back from the wars . . ."

She felt like crying. "Are you saying it's unrealistic?"

"At the present time, but that's only my opinion. You mustn't let it discourage you. I—"

"No, I trust your judgment. I am certain you're right." She sagged, dispirited.

"We could change the proposal to deflate the figures, but then the compensations will be so small, the toll on the public purse will outweigh the benefit to the compensated population."

"I see your point." Her entire work had been for naught.

He caressed her cheek. "Sweetness, I'm certain you can help these women in other ways. You are determined and bright and have the biggest heart in all of England."

His words warmed her to the depths of her soul. "Thank you for saying that."

He took her head in both hands. "It's the God's honest truth, my lovely lioness, and one of the reasons I admire you so much."

She gave a small smile. "You admire me?"

"I adore you," he whispered.

She experienced a fierce desire to kiss him, but her desire to see his face overrode the first. It dawned on her what their wager was all about: Trust, but not the kind she had assumed it was. They both sought proof of the other person's feelings. He wanted to ascertain that she would accept him despite his injuries, and she wanted to ascertain that she could entrust him with her love. It was an impasse, until one of them capitulated, or until the end of the week. Therefore, as much as she was tempted to devour him with kisses, she had to hold back and persevere.

"I might be able to help these women after all," she mused, rising off his lap.

His arms locked around her waist. "Where are you going?"

"Nowhere. To sit beside you on the sofa. I have something astounding to tell you."

He pulled her much closer. "Tell me. I enjoy holding you."

Her breasts pressed to his chest; she felt a distinct hardness beneath her bottom. A sharp spasm of desire shot to her feminine core. "You are a devious blackguard and I won't kiss you."

"If I must endure a constant state of arousal, so must you." He grinned devilishly. "Speak."

"Fine." She cursed him under her breath, making him chuckle. "Do you recall my telling you about my maid's cousin, the one I took from the workhouse in Spitalfields? Well, I found her a position in a millinery shop. The kind lady who owns the shop was so pleased with her new employee and moved by my involvement that she told her entire clientele about this, and, well, look at this list." She took it out of her pocket. "These ladies wish to hire women like Mary."

He perused the list. "You should open an agency—the Widows, Mothers & Sisters of War Employment Agency. A bill may get stuck in Parliament for years, but this is a simple, practical, immediate solution. You can advertise in the papers, rent office space . . ."

"You're brilliant!" She bent her head to kiss him, and stopped. "Drat."

"My thought exactly." He caressed her lips with his thumb. "I want to taste you so badly."

A dizzying craving possessed her. "Stop that."

"Imagine how sweet it will be, slow and pleasurable like a drug, only better." He made her eyelashes sink as she listened to his seductive drawl. Vaguely she sensed his long fingers closing around her left ankle and beginning to move up her stocking-clad calf. "We could kiss for hours, you and I. We won't even notice when the sun sets. We'll forget time, everything, in each other."

His warm hand came to rest on her thigh. She shook herself, gripping his wrist. "When I said no kissing, I neglected to specify no ungentlemanly caresses under my skirts."

He gave that slow, dark smile of his. "No ungentlemanly caresses, eh? That puts me in the clear, then. I'm absolutely convinced there isn't a single thirty-five-year-old gentleman alive who doesn't explore under some woman's skirts on occasion. Unless he has other tastes."

"Paris." She tugged on his wrist. "We were discussing my agency."

He gazed at her, his blue-green eyes overly bright. "Right." He pulled his hand from under her skirts and rested it on the same clad spot. "I'd be happy to administer the logistics—advertise in the newspapers, find you a suitable location, and finance the entire operation."

"You would?" Her eyes widened in surprise. "Why?"

"Wasn't it you who told me that by helping others one healed oneself? I believe in your cause. It's just and humane. And I will support you every step of the way."

She traced his strong, smoothly shaven jaw. "You're making it very difficult for me to win this wager."

"Good."

"How long do you suppose it would take you to find a suitable location?"

"A week, at the most."

"And until then I would be working with Sophie and Iris on the list. *Elsewhere.*"

His lips twitched wryly. "What else are you trying to extract from me, chit?"

"I want to commandeer your house for the time being. You have several sitting rooms—"

"Absolutely not." He shook his head.

"I understand." She threaded her fingers through his straight dark hair. "I only regret that I won't be able to see you, considering how busy I will be. I'll probably even . . . win the wager."

He shut his eyes and blew out his breath. "Fine. For the time being."

She wrapped her arms around his neck, whispering in his ear, "I adore you, too."

Chapter Seventeen

"You personally inspected each and every one of them?" Ashby asked his solicitor, as he went over the property reports spread on the worktable in front of him. After Isabel banished him from his office, commandeering it herself, her two-day operation having taken up every sitting room on the first two levels in his house, he retired to his cellar, where he pretended to be calm.

His foyer was now a crowded henhouse, every egress barred with rows of cackling females waiting to be admitted by their angelic savior or her lieutenants. But worse than that, time was running out. By the end of the day he would know whether the woman he craved would be his—or not. For the life of him he couldn't recall why the wager had seemed a good idea at the time. All it accomplished was putting a halter around his neck, with a sandglass attached to it.

"I did, my lord." Fitzsimmons pulled out a file from the pile. "That one on the Strand has twenty rooms and is offered for a reasonable price. I would have to say it's my favorite."

Although the large building appeared to be suitable for Isabel's operation, Ashby preferred a location closer to his house. He wanted her—*needed her*—within reach, whether she ultimately became his wife, or not. He already knew that if Isabel scorned him, he would still want to be there for her, always, no matter whom she married. A cold fist of dread gripped his insides at the thought he might have to go through life watching her from the shadows while another man got to hold her in his arms at night, early in the morning, whenever he desired . . . *Tick-tock, tick-tock.* He forced himself to concentrate. "How about this one, on Piccadilly?"

"Fifteen rooms, including a ballroom opening to a rose garden, but . . ."

"What?" Ashby demanded impatiently.

"The price is thirty-five percent steeper, my lord."

He didn't mind paying an exorbitant sum, so long as Isabel was near him. Christ, he would have gladly put down ten times as much, if he could purchase her from Stilgoe and be done with this torture. Alas, Isabel's brother was not an Arabian sheik. "Make the transaction. Today."

"Today? But, but, my lord—" Fitzsimmons began sputtering.

"Today. I want the deed in my hands before sunset." He looked at Phipps, unobtrusively lurking in the corner and pretending to be a wall ornament. "Please show Mr. Fitzsimmons out."

Phipps looked pained. "Out there?"

"Haven't you been complaining about not getting enough exercise?"

Stifling his grievance, Phipps led the solicitor to the upstairs frontier, where no man should go unaccompanied.

"What of my two boys, ma'am? I can't bring them to work and they're too young to be left on their own." The gray-faced young woman sitting across the desk from Isabel fidgeted with her frayed pelisse, a haunted expression etching her gaunt face. "My brother, Niles, sent us half his wages from the frontline, and we did well by him, but now he's gone—"

With a broken sob, the woman brought the edge of her sleeve to her eyes. "My husband was deported, you see. I—"

"Are you an honest, hardworking woman, Rebecca?" Isabel inquired softly.

Rebecca looked up, her eyes wide and desperate. "Aye, ma'am! Never stole a penny in my life! I am ashamed to say, my husband was a great villain, though. And he had a temper on him."

"There, there," Isabel soothed, casting a smile in the direction of the two small boys, sitting demurely on the sofa, their faces smudged. Her heart went out to them. They looked so . . . thin and sad. Danielli ate more than these two. "You needn't be ashamed of your husband's past. You have to think of yourself and your boys now, improving *your* lives, beginning afresh."

Rebecca smiled tearfully. "I would like that, ma'am, to begin afresh."

"Splendid." Isabel entered a commentary in her agency ledger next to Rebecca's name. "I will find you a position according to your skills and needs. Your task is to do your very best. Nothing more." She took a shilling out of a mahogany box and offered it to Rebecca. "Treat your boys to an ice. I'll send you a note as soon as I find you a position. Five days at the most."

Rebecca accepted the coin and clasped Isabel's hand. "Thank you! You are a Godsend."

Ashby was their Godsend, Isabel acknowledged privately. "You are welcome." She smiled. "Good day to you, and remember our chat."

As Rebecca took her boys' small hands in hers and walked out the door, Isabel sagged in Ashby's chair. Running a charity agency was logistically and emotionally taxing but also vastly rewarding. Within two days she had managed to find employment for thirty women, while Iris, Sophie, and Molly—little Joe's mother, the widow Isabel had been helping and now worked with them—were just as successful.

Owing to the advertisement in the newspapers, job offers poured in and more applicants arrived each day. All thanks to Paris. She ran her fingertips over the lion-carved mahogany box he created for her, the same one she returned to him weeks ago. She found it on the desk yesterday morning with a note explaining that the funds inside were to be spent as she saw fit. This morning she found a figurine—a lion and a lioness, kissing. The lion, she noted with a smile, was fashioned after his family crest. If she weren't careful, she might be tempted to believe that the Earl of Ashby was courting her. He'd certainly turned out to be her charity's knight in shining armor. The question was: Would he become her knight in shining armor?

Today was the final day of the wager. That morning, when she visited Paris in the cellar to regale him with their achievements so far, he took her in his arms, hoping she would succumb to the desire to kiss him. Fresh after his morning ablutions, his hair was damp, the crisp scent of shaving soap clung to his skin. She wanted to gobble him up. When she didn't, his green eyes became terribly somber. Did he really want her that much? It was almost too fantastic to believe.

She was surprised when someone scratched her door. Rebecca was supposed to be her last interviewee for the day. "Come in," she called, and a moment later Stilgoe strolled in.

"Izzy!" Her brother took in her lavish surroundings with a sweeping glance, smiling from ear to ear. "Damn me! It is true! I couldn't believe it when Leitrim told me over luncheon at the Society Club that his wife had hired a chambermaid through your new agency."

Isabel came over to give him a hug and a kiss. "I told you over dinner two nights ago."

He scrutinized her carefully. "I must say, I was somewhat surprised to discover that—"

"Ashby was involved? He volunteered to help."

"How did it come about? Have you been secretly in touch with him all these years?"

"No, Charlie. I called on him—with my personal maid, mind you—as Iris, Sophie, and I do all the time, with the hopes of enlisting supporters to our cause. Lord Ashby generously offered his assistance. Unlike you, he is willing to contribute his time and effort—"

"And his house, Lancaster House," Charles interrupted pointedly. "Quite a posh agency."

"For the time being, a week at the most, until we rent suitable office space."

Her brother still looked skeptical and concerned. "You're certainly determined, and daring. Of all the men in England, you went to him." He sighed. "I can't say I'm surprised, but . . ."

"What? Obviously you have something on your mind."

"I don't want to see you hurt, or disappointed, Izzy. Several years ago, I would have been pleased. Hanson is a good match, but Ashby is unquestionably the better man. Yet in view of his injury and consequent withdrawal from Society . . ." His brow furrowed. "Wait a minute—you *saw* him? Where is that devil?" He grinned. "I should like to say hello to him, myself."

"You shall have to consult his butler. Phipps manages Ashby's appointment book."

"I gather he hasn't completely come out of hiding."

"Not really. He keeps to himself."

"Does Mama know about this?"

"I am not on speaking terms with her at the moment," Isabel clipped. Or with her sisters.

"She only wants the best for you." When Isabel said nothing, he straightened. "I'll go see whether Phipps allows me a word with his employer. Afterwards, I'm heading home to kiss my wife and baby daughter." He kissed her cheek. "I'll see you at home."

As Isabel closed the door after him, she heard female

chatter in the hallway. Her friends were still interviewing. Yesterday, after the interviews, the four of them held a long meeting in which they assigned potential employees to potential employers and discussed their new agency. Paris didn't participate, preferring to maintain his involvement through her. As expected, Iris and Sophie were ambivalent as regards to him: they were happy with this new development in their work; they were concerned about her. Isabel resolved to try to talk him into meeting her friends.

She paced agitatedly, staring out the window. In a few minutes the sun would set and the time limit on their wager would expire. Her heart thudded excitedly; tension turned her stomach. Odds were, she won. Soon she would see his face. That wasn't the reason she was out of breath.

The wager kept their encounters tame and their dangerously heating, mutual desire in check. In a few moments, though, the restrictions imposed by the wager would lift, the barriers would fall. What would happen between them when they found themselves alone together?

"How was your day?"

Isabel spun around, her heart in her throat. "Paris."

He closed the door, bolted it, and strolled toward her. His bluish-green eyes glittered in the slits of his black mask. "I've something for you." He offered her a parchment.

"What is it?" she asked in an unsteady voice.

A faint smile hovered on his sensual mouth. "See for yourself."

She accepted the parchment, careful not to brush his fingers. If she touched him now, she wouldn't be able to stop. Then she would lose the wager, not see his face, and be rendered naked. Her pulse skipped a beat. "Stilgoe was here. He wanted to say hello to you. Did you see him?"

"No. Read the first page."

She commanded herself to focus on the print. "It's something concerning a house."

"It is being scrubbed, furnished, and prepared for tomorrow morning as we speak. I've also posted a change of address in the newspapers. You have an official charity agency, love."

Blinking, she read the entire page. "This is a deed for a house with my name on it. Paris!" Her eyes flew to his, her heart hammering furiously. "You *bought me* an entire office building?"

"Complete with fifteen rooms, a rose garden, and a ballroom, in which you will hold your fundraising balls and soirees." He smiled a rare and fleeting smile, gauging her reaction.

Tears filled her eyes. And she'd thought his initial donation was extravagant. The building must have cost him ten times as much. *No one* was ever this generous to the underprivileged. But he was. "I . . . if word got around that you purchased a house for me, I'd be utterly ruined."

"Damnation, Isabel! I bought it for your charity, not to set you up in it as my mistress!"

She must be demented, she decided, and as shameless as her sisters—a serious flaw in their upbringing, no doubt—because as soon as he'd uttered the word "mistress," the glittering shards of her recent dreams were pieced together, manifesting the feverish, indistinct yearnings ruling her nights. She *craved* him—this tall, dark, enigmatic man, this force of nature—with her entire being, so much that it hurt her heart just to gaze at him. She ached to embrace him and kiss him.

"What do you suggest I do with it, then?" he asked grimly, misinterpreting her silence.

Trembling with the intensity of her feelings, she let the parchment drop to the floor as she slipped her arms around his neck. "Put the house in your name. You are now an official member of the board of trustees." She covered his lips with hers, something ragingly hot coursing through her bloodstream. He groaned with pleasure and relief. The electricity that had been building between them over the past week broke. Their mouths melded passionately, desperate to make up for lost time. His tongue rode hers like velvet, eliciting deep moans from her with each caress. It was the headiest kiss, rough and sensual, rampant with physical and emotional cravings.

His mouth paved a scorching path to her throat. "You're spending the night with me."

Dazedly, she forced her eyelids to lift so that she'd be able to look out the window. It was dark outside. Sometime while she'd been waiting for him, the sun had set. *He lost.* Paris was also staring at the unraveling mat of nighttime. Their gazes locked. Sudden apprehension etched his eyes as, belatedly, he realized that he had miscalculated time. "You won," he said, stunned.

The anxiety she perceived in him made her question her resolve to unmask him. She felt as though she were holding a pistol to his head. Clenching his jaw, he peeled her hands off him.

"Where are you going?" she cried, as it dawned on her why she wasn't as ecstatic with her win as she ought to have been. *She wanted to be rendered naked and spend a night with him.* Winning the wager had robbed her of her only solid excuse to yield to the call of her dreams and engage in intoxicating sin with him. She watched him lean across the desk and extinguish the lamplight, throwing the room into blackness. "What are you doing?" she whispered.

His voice came right in front of her. "Removing my mask in your presence."

"You're cheating," she pointed out.

"We didn't specify the visibility conditions required at the moment I unmasked myself."

"You might as well keep your mask on, because I can't see a bloody thing."

"Yes, you can." Tension vibrated in his voice as he took her hands and placed them on his slightly beard-roughened cheeks. "You can see me with your hands, love."

She drew in a breath, and slowly, delicately, like a blind person, moved her fingertips over hard, masculine, perfectly sculpted features. He had high cheekbones, long eyelashes, and flaring eyebrows. His profuse hairline curved into a point at the apex of his tall, wide forehead. His nose was straight and proportioned, with the cutest, upturned slope to it. She traced his square jaw to his strong chin, then moved upward to outline his lips. She'd always been fascinated by these soft, pouting lips, but never like this, never in the dark. A startling fancy possessed her: To lie flat on her back and feel them gliding over her nude body, covering her with warm kisses. . .

His breath came sultry and harsh against her fingertips. "Well? Would you set me loose among small children?" He tried to sound blasé about it, but she sensed the muscles of his cheeks bunching beneath her exploring fingers.

"You look exactly the same," she murmured with a smile. In her mind's eye she could well envision the dashing, charismatic, staggeringly handsome hussar she had fallen in love with.

"You sound relieved." His tone was flat, but she heard the reproof in it. "Look again." He covered her fingers and guided them along his cheeks and forehead. This time, she felt the scars.

Long, thin lines slashed his skin. She finally understood why he felt such acute reluctance to reveal himself. Paris Nicholas Lancaster was born beautiful, clever, rich, and titled, but he had no loving mother, no sweetheart to kiss his wounds and make them go away in his mind upon his return from the wars. Despite and because of what defending his country against Bonaparte had cost him, she loved him even more. And after everything he'd done for her charity, mapping out every blemish on his face seemed petty and ignoble to her. Leaning up against him, she draped her arms around his shoulders and pressed her lips to his scarred cheek. "Paris, I lo—"

"Don't . . ." He jerked his head aside. "No pity, Isabel."

"You think I pity you?"

Silence filled the darkness between them.

"What would it take to convince you otherwise?" she asked quietly.

He lifted her waist and set her bottom on the desk, then moved to stand between her thighs, hiking up her skirts as he drew nearer. She felt the evidence of his arousal burrowing against her, setting her senses aflame. His warm, seductive breath filled the whorls of her ear. "Spend the night with me, anyway. I'll make you shudder and sigh with pleasure."

An electric tremor snaked up her spine and tickled her neck. She was seriously, deliriously tempted to say yes, to feel his mouth on her skin, to touch him as she did that night in the gazebo, to unleash his desire. "I cannot," she said regretfully. "John and his sister, Olivia, are escorting me, my mother, and my sister-in-law to Drury Lane this evening to see—"

"Hang Hanson! I don't want you to see him anymore, or his damned sister!"

She flinched. "Why do you find his sister objectionable?" she inquired suspiciously.

"I don't find his sister anything. Promise me you'll stay away from Hanson."

"Are you jealous?" She kissed a soft area of skin beneath his jaw and worked her way to his neck. *Goodness*. He was scrumptious, and she wanted to devour him.

He let out a low growl, letting her know he enjoyed being devoured. "What do you think? He is prowling after you with the intention of wedding and bedding you. Yes, I'm jealous, damn it! Haven't I proven how much I want you for myself?"

Her heart fluttered. "You could . . . come visit me," she offered tentatively.

His fingers thrummed her back, moving nimbly along her spine. "Are you suggesting I climb into your bedchamber tonight?" He sounded vastly intrigued by the proposition.

She felt her gown loosening. "I was referring to a visit during the daylight hours."

He tugged her gown and chemise off her shoulders and fastened his hot mouth to her skin, making her sigh with pleasure. "You run a charity agency during the daylight hours, love."

"Not on the weekend. A ride in the park in the early hours of the morning, or a . . . picnic on a patch of green would be delightful." She didn't think he needed instructions in wooing women, but he seemed to be in a dire need of a nudge in the right direction—or rather directions. It was about time the Gargoyle emerged from his cave into daylight and readjusted in Society. Though at the moment, being alone in the dark with him suited her just fine—and was sinfully arousing.

"I don't go out in public, love. You know that." Cool air whispered on her breasts, then she felt his open palms rubbing her nipples in slow circles, sensitizing them into tingling pebbles.

"You like keeping it that way, don't you?" she accused breathily, the thrilling sensations he stirred within her making it very difficult for her to concentrate on and stick to her side of their argument. "Sneaking about with me in the dark, where no one can see us, or know that we . . ."

"Are crazed with lust for each other?"

"Bear affection for one another." He wouldn't even see her brother today.

"Other people be damned. I want you all to myself." He bent his head, took her breast in his mouth, and suckled hard. Intense desire shot to the secret place between her thighs. She caught his head, barely able to sit still, as his tongue swirled around and lapped at her nipple. He filled his hands with her breasts, shaping and kneading, making her arch up against him, as her mind thawed into a sensual haze of heat and yearning. "Your breasts are so soft, so . . . perfect."

His teeth gently bit her nipple and tugged, shooting ripples of heat up the back of her legs. His large hand delved beneath her skirts, caressing her thigh. As it passed the garter holding her stocking in place, the shock of his hand on her bare skin was deliciously wicked. His hand sailed inwardly, deep between her thighs, located the slit in her drawers, and slid in to touch her flesh.

"My goodness!" she gasped, as the most excruciating pleasure shot through her body. As soon as it diminished, she craved more, a lot more of this electrifying sensation of heaven and hell aroused by one stroke of his hand. She edged closer, seeking the sinful magic of his touch.

"That's an appetizer of what you'll experience if you come to me tonight." He thumbed the sensitive nub of her desire, and she all but lurched off the desk. Clinging to his shoulders, she let him capture her mouth in a rough, hungry, tongue-tangling kiss. His fingers stroked her expertly, until she felt slick and hot and aching for him. He kept a hand on her breast, stoking her desire on three fronts, while they kissed deeply, uninhibitedly, burning for one another.

Gasping and moaning in rhythm with his caressing hand, she surrendered to the havoc he wreaked on her senses. The more pressure he applied, the faster he tended to the sensitive spot already beating with a pulse, the less she felt inclined to refuse his invitation. She already knew he was the man she wanted; she'd practically known it since she was twelve years old. LJ, she primly held off, but with Paris, virtue and propriety were empty words to her. "I . . . I . . ."

"You want me," he groaned against her parted lips, dipping a finger inside her. He located a deeper, more responsive spot and flicked his finger against it. Raw lust blazed through her taut, eager body, saturating her mind. She cried out, begging for more of the exquisite torture. "You want me inside you . . . Say it, Isabel. Say you want me inside you, my angel, my lioness . . ."

"I . . . I want you inside me," she cried softly, rolling her hips with his hand, emitting lava.

He knew precisely what she panted for. Yet once he slaked one need, another awakened, more acute, more demanding than the former. She was no longer the mistress of her own body.

"Remember how hard I was for you in the gazebo?" he breathed haggardly. "That was nothing compared with how much I need you right now. I want to bury myself deep inside you, pleasure you so thoroughly that you would sing an entire operetta by the time I'm through."

In the deep recesses of her misty awareness, she wondered why he doggedly withheld this promise of divine pleasure from her. She hardly possessed the power to resist him at the moment. Sizzling under her skin, however, was anger at his proclamation. She'd heard of his penchant for opera singers, but that he should dare compare her to demireps was unpardonable. "By the time I'm through with you, Paris Lancaster, you'll have something in common with Hector."

"What?" He half chuckled half groaned against her cheek. "A lolling tongue? A wagging tail? Believe me, my dear, I'm half way there already."

"You're forgetting, my darling," she whispered in his ear, half dazed by the molten desire licking at her insides, "that I know what you have always longed for, what your secret desire is."

"How would you know what my secret desire is?" His voice was deep and hoarse with hunger for her. He was groaning heavily now, sounding like a man in pain.

A feminine smile curled her lips. "You want a caress."

He drew back. She tried to distinguish his features in the

dark. All she saw was a pair of twinkling gems—his eyes. "Where are you off to?" she gasped in alarm, trying to pull him back.

"To find *your* secret desire."

She had no idea what he aimed to do. She was about to perish from sheer frustration. In the pitch black silence of the room, though, all she could do was feel. He braced her knees farther apart, tipped her back to lie on the desk, then put his head between her thighs. "Paris, what . . . what are you . . ?" He parted her slick folds with his fingers and tasted her. *"Paris!"* She became very vocal, indeed, particularly as he rubbed her sensitive, throbbing nub with the raspy velvet of his tongue, lancing her with shocks of dark, erotic pleasure. Next he sucked it with his lips.

Objects flew to the carpet as she thrashed and bucked, the resistance coiling in her making her whimper in sweet agony, begging for release. Undeterred, he licked her, sucked her, grazed her with his teeth, and drove her to the edge of endurance. Her heart thundered in her ears, her limbs shook uncontrollably, her hips swiveled wildly against his plundering mouth. "Oh, God . . . *oh, God*—Paris!" The tight knot snapped, and roaring contentment surged through her veins like lightning, like honey, like a potent opiate, flooding her brain with pure rapture. *She liquefied.*

Strong hands pulled her limp body up against a comfortable chest, tucking her head against a broad shoulder. She hugged his waist, her face buried in his neck, as bliss settled like stardust in her sated mind. Thank goodness for the darkness, she thought, mortified at her wantonness. At fifteen she'd pounced on him with a kiss; now she'd practically melted against his mouth—in the most shocking, scandalous way. "You were glorious in your passion," he said, "sweet as nectar."

"And several other things, as well," she mumbled into his collar.

"Are you embarrassed?" He chuckled. "Well, if you are, don't be. I love that about you."

She turned her face up. "What do you love about me?"

"Everything."

Did this mean that he loved her, she wondered. "Your heart is pounding terribly fast."

"You're driving me insane, love. If you don't take pity on me soon, I might suffer from an apoplexy or become a Bedlamite, I haven't decided yet. But as either mishap will be your fault, I expect you to visit me often, or I'll tear the place down around everyone's ears."

"Poor you." She chuckled. She threaded her fingers through his thick, silky hair and pulled his head down for a kiss. "*You* are my secret desire, Paris," she confessed as her lips touched his.

"Miss Aubrey!" Phipps called, knocking on the door. "Lady Chilton and Mrs. Fairchild are requesting your presence in the green drawing room."

"No rest for the wicked," Paris muttered irately. "Thank Lucifer I bolted the door. Come, I'll help you put yourself back together." He set her on her feet and turned her around.

"Turn on the light," she suggested, arranging her bosom as he buttoned up her back.

"No."

"You've lost the wager, you've touched me in every possible way, and you still insist on hiding yourself from me?"

"Sweetness, I haven't begun to touch you. What time should I expect you tonight?"

She was tired of playing this game with him. If he insisted, though, she would up the ante and see if he still wanted to play, by her rules. "I already told you. I can't come. Not that I would if I could. I've no wish to be ruined." Not that it would have stopped her . . . shameless as she was.

"You won't be ruined unless someone sees you, and no one will. I'll come get you myself in my carriage after midnight.

All you have to do is sneak out of the house. I'll wait around th—"

"I'm not sneaking about with you anymore. And that's final."

"Isabel." He spun her around. "I'm all out of patience."

"That is unfortunate," she returned. She was all out of patience, herself. At the beginning of this little game her worst obstacle was his seclusion, as it forced her to take the initiative each time she cared to see him, casting her in the role of the pursuer. Since then she'd learned that the flipside of the coin was her strongest suit, her trump card. However, so long as she visited him, he would never venture out into Society; and as long as he remained holed up in his luxurious cave, he would have no incentive to reveal his face to her or to declare himself. "If you wish to see me, Lord Ashby, you may call on me at Seven Dover Street Saturday afternoon and escort me on a ride in the park. I shall expect you at four o'clock."

"Isabel . . ." he gritted out.

"Miss Aubrey!" Phipps called again, knocking urgently.

"Damn. I'll take care of him." Paris strode to the door and opened it. "Do you mind—"

"What's going on in here, for heaven's sake?" Iris's angry voice filled the doorway.

Oh, dear. Isabel lit the wick and took out a few pins to quickly tuck her straying curls back in place. She had no idea why she bothered. Iris had probably guessed by now what she and Paris had been up to alone in the dark. Yet Iris would never tell a soul. She would keep Isabel's secret.

Paris was standing with his back to her, unmasked, his tall frame blocking the doorway and shielding her from outside viewers. Part of her warmed at his self-sacrifice in affording her a few extra moments of privacy to collect her bearing. The other part resented his letting Iris see him while he hid himself from her, especially after what had just transpired between them.

"Good evening. Lady Chilton, I presume?" he drawled in a composed, cultured, slightly gruff tone of voice that—to Isabel's practiced ears—attested to his discomfiture. "I'm Ashby, the new member of your happy charity board. I'm pleased to make your acquaintance."

"Lord Ashby." Iris curtseyed. Shock and then curiosity thrummed her voice. "Please allow me to welcome you aboard and thank you for the generous use of your magnificent home."

"My pleasure, madam." He tried to head off, but someone else materialized before him.

"Allow me to introduce my friend and colleague, Mrs. Fairchild." Iris presented Sophie.

"Mrs. Fairchild," he drawled charmingly, veiling the edge to his voice. "I had no idea Miss Aubrey's colleagues were striking young ladies, or I would have made a point of introducing myself earlier." Poor Ashby, Isabel thought. Iris and Sophie truly had him cornered.

"Lord Ashby." Sophie smiled engagingly, sweeping a curtsy. "You are too kind."

Tittering! Isabel heard distinct tittering in Sophie's voice. Recalling her false-hearted offer to play matchmaker between Paris and Sophie, she couldn't help wondering if his compliment to Sophie was his way of getting back at her for refusing to return to him tonight.

"I conserve my kindness for our cause. In this instance, I am merely being honest."

"I would also like to thank you for opening your doors and heart to us," Sophie sing-sang. "I'm certain it's a great inconvenience, which makes your contribution greater."

"I am glad to be of help. Tomorrow we shall relocate the agency to its permanent location. I have purchased us an office building a few blocks away from here, on Piccadilly."

Ohhs and *ahhs* ensued, and several other worshipful comments. Isabel wanted to scream at them that he was *hers*, that no one was allowed to gush over him but her. Instead she marched forward to join the conversation. Hearing her approach, Paris stirred. "I'll leave you ladies to your business. Good evening." Before Isabel reached his side, he vanished down the hallway.

Isabel froze in shock. First her sisters and now her friends? Enough was enough! The game was up with this. The next time she saw him, she would walk up to him and snatch the damned mask from his duplicitous face. Sneak about with her in the dark. Ha! She would show him. *Upon thy belly shalt thou go, and dust shalt thou eat, before I let you touch me again.*

As she stood motionless, more infuriated than she'd ever been in her life, Iris and Sophie breezed in past her, chatting excitedly about the dashing gargoyle. "Look!" Sophie exclaimed, picking up the parchment. "He did buy us a building. *Mon Dieu*, he's so generous . . ."

"And kind and charming," Iris murmured with awe. Papers rustled. "And wealthy!"

"And stupendously attractive . . ." Sophie stared at Isabel. "I understand why you like him so much, Izzy. Your Ashby is a man in every sense of the word, the good sense."

Grudgingly Isabel speculated on the reason he wouldn't let her see him. True, she was not as mature or worldly as her friends here, but her sisters were younger and more impressionable. The only plausible explanation was that he feared rejection—which was an insult in itself. She was far less judgmental than Sophie and Iris put together! They would never believe her if she told them she was the only one still kept in the dark. *Literally.* Not that she had any intention of enlightening them. It would make her look positively silly. Well, if Paris Lancaster wanted her in his bed, he had best start cultivating patience, because he was looking at a very long wait!

She didn't delude herself into anticipating his prompt

knock on the front door of Seven Dover Street at four o'clock this Saturday. But neither should he delude himself into expecting her call anytime soon. She had won one wager; she could win this standoff as well, blindfolded.

"You certainly seemed to like him well enough," she finally said. "I take it you've altered your opinions now that you've met him in the flesh." She paced in front of them, too troubled to conduct a meeting. She'd much rather go home and plot the downfall of the mask.

"I must say he's not what I expected," Iris admitted. "He's a distinctly amiable gentleman."

"You look . . . in a state." Sophie remarked with a chuckle. "Has anything interesting come to pass between you and the dark knight while we were conducting our little interviews?"

"We quarreled," Isabel muttered, blowing a curl off her face as she continued pacing.

"A domestic squabble, already?" Sophie's chuckles matured into laughter.

"He bought you a building for the agency and you quarreled with him?" Iris inquired.

"He exasperated me!" *And made her shudder and sigh with pleasure.*

"He exasperated you on top of the desk?" Sophie raised an eyebrow, indicating the clutter of deskware strewn on the carpet around the large oak table. "Must have been some quarrel."

"If you're worried that he . . . compromised me, then the answer is no."

"If he continues to exasperate you, let me know. I'll be happy to take him off your hands."

Isabel refrained from baring her teeth. She was still counting her blessings that despite her tousled appearance, she wasn't facing the Spanish Inquisition. Loath to reveal her ignorance on the topic of his face, she trawled, "What did you find stupendously attractive, anyway?"

Sophie smiled broadly. "I imagine it's precisely what you do, my dear."

Isabel doubted that. Paris's physical attributes were merely an added bonus. What she liked most about him was his generosity, strength, and compassion. He was the rare sort, especially in Mayfair, who wouldn't close the curtains to the suffering out there and pretend it didn't exist. And what made her yearn for him was the haunted look in his eyes when he gazed at her, as if he believed her the only person in the world capable of saving him. "May we please leave? John and Olivia are to collect me in less than two hours." She had planned to cancel the engagement, but that was before Paris had put her all on end. Served him right to be jealous! She hoped he turned cheerfully green behind that mask of his!

As her friends went to retrieve their wraps and bonnets, Isabel lifted the black satin mask from the floor, but before she shoved it inside her reticule, she closed her eyes and sniffed it for Paris's scent. In a way, inhaling the mask he'd worn on his face felt as intimate as doing so with his shirt, anything that had contact with his skin. *Dash it all*. Things were getting out of hand, if she considered coming to his bed regardless of who won the wager. Behaving as a lightskirt and a hoyden would not induce him to make an offer of marriage, but it would surely ruin her.

Reckless though she was, she did not care to be ruined. That would be the end of a life she enjoyed, and most likely, her agency. Her reputation was her future, and her present. Therefore, as much as she desired her dark knight, she would have to practice restraint and prudence—and stay away from him for as long as she could, or until the glow he lit about her subsided.

When they were comfortably ensconced in Iris's carriage, Sophie met Isabel's gaze in the shadows. "Has he proposed to you yet?"

"No," Isabel replied testily.

"He is in love with you."

Despite the flutter in her belly, Isabel doubted that. He wanted her, but she suspected it had more to do with need rather than with love. Apparently she possessed something that he veritably craved. She'd merely been teasing him with her pronouncement about his secret desire. In truth, she had no idea what it was. Unless Iris had been right all along and he did have a secret agenda concerning her. His self-restraint was disconcerting. Perhaps his maneuverings were designed to draw her in so that he could manacle her to the medieval bed with the decadent-looking scarlet counterpane in his cellar, or something equally gothic. It would have been . . . intriguing, if not for the lack of fresh air in that chamber of his. If he did have a nefarious scheme in mind, though, he would do well to consult with her sisters first. They would happily regale him with horror tales of how poorly she responded to confinement. It was not something he should attempt at home.

"I have a splendid idea," Iris announced. "Since there's a ballroom in our new building, I propose we throw a ball to let everyone know that we expect their donations and support!"

Isabel's eyes lit up. "Let's make it a masquerade ball," she suggested slyly. "With masks!"

Her friends liked the idea. Everyone enjoyed a good masquerade, and once their peers saw their sponsor's name on the invitation, they would be unable to resist a glimpse at the Gargoyle.

After dropping Sophie off, the carriage rolled to a stop on the front drive of Seven Dover Street. Isabel took out Ryan's letter from her reticule and handed it to Iris. "I've been carrying this for several days now. I didn't wish to give it to you in front of other people. It's from Ryan."

"Burn it."

"Don't you want to know what it says?" Isabel asked quietly. "He came to see me before I left for the country. He still loves you, Iris, and he wishes to apologize for his . . . misbehavior."

Iris swiped a tear off her cheek. "Burn it."

Isabel clasped Iris's hand. "You deserve to know the truth, dear heart. You have nothing to lose by reading his letter."

"Yes, I do," Iris clipped. "My hate for Ryan is all I have left of him. It keeps me warm at night, when I compare my life to what it should have been." Her voice shook. "I'm glad your Ashby isn't the monster I feared he was, but there is a reason why women came up with rules for behavior around men. I, too, believed that Ryan was my one true love, my savior. I trusted him so blindly that I allowed myself to . . ." She shut her eyes against a sudden flow of tears. "Don't repeat my mistake. Make certain he is the man you hope he is before you give yourself to him."

Isabel leaned over to hug Iris. "You're the best friend anyone could hope for. Thank you for sharing your secret with me, for trying to protect me. Ryan doesn't deserve you, dearest." She held Iris until her tears subsided, then handed her the letter. "Burn it yourself, if you wish. I'd be too curious not to read it, myself, but then, curiosity did kill the cat."

Iris smiled. "At least I can console myself with the knowledge that Ryan's life isn't a bed of roses, either. Or he wouldn't have gone to all that trouble to see this letter delivered to me."

"That's the spirit." Isabel kissed Iris's cheek and let the liveried tiger hand her down. "I'll see you tomorrow morning." She couldn't wait to begin putting her plan into motion.

Chapter Eighteen

Your voice alone declares your flame,
And though so sweet it breathes my name,
Our passions still are not the same.
—Lord Byron: *To Caroline*

Once again Isabel refrained from coming to see him—for a whole bloody week! Nursing a piss-poor disposition, Ashby poured his frustration and sweat into sanding the new project he'd begun since his return from Ashby Park. It smacked of servitude, as it was a surprise for Isabel, but he kept at it anyway. He enjoyed creating things for her. Her delight in whatever he gave her was exhilarating and highly addictive. He couldn't recall which Muse inspired him before Isabel reentered his life five weeks ago. Now he could hardly stand it when they were apart. Will once told him that people instantly grew accustomed to good things and never to bad things. Isabel Aubrey was the best thing that ever happened to him—and the worst, if it didn't happen.

The first two days Ashby assumed she was too busy converting the pretty town house he'd purchased for her charity into a proper agency. Then came Saturday, and as he failed to show up for their designated ride in the park, he allotted her two more days for sulking. The sixth day, when he sent her a note, inviting her to have luncheon with him, and was cordially refused, he knew the truth: Isabel didn't miss him half as much as he missed her.

He felt like those women he used to seduce. He, too, was frequently otherwise engaged to spare time for those he didn't care to see again or as often as they would have liked to see him. If this was how they had felt, then he had put them through hell. He'd never felt anything remotely similar to this choking need before, this constant pain beneath his ribs. Being unable to see her, touch her, or talk with her was transforming him into a pitiful wreck. He hated the feeling.

He strongly suspected she was making a statement. The little extortionist thought she could twist his arm into making a grand public appearance. She might settle for a private one, so long as it didn't feature a mask, but then he'd risk losing her altogether. In all fairness he should have let her see him by now. Each time he considered doing so, however, his hands grew clammy and a sensation similar to panic gripped him. If her friends' compassionate looks were any indication, then they, too, were concerned about Isabel's reaction. Hence, before he unmasked himself in a brighter setting, he needed to make certain that she cared for him enough to see past . . .

Hell and damnation. It was her damned fault that he felt pathetically insecure. All that talk of love and alterations was turning him into an antithesis of the hardened rake he once was. He'd served enough years as a field commander to be able to tell when the balance of power shifted against him. It was the damnedest thing. Usually after he made a woman cry out his name while in the throes of passion, he owned her; all he had to do was snap his fingers and she would come running. Not his Isabel. Oh, no. Isabel the Lioness had convictions, goals, and other suitors. The Lioness wanted to bring him to heel. Nothing he did had the power to sway her, except revealing his face. And that he couldn't do. Not before he made proper, slow, tender love to her.

Not that he had the foggiest of how to go about it. In roughly two decades of maintaining a sexually active lifestyle, he'd never once made love to a woman. Sex was a pleasurable activity that didn't require emotions—or planning or self-discipline or a forty thousand quid investment. Yet he didn't want to seduce Isabel on a desk, or in someone's gazebo, or in a plush hotel suite, or in any of the ad hoc locations in which he'd had sexual intercourse with former lovers; he wanted to seduce her in *his* bed, when they had all the time and privacy in the world. Nor did he select Isabel as his future wife because he was hungry, though he was, but his hunger was for the unique quality she possessed, the one he'd been searching for his entire life: His secret desire.

Since he was four years old, a little earl with a bottomless income and no one to answer to, people sought his company for two reasons: power and money. If he forgot it for an instant as he began to attract the fairer sex, the women let him know soon enough that—while he possessed other appealing qualities—they still expected a bauble or two. So he indulged them, as long as he got what he wanted from them, namely a short-lived, no-strings-attached exchange of physical pleasure. Inevitably he grew up to be a worthless degenerate, pampered and spoiled, who made a habit of getting what he wanted while doing as he pleased. His so-called friends and allies were wastrels and bounders, dissolute creatures with reputations as black and empty as his own, who, like him, went through life catering to their whims. It was a sad day when by the time he reached his twenty-fifth year he'd run out of whims. He felt like—*he was*—a damned cliché.

Meeting Will was a turning-point in his life. Will liked *him*. Even more peculiar, his new friend's self-worth stemmed from within. As a second son and brother to a fairly young member of the nobility, Will was expected to make his own

way in the world with nothing to his credit but his family connections. That did not stop him from strutting about with a
jaunty smile and an innermost belief in his uniqueness. He
forced Ashby to do some unpleasant soul-searching, but it
wasn't until Will brought him to Seven Dover Street that a
new whim budded within him. Only this whim was not as
easily satisfied, if at all. Thus, it grew into an obsession, a
hunger so deep, so persistent, that it occupied his every
thought and dream: He wanted to know what love was.

This illusive beast the entire world worshiped and wrestled
with and was enthralled by—*he wanted to feel it*. However
much he yearned for it, though, however hard he sought it, the
beast eluded him. Until he glimpsed it seven years ago on a
dark bench with a chit nearly half his age.

He had never met anyone more passionately devoted to and
protective of those she loved: a veritable lioness. Being the
object of her love even for that fleeting moment had invigorated him, made him feel special, invincible, and alive—a lion.
Whatever Izzy saw in him that merited her affection, he wanted
to be that man, for her and for himself, because he liked the
feeling. It made his life worthwhile. If he'd known she would
accept him—scars, black conscience, and all—he wouldn't
have considered putting a pistol to his head after Waterloo.
He'd have ridden straight to her. But she hadn't seen him since
Sorauren, and she didn't know he'd killed her brother.

The odds that he might end up as one of the hopeless sots
drooling after her terrified him. He would wager everything
he owned that Isabel wasn't even aware of the powerful
weapon she wielded so artlessly. He'd watched her do it with
the swags at the Barrington ball—innocently radiating her
magnetic warmth while keeping herself beyond reach because
she wasn't interested in any of them. Her weapon was neither
her beauty, though she was beautiful, nor her dowry, which
was handsome but not as those of other females in her circle;

it was the promise of unconditional love she unwittingly dangled before the love-starved men of the *ton*. Men like him.

They lived in a cynical, mercenary, hypocritical society, addicted to pleasure and gin, but if one scraped the surface deeply enough, one would see they were victims of a failed system. Like infants, grown men and women yearned for love. However, since it was a rare commodity, they trawled for artificial substitutes. "Like phantoms huddled in dreams, the perplexed story of their days confounded," Aeschylus wrote. Well, he was sick of Society and its sad pretense. He'd long ago realized that he would settle for everything—or nothing at all. Isabel's unaffectedness, her gift of love, dazzled and enticed him, as the wink of a sovereign in the mud bedazzled a beggar.

No wonder he felt deprived. After reading her letters to Will, after everything he'd done for her, he'd expected to be on the receiving end of her affection. Yet the infinite love she carried in her heart for her family, friends, and every ill-fated soul on earth, he didn't see a trickle of it. Not since his ungainly flight from the Barrington's gazebo, since he'd hurt her. These days, even as a charity case, he ranked lower than a street cat. All because of the damned mask. She didn't want a barrier between them. Fancy that. He'd been naked with women who hadn't known the first thing about him. Even the rare few he'd bedded over a period of time hadn't gleaned a fraction of the information he openly dispensed to Isabel about himself. Sex and a casual acquaintance didn't earn chits a peek into his soul. Isabel read him like an open book. She knew what his secret desire was. And she held it well beyond his reach. Intentionally.

For this reason he was well into his eighth day of solitary misery and doing nothing about it. What could he do but stomp over to the agency and throw a tirade like some spurned lover? Considering that any stomping on his part would be done in private, he shelved the option as a last resort. He could sneak into her bedchamber tonight, but if she shrieked for help, Stilgoe would shoot first and ask questions later. Perhaps he should kidnap her, whisk her away to Spain or Italy, buy her a little palazzo by the sea, where he could have her all to himself . . . Except that he had no assurances as to how she would react once she saw his face. *Damn. Damn. Damn.*

The rasp slipped his grip, and he ended up scraping the skin off his finger. "Bloody hell!" Growling, he lifted the box he'd created and smashed it against the wall. He couldn't stand being alone anymore, not for another damned minute. If she didn't love him, he was doomed, he would go stark, raving mad. Because she was the only woman he wanted. Cursing profusely, he went to dip his burning finger in cold water. Phipps materialized in the arched entry. "What?" he barked.

"My lord, you have a visitor." Phipps wriggled his eyebrows. "A certain young daisy . . ."

Ashby's heart kicked into a mad cadence. He grabbed his mask. "Show her in."

A moment later, sunlight flooded his candlelit cellar as Isabel walked in, her pretty bonnet and reticule dangling off one arm. Tall, lithe, and slender, she wore a pale apricot muslin gown, high-necked and prim, the same shade as her soft, rounded cheeks. He wanted to eat her alive.

It was by sheer willpower that he didn't stalk up to her, sweep her into his arms, and carry her to the antique bed at the far side of the chamber. She needed to know that he had other things in his life besides her. He had his thoughts of her. They occupied him a great deal. "Hello."

She stepped forth. "You're angry."

Yes, angry at himself for behaving as his less sportive conquests. If Isabel sold seats to this dismal scene, the cellar would be full to capacity with his former mistresses and lovers clapping their hands and cheering her on. Olivia accused him of being proud. Maybe he was, but at the moment he felt trounced. He would have returned to rasping his project, except that he'd skinned his forefinger and smashed the damned crate to pieces. He wished he could tell her something along the lines that he was done in after a night of carousing, but since she was all too aware he didn't go out in public, she would realize that he'd been spying on her again, watching her go out every night with Hanson and his sister, and with her friends. But she didn't have time for him. "How's the agency coming along?" he asked instead, distractedly blowing on his stinging finger.

"Very well, thanks to you. We are a smashing success. We receive bagfuls of requests for employees daily. Applicants are arriving from out of town, having heard about us. We took on a housekeeper, a sweet woman called Rebecca, who moved in with her two young boys. We hired assistants to help with the workload. And I contacted the families on the list you'd sent me." She smiled. "I should have thought of that, myself. After all, I'm one of them, the family of the 18th."

"I scratched Will's name off. I didn't want to upset you." He shook his finger. The bloody thing burned like the dickens.

She came over and took his hand. "My poor darling, did you hurt your finger? You should rinse it in cold water. It will remove the sting."

He wasn't feeling too charitable with her at the moment to appreciate her concern; mostly because he had other, more urgent stings he needed removing. "I already did. It didn't help."

"Then I have a better remedy." Smiling, she lifted his finger to her lips and kissed it softly.

His heart jolted. He must be rabid already, to have given her so much power over him. He couldn't help it, though. He'd tried to escape it before, and it came back to haunt him. He tilted his head forward to smell her hair. *Christ*. Her scent obliterated his brain. "Do you love me?"

A startled look etched her eyes. "Do you love me?" she countered. "Or do you need me?"

Her riposte confounded him. How the devil was he supposed to answer this trick question? Wasn't love a need for another individual? *Damnation*. He wasn't incapable of love! He loved his parents, didn't he? He loved Will. He desperately wanted to ask her, the resident expert, what deuced difference it made, but he wasn't *that* daft that he didn't predict she would construe his question as a disclaimer of sorts. "I need you very much," he confessed, feeling like a halfwit.

Judging by her pursed lips, he got the answer wrong. "Why should I love someone who needs me but doesn't love me?"

"I didn't say I didn't love you, damn it!" He snatched his hand from her grip and went to pour himself a healthy dose of whiskey. The woman was determined to see him institutionalized. "Do you want some whiskey?"

"No, thanks. There is a difference between love and need, Paris. Don't you know that?"

"Explain it to me."

She sent him an odd look. "Very well. Love means that one would overlook his own needs and put the needs of the one he loves before his own."

He looked at her. "You're joking, yes? I'm supposed to understand a bloody thing from the tangle you just described?" Cursing softly, he knocked back the entire contents of his glass.

"I can't explain love to you. You either feel it, or you don't."

"And you don't feel it for me. Not anymore." He refilled his glass. Getting drunk seemed such a splendid idea, he wondered why he hadn't thought of it earlier.

Her fanlike eyelashes fluttered—a telltale sign that she felt ill at ease. "I don't understand why we are suddenly discussing this. What's gotten into you?"

"You have." He slammed the glass on the side table and started toward her. "You . . . burst into my perfectly peaceful existence, disrupted everything, seduced me with your honeyed voice and your glowing blue eyes and your soft lips . . ." As he neared her, he felt very predacious all of a sudden. Instinctively she edged back in alarm, but he was slowly backing her against the wall.

"Stop this. You're frightening me," she admonished, not looking the least bit cowed.

"I bent over backward to atone for my behavior in the gazebo, but nothing is good enough for you, is it?" When he reached her, he flattened his hands on the wall on either side of her face, caging her, commanding her defiant gaze. "You won't rest until you bring me to heel."

"You've lost your mind," she retorted. "You've been stuck in this airless cellar too long."

"You wanted the lists, I got you the lists. You wanted my commentary on your reform bill, I offered it to you. You needed another direction in how to help your destitute females, I handed one to you on a platter. I gave you everything you desired and asked for one thing in return—something *both of us* wanted—and what did I get? Indifference. Coldness. Utter disregard."

"I am never cold to you."

"You aren't too warm, either." He watched the play of emotions on her heart-shaped face: her cherry lips were puckered, her soft cheeks puffed, her pert nose wrinkled, her innocent, sky blue eyes deep in thought, with a tiny crease between her fine, dark blond eyebrows. *Christ.* This wasn't a problem in Aristotelian Philosophy! All he wanted was a bloody kiss. To begin with . . .

"Are you saying that everything you did for the charity was . . . just for me?" she asked.

"It wasn't for my health." Though, surprisingly, it felt more than rewarding—it felt right.

"I thought you cared about our cause. You said the reason you decided to become involved was to heal yourself by helping others." Disappointment crossed her brow. "You don't care a fig about those poor women and their starving children! All you care about is fulfilling your needs!"

"I care a great deal about your cause. Perhaps I'm not gifted with your propensity to care about everyone else all the time, but you pointed me in the right direction, and I helped. I fail to see why it is a crime to do something good for someone you want to please!"

"You are just like everyone else." She fought back the tears swimming in her eyes. "Only you play the game better, because you've more intelligence and determination and . . . money."

Exasperated, he hissed, "Does everyone else adopt a stray pup because you couldn't bear to see it tossed back to the streets? Does everyone else go out of his way to help you accomplish the goals you set for yourself? Does everyone else absorb himself in helping destitute females?"

"You did all that because you needed something from me."

"Yes. *You*. Is it so bad? Does doing things for you make me out to be a villain?"

"No," she acknowledged quietly, lowering her eyelashes. "But I thought—"

"You thought I was exactly like you." He heaved a sigh. "I wish I were. Believe me, I'm doing everything within my power to become the man you want me to be, Izzy, and I'll do more, but I need you to . . . guide me." He bent his head and softly kissed her lips. "I want you. Don't you want me?" When she merely gazed up at him with her expressive eyes, he raised a hand and traced her doll-like features, as if in a trance. "Does everyone else make you burn with desire, as I did?" She looked away, blushing scarlet red. This was going to fry him, but he had no choice. He put his lips to her ear, caressing, whispering, "I can still taste you. And I want to taste more."

"Stop that."

Thank Lucifer, he affected her. It wasn't very subtle, but he was all out of subtlety where she was concerned. He decided to be relentless. "Do you touch yourself, as I touched you, when you're alone in your bed at night? I touch myself sometimes, when I can't bear the craving, and I think of you. I imagine your sweet lips, your soft breasts in the palms of my hands, your graceful body, nude and welcoming beneath me, and I find my release. Not as I would like to. That would have to be with me inside you, with you wet and on fire for me, clawing at my back, my lioness." He kissed her throat, hot blood rushing in his veins, every inch of him burning for her. When she moaned, digging her fingers in his waist, he wanted to take her right there against the wall.

Her voice was a shaky string of gasps. "Would you do something for me? Just for me?"

In his condition, he would agree to anything. He only prayed she wouldn't send him to the devil. "I'm listening." He raised his head and was confronted with an envelope. "What's this?" If it was an invitation to her upcoming wedding with Hanson, she was never leaving his house. He took the envelope and drew out a card illustrated with black-and-gold Venetian masks.

"We're throwing a ball this Friday to celebrate the opening of our agency. We hope to raise money and awareness among the *ton*. I came here to invite you in person."

He noticed his name was embossed below the title *sponsored by*. "I'll think about it."

"It's a dress-up masquerade ball. Everyone will wear a mask, not just you." She gazed into his eyes. "I want you to come, Paris. For me. Will you do that, *for me*?"

It was the first time she asked him for something for herself, not for charity, or for the sake of some poor creature. If he refused, he doubted he would be asked to do anything for her again.

Her hands slid up his chest and circled his neck. "Please attend my ball, my darling. You're the only person *I* would like to see there and dance with." Surprising him, she perched on tiptoe and kissed him, softly, deeply, distilling her heart and soul into her kiss. When she put it this way, he was up for anything. "I do want you," she murmured between slow kisses. "Even when I want to cheerfully strangle you. You are the most exasperating, secretive . . . wonderful man." She hugged him—*just hugged him*—tightly, and he could feel her heart beating against his.

"Isabel . . ." He held her close, the wind knocked out of him, as her warmth seeped into the cold chambers of his heart, evoking memories and feelings he'd long since forgotten. He hadn't been embraced like this since he was four years old. And although she felt so small and fragile, the strength of her spirit humbled him. He would never be able to let her go, even if she spurned him, mocked him, and retched upon seeing his face, because he would never survive without her.

"Before I forget . . ." She ended their embrace—to his dismay—and extracted a small box from her reticule. It was prettily wrapped as a gift with a blue bow. "This is for you."

"What is it?" He frowned.

"See for yourself." She smiled, offering him the box on the palm of her hand.

He removed the bow, the paper, and the lid—and stopped breathing. "It's a pocket watch."

"I know. No doubt you have lots of them, but . . . I spotted it in a shop on Bond Street and . . . couldn't resist." She sent him a timid smile. "Look at the back. I had it engraved."

He felt . . . faint. "You bought me a gift? Why?"

She shrugged, blushing. "Why did you make me the box with the lions?"

"Isabel, if this is for the agency building . . ." he stammered awkwardly.

Her color rose. "I got you this gift because, well . . . I like you, silly. Must I have a reason?"

His hands unsteady, his pulse turbulent, he reverently scooped the lustrous gold watch and its chain and looked at the back. His family crest, a lion, was beautifully engraved in the white gold, along with an inscription: *To P. N. Lancaster, Cœur de Lion. With affection, Isabel.* He sucked in a shaky breath. "I . . . don't know what to say. It's beautiful. I'll treasure it. Thank you."

She bit her lip on a smile, her eyes shining. "You don't mind the French?"

"Lionheart. No, I don't mind." He swallowed. "Is that what you think of me?"

Her eyes said "yes." Hastily, she asserted, "It isn't bribery and has nothing to do with my invitation to the ball—"

"If you say one more word, I'll start weeping." He silenced her with a kiss, conveying how deeply she moved him. The last gift he received was from his parents. *She was killing him.*

"Now put it aside because I am not finished discussing the ball."

Overwhelmed by her sweet gesture, he put the watch gently back in its box and set it on the wine table. He came up in front of her, his heart thumping madly. "Yes, Your Majesty."

She curled her fingers around his neck and pulled his head down for a soft, slow kiss. The supple warmth of her full lips, the velvety caresses of her tongue held him completely in thrall. This was Isabel's signature—kisses that sucked his soul and turned him into a blithering idiot.

"One gesture of good faith is all I ask," she whispered. "Think about it."

If she only knew what she was asking of him . . . but what could he tell her? How could he explain that his atrocities followed him everywhere? That he was a living battlefield of hundreds of thousands of mutilated ghosts. That he wasn't fit to move in Society. She would only egg him on harder, eager to heal his torments and make a new man out of him. Perhaps she did want him, but she'd mapped out a Via Dolorosa for him to undertake before she pronounced him worthy of her unconditional, uninhibited, unaltered love, and he wasn't certain he would prevail.

Chapter Nineteen

Oberon. *Ill met by moonlight, proud Titania.*
Titania. *What, jealous Oberon! Fairies, skip hence;*
I have sworn his bed and company.
Oberon. *Tarry, rash wanton: am I not thy lord?*
—Shakespeare: *A Midsummer Night's Dream*

"What a splendid crush!" Disguised as a bird of paradise in a blue silk gown with colorful feathers and a matching mask, Sophie bubbled with delight upon surveying the richly decorated, crowded ballroom. "I worried the rain would keep everyone at home, but it appears that every peer and none-such is present this evening. Our ball is a success, if I do say so myself."

"I hear Prinny is on his way," Iris whispered with equal enthusiasm, looking glamorous in an emerald silk Celtic costume. "Oh! And I see the Duchess of Devonshire gobbling chocolate balls at the refreshments table. That's always a good sign."

"Everyone seems to be having a marvelous time," Isabel conceded. *Everyone but her.* She sighed glumly as masquerading couples swirled by her in a country dance. As hostess, it was her prerogative to decline to dance without offending anyone. Thus, she stood at the edge of the parquet floor, wishing she were somewhere else, and with someone else. Unfortunately, she had used up all her trump cards: staying away from his house, begging him to attend her ball, letting John and Olivia escort her to every soiree this week while knowing full well Paris lurked in the shadows outside her home. Yet nothing seemed to faze him. On the contrary, he seemed more entrenched in his position— and behind his mask—than ever. What else could she possibly do?

Her machinations exhausted to no effect, her hand had slimmed down to two cards: either unmask him when he least expected it, or spend a night with him. But she didn't want to do the one or the other. Resorting to desperate measures might very well cost her the man she loved, her reputation, the agency, and perhaps even her freedom. She was losing the dratted game.

Although she'd rattled his confidence in her being an easy mark, Colonel Lord Ashby, the brilliant tactician, was biding his time, waiting for the fruit to ripen and fall into his hand. That was well and good, except that she didn't have the final vote in determining her future. John had stopped teasing after other females, concentrating his attention on her, and as a result, her mother and brother were expecting a marriage proposal any day now.

"Everyone has donned a mask and come for a peek at our sponsor," Iris asserted. "Even Chilton is here somewhere."

"Your husband, along with everyone else, will be sorely disappointed this evening, because he's not coming," Isabel said. After two hours of searching the masked throng for *the man* with a mask, she was beyond disappointment. She was utterly miserable.

"Who's not coming?" a low voice spoke beside her.

Isabel jumped, but before she even glimpsed the tall, auburn head, her mind recognized the voice as the one belonging to Ryan Macalister. Iris was quicker in discerning it, for she excused herself thereupon. Sophie sent Isabel a look that told her she would be strung up as a traitor for consorting with the enemy and followed their fleeing friend. Isabel stayed put.

The masked hussar took her hand and bowed. "Bottom, at your service, Your Majesty."

"How did you know?" She smiled behind her silver-dusted, pastel-colored mask.

"What? That you are Titania, Queen of Fairies?" Appreciative light blue eyes, seen through slits in his dark half mask, took their leisure sweeping the length of her, from her silver sleepers, past her multi-hued gown of shimmering yellow, pink, and light blue gauzes, lingered briefly on her bosom— displayed more generously than usual above a silvery corset—and reached the top of her head, where her burnished curls cascaded from a tiny silver tiara. Alas he was not the man she'd had in mind upon choosing the provocative costume. "It was a safe enough bet. Safer than suggesting you were disguised as . . ."

"As what, pray tell?" she demanded challengingly.

"At the risk of getting my knuckles rapped with your fan, my next guess would have been a creamy *millefeilles*, a puff pastry cake of a thousand layers thin as paper with rich, sweet—"

"For shame, major!" She lightly put her fan across his knuckles, unable to hide her smile. "Comparing a lady to pastry, indeed! What does that make you?"

"Not a Frenchman, I hope."

"The French lost the war, major, and you are tottering on losing your own."

He leaned closer. "She returned my letter?"

"No," she whispered back, "but you've just made a critical error."

"How so? What do you mean?" he asked in alarm.

"First, you should have approached her, not me. Also, you

should have taken advantage of the crowded setting and of the fact that everyone is in disguise to draw her into a private tête-à-tête, but you've unwisely alerted her to your presence. Now she'll do her best to avoid you for the remainder of the evening."

"You're right. I'm an idiot." He ran a hand through his hair, tousling it. "It's just that she . . . took my breath away in that emerald gown. She made me nervous," he conceded ruefully.

Sadly, Isabel had no advice to dispense to him. Even if Iris forgave him, they would never be together, as she was beginning to fear neither would she and Paris. "Whatever you do, please know that her husband is in attendance. Don't cause trouble for her. Chilton is the jealous type. If he sees you with her, Iris will eventually pay the price for it."

Ryan set his jaw, anger and pain darkening his eyes. "I wish I could swoop in and rescue her from the ogre, but I can't. Not that she would let me, if I could."

"Izzy!" Her mother's cry nearly deafened her. Lady Hyacinth gripped her arm, her lips in Isabel's ear. "John is looking for you, and I have it from an excellent source that he's about to declare himself tonight. Oh, my dear! I can scarcely contain my tears!" She sniffled dramatically.

"Neither can I." Isabel drained her champagne glass and handed it to a passing footman. Her mother's excellent source was no doubt Lady Fanny, John's mother—which meant that a marriage proposal was indeed pending. She wasn't looking forward to the ensuing row at home, when she informed her family that she would sooner join a nunnery than wed the non-pulse-quickening John Handsome. Ryan was still standing on her other side. "Mama, this is Major Macalister. He served with Will in the 18th. Major, my mother, the Dowager Lady Stilgoe."

Her mother shook Ryan's hand, looking none too happy with his hanging about her soon-to-be-married daughter. As soon as she left, Isabel turned to Ryan with a ready apology, but his gaze was fixed on a ruby mask heading their way: Sally Jersey. The orchestra struck up a waltz.

"Dance with me," he murmured in supplication, wrapping her gloved hand around his arm. Isabel let him escort her to the dance floor, grateful for the diversion. If John was hunting for her with a ring in his pocket, dancing presented a new appeal all of a sudden. She faced Ryan on the floor. "We make a fine couple." He smiled grimly, taking her hand. "I wonder whether either of us will have a happy ending. They won't allow you to refuse him, will they?"

Obviously, he'd heard her mother's poorly whispered alert. "No, they won't, but I'll fight them tooth and nail, if I must. I won't become the wife of the man I don't love."

He curled his hand around her waist, curiosity twinkling in his eyes. "Whom do you love, my scintillating Titania?"

A large, gloved hand settled on Ryan's shoulder. "Step aside, Macalister," a baritone voice drawled. "This waltz is mine."

Isabel's pulse leaped in a frenzy.

"Who the devil—?" Ryan swung his head aside and his jaw dropped open. He snapped to attention. "Colonel Ashby." He released Isabel, a grin forming on his lips, and offered his hand.

"Just Ashby." As he shook Ryan's hand, Paris's emerald gaze veered to Isabel. He was dressed entirely in black, his unfashionably long hair a dark gloss in the light of the chandeliers. Heat ran under her skin. The message in his eyes was loud and clear: *I want you this much.*

His curious gaze darting between the two of them, Ryan bowed out. "Any time you feel the need to share a drink while listening to embellished war stories, drop by the old captains' club."

Paris's teeth gleamed a wicked white beneath his black mask. "Thanks."

As soon as Ryan strolled off, Paris stepped in front of her

and slipped one hand around her waist. She caught her breath. Taking his proffered hand, she joined him in a swish of skirts across the crowed floor.

With the fluid grace of a black panther, he navigated them among colorfully disguised couples, his glittering gaze commanding hers with its intensity. She wanted to thank him for coming but couldn't find her voice. She might have imagined herself floating in a dream if not for the heartbeats clamoring in her ears. He spellbound her. His highwayman costume was sewn onto his tall, lean, broad-shouldered form, making him look . . . lethally desirable.

Paris echoed her silence, rendering her physically faint. It was the oddest thing. After constantly sneaking about with him, in the dark or otherwise, at that moment, surrounded by all these people, she was practically swooning with lust for him.

He leaned a little closer, nipping her earlobe with his lips. "Me, too."

Her knees all but folded beneath her. "Balcony."

"Lead the way."

She indicated the balcony doors with a glance, and he instantly changed course, waltzing in that direction. They reached the rear of the floor, and with a nudge of his shoulder, the French doors opened. He pulled her after him, kicking the doors shut. The crisp scent of recent rain hung in the air; drops resounded through the drainpipe. He embraced her closer as she looped her arms around his neck. Throatily she inquired, "Why did you accept my invitation?"

"Do you really need to ask?" His mouth crushed hers, intoxicating as brandy. With a sigh of pleasure, she delved her fingers in his hair and drew him closer, deeper. He tasted her with the instinct of a lover, stealing her remaining strength, heating her blood. Their masks kept bumping as he slanted his mouth over hers again and again, melding their bodies. She couldn't stand it, the melting, the craving, the layers of clothing separating their smoldering bodies, the barriers . . .

She pushed her mask off her face and—without thinking—removed his as well.

Paris froze for a heartbeat . . . and brutally tore his mouth away, stumbling backward. Shocked by what she'd done, Isabel steeled herself, then opened her eyes a fraction and peeked at him. He was shrouded in shadows, both hands splayed across his face. His eyes glinted through the gaps between his fingers, hard with fury and betrayal.

"Damn you," he rasped. "You couldn't resist, could you? You had to humiliate me in a public place."

"No!" she cried, her stomach plummeting with dread. *Oh, God.* He would despise her now.

"Look your fill, then," he growled. He took another step back and with fierce reluctance lowered his hands to his sides. A patch of moonlight fell on him, and she saw his face.

A soft gasp escaped her lips. She covered her mouth, blinking. It hadn't been a trick of the dark or of touch versus eyesight—he did look the same! The unforgiving face before her was the exact one she remembered: perfect lines, godlike masculine beauty, with two long, thin scars shooting up from the bridge of his nose to his hairline in the shape of a V. He had two additional pairs of equally fine lines slashing his cheeks slantwise from the bridge of his nose to his ears. A master surgeon had done a spectacular patch-up work on him with symmetry and precision, so that only six fine streaks showed on his face. If anything, she mused, he looked more like a lion than a gargoyle, and there was nothing hideous about him, no matter what he'd said.

Why in blazes did he feel compelled to conceal himself? It made no sense.

She couldn't stop gawking at him, as she'd seen people staring at the Greek marbles in the museum for hours. Just standing and staring. The Earl of Ashby looked the same but . . . different. At twenty-eight he had been too beautiful, almost pretty, like John. At thirty-five he was all man. He had the face of a Spartan: hard, well-defined, full of character and magnetic allure. But the significant change was in his eyes. Strange she hadn't noticed it until now. Gone were the boyish charm and the rakish sparkle. His dark expression held secrets and pain beyond her ken.

"Satisfied?"

His sharp tone plunged the knife of guilt deeper into her conscience. Sensing the ground slipping from under her feet, she stepped forward and fisted his coat lapels. "Forgive me. It was wrong of me to put you in this position. I—"

He looked down at her coolly. "I told you once before. Never apologize to me."

"Why? Why can't I apologize to you? What I did was insensitive and—"

A familiar voice snarled, "Leave her alone, Gargoyle!"

"John!" Isabel winced. *Oh, no, no, no. What an unmitigated disaster!* She stepped between the two men as John advanced on Paris. "Apologize to Lord Ashby—now!" If they brawled over her on the balcony with no other female as chaperone, she would be utterly ruined, her agency would never survive the scandal, and all those poor women would have nowhere else to go.

"Apologize? *To him*?" John smirked, cynicism written across his face. Behind her, she felt Paris's large bulk stiffening, but he didn't utter a sound. "I'd soon cut off my very own tongue."

She wasn't certain regarding Paris's ability to control his temper. She knew he had one, but she'd never seen him in a confrontation with someone other than herself before. "Your tongue is in dire need of disciplining, John. Lord Ashby is the founder of this agency, our most generous benefactor. You've just interrupted a most important conversation related to our work."

"Don't defend him! I saw him dragging you out here!" Moving with surprising speed, John circumvented her and shoved at Paris's chest with insulting force. "Are you deaf?" he snarled. "Be off, Beast, before I beat your hideous-looking self into a better looking pulp!"

Paris stumbled back a step, saying nothing, his expression inscrutable, his hands coiled into fists at his sides.

"Coward," John spat with contempt.

Isabel felt panic rising in her throat. "Enough!" She glared at John. "How dare you insult our sponsor so cruelly? You are the beast! Apologize at once!"

The Golden Angel looked livid. He stood toe to toe with Paris, the top of his head barely clearing Paris's nose. It struck her as odd—Paris's complete inertness, his meticulous silence. He was bigger and stronger than John; he could smash the man's pompous face, if he wanted to. But he didn't. And thank goodness for that, or the entire ballroom would stampede to the balcony.

"I am the beast?" John sneered, his gaze on his rival. "Why don't you ask *him* what sort of man he really is? Ask him why the French called him *Le Boucher*."

The Butcher? Scowling, she looked at Paris. "What is he talking about?" she whispered.

Paris's gaze collided with hers for a heartbeat before he edged back another step, but it was enough for her to perceive the guilt and vulnerability in his eyes. Her heart constricted. No, she refused to believe he had anything to be ashamed of! He was her dark knight in shining armor!

"Go on, Ashby." John smirked. "Don't be a spoilsport. Regale us with your heroic feats. Tell Miss Aubrey, who lost a brother in the war, how bravely you scoured every battlefield for wounded enemy soldiers and slaughtered them when they couldn't defend themselves against the scavengers, let alone your bayonet!"

"How dare you!" Isabel exclaimed. "That's the foulest lie I've ever heard!"

"Is it?" John commanded her dismayed gaze. "Imagine your

beloved brother lying hurt and bloody after battle, and some filthy French soldier stabbing him while he begged for mercy. This is the gentleman"—he spat the word out like a curse— "you extol as your benefactor. And you thought his face was his only deformity. *Le Boucher*," he bit out caustically.

"Ashby?" Isabel sought Paris's gaze in the shadows of the balcony. Though he stood tall and proud, dark strands of hair falling over his eyes, his gaze was fixed on nothing in particular. Why wasn't he defending himself against these awful accusations? Surely John was lying.

"Go on!" John waved his hand condescendingly at Paris. "Go off with you now—shoo!"

"Stop that!" Isabel rounded on John, sickened with him altogether. "This is my agency, my ball, and you are no longer welcome! Please leave!" Something stirred behind her. Swiftly she turned around. Paris was gone. "Ashby!" She dashed to the railing overlooking the shadowy, rain-dripping rose garden. There was no sign of him anywhere. He had vanished into the night.

Her heart pounded frantically; heat flushed her face. *What had she done?*

"Good riddance," John muttered beside her, following her gaze to the murky shrubbery. He touched her hand. "My lovely Isabel, I've been meaning to speak to you—"

"Leave me," she hissed, shaking with fury—at him, at herself—with dread, with sheer panic, unable to grasp the magnitude of tonight's catastrophe.

"There you are!" A bright blue savior with colorful feathers wedged herself between Isabel and John. Sophie gripped Isabel's arm and towed her toward the French doors. "We're down to the last bottle of champagne. I need your key to the storage room." She dragged Isabel back into the ballroom, elbowed a path for them through the multicolored crowd, down the hallway, all the way to one of the offices, and only let go when they were out of sight with the door closed.

"Have you lost your senses?" Sophie exploded. "What in blazes were you doing alone with Hanson on the balcony? If anyone saw you with him, you'd have to marry him, you silly goose!"

"I wasn't alone with Hanson. I was with—" Isabel sat in a chair and covered her face with her hands. "Oh, Sophie. I've made such a mess of everything. I invited Ashby to the ball, and he came. Then John surprised us on the balcony and insulted Ashby most cruelly, and now he hates and despises me, and I can't blame him because I hate and despise myself. He'll never forgive me. I've lost him." She sobbed, tears soaking into her gauzy costume. An unpleasant feeling assailed her as the words *Le Boucher* reverberated in head. *No!* It had to be a lie. The Ashby Will loved and admired so much could never resort to such vile, dishonorable methods—butchering poor, wounded, defenseless soldiers lying in their own gore on the battlefield, even if they were French. The man she loved removed thorns from puppies' paws, played with her year-old niece, was Will's hero. He donated a house for their charity. He was good and kind and thoughtful . . .

Sophie's hand squeezed her shoulder. "You haven't lost him, Izzy. Go see him tomorrow morning. You'll straighten this mess out easily. It was Hanson who insulted him, not you."

"Hanson would not have had the opportunity to insult him, if I hadn't compelled him to attend and then—" *Exposed him most unfeelingly*, she finished silently.

"What?" Sophie chuckled softly. "What did you do? Steal a kiss with him on the balcony? Ah, yes. I can see why he should hate and despise you and never forgive you for that."

She would never forget the look in his eyes after she'd unmasked him. *You couldn't resist, could you? You had to humiliate me in a public place.* Tomorrow would be too late. If she didn't go to him now, he would have the whole night to trial her, find her guilty, and execute her in his head. She stood. "I need you to go find my mother and tell her I felt ill and have gone home."

"Oh, no, you don't." Sophie shook her head. "You are not going to him tonight."

"But I must!" Isabel cried. "Don't you see? Tomorrow will be too late!" Somewhere in this little room she had left her cape and reticule. She found the items and headed for the door.

"No! I forbid it!" Sophie gripped her arm. "Iris was right. A woman should never put her honor and liberty in the hands of a man, particularly a tormented man. Wait until tomorrow."

Refusing to hear that, Isabel shook free of Sophie's grip and opened the door. She hastened to the foyer, ignoring the curious eyes of guests milling about the place. A footman opened the front door for her. "Wadley, would you please stop a hack for me? I'm feeling quite ill."

"At once, Miss Aubrey." The man stepped onto the thoroughfare, holding up his hand.

It was raining again. Isabel pulled the hood over her head as someone rammed into her.

"Stubborn goose. Wadley!" Sophie called. "Miss Aubrey is coming home with me. Please find my coachman and ask him to meet us out here. He's waiting across the street."

As they waited for the carriage, Isabel looked at her friend. "Did you find my mother?"

"No. I found Iris and told her to find your mother and tell her that my Jerome is terribly ill and that you took me home because I was too distraught to go by myself."

Despite the tension knotting her stomach, Isabel was able to smile at Sophie's deviousness. "Thank you. The next time I feel the need to commit a felony, I'll ask you to be my accomplice."

"A reluctant accomplice," Sophie muttered reproachfully, as her carriage rocked to a halt in front of them. The footman handed them inside, and they took off. "By the by," Sophie said, "I found Iris on the balcony with the major. I should very much have liked to be a fly on the busy balcony's wall tonight. It appears all the entertainment is taking place out there."

"Iris was with Ryan?" Isabel was all in favor.

"Was this why Macalister approached you before? You plotted this reunion together?"

"Iris needs to know the truth, why Ryan left her in that hut. She carries too much pain and bitterness to go on like this forever." Talking and thinking about Ryan and Iris was distracting her from the tension and distress whittling away at her conscience. She wouldn't be able to draw a full breath until she saw Paris, until he held her in his arms and said he forgave her.

"Lancaster House!" Sophie's driver announced from his perch. A sodden tiger opened the door, but Sophie raised her hand. The carriage door closed.

Sophie leaned forward, taking Isabel's hands in hers. "Listen to me, little girl. There is still time to change your mind. If you go in there, all will be over. There will be no way back."

"For heaven's sake, Sophie! I just want to talk to him, to explain . . . Nothing will happen!" Isabel insisted, as her heart beat like a drum and her stomach churned with anxiety. She wanted a proper proposal of marriage, a respectable life, with friends and soirees and a thriving charity agency. She wasn't about to risk everything because she lusted after the man she'd been in love with for ten years! She was not about to commit any such folly, she shouted at herself.

Sophie shook her head, sighing. "You're too reckless, too impatient. He will come to you."

"No, he won't." A tear escaped the corner of Isabel's eye. Making an appearance at the ball tonight was his grand gesture, and she had abused and mishandled it. She had to set it to rights.

"I will wait for you here. Don't stay too long."

Isabel knew precisely what her friend was doing—appointing herself as Isabel's chastity belt. "You don't need to wait out here in the rain for me. Your son is expecting you at home."

"Ah, *chérie*." Exhaling forlornly, Sophie squeezed her hands, her eyes entreating Isabel to reconsider. "Do you think this old opera singer doesn't know about love? If he is hurting, you'll console him as a woman consoles the man she loves, because you won't be able to bear his pain. Don't go to him, Izzy. If he is the right man, he will come to you. If he isn't"—she shook her head gravely—"then you mustn't go in there at all."

Isabel refused to listen. Yes, Paris was dangerous and enigmatic and unconventional. He preferred moving mountains for her over taking her for a ride in the park. But tonight he came to the ball, because she'd asked him to. How could she let him hurt alone, when she was the one responsible for his pain? All this time he was convinced she wouldn't want him because of his scars. She needed to set him straight. He needed to know that his injury didn't stand between them, that his uncertainty had been for naught, that he could come out of his cave and live a normal life. And if he wanted her as much as he claimed to, she would take him with open arms.

"Go home to Jerome." Isabel opened the door and stepped out into the rain.

"I'll send the carriage back. Don't stay too long!" Sophie called after her.

Paris. Paris. Isabel rushed up the front steps and banged the knocker against the door.

Chapter Twenty

Come to me in the silence of the night;
Come in the speaking silence of a dream;
Come with soft rounded cheeks and eyes as bright
As sunlight on a stream;
Come back in tears,
O memory, hope, love of finished years.
—Christina Rossetti

Isabel paced the small sitting room in which Ashby had received her the first time she'd knocked on his door. She was twice as sick with anxiety as she'd been then.

"Miss Aubrey." Phipps returned. His expression was inauspiciously glum. "His lordship begs you to leave. My apologies."

Leave? It was unacceptable! She would not let him dismiss her and retreat into the depths of his solitary cave as he'd done after the Barrington ball. He had come after her then; she would come after him now. "Is he in the cellar?" she demanded to know.

The butler's eyes darted in the direction of the stairway. "Fourth door to your right, second floor," he murmured conspiratorially.

Smiling gratefully, she hurried past him out the door, grasped fistfuls of her silk train, and dashed up the stairs. Her slippered feet were soundless on the hallway thick carpet as she entered the quiet grandeur of the private wing. She counted four doors to her right and halted. *Just to talk*, she vowed and lifted her hand to knock, then changed her mind and tried the handle instead. The door was unlocked. She pushed it open a crack. "Paris."

Silence.

Drawing a steeling breath, she opened the door all the way, praying he hadn't disrobed yet. She would be in deep trouble if he had. She already entertained sufficient concerns regarding her self-control where Paris was concerned without the added lure of his mouthwatering body.

A fragrance of burning firewood welcomed her inside the softly lit bastion of masculinity. Royal blue draperies and mahogany furniture decorated the spacious room. Paris lay sprawled on a four-poster bed, fully clad, staring morosely at the canopy. Fire-glow and shadow played on his fine, patrician profile. She watched him for a while, her gaze hungering for every detail.

If the Earl of Ashby felt compelled to hide his appearance from the world, what should the rest of the population do, she mused, reside in subterranean holes? He was bloody gorgeous.

She closed the door, tossed her reticule and cape on a chair, and ambled inside.

"You shouldn't have come," he stated tersely. "Too many people will notice your absence from the ball."

She came to sit on the edge of the bed. "Are we back to worrying about my reputation?"

He wouldn't look at her.

"Paris . . ." She reached out to caress his cheek.

"Don't." He turned his face away from her.

She *would not* lose him. She took his hand in hers and brought it to her lips. "Forgive me."

"For Christ's sake, Isabel! Don't apologize to me." He pulled his hand free from her grasp, lunged up, and twisted sideways to sit beside her. With a sigh, he buried his fingers in his veil of dark hair, propping his elbows on his knees. "You had every right to want to know how I looked, to discover what you were getting yourself into. I . . . You deserve to know everything." He stared at her, the haunted vulnerability etching his eyes again. "Hanson spoke the truth. The French did call me a butcher. After each battle, we pounded after the runaways, trampling them with our hooves, slashing them on the ground, shooting them in the back . . . whatever was necessary to ensure we wouldn't encounter these same troops on a different battlefield the day after. We were so sick of this damned war." He got up and sauntered to a side table, where several bottles were juxtaposed with glasses and snifters. He selected a bottle and filled a glass.

Shaken by his confession, she fixed her gaze on his broad back. "When you said 'we'—"

He turned around, and she caught her breath. Just being able to scrutinize his countenance instead of guessing it sent her senses reeling. The myriad expressions playing over his striking features captivated and alarmed her at the same time. He was singularly beautiful, and contrary to the Golden Angel, Paris's brilliant emerald eyes, his flowing dark hair, his imposing frame, and innate intensity rendered him quite ferocious-looking. "I meant the entire regiment."

Horror rounded her eyes. "Dear Lord," she murmured. *Will, too.*

The lines in his forehead deepened. "I'm sorry, Izzy. I shouldn't have told you—"

"I don't understand. How could you and my brother become butchers?"

"How?" His expression turned as black as the mask he

usually wore. "Because Napoleon Bonaparte was the maddest butcher that ever lived. Someone had to stop him."

"That's true." She stared at him sorrowfully. "I am sorry it had to be you and Will."

"When I made my tour of the Continent years before the war, I watched from a balcony as General Bonaparte lined up cannons and blasted at a mob of disgruntled Parisians. He didn't send a few squadrons to drive back the hotheads. He brought cannons! He didn't even blink! He took eight-hundred-thousand men with him into Russia and brought back less than a hundred thousand! For years he massacred the poor Spanish people! He obliterated towns, villages, farms, families . . . For what? The glory of France? To enter his name in the history books?" Scowling, he took long breaths. "I'm not trying to justify or defend my actions. I've no excuse. I took lives, and for that I must pay. I must remember and pay every day for the rest of my life."

She regarded him in stupefied silence. If good men such as Will and Ashby had to become butchers to restore the peace in the world, then they lived in a sad world, indeed. "How you must have suffered, you and my poor brother. Brutality was distinctly against his sweet nature." She wiped the moisture coating her cheeks. "As I'm certain it is against yours," she amended.

"It's all right, Isabel. I know your high opinion of me, but in this instance, I may be forced to shatter it. Unlike Will, my past and character are a trifle more . . . complicated. Come. Let us sit over there." He indicated the pair of wingchairs by the fireplace. "I need to tell you something."

His serious tone unnerved her. She rose from the bed and approached him. Her hands were shaking; chills coursed through her veins. "May I have some of what you're drinking?"

"Certainly."

She took a seat close to the fire, watching him fill another glass with a bright amber fluid. He handed her a glass and dropped into the opposite chair, contemplating her over the rim of his. "I'm not certain how much you know about me, about my years as a young man on the town. I was not always the 'upstanding character' your brother brought into your home."

He'd been a scoundrel and a rake, everyone knew that, but she wasn't about to say it to his face. She sipped her drink and coughed. "Whiskey? How can you drink this . . . vile brew?"

"Like any good poison, one builds a taste for it with time." He drank some, his expression shuttering. "Will pulled me out of the black heart of London to which I had sunk. He introduced me to you lot"—he smiled fleetingly—"and gave me a purpose: 'vanquish the monster,' 'rid the world of the tyrant,' 'make England safe for our children.' His zeal was contagious."

"I remember his patriotic speeches," she said wistfully. "Mama was hysterical over his joining a regiment during wartime. Stilgoe offered to obtain him a cabinet post, but Will would hear none of it. Nothing they said had the power to sway him." She gave him a gimlet eye. "I often wondered why you chose this career. The military is for poor folk, younger sons, and lower gentry. Men with titles and fortune and no heirs don't risk their lives on battlefields."

"Do you deem it reasonable that the best educated men in England should sit in their clubs, twiddling their thumbs, while the underprivileged, men with families to feed and nothing to their names, the ones to whom England has given so little, shed their lowborn blood for the Ten Thousand's properties? Being a peer didn't absolve me of my duty to my country. It bound me to it. I had no dependent relatives to support, no family to mourn my loss. I was expendable."

Goodness. "You were *not* expendable."

"I thought that you, of all people, would understand."

"I do . . . What I meant was . . . well, to me you are not expendable, or replaceable."

His gaze burned into hers. "You may feel differently after you hear what I must tell you."

She braved another sip of whiskey and understood what he meant about acquired tastes as a rush of warmth banished some of the chill in her bones.

"We were talking about butchers." He knocked back his drink and poured himself another. "As you've pointed out, your excellent brother had a sweet nature about him. Kind, courteous, honorable. Everyone loved Will. I looked up to him. He was everything I always wanted to be. Until Sorauren." His expression darkened. "When I recovered, I began to enjoy the battles, the killing. I wanted the French to suffer as I did, to pay for the 'present' their guns had bestowed on my face. Since my hatred was directed at the enemy, my superiors failed to see a problem and continued lavishing praise, higher ranks, and medals on me. Everyone wanted Napoleon bested and I kept delivering the goods." He stared at the flames leaping in the fireplace. The hollowness of his tone, the bleakness written across his face tore at her. "I killed babies, Isabel, French boys not older than your sisters, who didn't know the first thing about fighting. All they knew was that they would follow their emperor to hell and back. Napoleon had the uncanny charisma to inspire the same people he'd barraged with cannons into marching to their deaths upon his command."

He sipped his whiskey broodingly. "The only person I felt sane with during that time was Will. In retrospect, I know it was a mixture of the bitterness I felt over what my injury had cost me and this deformed image looking back at me in the mirror that transformed me into an ugly version of myself— the monster I'd come to resemble. Will understood what I was going through even better than I did, and he refused to let me go on exacting punishment on myself. We talked for hours, for days, about everything and nothing at all. We talked about you." He hid his expression. "If I had a sister like you, I wouldn't want her to end up with someone like me."

It was an odd statement, which led her to wonder whether Will—who'd known precisely who and what his best friend was—thought her and Ashby well-matched. In spite of everything.

"Would you have told me any of this if Hanson hadn't—?"

"Probably not."

"Why didn't you say nor do anything when he insulted you?"

His emerald gaze glinted with fury. "Because I wanted to bloody him—and I couldn't."

She stared at him questioningly.

"After Waterloo, I . . . vowed that I would never, ever do violence again." Iron-hard resolve solidified his features. "I don't handle weaponry. I don't raise my hand with aggression in mind, no matter the provocation. I'm a man of peace." Clearly he felt the weight of his vow keenly.

"You disregarded his provocations out of strength, not weakness," she concluded, sending him a small, gentle smile. "After everything you just told me, I still think highly of you."

"You won't once I tell you how your brother died." Self-loathing and sorrow looked back at her. "I killed Will. I put a ball in his head and didn't have the mettle to do the same to myself."

A punch of ice knocked the air out of her lungs. "What?" she cried, horror-struck. "Why?"

So he told her, recounting the last three days in her brother's life, spent near a small village in Belgium called Waterloo two years ago. As he spoke, vivid scenes of savagery, anguish, and despair came to life in her mind, as if she had been there herself. He didn't spare her sensitivities; he laid bare the whole truth, unburdening the ugly secrets tormenting his soul. She was grateful for his honesty, because worse than losing her dear brother was the not knowing how he died and not being there when he needed her. But Paris had been there for Will. As he took her back in time with him to the field of carnage, she could finally say goodbye to William Daniel Aubrey.

When he finished his tale, her face was wet and a pain so deep wrenched her heart that she couldn't speak. He killed Will—a mercy killing, but he was the one who shot her brother in the head, nonetheless. Unshed tears glimmered in Paris's eyes. "I sat there with Will in my arms," he whispered, "pressing the muzzle to my head, and I couldn't do it. I didn't have the courage to do it. A bloody coward." He shut his eyes, monstrous guilt and misery furrowing his face.

"You're not a coward," she said softly, sniffling. "It doesn't take courage to kill oneself. It is an act of despair. Will knew he was dying. My poor brother." She covered her face and wept.

For several moments the only sounds thickening the air were of logs being consumed by fire and her soft sobs. Then a broken murmur came from the vicinity of her knees. "I am sorry, Isabel. I'm so very, very sorry. Your brother was the finest man . . . I'm so sorry." He squatted at her feet, his eyes begging forgiveness. With a terrible sob, she collapsed in his arms and buried her face in his neck. He embraced her to him, shock thickening his voice. "You don't hate me?"

She raised teary eyes to his. "Hate you? You took my brother's pain upon yourself. I would never have had the courage to do what you did. Will died in the best of hands, the bravest, most honorable hands . . ." She cried on his shoulder, beset with longing and grief for her Will.

"I made so many mistakes. If I hadn't sent Will to the center, if I had ordered Ellis to fetch a cart instead of sending him off with that soldier—"

"Don't." She lifted her head from his shoulder and commanded his rueful gaze. "It's over. Stop blaming yourself. You saved another soldier's life. Will could have died anyway, alone in the dark, prey to the scavengers and the elements, but he didn't, because he had you. How many men do you suppose went in search of their dying friends after three days of grueling battles and sat with them while they drew their last breaths?" It astonished her that she could still speak lucidly while inside she was dying a little all over again, while infinite tears swam in her eyes.

Paris's eyes were none too dry, either. Who'd ever come up with the stupid assertion that men didn't cry? Real men cried, quietly, privately, as Paris did, because his heart was crying.

"Do you understand why I didn't come to call on you upon my return?" he asked quietly.

"What I don't understand," she whispered, "is how you even considered killing yourself."

He stared at her. "Without Will, I had no one. Just . . . blackness."

His loneliness clawed at her heart. He was like a rock, she realized: Steadfast and strong, yet frozen in his ill-fated solitude. She laid her hand on his cheek. "You had me."

As their gazes locked in silence, something rare and extraordinary happened between them: She felt his soul, and he felt hers. Their spirits touched. It was a bond forged by their mutual love and grief for her brother, as though Will himself had swept by to unite them and then vanished.

He touched his lips to hers. His kiss was sublime, purified of lust, distilled with emotion. Then, before it had even begun, it was over. He ended it.

"Paris."

His jaw clenched. "Look at me," he rasped, his tone harsh and commanding. "Is this what you wish to encounter every day for the rest of your life? *This gargoyle?*"

This time he didn't recoil as she traced each and every scar. She met his hard gaze, a smile of the heart tugging at the corners of her mouth. "Yes. I'd like that very much."

"You deserve better than me, Izzy—a whole man, a

younger one, a man who shares your passions, your vivacity, your enthusiasm . . . I'm not much of anything anymore."

Tears threatened to obscure her vision. She did feel sorry for him, a man tormented by the horrors of war, austere and alone, living in his private hell, bereft of family and friends. She wanted to become his family and heal his torments. Yet her motives were anything but altruistic. She coveted him— every fierce inch of him—for herself. Summoning her courage, she decided to risk a third and ultimate rejection. "I love you, Paris. I've always loved you, no one else. Don't ask me to choose another man over you. I won't be able to bear it."

"Love alters when it alteration finds, remember? I'm much altered, Isabel."

His resigned tone of voice sent one diamond-like tear cascading down her cheek. "'Love is not love which alters when it alteration finds, or bends with the remover to remove,'" she recited softly. "'Oh, no; it is an ever-fixed mark, that looks on tempests, and is never shaken.'"

For an interminable moment he just looked at her, his breath coming hot and swift. Then a violent, irrepressible need sparked his irises. "I want to be selfish. How I want to be selfish . . ." He captured her mouth in the hottest, deepest, hungriest kiss, igniting a furnace of sensations and feelings inside of her. He tasted of whiskey and passion, smelled of forests and rain, felt solid, warm, and strong, and she wanted to crawl into him and never emerge. She kissed him with pure abandon, terrified that if she let go of him now, he would be lost to her forever. Her arms locked around his neck, she rained countless kisses on his brow and cheeks, branding every scar with love and banishing the memory of pain. "You don't find me repulsive?" he murmured hopefully.

"Repulsive?" She smiled in astonishment. "Are you blind? Should I hold a mirror to your face? My darling, you are the handsomest man in England!"

He drew back, scowling. "Perhaps you need spectacles?"

"There is nothing wrong with my eyesight." She chuckled.

He eyed her critically. "It is a miracle you haven't walked into a lamppost yet."

"You're a lunatic—" He swallowed her mirth with a rougher, more arousing kiss, one with a mission to seduce. Her body responded as kindling to a spark, desire combusting in her veins.

He removed her silvery tiara, and a cloud of burnished curls in sunset colors puffed out and tumbled to her waist in glorious disarray. "My God, Isabel." He caressed her undulating cascade of silken locks, his eyes marveling at the sight before him. "You *are* a lioness."

His open admiration brought a blush to her cheeks. "Female lions don't have manes."

"Mine does. You are beautiful," he whispered. "You must know that."

Her blush deepened. "Beauty is in the eyes of the beholder."

"Not in your case." He cupped her face. "You are every man's dream, Isabel Jane."

This from the man who could have any woman he wanted. She wondered if other women felt as electrified by his attentions, or as privileged to have attracted them. Her heart was full to bursting. There was no other man like him, and she sensed, she hoped that he was hers.

"Isabel, I doubt I'll be able to let you go tonight."

"You were about to send me away forever a moment ago."

"That moment is long gone." He pushed to his feet, drawing her up with him. She swayed and he had to steady her with a supportive hand around her waist. "You are not drunk, are you?"

"No, I—"

"Touch the tip of your nose. Stand on one foot."

"Am I joining the circus?" she asked wryly.

He pinned her to him. "You're joining me in bed. Are you coherent?"

She nodded, his sultry announcement rendering her speechless and weak in the knees.

"Do you want to be with me, to make love with me?"

"I do," she whispered, seduced by the promise in his enigmatically glittering eyes. She had waited seven years to become woman enough for him. Tonight was the night.

His hand delved beneath the weight of her hair, curled around her nape, and drew her for a long-drawn-out kiss. Her eyelashes sank as he kissed her softly, sweetly, slowly. *Goodness*. She all but oozed to the floor. "I need you," he murmured. "I need you so badly."

"I need you, too," she said, trembling a little, and yet he made her feel so cosseted and safe in his embrace, it was addictive.

Holding her gaze, he shrugged out of his coat and then tugged on his neckcloth.

"Let me do this," she whispered, taking over. She'd been fantasizing about his body ever since she'd spied on him laboring in the cellar, shirtless and Herculean. Her hands shook, yet she savored every little thrill. "You thought I was a milk and water thing, didn't you? Who'd balk at your battle scars, scorn you for bloodying your hands to keep the rest of us safe in our beds, and blame you for my brother's death. You underestimated me, Ashby. Shame on you."

He smiled glumly. "What do you Aubreys have flowing in your veins?"

"Exactly what you do—which is why my brother admired you so much. Why *I* love you so much." She exposed his throat and pressed her lips to his warm, smooth skin.

He shut his eyes as she kissed him sensually, devouring his neck. "This feels so good."

She dispensed with the waistcoat and started to unbutton his lawn shirt. Beneath it, his chest felt hewn of steel, yet warm and rippling with muscle. In her haste to bare it, she tore off one of his buttons, making him chuckle. "Why don't you rip it altogether?" he suggested huskily.

Smiling, she pushed the shirt open and splayed her fingers across the powerful expanse of his chest. *My goodness.* No wonder so many women had lusted after him, she thought. He was masterfully wrought to be worshiped by her persuasion, the finest specimen of masculinity.

He watched her beneath long eyelashes as she explored his chest, caressing and kissing. He was an embarrassment of riches, and she felt painfully inexperienced to deal with all this loot. Recalling how he'd pleasured her in the office, she flicked his flat, velvety nipple with the tip of her tongue until it stiffened into a tiny kernel. A groan of satisfaction resounded in his throat.

The knowledge that he no longer moved in Society, that she had no competition over him, instilled her with confidence, which in turn emboldened her. She smoothed her hands along his hard abdomen, marveling at the perfectly symmetrical dices carved into his flesh. The laborers she'd seen without their shirts on were hairy brutes; Paris's torso was elegantly lean and hairless.

Her gaze traveled lower to the unmentionable part of his anatomy, the part she'd brazenly fondled in the gazebo. It seemed to be in the same condition: very large and very conspicuous. Once again her deplorable curiosity reared its naughty head. She unbuttoned his breeches, letting them slide down his hips and expose the wing-shaped muscles of his waist. She sought his eyes.

"Go on," he breathed haggardly, his voice sounding hoarse. "Touch me, Isabel."

Sustaining his heavy-lidded gaze, her heart beating staccato, she pushed her hand inside his drawers. A thick, hard rod jolted at her touch. She snatched her hand back. "It moved."

He made a choking sound. "I'd better concentrate on you awhile before it shoots, too."

"No, I want to touch you," she whispered, seeking reassurance in his eyes. They resembled sparkling green pools of yearning—and it was all the encouragement she needed. Observing his taut face, she put her hand inside his drawers again and clasped him. He felt warm and smooth, growing thicker and harder as she caressed his silken length. Paris cursed softly, an expression of agony crossing his features; his whole body tensed. *Oh, dear*. "Tell me what to do."

"You are doing just fine on your own," he groaned, his chest heaving. "Just . . . stroke me."

She did, her confidence maturing along with his reactions. "What is it called, this organ?" she inquired, feeling terribly brazen and free. "It wasn't in the curriculum in finishing school."

"Mr. Jones, er . . . a penis." His voice was strained, his breathing harsh. He stood very still.

"Mr. Jones?" She wrung it slowly. "Nice to make your acquaintance, sir."

Paris cringed, grating his teeth. "Impudent witch. You're enjoying this, aren't you?"

Her eyes flew to his. "Aren't you enjoying this?"

He sent her a heated look. "Can't you tell?"

Fascinated by his male member, she thumbed the rounded crest, wringing a shudder from Paris. "Should I go slower? Faster? Farther?" Her hand slid all the way to the soft sac at its root.

"*Sweet Lucifer*." His head fell back as he dragged in a hissing breath. This was the essence of power, Isabel decided, being in command of a man like Ashby, allowed to do whatever she pleased with him. He gripped her shoulder. "If you do it any better, I'll go off in your hand. I'm mad for you, and Mr. Jones has been suffering of a very long drought, himself."

"Poor fellow," she mocked tartly. "No opera singer in sight for months."

His eyes snapped open. "Have you been listening to idle gossip? No, you needn't answer. I can't blame you if you did. God knows I've been feeding the gossipmongers with material for years." He removed her hand from his drawers. "My turn now," he murmured, undoing the front clasps of her fairy costume. The multi-hued material spilled to her feet, exposing her tightly laced corset. "My, aren't you wrapped up like some delectable dessert." He turned her around.

"That's what Major Macalister said." Kicking off her slippers, she gripped a bedpost for support as he loosened the laces. "What is it with you men, always comparing women to food?"

"I don't know about other men, but you, my sweet angel, are decidedly edible." He licked her ear. "I should know. I've had an appetizer."

Her spine liquefied as she recalled the wickedly satisfying pleasure his mouth had given her. She couldn't help wondering what pleasures awaited her still. Somewhere at the back of her mind she could hear Iris and Sophie's matronly voices scolding her for not waiting until she was properly wedded. Unfortunately, she couldn't wait any longer. He'd been priming her body to engage in sin with him for weeks, and her every nerve-ending hummed in anticipation.

Once her corset slid off, his arms circled her waist, pressing her back to his bare chest, her bottom to his aroused groins. With only her silk chemise on, his embrace felt very intimate. "Is Macalister still tomcatting after you? Are you welcoming his attentions?"

"Ryan and I have an understanding," she explained, out of breath.

He swept her wild mane aside to kiss the curve of her neck, while kneading one breast over her thin chemise, his thumb rubbing her nipple to raw sensitivity. "What sort of understanding? I'd hate to break my vow of non-violence to rid myself of this heap of competition."

"It's nothing like that. It concerns my friend, Iris." She sighed, letting her head drop back onto his shoulder. Desire blazed through her, manifesting itself in the warm moisture issuing between her thighs, where she most ached for his magical touch.

"Lady Chilton? She's a married woman."

Though she would hardly criticize Iris for having an affair with another man, when she had to constantly endure Chilton's cruelties, the flinty edge in Paris's voice told Isabel that he would most likely construe her opinion on this matter as a wide-ranging approbation of infidelity. "It's an old feud, that's all. They've known each other for years."

"I see." He hooked his fingers in the chemise's straps and tugged them off her shoulders, exposing her torso. "Isabel." He groaned against her ear as he filled his hands with her soft flesh, molding and squeezing her bare breasts covetously. "I've waited so long for this. *For you.*"

He moved his hand down her belly, beneath the folds of the chemise clinging to her hips, and caressed her all the way to the moist cleft between her legs. Lava flowed out of her. She tilted her face to his, and he caught her mouth with a languorous kiss. His whiskey-spiced tongue tangled with hers in the most sensual of kisses; the large palm of his hand fondled her breast until her nipple puckered and tingled; and all the while he stroked her, intensifying her desire until her body clamored for his. She melted against him, losing herself in their trancelike embrace. She moaned and swayed, begging for more, yet he was determined to prolong the wait, arousing her with meticulous patience, dissolving her bones until she could barely stand on her feet.

"Don't move," he whispered, releasing her unexpectedly. If it weren't for the bedpost, she would have spilled to the floor. He sat down in one of the wingchairs and yanked off his boots. He stood, and without ceremony, shed his breeches and drawers in one motion.

Isabel's eyes grew round as saucers. He had sterling physical proportions: his magnificent broad-shouldered torso tapered to narrow hips and the longest legs, lean and muscular, covered with a sprinkle of dark hair. But it was the sword-like Mr. Jones saluting her from a springy nest of hair amid his groins that sent her heart thundering in her chest. *My goodness,* she thought.

"Let go of your armor, golden fairy. Let me look at you." His voice brooked no refusal.

Mustering her resolve, she shimmied out of her chemise and stool tall and nude before him.

His gaze roamed her ravenously, heating her skin. "You're the loveliest, most desirable woman I've ever laid eyes on," he declared huskily. He lifted his whiskey glass from the mantel and ambled toward her, all man and irresistible, his skin dyed bronze by the firelight.

The sexual potency he exuded was magnetic. The scent of his skin filled her, beckoning her to caress the velvety width of his shoulders down to his sculpted chest. Absorbed in the feel of him, she hardly sensed the drop of whiskey plopping on her skin and rolling to her nipple.

With perfect timing, he bent his head and suckled the bead and her nipple into his sultry mouth. She shut her eyes, relishing the exquisite turmoil he kindled in her. This was rapture—the heat of his hands and mouth on her, the rasping caresses of his tongue . . .

Paris released her breast to gulp the last mouthful of whiskey and tossed the empty glass on the chair. His mouth covered hers, and warm whiskey flowed from his tongue to hers. Their kiss became richer, needful. He caught her waist and lifted her up. She twined her limbs about him, her breasts compressing against his chest. Her pulse raced. She felt weightless in his arms.

He strode to the bed and lowered them both to its center. They lay chest to chest, heartbeat to heartbeat. He stared at her as if it were for the first time, his dark hair spilling around his face, his glinting gaze holding hers completely in thrall. The possessive gleam in his eyes reflected more than lust— it radiated a need of the spirit, a hunger so great, she had serious concerns whether she would be able to satisfy it. "Why me?" she whispered. "Why did you let me in?"

"You don't know?"

She shook her head. "Was it because of Will?"

"No."

"Why, then?" Women had been throwing themselves at him for years. Why was she the fortunate one? Was it because he was a recluse now and she had made herself available, or was it something more meaningful?

He grinned wickedly. "Are you always chatty when you're nervous?" When she began to protest, he silenced her with a kiss. "I'm nervous. I've never been with a woman who meant this much to me before. I want to make tonight the finest night of your life, for it's certainly mine."

She swept the shock of dark hair off his brow, unveiling his uncommonly handsome face. "You still haven't answered my question, Paris. Why did you choose me and not someone else?"

"You chose me, Isabel." He slanted his mouth across hers, seducing her, absorbing her, until she forgot her question. Immersed in the heady pleasure of lying beneath him, kissing him, breathing him in, she explored his body with her hands and legs, and realized she'd reached heaven. Who would have guessed that one day she would find herself in his bed, the focus of his admiration, about to make love with him? He made her feel soft and feminine and natural, as she imagined Adam and Eve had felt in the Garden of Eden. Even the black serpent was there, taking shape in the erotic undercurrent winding between their entwined bodies, goading and enticing.

His mouth broke from hers to travel lower. He kissed her throat, the velvet of his tongue dragging along her skin to tantalize a dusky pink nipple with slow ministrations. His lips closed around it and tugged, shooting fire to her loins. His mouth drifted farther, his dark head a stark contrast to the alabaster flesh beneath him, torturing and worshiping her trembling body. Finding the silk stockings attached to her legs, he peeled them off one by one, kissing every patch of skin he exposed. He spread her knees wide apart, kissed a path of fire up her thigh, and tasted her.

With a cry of need, she lurched off the bed in a perfect arc, writhing and tossing her head. She tugged on his thick hair, her throaty moans begging for more, for something she couldn't put into words, yet she knew it existed. The unappeasable desire raging in her blood confirmed it.

He didn't guide her toward the light this time. Instead, he pushed upward, coming to hover above her. His sea eyes reflected bottomless need; beads of perspiration clung to his forehead.

Submerged in a haze of yearning, she felt him entering the slick, aroused flesh between her legs, heard him groaning her name. . . "Yes," she whispered back, her senses filled to the point of intoxication. Her arms slid around his neck; her body rose to his as if it ached to receive him.

"Your delicious musk drove me a little crazy," he confessed. "I can't wait anymore. I need you now. Take me inside you, sweetness. Open yourself to me." He shifted his weight to his forearms and drove his hips forward, taking her in one swift almost savage motion.

The sudden fullness, the pressure, the joining of their bodies overwhelmed her, blotting out the fleeting stab of pain. She felt utterly possessed by his invasion, subject to his will and superior strength, and she loved it, for therein lay her power: the completion her softer body offered and of which he hungered to avail himself. Her loins melted to receive him, drawing him deeper, enfolding him with luscious heat. Sweet, dark pleasure flowed in her veins, awakening the sensual wanton, who blazed with an appetite so rampant that her body shook with it. Clawing at his back, she pressed her hips to his, urging him on. "More, Paris, more . . ."

His chest rose and fell with his laborious breathing. "You're not in pain?"

She moaned. "*I'm in agony*. I feel as if I'm about to die. What sort of torture is this?"

"The best sort, which is why it's called the 'little death.'" He pulled out and repeated the thrusting motion, plunging harder, deeper. Her arms and legs wrapped around him like a vine, she welcomed his escalating rhythm with guttural sounds that kept pouring from her throat. His hips pumped strongly against her, rocking them faster, relentlessly driving in and out, pushing her toward oblivion. The more aggressively he pounded into her the more she ached for him. His groans filled her ear. Her moans became cries of urgency. Her insides coiled tighter and tighter. She shuddered all at once, crying out her pleasure, as her senses submerged in a pool of bliss.

He never broke rhythm. His eyes burned through her, devouring and insatiable. He moved against her like a man possessed, thrusting repeatedly, pulling her back into the storm with him. Semi-delirious, her body undulated with his, as tidal waves about to crush onto a golden shore.

"Don't stop . . ." She moaned, gripping his shoulders, wanting, *needing* . . .

A growl tore from his chest. "*Christ*. You're killing me." He stilled against her, panting.

Gasping in protest, she tumbled back to earth. "What's wrong? What am I doing wrong?"

"Nothing. It's me. I can't hold back." He hung his head,

blowing out his breath. "If I move, it's over, I'll be spent, and I don't want it to end."

"Is it because of the 'drought situation'?"

"No, angel." He chuckled. "It's because you feel too bloody good, like a sweet, hot glove, wringing me toward ecstasy. I feel like I'm burning inside you."

Ah. "It's a compliment."

"It's a confession," he whispered. He rolled onto his back with her, positioning her astride him. His large hands planted on her hips, he set her into motion. "Ride me, Isabel."

Impaled on top of him, she found her pace with an instinct she had no idea she possessed. Her pleasure was instant and intense; the sense of power was unimaginably thrilling. He watched her intently, riveted. "If you could only see how gloriously beautiful you are right now . . ."

She was thinking the same thing. Sprawled on his back beneath her, he looked like a pirate, his dark mat of hair spread on a pillow, his body made for sin, his green eyes ablaze. He wrapped a hand around her nape and pulled her forward for a kiss. Her taut nipples grazed his chest as his tongue plundered her mouth. Her hips continued to roll atop him, increasing the friction between their coupling bodies. Her eyes half shut, she pushed upward and concentrated on conquering the illusive peak, shifting experimentally. Heat filled her belly. She moaned. "*Yes*, oh God, yes . . ."

He raised his hands and fondled her bobbing breasts. "Ride me harder," he whispered, as he thrust his hips up, again and again. It was the most turbulent, exhilarating ride of her life. His hands sailed down the curvy sides of her body and cupped her buttocks. He increased her pace, spearing her with forceful plunges. He groaned. "*Yes*. Like that. Faster."

She tossed her head back and galloped, curls whipping at her back, every responsive nerve in her body pulsing with tension, every muscle bunching and straining. A tremendous explosion was building inside of her, squeezing her like a fist, thundering toward its peak, screaming to be released . . . A cry of surrender tore from her throat as raw pleasure surged through her quivering body, saturating her mind with exquisite contentment, stronger, higher than ever before.

Paris caught her to him, flipped her over, and buried himself deep inside her one last time. As his powerful body tensed over her, his growl of surrender was her name spilling from his lips.

A sweet afterglow descended on her, lulling her to sleep. Slick with sweat, she embraced his limp, heavy frame, her fast heartbeats echoing his. She wanted to stay that way forever.

He rolled to his back, his arms gripping her to him, as though he were afraid she might flit away. "You belong to me now," he stated vehemently, covering her damp face with feather light kisses. "You're mine, Isabel. Mine."

Chapter Twenty-One

Ruin hath taught me thus to ruminate—
That Time will come and take my love away.
This thought is as a death, which cannot choose
But weep to have that which it fears to lose.
—William Shakespeare: Sonnet LXIV

What was this goddess of love and warmth and light doing with him?

Ashby couldn't take his eyes off Isabel's innocent countenance as she slept peacefully in his arms, lit solely by the fire dimming on the hearth, her legs tangled with his under the covers. He finally knew what it meant to make love to a woman. It wasn't about the actual act—though he'd come harder and richer than ever before—but about what transpired between them prior to, during, and after: The companionship, the connection, sharing the experience together, as one, not as two separate beings absorbed in themselves, lost in their own little worlds.

With Isabel, for the first time in his life, he *felt* the person he was with: He breathed her, knew her, and tasted her on his tongue; he experienced what she did, because he cared, because he wanted to know her sweet body better than he knew his own. Because she bewitched him.

Even now, he wanted her again. She was like a drug, a powerful opiate, and he had become a Dragon Chaser. Usually, at this stage, he was making excuses and hunting for his boots, if he weren't already gone. This woman . . . she held his soul in shackles. She ruled his thoughts. She intoxicated his senses. She humbled his pride. She made him smile. She aroused him to the point of wanting to make love to her constantly, repeatedly, until he figured out why she loved him.

Isabel loved him. She loved his ugly scars and his black past and didn't balk at anything he threw in her path. It was ungraspable, bordering nigh on a miracle. What was there to love? What was there to admire? His generosity? Since his self-imprisonment, he'd trebled his fortune and had blunt to spare. His kindness? He was kind to those he liked. His gentleness? She hadn't seen him on a battlefield with a saber in hand and blood smeared on his face and jacket. His act of mercy toward Will? Her brother saved his life; whereas he failed Will at his crucial moment.

It seemed to him that Isabel had created a superior image of him in her mind and had fallen in love with her own creation. Nothing else explained the vision of loveliness resting on his shoulder. He was terrified that once she awoke, she would see the real him, realize her mistake, and flee as fast as her legs could carry her. Therefore, as a precaution, he would let her sleep till morn, and when she opened her eyes to a new day and discovered she'd spent the night with him, there would be no going back. Isabel Jane Aubrey would finally be his. Irreversibly.

The grandfather clock in the foyer rang three times. His angel stirred. *Damnation.*

"Hmm." She smiled sleepily, her eyelashes fluttering in an attempt to open her eyes.

"Shh," he murmured, kissing her eyelids, stroking her hair.

With a sigh of contentment, she snuggled closer to his chest and drifted back to sleep. He exhaled carefully. He was determined to stay awake. He didn't want to miss a single sigh she emitted, a single moment of feeling her warm, slender body lying flush against him, soft and quiet, ensconced in dreams.

He never dreamed; he was subject to nightmares. The last thing he wished to put Isabel through was awakening to a bloodcurdling scream and a sweat-drenched body shuddering beside her with haunted eyes and a parched throat. One of his lovers had accused him once of rousing her quite rudely— wild-eyed and pressing a dagger to her throat. It was one of the rare few times in which he'd allowed himself a catnap after sex. He'd never repeated that mistake again.

A log popped in the fireside. She stirred again, mumbling unintelligible words. Suddenly she bolted to a sitting position and stared blankly into space. He hesitated over whether to coax her back to sleep or simply leave her be, for fear he might snap her back into full awareness. Her gaze swerved toward the undraped windows. "It's stopped raining," she remarked, unconsciously stretching her arms over her head and letting the blanket drop to her lap. "What time is it?"

He sat up beside her, entranced by the sight of her nude upper body silhouetted against the silvery moonlight. Her tangled curls shimmered down her willowy back; her perfect breasts jutted out over her flat belly like ripe pears. His semi-arousal swelled to a full-blooded erection.

"It's three o'clock," he murmured. Temptation overtook him. He reached out and outlined one breast with his fingertips, then traced the contour of her dusky nipple with acute absorption.

She allowed her head to fall back, her eyelashes sinking languidly, her cherry lips parting on a sigh—and it was all he could do to keep from pouncing on her like a randy bull.

Clamping down on his lust, he ran the back of his fingers along the milky skin of her throat down to her breastbone, drinking the view of her profile—those full, tempting lips, the pert little nose, the smooth brow. He was not immune to the power and beauty of her youth, and the realization resurrected his earlier fears. What if she deserted him? No Isabel and no capacity to off himself left him cold and shaking inside. He often wondered what his life could have been like if his father hadn't loved his mother to distraction. The story he told Isabel about his parents' death was the official version, the one Phipps had made up after his father's solicitor had crossed the servants hands with silver to secure their silence. He'd stumbled upon the truth years later, when the previous butler died. The nasty old bugger left the hush money in a box at his deathbed, with a note for the young earl detailing the true horrid version of the affair and claiming he couldn't in clear conscience pass on to the other life without speaking the truth.

That was a day to remember. He was packing off for Cambridge, hardly a man. No wonder he chose the black path to rakedom. That day he resolved *not* to model his life after his estimable albeit unfortunate father. And yet, here he was. Retrospectively, perhaps his father was better off dead, instead of living like a madman, caged in his secret hell—which was what awaited Ashby if his goddess of love and warmth and light abandoned him to his fate.

"It's terribly late. I should leave."

His hand curled around the side of her neck and drew her closer. "Stay with me."

She smiled at him, her eyes large and luminous in the dying glow of the fire. "My mother will have a fit if she wakes up to discover my bed has not been slept in. She will dispatch a thousand runners to locate me, and when they eventually find me here—"

"I meant . . . stay with me forever." He swallowed hard. "Live with me, marry me, be my countess . . ." His heart hammered as he waited on tenterhooks for her response.

She drew back, her eyelashes fluttering. "Are you . . . proposing marriage to me?"

"I thought I just did."

A huge smile broke on her face. "I'm not dreaming, am I? I would hate to wake up and discover this was all a dream."

Dazed with euphoria, he playfully pinched her cheek. "Will you marry me, Miss Aubrey?"

Her shriek of delight was a song to his ears. "Yes, I'll marry you!" She threw her arms around his neck, toppling them onto the pillows, and smothered him with kisses.

Perhaps he was dreaming. He swept soft tendrils off her face, his throat clogged. "Thank you. You've saved me." He kissed her with all the aching need in his soul. When she lifted her head to draw in a breath, he asked, "Are you sore?"

"Sore? No. Why?"

"Because I'm not nearly done with you tonight." He pushed her onto her back and lay atop her. He was so hard for her; he worried he might go off between their pressed bodies. His knee forced apart her satiny thighs. His hand reached between them to prime her body to his.

"No, I can't." Laughing, she shoved him aside and scrambled to the edge of the bed.

"Come back here, agile cat!" He caught her hips just as she started to rise and pulled her back. With a shriek of laughter, she landed on her belly, choking out a protest. He covered her, breathing in her ear, "You are not going anywhere. You belong to me now." Lodged against the enticing cleft of her bottom, Mr. Jones increased to maximum proportions.

"Mama will be hysterical," she blurted out throatily, as he slid his hand around and beneath her and fingered the tiny nub that was sure to make her reconsider.

"She won't be up till noon." He continued tantalizing the pink bud that was the heart of her desire, knowing that if he weren't on the brink of losing his control, he'd be rolling her raspberry on his tongue and making her pulsate with pleasure several times in quick succession.

Her breathing became rugged and swift. She melted against his hand like a river of fire. He raised her pelvis and penetrated her slick feminine tunnel from behind. They groaned in unison.

"Yes." She moaned, as her lithe body undulated with his in perfect accord. "Oh, Paris."

This was paradise, he thought, moving inside her, engulfed in her vanilla scent, knowing she belonged solely to him. He shut his eyes and accelerated his rhythm. He was going up in flames. Her little whimpers of pleasure, the eager pumping of her bottom against his groins catapulted him over the edge. He drove into her like an iron ram, losing himself entirely in her snug heat. His heart pounded in his chest, in his ears, in his blood. Her whimpers turned to cries of culmination. She pulled him in, consumed him, convulsed around him, milked his release . . .

Sweat broke on his brow as he fought the urge to explode. He groaned in torment, delaying his orgasm as long as he could, and the instant he felt the shudders of climax rock her, draining the tension from her body, he erupted with a powerful jet that left him headily sated and gasping for air. He collapsed over her, lax and spent. He couldn't move to save his life.

Isabel found his hand, laced her fingers through his, and pressed it to her lips.

"Am I squishing you?" he asked, struggling to catch his breath.

"No. Stay," she whispered. "I want to memorize the feeling."

He rested his cheek over hers. "What feeling?"

"Perfection."

His heart stirred in his chest. "This is perfection." And so much more than he deserved that it scared him senseless. He couldn't believe his good fortune. He knew she was passionate—and would have been content to learn she wasn't the sort who disliked sex—but he never realized just how fiery she was. He had never known a female more comfortable in her skin or more natural about the act of lovemaking. Visions of long, sweaty, messy nights steamed his brain. *She was made for me*, his inner self acknowledged with a smile, but another voice, the one that wouldn't shut up, filled him with a terrible foreboding. Suddenly he knew what the perfect solution was.

"Don't you dare move a muscle." He vaulted out of bed and sauntered to his writing table.

"Where are you off to?" she called after him, turning her head on the pillow.

"Nowhere." He lit a beeswax candle and opened a drawer. He gathered a few sheaves of foolscap, a quill, and ink, and returned to the bed. He set the candle on the console, sprawled on his stomach, and placed the sheet of paper on her curvy back. He dipped the quill in the inkwell, cleared his throat, and started scribbling. "My Dear Lady Aubrey—"

"What are you doing?" She giggled, craning her head past her shoulder. "It tickles."

" . . . although the following may come as a surprise to you, I pray your ladyship will be as joyful as I am upon learning that early this morning your delicious, er . . . strike that out . . ."

"Paris!" Isabel choked with laughter.

"Hush. And stay still." He planted a kiss on her beautiful bare bottom, making her wriggle and giggle. "Well then, where was I? Ah, yes. 'Your delightful daughter has kindly accepted my offer of marriage.'" He punctuated his sentence and accidentally punctured the paper, a slip that resulted in an ink dot on Isabel's ivory skin and more peals of laughter. "'We have spent a most scandalous night of pleasure together in my bed and are on our way to Gretna Green—'"

"*What?*" Isabel flipped over, snatching the sheet of paper. It was only thanks to his sharp instincts that the ink didn't tip aside and spill across the bed linen. He set the writing tools on the console and lay back beside her, hands tucked behind his head, grinning as she carefully perused his letter. "You didn't write any of that scandalous nonsense."

"Nonsense?" He pulled her to lie flush on top of him. "If that's your interpretation of what we did tonight, I'll rectify it at once." He nuzzled the graceful curve of her neck while his hands roamed her silken skin. He wasn't surprised he craved her again. She had transformed him into a lust-crazed savage. It seemed imperative that he feel her body against his all the time.

With a sigh, she rested her head on his shoulder. "I really do need to return home now."

"No, you don't. I'll send the letter to your mother, and we'll take my coach to Scotland."

Her head came up. "Tonight?"

"Or first thing in the morning. Whatever you wish."

"You are serious, aren't you?"

"Very serious. We'll elope."

Disapproval crossed her brow. "But I don't want to elope. And there's no reason to."

"There might be."

Her eyes widened in shock. "A baby? Oh, no, no, no."

His chest constricted. "Don't you want to have babies with me, Isabel, a family?" *A home, with laughter and mayhem and life*, with Izzy—what he always wanted but didn't dare hope for.

"I do, but we don't know . . . yet, and I should like to have a proper courtship first."

"A proper courtship lasts a year, if not two, and I don't want to wait."

"Why not?"

Because you could change your mind. "I'm too old to wait. By the time we marry, I'll be a doddering old fool, who can't take his wife to bed, or lift his children. I'll be a papa-grandpapa."

Her lips twitched. "Seeking refuge in decrepitude, are we? Ha, ha."

He cupped her face in his hands. "So lovely, you are." She opened her mouth to protest and he kissed her. "I want to marry you. I want to make love to you every night, every morning, in the afternoon, and spend the rest of my life with you. Why must we wait, for Christ's sake?"

A wrinkle of chagrin formed between her eyebrows. She sat up, frowning. "Because I want my family with me when we marry. I want a church wedding with flowers and a champagne reception with friends around us, wishing us very happy."

Her simple request lit a burn of frustration in him. "How many times must I tell you that I do not go out in public?" he snapped, more harshly then he intended.

She stared at him frostily. "Are we to sneak about forever, then?"

He had no good answer to that.

"I want a respectable courtship, Paris, and I don't care to be ruined!"

The burn grew hotter. "You are ruined. I've compromised you quite thoroughly tonight."

"No one but us knows anything about it, but if we elope—"

He sat up. "When we return from Gretna Green a married couple, the rumors will peter out. You will be a properly married lady of rank. No one would dare cut the Countess of Ashby in public or otherwise. Furthermore, you could come live with me straight away. Why wait?"

"You didn't elope the first time you were engaged, did you?"

Hell and damnation. "If I did, we wouldn't be here now, would we?" And thank God he hadn't, for it would have been the worst mistake of his life. "Postponing our marriage could lead to all sorts of trouble. Trust me. I've been through this before. It wasn't a pleasant experience."

Her eyes narrowed. "Who was she, your former betrothed?"

"The wrong woman." He couldn't risk telling her about

Olivia. She'd rush over to question his former fiancée, and he dreaded to imagine what lies the cold-blooded bitch would fill Isabel's ears with. Olivia would pounce on the opportunity to separate them.

"Am I the 'right woman'?" she inquired with deceptive sweetness.

He held her gaze. "Yes."

"Then why won't you do this for me?" she exploded. "Why can't we have a lovely, normal wedding? Why must we hide from the world?" She waited for his response, and when he offered none, she ground out, "You are the Earl of Ashby, a war hero, a—"

"There are no living war heroes. Don't you know that?" he spat with derision.

A fierce glint entered her eyes. "Listen to me. My brother is dead. You are alive. You must forgive yourself for it. You have to stop hating yourself," she enunciated heatedly. "I don't know why men butcher each other, but it's time you put the war behind you, or you'll never have peace. Living your life shut away from the world will neither bring Will back nor any of the men who died in it, and it's unhealthy. For heaven's sake, look at what it's done to you!"

"You certainly know how to rake a man down." But she was right, and it galled him.

Her blue eyes softened. "If it's because of your face—"

"It's not because of my face, damn it!" He swung his feet to the floor and ran his fingers through his hair. What it was about, however, he dared not delve into, not even privately.

She came up behind him, pressing her breasts to his back and sliding her arms around his shoulders. Her warm lips glided like silk along the curve of his neck. "Paris. What torments you, my love? You've shared so much with me already, and yet I feel there is a place inside you that a single ray of light couldn't breach. I may not be as experienced as you are, but I'm here for you."

He peeled her hands off him and stood, exasperated with her, with himself. But how could he tell her? How could he explain? "Why can't you respect this one thing? I respect everything that concerns you. So I am not much for Society, but within these walls I'd do anything for you!"

"Anything?" She eyed him in trepidation. "Will I be permitted to host balls and soirees, to invite my family over for holiday feasts? Will you come to dinners at Seven Dover Street?"

The maddening woman knew precisely where to stick her needles. "You knew bloody well how I lived my life from the start!" He strode to the side table to pour himself another drink.

She twisted to face him, her legs folded beneath her. "I didn't ask you to become a social creature, blast you! I asked for a family wedding, for a normal family life! Why ask me to marry you, when you can keep me fettered in your cellar? It would achieve the same goal."

"I thought you didn't like my cellar," he riposted irritably. "But the idea has merit."

She let out a shriek of rage, her gaze shooting daggers at him. "You are impossible!"

He sipped his drink, regarding her with a mixture of annoyance, lust, and awe. Balanced on her haunches, sky blue eyes glinting, her golden curls tumbling around her slim upper body, his infuriating lioness seemed oblivious to her nudity—and magnificently ferocious. He couldn't recall a single instance in which a woman quarreled with him in the buff. He wanted to ravish her all over again. He decided to relent a little, give up some ground, perhaps a private wedding, with only her family present. "Do you wish to be married by a special license?"

"What would it change?" she railed at him. "You'd still keep me locked in here with you, as some . . . pet in a cage! No family gatherings, no friends. What sort of life is this, Paris?"

Her insulting doubts cut him like a knife. "Did I say I'd keep you a prisoner? What the hell do you think I am—a bloody monster? Come and go as you please. I'll even give you the key."

"But you won't accompany me anywhere. I'll come and go as though I have no husband. Will I have to submit my schedule to you each day and beg for your approval? Will I have to recount every outing to you? Will you forbid me to dance with other gentlemen at balls?"

Her questions hit him like a cannonball. "I'm asking you to be my wife," he bit out angrily, "and you're concerned over whether you would be *permitted* to dance with other men?"

"You might not mind it at first, but after a while, when your Phipps comes gossiping to you about the number of gentlemen I conversed with, while you sat alone at home, waiting for me to return, you will care. You'll become a jealous tyrant! I know you, Ashby!"

The idea of her dancing and flirting with the wolf pack at social affairs made him see red. "One would think that a woman in love would rather spend her nights with her husband!"

"Why must I make the ultimate sacrifice? Why can't you sacrifice your habits for me?"

"You don't know what you're asking of me!" he growled in frustration.

"Then my answer is no."

His mind went numb. "What?"

Tears trembled in her eyes. "You don't care a fig about me. You never did. It was all about your *needs*—which I now know what they are. You want a brood mare that'll give you an heir and a spare and share your bed at night. But what about *my* needs? Or don't they fit into your perfectly nefarious scheme?"

If their squabble proved anything, it was that nothing on earth could ever make him strike a woman. "*Nefarious scheme*? You came to me!" he roared.

Tears spilled over her cheeks. "Lord, I was so stupid. I thought . . . I convinced myself that you cared for me."

Imbued with contrition, he set the glass aside and approached the bed. "I do care for you. And I'm very happy you came to me."

Anger sparked her glistening eyes. "You would!" She climbed off the bed and started to collect her scattered garments. "I won't spend one minute incarcerated with you!"

"You're rejecting me?" he asked incredulously, his mind refusing to register her words.

"Yes, I'm rejecting you! Find some other pea-goose to keep you diverted in your solitude!"

His heart hammered violently. Christ, she was killing him. "What if you're pregnant?"

"Then I'll be thoroughly ruined, but at least I'll have my family around me." She sniffed.

"I never said you couldn't be with your family, confound it all! And if you think I'll let you raise my child, *my heir*, as a byblow, alone, out of wedlock, then you don't know me by half!"

She sent him a disparaging look. "What would you do? Shackle me?"

"If you truly believed I'd shackle you, you wouldn't be joking about it."

"I won't marry you under these conditions, Paris. I won't become your private pet."

Irrational fear possessed him, and a voice he didn't recognize said, "If you deny me, I shall be forced to have a word with Stilgoe. How would your brother react to the news that his dainty sister paid me a nocturnal visit and that as a consequence she may be enceinte?"

She reacted as though he'd hit her. "You're threatening me?"

"I'm urging you. Reconsider."

"If you speak to Stilgoe, I'll be ruined, my charity will be ruined, and I'll hate and despise you for all eternity!"

"Eternity is a very long time, Isabel."

"Precisely!" She clutched at her chest, breathing with obvious difficulty.

The consternation in her eyes unnerved him. "How did we come to this? A moment ago we were making love."

"*Love*? You don't even know what love means! You ruined everything . . . Everything!"

He took a step forward. "You can't walk out on me. We belong together!"

"Watch me!" Panting, she sat down on the edge of the bed and pulled on her stockings.

"In the middle of the night? I'll take you in my coach in the morning." Straight to Scotland. How long would she cling to her irrational umbrage? Once they were on the road, spending days and nights in each other's company, she would come around. He would make her come around.

As he materialized before her, she stood and stumbled to the wall of windows. "Leave me be! I can't breathe with you around me. I need air . . ." She was crying so hard, she was wheezing.

Anxiety gripped him. He caught her shoulder. "Isabel, what's wrong?"

"Let go of me!" She threw open a window and leaned out of it, letting the chill of the night assault her naked body. He grabbed the blanket and came over to drape it around her shivering frame before she caught pneumonia. "Don't touch me!" she panted, cringing away from him.

She was having some sort of attack, and all she allowed him to do was stand and watch. Her choked sobs eviscerated him. "I'll have my carriage brought around and take you home."

Her sobs quieted. Hugging herself, she left the window and found her chemise. "Sophie's carriage is waiting for me across the street. I'd like to put my clothes on. Please wait outside."

He was a blackguard, an unfeeling brute. He deserved to rot in hell. "Isabel, I apologize. I didn't mean to frighten you. We can discuss this calmly. I'll fetch you a glass of w—"

"Get out!"

He stiffened. Her tossing him out of his own bedchamber, as though she were the mistress of his house, instilled him with sudden hope. "Fine. I'll wait outside while you dress. Then we'll talk." He pulled on his breeches and stepped out barefoot into the hallway. He leaned against the wall, hearing silk rustling and her crying. Her misery shredded what remained of his soul.

She emerged wrapped in her cape, the hood drawn over her eyes, and dashed downstairs.

"Isabel!" He pounded after her. He reached the front door first and put a hand out to bar her exit. "Please don't leave," he implored softly, dying inside. "Reconsider."

She looked up at him, her blue eyes gloomy and tired. "I have one question for you. Would you have ultimately sought me out if I hadn't called on you in the first place?"

He should have liked to think so. He'd always wanted her. She'd never been far from his thoughts, even when she'd been too young for a romantic involvement. But his face . . . his past . . . things had always gotten in the way. They still did.

"I didn't think so."

Hurt and resentment wound tightly inside him. "You'd throw away what we have between us for your social affairs and you say I have no notion of love? You're the one who's heartless."

"You're selfish and despicable! You threatened me! I never want to see you again!"

Black panic struck him. "*Never?*"

"Never." She tugged his hand aside and opened the door. "Goodbye, Ashby."

Chapter Twenty-Two

Passing away the bliss,
The anguish passing away:
Thus it is
Today.
—Christina Rossetti

"Will you sit still for two seconds together? You're making me dizzy."

Pacing back and forth before the garden window in Sophie's morning room, Isabel wished someone brained her with a bludgeon, knocked her out cold, and silenced the incessant turmoil in her mind. Her every thought was of him, her feelings fluctuating between terrible longing and sizzling fury. Last night, upon leaving Lancaster House, she'd made the quick decision to go to Sophie's. Her friend would make a sterling alibi should any gossip arise or in case Paris carried out his threat. She'd also be spared her mother's queries. As for Sophie's servants, muteness was their forte, as they were paid for that rather than for their efficiency. She'd slept a few hours and woken up with a splitting headache and the desire to die. She had taken a bath and changed into one of

Sophie's day gowns, but her lover's scent encompassed her, a torturous reminder of how their bodies had joined in intoxicating delirium, finding pure rapture together.

Making love with Ashby had been . . . wild, hot, beautiful. If she didn't know better, she might imagine his feelings for her ran as deeply and strongly as her feelings for him. What he'd let her feel, though, was the force of his *need*—his need for a home, a family, a woman who'd share his bed and provide him with the aforesaid. He'd laid bare the magnitude of his loneliness.

She'd spent nearly half her life pining for one man, for Ashby, wanting him all to herself. Last night, seeing his face, listening to his voice, and then lying in his embrace, was magic. He'd shared his deepest secrets with her and enfolded her in a cocoon of love. Or so she'd presumed.

You chose me. Of course. When she spoke of bearing affection for one another, he spoke of lust. When she wanted to shout her happiness to the world, he wanted to keep it a secret. And when she tried to parley, he threatened. The truth of their relationship was clear as crystal: She was the female who happened to knock on his door when he was at the end of his tether.

"Have some tea and biscuits," Sophie suggested. "I can hear your stomach growling all the way over here." She patted the cushion next to her on the sofa and poured Isabel a cup of tea.

Reluctantly, Isabel complied. She sat down and dipped a biscuit in her teacup. "Did you send my note to Seven Dover Street?" she asked, forcing down a nibble of soaked biscuit.

"I did. No one will find out about your previous night's escapade."

Anxiety twisted Isabel's stomach. "Not unless Ashby decides to ruin me."

Sophie rolled her eyes. "Now, why would he do that?"

"I don't know what he will do," Isabel replied quietly. "He

frightened me last night. For a moment I feared that if I didn't get out of there straight away, I would never be permitted to leave." She had trouble figuring out his possessive attitude toward her. She wasn't the only pretty pet in London. Through discreet exchanges, the Earl of Ashby could convince at least half a thousand English noblemen to relinquish their daughters to him. Why threaten her? Although she'd been readily available to satisfy his needs, she was hardly the most amenable woman.

"You fear him?" Sophie inquired in astonishment, then understanding dawned in her eyes. "He is not Chilton, Izzy. Don't let Iris's gothic tales destroy your life. Iris loathed Chilton long before they married. And she was in love with another man, who'd left her. Ashby is different."

Ashby was different. He was predictably unpredictable. She polished off her soggy biscuit, and it dropped like a chunk of wet clay into her stomach. "He is too . . . complex for me."

"That's what makes him interesting." Sophie smiled. "Or would you rather he were dull? If you were after dull, *ma chère*, you'd be married to Lord Wiltshire or to Ailsbury's son or to any of the dozen or so bucks who slobbered after you since your debut."

Isabel drew a deep breath. "I turned him down, Sophie. I declined his offer of marriage."

Surprise, shock, and anger flashed in Sophie's eyes sequentially. Her lips compressed in a thin line. "You foolish, impetuous girl! You turned down the man you adore to marry a peacock you don't care a straw about? Your brother will brook no more refusals, Izzy. He will force you into an alliance with Hanson, and you will spend the rest of your life regretting your mistake."

Numbness spread through her body. "All he wanted was a female companion to ease his solitude. I won't be amazed if the milkmaid becomes the Countess of Ashby by Easter."

"*Mon Dieu, Isabel*. That is the cruelest thing I've ever heard you say."

Moisture blurred her vision; her voice shook. "I was blinded by him. I melted at his feet . . ." With a great shuddering sob, the dam broke, and she poured out all the anguish in her soul.

Sophie offered her a napkin to dry her face. "On what grounds did you decline his suit?"

Sniffling, Isabel dabbed the napkin at the watering corners of her eyes. "He suggested we elope. I begged for a traditional wedding with family and friends. He adamantly refused, and we remonstrated. Then he threatened to ruin me if I left him—the bully—so I did. He gave me no alternative but to reject him. He admitted that"—her voice broke on a sob—"had I not come to him, he wouldn't have . . . have had any interest in me." Struggling to regain her composure, she sought Sophie's gaze for signs of compassion, but her friend was frowning in thought.

"That is what I told George when he proposed to me," her friend finally said. "With mock superiority I informed him that had he not pursued me with all the ardors of a schoolboy, I would not have given him a single thought. Can you imagine the reason for my vain and callous retort? I was petrified. That the second son of an English marquis should fall in love with an ignorant, unchaste, poor French opera singer was . . . ridiculous! A fairytale. Immediately I set upon him. I examined him for faults that would explain his odd sentiments and could find none. Indeed, he was neither striking nor dashing nor titled nor wealthy like your gargoyle, but he loved me well. A blessing in disguise." Her black eyes sparkled. "Perhaps the fact that Ashby is not a pink of the *ton* is also a blessing in disguise."

Isabel blinked in astonishment. "You think I should have given him my consent?"

"Most assuredly. Nothing is permanent in life, except

death. People change. Needs change. Time and love are the strongest healing forces in the universe. Lost confidences can be restored, same as one's *joie de vivre*. So maybe you had to chase him a little bit to secure his interest, and maybe you will not have your dream wedding, but that is nothing." She took Isabel's hand and squeezed it. "I wasn't in love with George when I wed him, but I was devastated when he died. I felt that the best part of me had been ripped out and lost at sea. Shall I explain mature love to you, dear friend? It is respect, friendship, comfort, stability, and mutual fondness. You have that with Ashby. Today you love him more, tomorrow he will love you better, and vice versa."

Isabel pondered Sophie's pronouncements. "How could *I* live in seclusion, Sophie? Did I mention I had an unfortunate attack of the vapors in his presence? I felt caged, out of breath . . ."

"Poor Ashby. He must have been out of his wits, reproaching himself for having scared you into hysterical suffocation. Did you explain about your ailment?"

"It is none of his concern."

"Was he concerned?" Sophie inquired delicately.

Isabel lowered her eyes. "Yes. Very."

"Izzy, I doubt his situation will remain unchanged forever. He will, in good time, return to Society. Marry him, open your enormous heart to him, and help him heal."

"It may take years," Isabel protested feebly, Sophie's words beginning to sink in.

"Must everything happen according to your timetable? Must everything be now or never?"

"I feel like a silly sheep that wandered away from the flock into the gargoyle's cave and was thereupon selected for dinner." Only that . . . Paris wasn't a gargoyle. He just thought he was. But she had said her piece, and he had unleashed his demons on her. So now it was up to him to untangle his emotional and moral conundrums and decide whether to return to Society, or not.

"Don't be a goose." Sophie grinned. "He adores you. He will lavish his riches on you and seduce you with every vice at his disposal. I daresay you will be a well contented sheep."

Isabel's face warmed as she recalled how very content she'd been with his seductions last night. "He asked me to reconsider," she admitted with great ambivalence.

"This alone should tip the scales in his favor, *chérie*. Remember Moreland and what's-his-name, the Duke of Salisbury's nephew, how they stomped off in a flame because you said 'no'?" Isabel nodded, not quite following. "Tell me, what induces an eligible gentleman to swallow his pride, keep himself pending, and thus condemn himself to the tortures of uncertainty?"

Isabel shrugged weakly. "He wants a wife."

"He wants *you*."

With a hearty sigh, Isabel propped her chin on her fists and rested her elbows on her joined knees. "Sophie, why must you always play Devil's advocate? It is most annoying." Her friend was methodically fraying her counterarguments. But she still had one left. "I should like to be chosen from a crowd . . . of beautiful, accomplished ladies, not as the only convenient sheep." At the charity masquerade ball, he had eyes for no woman but her, and it was dreamlike, floating in his arms as though they'd waltzed together a million times before. She wanted to feel that way again with a keen yearning that brought tears to her eyes. Alas, Paris could neither claim to love her nor not to. Why should she live this way, perpetually off balance, looking for signs of affection, removed from her family and friends, while he surrendered nothing? It was intolerable.

And yet . . . she'd never known such happiness as when she was with him.

"Izzy, you are chosen from a crowd daily," Sophie reassured her. "Society's Golden Angel dances attendance on you, with a gaggle of young swags trailing behind him, all of whom you have bewitched and none of whom you want. Ashby is not blind. He knows—"

"You have no idea who he was before his injury!" Isabel disputed. "You think Hanson is popular with the ladies? It's nothing compared with how they fawned over Ashby. Every mother wished him for her daughter and secretly fancied him in her own bed. Will said that Ashby was the worst suitor in existence because the women did all the wooing. He had more mistresses than Don Juan. Now he is a recluse and a hermit and you think he *chose* me? I tell you, *I–was–at–hand!* He told me himself that he was not much of anything anymore. Were he the same man he was four or seven or ten years ago, he would not have given me a second glance."

"Did you tell him how you felt about him?" Sophie inquired, and Isabel nodded. "And then you left him?" Again Isabel nodded. Sophie stared at her disbelievingly. "Ruthless, you are."

Tears rushed to Isabel's eyes. "I am not heartless," she whispered. "I told him that I loved him, as I would never love another. Would you like to know what his response was? He said, 'I need you,'" She hugged herself, beset with shivers and nausea. *I need you, too*, her heart wept.

Sophie wrapped her arms around Isabel's shoulders and rocked her. "Heartless beast."

Isabel nodded against Sophie's shoulder, dampening the deep purple muslin.

"All men are stupid imbeciles."

Isabel nodded concurringly, though she suspected Sophie was teasing.

"They should lose their private parts on the guillotine and die screaming in agony."

This time Isabel smiled.

Chapter Twenty-Three

My life closed twice before its close;
It yet remains to see
If Immortality unveil
A third event to me.
—Emily Dickinson

The grandfather clock in the foyer chimed nine times. "Damnation," Ashby muttered. Why did it feel as though it was past midnight? He prowled his vast, empty house, striding from room to room like a caged lion. She would not be coming back this time. She stood pat. It was all over between them. Then why could he not quit obsessing over her?

Her grounds for declining his marriage proposal hammered at his conscience. Although he sorely begrudged her reasoning, he understood it nonetheless. Why should he subject her to a life even he found difficult for the most part, and in the last three days downright insupportable?

Because he'd presumed—hoped—that she felt as he did. When he was in her presence, he no longer stood in the shade but in the sunlight and everything was fine and good with the world. In his current sad state, he would have contented himself with just sitting in front of the fireplace with her, holding hands, like some old married couple. *Christ*. There had to be *something* he could do to keep his mind off of her. He was going mad, wishing she were here with him.

Isabel, Isabel, Isabel. She consumed his thoughts, day and night, and wouldn't give him a moment's repose. His usual pursuits, whatever he used to do to pass the time before she barged into his life—and into his bedchamber—had lost the capacity to hold his attention for more than mere moments at a time. He took perverse pleasure in inhaling the vanilla scent still clinging to the wool blanket while tossing about in his bed at night, burning to hold her in his arms.

There was only one plausible explanation for his dismal condition: He was possessed.

He couldn't remember what his life had been like before Isabel brightened his doorstep. Nor could he remember what *he* had been like before first setting eyes on her—a twelve-year-old infant, for Christ's sake! Perhaps dementia did run in his family. He'd always assumed his father had killed himself over love. Now he knew better. The Lancasters were a clan of lunatics.

If only he hadn't tried to force her into a marriage with him, she wouldn't have begged him to leave her be and then bolted out of his house like a scared animal. The odds that she would accept him were abysmal to begin with. Once he'd voiced his threat, they'd become nonexistent. Which made him twice the idiot that he was, since he'd never meant to speak to her brother in the first place. But when she'd trampled over his proposal, she'd unwittingly roused the dormant beast inside of him—the one Olivia had scarred for life. Only this time it was worse. When news of Olivia's nuptials to Bradford reached him, he spent a week drowning his injured pride in a tun of whiskey. Isabel injured more than his pride; her refusal cut him to the core. He felt as though he were bleeding inside. How could she claim to love him and then leave him? It was inhumane!

Like his father, who loved his wife better than he loved his son, Isabel preferred her family and social life over him. Supreme hurt and longing gnawed at him until he couldn't eat, couldn't sleep, couldn't breathe, couldn't do a damned thing but howl in torment.

He found refuge in the billiards room and leaned against the closed door. "Curse you," he whispered with a shuddering breath, shutting his stinging eyes. "What have you done to me?"

Why must I make the ultimate sacrifice? Why can't you sacrifice your habits for me?

Anger simmered under his skin. He wondered how Isabel would react to his showing up at one of her precious social affairs and flirting with the easy game fluttering about. He'd been quite the rage once upon a time. Alvanely and Argyll, his cronies from the old days, had tied a dance card on his wrist during one ball and urged the panting females to line up for the privilege of signing their names next to a dance. "No stampeding and no brawling!" Argyll kept crowing, while Alvanely herded the eager flock clamoring for Ashby's attentions.

Those were the good old days, he sighed reminiscently. Would Isabel have caught his eye had she been of age then? Probably. Though back in those days, he would not have been thinking beyond lifting her skirts—and most certainly not lamenting her disinclination to marry him. He would have congratulated himself on a successful hunt and an easy escape from the altar. *Or not.*

Isabel Aubrey wasn't the sort of female one purged from his system in one night of sin. He would have continued lusting after her well until his luck had run out and he would have been forced to wed her. But obsessed as she was with altruism and propriety, she wouldn't have batted an eye at a selfish rake of his black reputation. Philanthropists and philanderers didn't mix well.

Still . . . surely she'd heard some of the rumors circulating at that time of the sort of man he used to be—and she'd still liked him. Then why couldn't she accept the sort of man he was now? He was ten times better than the wastrel who got sotted every night, bet huge sums of money on absurdities, and considered a monogamous relationship an unnatural condition.

Good God, he'd become a lamb!

Churning with self-disgust, he pushed away from the door, arranged the billiards balls, and selected a cue from the rack. No wonder she'd refused him. Women didn't appreciate inoffensive sods; they melted for rakes. They led the good-intentioned chaps by their pink noses, but when a perfectly able, heart-breaking blackguard walked by, they virtually swooned—which, of course, was one of the reasons he had been a damned successful rake at the time. *Bloody, bloody hell*.

He pocketed a ball with a cannon shot and then contemplated the balls scattered across the green felt table. If it weren't for his curst scars, he'd make her eat her rejection. According to Phipps's sources, Isabel had received twelve offers of marriage since her debut, five of them put formally before Stilgoe, and she'd rejected each and every one. Well, unlike her well-manicured, intricately neckclothed lapdogs, *he* didn't spout marriage proposals with every breath.

He pocketed balls for what seemed like an eternity but lasted no more than an hour, while indulging in fanciful scenarios in which he was back to his old lifestyle and making Isabel burn with jealousy. The visions became so sweet that he was grinning by the time he'd cleared up the table. Perhaps she was right, after all. He was hungry, and when she turned up on his doorstep, bright-eyed and eager for his company, his unappeased hunger focused on her. That must be it. It was unhealthy to live as he did, starving his mind and body of basic needs. Even playing billiards *à la solitaire* had begun to pall. He desperately needed to do something to recover his old self, and he needed to do it immediately, for when a man reached the point where he couldn't stand his own company anymore, no one else would care to withstand it either. Not even his servants.

He threw the cue on the table and headed purposefully toward his private rooms. By Jove he would make her regret her decision, even if it killed him. He rang the bell cord for Phipps and strode to the wardrobe. He grabbed a waistcoat and a jacket and pulled them on with cold single-mindedness, not allowing himself a moment to consider the rash course of action he had settled upon. He would not get past the front door if he dwelled on what he was about to do.

True to form, Phipps skidded to a halt at the open doorway. "My lord?"

"I'm going out." He reached for a new, starched cravat and knotted it around his neck. That he still remembered how to do it was a shock in itself. He'd been dressing himself in regimentals for as long as he could remember, and in the past two years, it was his valet who'd taken over the task of packaging him in a semblance of decorum for an audience with one of his administrators.

"I'll have Apollo saddled straight away."

"I'll be taking the coach." Ashby strode past the stunned butler out into the hallway and continued toward his office. By the time he found his purse and stuffed a stack of banknotes into it, Phipps materialized before him, his expression vacillating between concern and delight.

"The carriage will be brought around momentarily, my lord. May I—?"

"You may not." Ashby poured himself a shot of courage and gulped it down. His brittle resolve wouldn't survive one of Phipps's interrogations. But neither did the faithful retainer deserve to be ridden roughshod over in case his master's nerve failed him for no apparent reason, except its infirmity.

"My hat and greatcoat, if you please." He had no idea where the blasted items were stored. He hadn't used them in years. In all probability they'd gone out of fashion.

It took another boosting nip, and he was at the door. Phipps awaited him with an unfamiliar hat dangling from a white-gloved finger and an equally alien greatcoat hanging on his forearm. His butler didn't utter a sound, but Ashby clearly read "Good luck!" in the old man's kind eyes.

Isabel paced the carpet in her bedchamber, her nerves wound tightly, her heart drumming forcefully, and waited for the last door down the hallway to open and close. Twice she tiptoed downstairs to find the library lit and Charlie smoking a cigar, drinking a nightcap, and reading his newspaper. Wasn't her stupid brother eager to join his loving wife in bed? She would not be so lenient with her husband. She would go into his library, dressed in a silk negligee and nothing else, and seduce him right there in his favorite armchair.

Her mouth went dry, because the male protagonist in her imaginary, fire-lit scenario was, as always, Paris Nicholas Lancaster.

During the past three days she refrained from discussing him with her friends and kept her own counsel. They were both older and perhaps wiser, but Iris was angry and bitter, and Sophie had married a man for security rather than for love. Blocking out their contradictory voices in her head, Isabel searched within her breast for her absolute truth, her voice. The answer was simple and an integral part of herself: *She loved him. Nothing could change that. Ever.*

For this reason she had begged off from attending the ladies' charity soiree at Sophie's and stayed home. She missed Paris; she wanted to be with him; she wanted him back.

She stopped before her dressing mirror and removed her cape to check her appearance for the tenth time. She wore her hair down—a cascade of spiraling gilt locks—and a décolleté gown of deep sapphire satin that clung to her figure and glistened in the soft candlelight. It was carefully selected to overcome grudges, rancor, animosity, and any changes of heart or mind that might have arisen over the past three days. She pinched her cheeks to bring color to her pale, sleep-deprived complexion and put a clove in her mouth. Everything had to be perfect. *She* had to be perfect to convince the man she craved and had declined that he still needed her. Badly.

A last minute idea struck her. Since she was about to surrender to his wishes and phobias, she might as well pack a satchel with personal items, a change of clothes, and no nightshift. She hoped Paris hadn't discarded his letter to her mother. She would never separate from him again.

A door closed softly down the hallway. *Finally.* She opened her door and peeked outside. Darkness and silence welcomed her. She crept downstairs, her senses on the alert, but everyone was to bed, including the servants, and she reached the front door uneventfully. The key dangled on a ribbon tied to the doorknob, Norris's latest antic. The spare rested in a drawer in Stilgoe's office desk. She took the key, reluctant to leave the house unlocked, and stepped outside.

A hack drove by five minutes later. She hailed it and gave the man the required address. If Lady Hyacinth Aubrey got wind that her hoyden of a daughter took a hack alone at night, she would immigrate to the Colonies and beg one of the savages to slay both her and her shame.

As the hack rolled up Park Lane, Isabel fumbled in her reticule for the correct change but stared out the window in anticipation of glimpsing the tall white columns of Lancaster House.

"Stop!" she shouted to the driver with a start. A black town coach waited in the front drive. Ashby had a visitor at eleven o'clock at night? She stuck her head out the window and quietly asked the driver to advance but keep to the shadows. She soon made out the crest emblazoned on the coach's door. *A lion*. This was Paris's coach. She was fuming over where he could possibly be slinking off to in the middle of the night, when the man himself crossed the front threshold, unmasked, wearing evening clothes, a multi-caped black overcoat, and a hat. *He was going out.*

He never went out, except to sometimes lurk with Apollo in the bushes outside her house. Her mind ran a quick list of destinations a gentleman might visit after dark, dismissed most of them, and arrived at the only plausible conclusion: He was off to an old mistress. *The louse.*

So he never moved in public, did he? Well, he certainly moved a lot in private. Damn him. If she had arrived a moment too soon or too late, he would have known that she'd come to throw herself at his feet again. She would have been humiliated to dust for the God knows which time.

Devastated, she watched him stride to his carriage, more beautiful than the dark-blue night. She waited until the carriage drove off and then asked the driver to return her to Seven Dover Street. She was of a good mind to tell Sophie what she thought of her phenomenal powers of deciphering the male psyche but decided to keep her mortification to herself.

Major Ryan Macalister lifted brooding eyes from a glass of Hock and choked on his last sip. "Good God! I must be three sheets to the wind. Look what the Devil has dragged in!"

His good friend, Captain Oliver Curtis, chased his stunned gaze and suffered of a similar reaction. "Damn me . . . Colonel Ashby! I thought he never ventured out anywhere these days."

"Evidently he does, Oli," Ryan murmured, "and I think I may know the source behind his miraculous reemergence." He pushed away from their table and crossed the less-than-plush but well-appointed clubroom toward his former commanding officer. Unlike any of the pretentious elite clubs, this establishment catered to army officers. "Lord Ashby." He extended his hand for a shake, grinning. "I'm glad you accepted my invitation. Would you care to join us?"

Ashby swept the room with a cursory glance, nodding his head stiffly at old acquaintances. Most of the patrons were in regimentals, and for some reason, it appeased his discomfort. "Don't mind if I do," he said, returning Macalister's handshake while throwing in a fleeting smile. He followed the cocky major, envying his self-assurance. How long since he'd felt this way? Ages.

Curtis sprang up as soon as they reached the table and grabbed Ashby's hand. "Good to see you, sir. We've just started in on a fine bottle of Hock, but if you still prefer Spanish wine . . ."

"Whatever you're having is fine with me. And as you can see"—he gestured at his civies—"I'm no longer in regimentals, so Ashby would do." He took a seat while Macalister signaled for another wineglass. His cravat felt a bit tight, but he ignored the urge to tug at it. "So what are you two deserters doing out of India?" he inquired, as a footman came to pour him wine.

His tablemates chuckled. "I'm on sickness leave," Ryan explained, "and Oli here is in town for his sister's upcoming nuptials. Old Silvia has finally found a shortsighted chap—"

"Stubble it, Macalister," Curtis snapped. "Your humdrum jokes about my sister's nose haven't succeeded in tickling anyone, so you might as well stuff them in a dark place."

Ashby fought to maintain a straight face. In truth, Silvia Curtis's frightfully long nose, also known as "the bayonet," had provided them with an indefatigable source of hilarity throughout the final campaign. His effort held, until Ryan put on a deceptively innocent face, saying, "All I meant to say was that old Silvia is marrying a fine arms collector." He lost the fight thereupon, exploding with laughter together with Ryan, who nearly got his nose bloodied for his *faux-pas*.

"Would you wits stop cackling?" Curtis muttered. "That one wasn't all that amusing."

"Yes, it was," Ashby blurted between fits of irrepressible laughter. "Sorry, old boy."

Curtis stood. "I'm off to see what the stakes are at the hazard table." He stalked in the direction of the gaming room, wincing as another bout of laughter went off upon his departure.

"We're evil," Ashby declared, refilling their glasses. "Her nose was not all that long."

"You haven't seen her in a while. Bear in mind that the nose is the only organ in the human anatomy that never ceases to grow. I'm afraid we've been charitable toward it in the past."

Chuckling, Ashby eyed one of the finest officers he'd ever commanded. "So what sort of illness is keeping you away from the land of gold and ivory? You look fit to me."

Ryan grimaced. "I've pangs in my pockets and spasms in my heart. It's a deuced confusing illness, as the cure for the one ache contradicts the cure for the other."

"You, in love?" Ashby gave him an amused sidelong look. "Who's the unfortunate chit?"

"A lovely, blue-eyed angel. I'd be stalking her now if she weren't at a charity soiree."

Ashby lost his smile. "And is this heavenly creature returning your affections?"

Ryan fixed his gaze on the wine in his glass. "Some things a gentleman keeps to himself."

Jealousy struck Ashby, hard and raw. Isabel lied to him. She *was* encouraging Macalister. His hands curled into fists. *No violence*, he reminded himself. *Keep your head cool*. "I suggest you give her up, Macalister," he clipped in a low, none-too-friendly tone of voice; it was the one he had perfected during his military service. "The person being discussed is unavailable."

"I know that," Ryan muttered, narrowing his eyes on his companion, "but no woman ought to throw her life away on a monster that treats her no better than a pet in a cage!"

Ashby's muscles tensed at the direct offense. Slowly he gritted, "Who are you to determine what's good for her? Leave her be, Macalister. She is not your concern."

Surprise and suspicion flickered in Ryan's eyes. "Neither is she yours."

"You're wrong on that account, and if you ever come near her again, I'll make certain they ship you back to India on the subsequent tide."

Ryan pushed back his chair and stood. "I'm sorry it has come to this between us, but since I have no intention of following your 'advice,' I suggest we settle this at dawn."

With a swift glance about the room, Ashby pushed to his feet and muttered very softly, "I will not fight you, but if you do not heed my 'advice,' I will most assuredly exile you."

They locked horns for an interminable moment. "I thought you were a gentleman, Ashby. Men of honor settle their disputes over pistols, not in the backrooms of the War office."

Ashby clamped down on the old belligerent impulses egging him on. "As I said, I won't fight you, but stay the hell away from Isabel, or I'll make you wish you'd never left India."

"Isabel?" Ryan blinked. "Good God, man. I wasn't speaking of Isabel Aubrey. I was"—he leaned closer as not to be overheard—"I was referring to her friend, Iris, Lady Chilton."

It took a moment for Ashby's blood temperature to return to normal. He was out of control. Had he been using his brain, he would have realized it wasn't Isabel Macalister spoke of, as she was an heiress, who could solve both his problems. Nor would he have revealed his relationship with her, especially not to a devil-may-care, unattached major with empty pockets, a fair stock of charm, and the manners of a peer. He cleared his throat and offered his hand. "Apologies. May I depend upon your discretion? I offer the same."

With a relieved nod Macalister accepted his handshake. "Thanks. I'd appreciate it."

They regained their seats, exchanging sheepish scowls. At least they'd straightened it out, Ashby reflected, feeling more than a trifle foolish. He'd never imagined he'd come to blows over a female. Then again, he'd never imagined a full-grown Isabel would march back into his life.

Macalister retrieved his wineglass, looking pensive and, to a degree, amused. "A bit young, ain't she?"

"But not the least bit married," Ashby reposted with an equally condescending smile.

"Can't say I'm surprised. I suspected it the moment you swooped down on us at the charity ball. Though, I should warn you. That one has it hard for someone else . . . Wait a minute." A silly grin tilted the corners of his mouth. "You're the 'someone else.' And when I mentioned your name, she looked so sweetly bewildered." He drained his glass. "Women."

Ashby's heart did bizarre flip-flops. "When did you mention my name to her?"

"Weeks ago, when I spotted her having luncheon with, er, Lady Chilton and another friend. She told me about some lists she needed for her charity work and I suggested she go to you." He smirked smugly. "Obviously she did."

Thinking back, Ashby was fairly convinced that she'd initially come to him before that but kept his conclusion to himself. Ryan saluted him with his wineglass. "Pretty as a sunflower, she is. I tried, myself, but she gave me the brush-off, saying—"

"She gave you the brush-off?" Ashby repeated, suppressing the impulse to hoot.

"Most firmly. However, I think you should know that her

family is eager for her to marry the Duke of Haworth's grandson, and although she's resolved to fight them tooth and nail, you'd better hurry up before she runs out of nails. Her mother struck me as the persistent type, if you catch my meaning." He winked. "I hope you had the good sense to obtain those lists for her."

Ashby whirled the wine in his glass. "She declined me, nonetheless."

Ryan's wineglass stopped midway to his mouth. "You're pulling my leg, aren't you?"

Sighing, Ashby admitted, "She has no desire to be put in a cage, was her exact phrasing, which I now suspect she got from her friend, your friend, the unhappily situated Lady Chilton."

Anger and anguish etched Macalister's face. "That bastard, Chilton, keeps her under lock and key. From what I managed to glean from her personal maid, she must present him with a daily schedule and beg for his consideration, she is forbidden to dance with anyone but him, and I have reason to believe his abuses are not limited to mental or verbal ones alone."

"He beats her?" The very idea of a man beating a woman, regardless of his connection to her, turned Ashby's stomach. Were he in Macalister's boots—vow of non-violence or not— he'd tear out Chilton's heart and eat it. No wonder Isabel balked at the life he offered her. She feared ending up in the same dismal situation as her wretched friend. Good God. "I met Lady Chilton. She's a beautiful, delicate young lady. What sort of monster abuses a woman like that?"

"An old, powerful, wealthy monster, but she refuses to part with his blunt and station." He snorted with disgust. "Go on. Say it. What are you doing, you unhappy sod? Go back to India, put her behind you, and fill your empty pockets with gold and ivory."

"I'm hardly in a position to take the pulpit and breathe fire on anyone," Ashby stated. "My direct contact with the Almighty was severed years ago, to both parties' satisfaction."

Ryan smirked, shaking his head. "Aren't we two peas in a pod? I gave up my one true love, and you won't go after yours." He signaled for another bottle. "I say we get foxed immediately."

Ashby cast him an intrigued, sideways glance. "What do you mean 'I won't go after mine'?"

"You're sitting here with me, ain't you? I've already been handed my walking papers, but you may still have a chance. Unless you are not the 'someone else' after all. Bear in mind that I am not the only handsome and charming predator in London. Your sunflower is a prime target."

Oh, he was the 'someone else' all right, Ashby acknowledged with a secret, sad smile. She had come to him chaste as snow and with eyes melting with love. Of course she had left him in a very different condition. Ashby cleared his throat. "Hypothetically speaking, what would you do in my position? Keep in mind I'm not exactly"—how did she put it?—"a social creature."

"Hypothetically speaking?" Ryan smiled slyly. "Do to her the one thing that, if she did it to you, would annoy you the most. I believe it is a trick my colonel once taught me."

"Everything she does that doesn't include me annoys me, Macalister. Be specific."

"Pursue her best friend, my friend."

That had been his first impulse, but he didn't care to pursue or be pursued by anyone other than Isabel, however perfect a solution it seemed. Even the concept of paying his advances to her friend left a bad taste in his mouth. "Her best friend is your friend, Lady Chilton," he quibbled.

"What of the other one? The bedroom-eyes French chocolate soufflé."

Ashby made a face. "If I weren't already on my way to hell,

this would buy me a first class passage. Besides, females have this damnable silent code—no sharing among friends."

Ryan shoved to his feet. "Let me fleece you for a pittance of your net worth at the gaming tables, and I'll lay down a strategy for you that will put old Boney to shame."

Ashby gave a grim smile. "Lead the way. I'll just follow the smell of sulfur . . ."

Chapter Twenty-Four

Someone scratched her office door. "Come in!" Isabel called distractedly. This was odd, she reflected. Fifty pounds were missing from her charity box, but she'd counted the money this morning, before paying Rebecca her wages. Had she mistakenly paid the housekeeper more than she owed her? Impossible. She paid Rebecca in coins. She would notice handing over fifty pounds. She always kept the moneybox locked in the drawer of her desk. She checked the lock in the drawer. No signs of tampering. She replayed the day's events in her mind. The only time the box lay open on her desk was when . . . Inconceivable. It had to be someone else.

"Are you cross with me?" a gloomy, lilting voice asked.

Isabel looked up. "No, of course not. What's wrong? Iris, do sit down."

Iris took the chair in front of the desk. "I spoke to Sophie before she left for the day. I got the impression that my bad counsel may have cost you a most . . . desirable alliance."

Cold anger seized Isabel at the memory of seeing Paris leaving Lancaster House two nights ago. She put the coins, banknotes, and the tally sheet back in the box, turned the key in the lock, and returned it to the drawer, locking it too. "Sophie had no right to scold you. She has all the wrong notions. She thinks marrying George turned her into an expert on conjugal harmony."

"Ashby proposed, and you turned him down, because I had infected you with my disdain and loathing for my husband." Iris looked thin and pale and had a bruise on her left jaw.

Isabel couldn't possibly add to Iris's guilt. "Stuff and nonsense. Don't rake yourself down, dear heart. My problems with Ashby are more complicated than what it appears on the surface."

"What happens now?" Iris asked.

Isabel shrugged. She had no answer to give, not even to herself. She just wanted to crawl into a hole and put everything out of her mind. She was beyond depressed.

"He is our sponsor, Izzy, and a member of the board. You will have dealings with him."

"I'll send you." Isabel offered a smile she didn't feel inwardly.

"You're incensed with him, and yet he is the injured party, isn't he? You said 'no.'"

She said "no," then was about to say "yes," and it was too late. So now she was the rejected instead of a rejecter, though technically it never happened, and she liked to keep it that way. She decided to change the subject. "What happened to your jaw? It is swollen and bruised."

Iris averted her gaze. "Nothing. An accident. I, er, crossed a busy street and—"

"You used this excuse once already, dearest," Isabel remarked gently.

"Let's go home, Izzy. It's late, and we have a play to go to." Iris started to rise.

Isabel leaned over the desk and clutched her hand. "Come live with us. Stilgoe won't mind. Get a divorce, and if you are concerned with the scandal, I will arrange for you to spend the rest of the Season at Stilgoe Abbey. Don't go back to that monster. I beg you."

Iris's face transformed into a mask of dignified resignation. "I'm fine, Izzy, but thanks for offering. I made a mistake, but it will never happen again."

"What mistake?" Iris was so strong and yet so delicate. Isabel's heart bled for her.

"Chilton saw me coming off the balcony with Ryan behind me. He was displeased."

"Please tell me what happened with Ryan. I feel I am to blame. I encouraged both of you."

Iris patted her hand. "Perhaps a little, but some temptations are so strong one is bound to slip eventually all on his own. In a nutshell, Ryan's defense for having left me in that hut was that he realized too late how he couldn't support me and all that crock. The man never had a drop of imagination in his minuscule, self-absorbed brain."

"This is a pathetic excuse," Isabel concurred. "Anyone who knows you well enough is also aware you care naught for fortune or social standing."

The expression in Iris's azure eyes was flinty. "How terribly misinformed you are, Izzy. As of five days ago, I care for naught except fortune and social standing."

"So you took your revenge on him. You told him you are better off married to a wealthy peer than to a poor soldier. That's brutal, in a justifiable sort of way."

"More than you'll ever know," Iris murmured vaguely, then shook herself. "Did I interrupt you in the middle of something? You seemed distracted when I walked in."

Isabel explained about the missing fifty quid. "I was about to put away the box when Lord John came by to apologize for his behavior at the charity ball for the fifth day in a row. I left him for a moment to leave you the note about the play tonight, and when I returned, Sophie was here, chatting with him. Perhaps Sophie took the money, but for what purpose?"

"You shall have to ask her tomorrow. She received a mysterious note and dashed home."

Distractedly Isabel caressed the figurine of the lion kissing his lioness. "If Sophie didn't take it, one of us would have to consult our sponsor. He'd know how to solve this puzzle."

"One of us? Admit it, Izzy. You want to see him."

Isabel gave a negligent shrug. "What was it you said regarding temptations?"

"That some of them are too strong to resist."

Sophie Paulette Fairchild found it terribly vexing that the first green-eyed, dark-haired, tall, and broad-shouldered earl plowing a track in her sitting room carpet should be in love with her best friend—and the silly chit had refused him. Sophie sighed. Perhaps Izzy knew what she was about. The poor man seemed to be suffering of advance stages of a fatal lovesickness.

"Lord Ashby," she ventured, when he had been pacing for a good ten minutes and had yet to open his mouth other than to wish her a good evening or to groan and curse under his breath. "I have an excellent bottle of brandy I've been polishing off on my own. May I offer you some?"

He halted before the mantelpiece, his brilliant gaze colliding with hers. "Yes, please."

With an affable smile, she rose from the settee and poured them both a healthy nip. "There you are, my lord." She handed him a snifter and regained her seat. If it took more than two drinks to loosen his tongue, they would be in trouble, as brandy made her sleepy.

He drained his glass and put it aside. "Thank you for seeing me. I didn't think you would."

"Lord Ashby, please take a seat and tell me how I may help you. I'm all ears."

She was impressed how fluidly his massive frame sank into the overstuffed chair opposite her. Another sigh escaped her lips. Athletic men were her weakness, more's the pity.

"I want Isabel," he stated vehemently.

"Yes, I realize that." She smiled sympathetically. "And I am willing to assist—"

"—and you are the key." He shoved a hand through his overlong hair. It was the fashion in Paris, but she suspected Ashby wore it long to conceal the scars on his face. Men were a clueless lot. Didn't he have an inkling of the air of danger and mystery the scars added to his almost-too-fine-looking features? "My ploy requires that . . . you consort with the enemy."

She smiled. "I imagine you consider yourself to be the enemy, Lord Ashby."

"Ashby, please." He leaned forward. "Mrs. Fairchild, I—"

"If I am to be your co-conspirator," she interrupted, "I insist you call me Sophie."

"Very well, Sophie, I'm asking you to engage in the lowest form of subterfuge with me."

She grinned slyly. "Am I to become your pretend mistress?"

He blinked. "I was about to suggest a pretend courtship, but come to think of it, in the eyes of the *ton* it would seem—" He grinned. "Forgive me, but I must ask. How did you know?"

"I'm a Frenchwoman, *monsieur*. Romantic subterfuge is in my blood." She took a sip of brandy. "So you want to make her jealous. Not a bad strategy. Used it several times myself."

"Actually, it would serve two purposes." He drew in a breath, every line in his body rigid. "I've decided it was time I resumed my, er, social life. I've been out of circulation for years and I find myself a bit out of form." He smiled sheepishly. "I'm asking you to . . . chaperone my debut."

She took him in from head to toe. "Will my duties include fending off female admirers?"

"That remains to be seen, madam." He chuckled, the sound rich and warm. He sobered. "I confess, I am . . . somewhat skittish about reentering Society. I am sure you can imagine why."

She didn't believe it was just his scars he was reluctant to expose but nodded anyhow. She hadn't been entirely surprised to receive his note this afternoon. She was verging on sending him one herself. This was better. It spared her the effort of convincing him he needed assistance from a female ally, who also happened to be informed about the particulars of the affair and interested in seeing both parties happily reunited. "Why me?" she queried, just to hear his reasoning.

"You are the perfect choice. An attractive, sophisticated widow, who's seen the world and knows its imperfections, you enjoy more freedom than greener chits and are less likely to . . . feel uncomfortable in my presence."

"So long as we are straightforward with each other, I'll feel perfectly comfortable in your presence. But surely you are acquainted with other ladies who fit this description."

"I couldn't very well turn to an old female acquaintance, could I?" He sent her a sardonic grin that said it all. The scoundrel hadn't cultivated a single platonic alliance with a female in his life. No wonder, Sophie thought. What woman would care to adopt him as a mere bosom friend? "Furthermore," he went on, "you are Isabel's particular friend. You will know where to be, keep me from performing a *faux-pas*, and once our charade is over, reassure Isabel of my innocence."

"How very devious of you." She was beginning to appreciate why Izzy desired and feared him. The man thought of everything.

"As for my third and final reason." He rolled his snifter between his open palms, his eyes almost blue in their intensity. "A while ago, Isabel sought to provoke me by suggesting you as an alternative to her. She claimed we had much in common and would deal well together."

"She said that?" Sophie felt her face glowing. *Ventreblue.*

She never blushed. "Silly goose! Did she also mention I was a famous opera singer in Paris before the war?" she countered.

"No, she didn't." Amusement sparked his eyes, then surprise and understanding, as if he'd figured something out, and suddenly, he burst out laughing. "I'm such a bloody idiot!"

Mon dieu, Sophie thought. Perhaps this business of just pretending to like him wouldn't be so easy after all. She pursed her lips. "Might I inquire what you find so amusing?"

"It's me I find pitifully amusing. You see, I . . . I was convinced she found me, well, flawed, and that therefore the friend she offered to pass me off to must be flawed as well, but that wasn't it. She has it in her head that I'm partial to opera singers, but she . . ."

"Are you?" she asked with a raised eyebrow. "Partial to opera singers."

"Her notion is based on gossip. I've sowed my wild oats long before you took the stage."

She studied the beautiful planes of his face. "You are not as old as you pretend to be."

"I am five and thirty, madam, and certainly much older than you."

A year older, but that was between her and God. "If what you say about Izzy is correct, she will be more than jealous." She frowned worriedly. "She will believe you found her lacking."

All amusement vanished from his countenance. "Isabel is perfect," he whispered with such fervor, his eyes gleamed blue again.

Perfect but blind, Sophie determined. She felt happy for Isabel and sad for herself. Would another man ever look at her with such eyes again? "Well, I suggest you go home and change."

He swallowed. "This evening?"

She smiled at his obvious dismay. "*À la guerre come à la guerre, Colonel*. You didn't wait for battles to come to you, did you? Lord John and his sister are taking Izzy and Iris to

Covent Garden. It's the perfect setting for your debut. Instead of tackling a crowded ballroom, we'll sit in the dark for most of the evening. My in-laws rent a box, so I do not foresee any difficulty."

"I will take care of that. The theatre is an excellent idea." He forced a smile. "My thanks."

"You are most welcome." She stood, smiling brightly. And so was Izzy, though by the end of the week her friend would want nothing better than to drop a house on her head. She escorted him to the front door, pleased with their plan. "I'll expect you in an hour. Wear something dark."

"Yes, my dear." He swept an elegant bow. "Should I bring a notepad to the theatre, in case you come up with further instructions? I'm not a complete idiot, you know." He chuckled.

"We'll see. Be sure you are nice to Izzy. Behave naturally with her. But not too naturally!"

"She'll cut you," he warned. "You might even lose her friendship over this."

"No, I won't. Not permanently."

"I might," he acknowledged austerely, and walked down the front steps.

Chapter Twenty-Five

And thou, who tell'st me to forget,
Thy looks are wan, thine eyes are wet.
—George Gordon, Lord Byron

Isabel loved the theatre. Tonight, however, sitting still in the dark and listening to cultured tones performing Shakespeare felt more like torture than entertainment. She should have insisted on attending a ball, where she could dance, chat, and exhaust her agitation, but she hadn't been thinking when she had relented to LJ's incessant pleas. Correction: She had been obsessing over the unfathomable Earl of Ashby. Whom had he gone to visit that night? To think she'd actually worried about him, all alone in his house—ha! Good thing she'd told him "no," then. She had very nearly wedded the ficklest, shiftiest . . . And yet, the more she considered it, the less likely it seemed to her that he should rush off to see an old mistress three nights after making love to her, especially after openly admitting to a two-year long celibate existence. But the fact of the matter was: Paris had a secret life she knew nothing about, a secret self he would not reveal to her, and that was the real barrier between them. *Drat.* Her emotions seemed to be caught in an ever-spinning loop of longing, anger, and frustration. One minute she was imagining herself naked with him and in the next she was breaking something hard over his head.

Unwanted fingers curled around her hand. "John, please," she protested, pulling her hand.

"We're practically engaged," he murmured close to her ear. "It's allowed."

There was nothing offending about his scent or presence, except that he wasn't Paris. "We are not engaged," she muttered, and rapped his undeterred hand with her fan. "Please stop."

He chuckled softly. "We will be, my sweet. I'll come by tomorrow and speak to Stilgoe."

It was at the tip of her tongue to inform him that he should ask her first. Instead, she said, "How clumsy of me. I left my program in the coach. Would you be a dear and fetch it for me?"

"It would be my pleasure." He got up, making a point of touching his knee to hers as he did so, and left the box. Isabel sagged in relief. Stilgoe wouldn't give his consent without consulting her first, but she knew all too well she wouldn't be able to put either man off for long. But she desperately needed time to come to terms with the fact that she would not be marrying the man she loved and railed against and craved to the point of physical agony.

"I hear your charity is a great success," Olivia whispered, immigrating forward to John's seat. "Everyone is talking about it and in particular about your illustrious sponsor. How do you communicate with him? Does he visit the agency, or do you call on him at Lancaster House?"

"We correspond," Isabel prevaricated. She did send him bills and lists of contributions.

"Ashby was extremely fine-looking in his youth. We grew up together, did you know?" As Isabel's head swerved aside,

Olivia leered. "He didn't tell you, did he? Oh, we knew each other very well. My grandfather took pity on the boy and included him in our family feasts. Poor Ashby had no one, an orphan. He was never one of *us*, but we took him in nonetheless. I daresay if it hadn't been for our generosity, he would not have come down from Eton during the holiday seasons. He detested dining alone with ten footmen about him, the poor dear."

The way Olivia told it, Isabel felt deep sympathy for Paris. No wonder he liked *her* family; they never let him feel "not one of us."

"Naturally he fell violently in love with me," the iceberg went on with cloying smugness. "He wrote me countless letters. Oh, he was never one for poetry, but he had a way of expressing his feelings and . . . desires most eloquently. Those ardors! They say first love is a forever love." Olivia let out a sigh, and Isabel wanted to hand Olivia her teeth. The witch was as obvious as she was malicious. Yet she accomplished what she set out to do. Isabel churned with jealousy.

Paris had loved Olivia, had most likely been engaged to Olivia. The soulless ice queen had a boxful of his love letters!

From the self-satisfied look in her eyes, Olivia seemed to be warming to her *coup de grace*. "When he offered for me, I didn't have the heart to refuse him, and we became engaged."

She knew it! Olivia was Paris's mysterious betrothed. Will and Charlie must have known about his engagement to Olivia, and they'd kept it from her. Why? And why did Paris keep it a secret? Was he still pining for Olivia? Mustering her poise, Isabel inquired, "What happened?"

"We were engaged for three years, and although he made a point of coming to see me each time he was on leave in England, it seemed to me that the war would never end."

"So you cried off and married Lord Bradford instead," Isabel concluded with disgust. She finally understood Paris's inclination to elope. *Postponing our marriage could lead to all sorts of trouble. I've been through this before. It wasn't a pleasant experience*. While he was fighting Napoleon, the woman he loved accepted another fellow's advances. Stupid, impatient, heartless Olivia. Bradford was a poor substitute for the man Olivia could have had—the man *she* could have had. Was she as guilty of stupidity, impatience, and heartlessness?

"Poor Ashby was devastated." Olivia sighed. "His friends told me he got foxed for a month and was never the same after that. I was heartily sorry to have injured him, but well . . ."

How could anyone boast to breaking another person's heart? Disgusted with the coze and feeling very glum, Isabel raised her opera glasses to survey the occupants of the other boxes. She spotted Ryan Macalister being cooed at and pawed by Sally Jersey in her box and hoped Iris had not seen them from her seat behind her. Isabel doubted she would have survived spotting Paris escorting other women about town. The very idea instilled chill in her heart.

Distractedly she let her opera glasses drift along the boxes teeming with activity. As usual, the occupants were more interested in spying on each other and indulging in crisp gossip than in watching the performance. Curiously, everyone's attention centered on a specific box tonight. It was situated to her right, more expensive and closer to the stage than the one she sat in. She veered her lances toward it and gasped in shock, nearly dropping the binoculars.

Paris. Elegant and cool, dressed in black with an emerald pin stuck through his snowy cravat, his patrician profile betrayed no sign of his being aware of the stir he fermented. That was not all. A ruby gown, displaying generous wares, sat on his other side, her face unseen. What in blazes was he doing here, attending a play with some . . . strumpet? A secret outing two nights ago and now this? He was supposed to be a confirmed recluse, for goodness sake!

As she gawked in dismay, his head turned and his glittering gaze found hers, as if he had known where she was all along. Her heart jolted. The Gargoyle had come out of his cave and joined the world, but he did it with another woman. She lowered the opera glasses, her hands shaking. Was this intentional—his flaunting a prime article in her face?

His eyes sparkling enigmatically, he tipped his head at her and mouthed, "Good evening." He then turned to the woman in red. His companion stuck her head out and waved her hand.

"*Sophie*?" Isabel choked. What was *she* doing with him? Thunderstruck, she leaned back in her seat, murmuring over her shoulder, "Iris, look who's over there . . . to the right . . ."

Iris squeezed Isabel's shoulder. "It seems our busybody friend has become a matchmaker," she whispered. "Smile, wave, and keep your calm. We'll take her out and shoot her later."

Isabel didn't want to wave and smile and certainly couldn't muster her calm. "I hate her."

"Perhaps she believes she's doing you a favor," Iris reasoned in a hushed voice, but Isabel begged to differ. If Sophie Fairchild was doing her a favor, *she* would be sitting there with Paris.

"What did I miss?" John's hushed voice came from Olivia's former seat. He handed Isabel the program, smiling. "Come sit with me in the back. You don't mind, do you?" he asked Iris.

Isabel's eyes were attached to this evening's reigning couple. Paris met her gaze again, and she could have sworn she detected a glint of triumph in his eyes. Was he gloating? Was this his method of penalizing her for saying "no"—to reenter the *ton* with her best friend on his arm? She refused to accept that Sophie would go along with it. She must be misreading the entire situation. Paris was neither vindictive nor cruel, and Sophie would never stab her in the back. *Never*. But then the unthinkable happened. He grinned at something Sophie whispered in his ear and brought her gloved knuckles to his lips. *He kissed Sophie's hand.* Isabel stood. "Shall we switch, Iris?"

"We'll chaperone them from the fore," Olivia assured Iris when the latter dithered.

As they traded seats, Iris whispered in Isabel's ear, "I wouldn't hide at the back of an opera box with the man I don't want just to annoy the one I do. The whole world is watching."

It was either that or run home, thus announcing to the world that she was in love with the Earl of Ashby. Isabel sat down stiffly in Iris's former seat and fixed her gaze on the stage. *Think of something else,* she told herself as tears accumulated in her eyes.

A finger touched her chin and tilted her head aside. Before she realized John's intent, his lips met hers in a gentle kiss. *What are you doing,* her mind shrieked. She pushed him away and scrambled to her feet. She flounced past the heavy curtains at the back of the box and dashed down the vacant corridor toward the entrance of the theatre.

"Isabel!" a deep voice roared at her back, but she kept on running, sobbing and panting.

A hack drew up before the front steps as she came down. "Seven Dover Street," she called out to the driver and jumped inside. The hack lurched forward, and she collapsed back against the tattered squabs. The world had gone mad tonight, and the only sane place was home.

Paris came to a halt at the top step and watched the hack Isabel had climbed into drive off. He swore, wanting to break Macalister's bloody neck. Watching Isabel letting Hanson kiss her had nearly sent him leaping from his box. Yes, he wanted to make her jealous; jealousy made the heart grow fonder, but not toward a rival. *Damnation.* Everything had just gone to hell.

"Come back inside before the lights go up and the corridor swarms with people." A French accented voice spoke behind him. "We've come this far, let's not ruin it."

He whipped around, his muscles tense with barely suppressed fury. "I'm going after her! This is absurd! If her brother hears of that kiss, she'll be engaged to Hanson by breakfast!"

With a worried glance at a footman, Sophie whispered, "Calm down, and for God's sake, lower your voice. Do you think Stilgoe can make her marry someone she doesn't want?"

"She seemed to want to kiss Hanson very badly a moment ago, and in front of everyone!"

"Not everyone. *You.* Everyone else was staring at us. Anyway, she stopped the kiss almost immediately. Remember, Izzy has just received her first shock. Next time she'll be ready for us with her claws drawn, which is precisely what you want. Be patient."

If she let Hanson kiss her to get back at him for this one appearance, he dreaded to imagine what she might let the blond shark get away with tomorrow. He shoved a hand through his hair, a suffocating ache compressing his chest. "I begged her to marry me, to spend her life with me, and she accused me of being a despicable monster, who didn't care a whit about her and wanted to put her in a cage. A cage!" His harsh breaths swirled like smoke in the cool night air. This was killing him, wanting her to the point of insanity, while every word he said and everything he did to win her seemed to drive her farther away from him. "I never wanted any woman but her."

Sophie took his arm. "Come. Let us go back inside before intermission begins. We have an affair to bandy about and we should also exercise your rusty social skills."

He looked at her. "What's the point, Sophie?" He exhaled haggardly, this evening's events taking their toll on his spirit more than he cared to admit. "She doesn't want me, not really.

I was her girlhood fancy. My flesh and blood form daunts her. She'll keep coming up with excuses—"

"Then you must show her the man she came to know years ago, remind her that he's still there"—she jabbed a finger at his chest—"inside."

"Slap on my hussar regimentals and pay a visit to Seven Dover Street?" he quipped grimly.

"Why not?" She sent him a kindly smile and dragged him back into the torture chamber.

"What happened to me, Sophie? I was a man once."

"You are still a very fine man, but you suffered a traumatic experience in the war, and your mind has not yet completely recovered from it. As for Izzy, you need to woo her, dazzle her with your wits and charms and anything else you keep in your arsenal—anything that won't render her utterly ruined, that is."

"I thought I was supposed to woo you," he countered, wondering if Sophie had an inkling of how utterly "ruined" he'd already rendered her golden-haired friend. She probably did, the sly creature, but was clever enough not to allude to his and Isabel's transgressions openly.

"Ah, *mon petit ami*, I heard grand tales about your past exploits. Surely you won't let one fake mistress stand in the way of more important conquests."

"Escort you in public and woo her in secret, you mean?" The idea had merit, to be sure. Of course, Isabel would accuse him of sneaking about with her again, only this time they shouldn't be sneaking in the dark or behind the walls of Lancaster House. He could sneak about with her in broad daylight and in the open. First, however, as Sophie wisely pointed out, he needed to brush up his social skills. He'd come appallingly close to disintegrating a few moments ago, and he was simply too damned proud to use Isabel as a crutch on his return to Polite Society.

"Tomorrow evening," Sophie jarred his thoughts, "Stilgoe

and his wife are taking Izzy to watch the fireworks at Vaux-hall Gardens. We must go, too."

"If we must, we must."

"The day after that you will come to the agency and take me out for luncheon. It is very important that you go about town in the daylight hours, as well, you see."

"Yes, my tough drill sergeant."

"After that we'll undertake our first ball. By then, you'll be bombarded with invitations."

"I should have brought a bloody notepad after all."

"Now stop scowling and smile."

"Why?" he grunted, vaguely aware that they were no longer sitting in the dark.

"Intermission," replied the amused voice of Macalister, as he shoved aside the curtains and let the first circle of gossip-hungry vultures into the Lancaster family box.

Chapter Twenty-Six

The next morning Isabel stormed into Sophie's office. "Would you care to explain—"

Sophie signaled for her to wait a moment and returned her attention to the woman she was in the process of interviewing. "I think we've covered everything, Miss Billingsworth. As soon as an opening for a governess comes in, we will contact you. Thank you for coming here."

"Thank you, Mrs. Fairchild. You've given me hope." The young woman came to her feet, and with a wary glance at Isabel, hurried out the door.

Isabel slammed it shut. "What were you doing in the theatre with Ashby, Sophie?"

"He invited me. I saw no reason to refuse."

Isabel seethed. "The reason is standing right here in front of you!"

Sophie stood and went to pour herself a glass of water. "Be honest, Izzy. You don't want him. Not really. I gave you excellent advice, and you dismissed it out of hand. Did you expect him to remain alone forever? He wants company, and as you won't have him, why shouldn't I?"

Isabel felt she was about to explode. "Because . . ." *He is mine!*

"He told me it was you who thought he and I would deal well together. You were right."

Isabel blinked back tears of misery. "I also thought you were my friend, Sophie."

"I am your friend."

"You are nothing of the sort! You are an unfeeling, unconscionable . . . back-stabbing witch. You knew I loved him and . . . and you took him!"

"I didn't take anything you did not throw away," Sophie replied calmly. "However, if your feelings for him are unchanged, I suggest you go to him and tell him you've reconsidered. I will not stand in your way. Nor will I see him again if he rejects you. Is this acceptable to you?"

"I *have* reconsidered—you may both go to the devil!" Isabel spun on her heel and stormed out the door. Acceptable, ha! She would *never* crawl back to him. Three times she confessed her love for him. She sought him out; she surrendered her virtue; she convinced him to end his seclusion . . . but no more! If Sophie was what he wanted, then Sophie was what he would get.

Cursing under her breath, she stomped into her office and came to a halt when Lord John Hanson stepped forth to greet her. "Isabel, my dear, I came to apologize for last night."

She stared at him blankly, then remembered their flitting kiss. "Oh, that. Well, you should not have done it." She started for her seat behind her desk, but he gripped her hands.

Slowly he knelt down. *Oh, no.* She stifled a groan. Not now. "My lovely Isabel, I—"

"Good morning."

At the sound of the familiar deep voice goose bumps spread over Isabel's arms. She looked up, heat rushing through her body, and met Paris's inscrutable green eyes. What an opportune entry, she thought vengefully, gleefully, straight out of a Shakespearean play. "Good morning."

With palpable annoyance, John pushed to his feet. "Ashby."

"Hanson," Paris drawled, then dismissed the man, focusing on her. "Sophie tells me fifty quid are gone missing from the charity box. I came to look into the matter."

John stirred. "Do you attend the fireworks at Vauxhall this evening?" he asked her.

Isabel blinked. "My brother and his wife are escorting me."

"Splendid. I'll leave you to your charity business, then. Good day, my dear." He kissed her hand and left as if his tail were on fire. His behavior was very odd, she thought. He already knew that Ashby wouldn't pound him for the insult John had handed him at the charity ball.

Paris gripped the doorknob. "Please leave the door open, Lord Ashby," Isabel clipped and hurried to take shelter behind the desk before her wobbly knees buckled and she sprawled on her face. She was not ready to have this conversation with him yet. Her feelings were too jumbled.

He strolled in, circled the large desk to where she sat, and leaned back against it, folding his arms across his well-tailored chest. Green eyes studied her. "How are you feeling?"

"What?" Her heart jolted. He could not be inquiring about what she thought he was.

"When we were last together," he began softly, "you turned blue in the face and doubled over an open window in the nude. I am inquiring after your health."

She stiffened her spine. "I'm perfectly sound, thank you."

"I would appreciate an explanation. I was concerned."

How cool he was, she reflected. Or was he controlled? Ugh, she might as well tell him. "I dislike closed spaces. Sometimes, when I feel . . . trapped, my lungs compress and I suffocate. It is not a serious ailment. Our family physician insists that it's mostly in my head."

A muscle bunched in his jaw. "I apologize. I had no intention of making you feel *trapped*."

His emphasis on the word made her wince. Clearly he misunderstood. "I didn't mean with you," she clarified snappishly. "I meant trapped in the mental sense—anxiety, nervousness."

"I know what you meant." His eyes glinted.

Well, how was she to know that a week later he would be escorting her *former* friend about town? "What are you doing here? What are you doing outside in public?"

"I bought a ticket," he scoffed. "What the devil do you think I'm doing?"

Tomcatting after an ex-opera singer? "Disrupting my busy schedule," she muttered. How could he go to Sophie after their night together? Why didn't he come to her?

His jaw tightened again. "I seemed to have *interrupted* something else entirely."

Out of sorts, she got up, needing to escape his disturbingly close proximity. "Whatever you interrupted will probably be concluded this evening." That put her even more on edge. The way things were progressing, she would be better off barricading herself at home, as Paris used to do.

Steely fingers closed around her arm and jerked her back to face a considerably less self-possessed Paris. "I saw you kissing him last night. What answer do you intend to give him?"

She was shocked into silence by the swift surge of yearning that saturated her bloodstream. Staring into his lambent sea eyes, she could still feel him on her skin, caressing her, kissing her, moving inside her body, making her shudder with pleasure. It was more than she could bear.

"Isabel . . ." He leaned in, his gaze imprisoning hers. "What answer will you give him?"

The need to pull him closer and kiss him to oblivion rendered her positively mad—but he had Sophie now! "None of your affair! You made your choice. Now live with it!"

Black anger crossed his handsome features. "*I* made my choice? You said 'no'! What was I supposed to do, wait forever?"

"You asked me to reconsider and then you . . . you took Sophie to the theatre! I hate you!"

As she flew out the door to seek refuge in Iris's office, she heard him growling at her back, "Yes, I believe you've made *that* clear on several occasions!"

"Izzy?" Iris lifted surprised eyes from her newspaper. "What's wrong?"

Isabel latched the door and started pacing about the office, trembling all over. "He's here."

"Yes, I thought I recognized his voice. . . You are in a state. Has anything come to pass?"

Isabel swallowed. "Did you inform Sophie about the missing fifty pounds?"

"Last night, at the theatre, during intermission. I went to speak with her privately."

"What did she tell you?" Isabel inquired, dreading the answer, though in effect, there was nothing to dread anymore. The worst had already come to pass: Paris rejoined Society and was courting another woman. Was Sophie the appointment she'd seen him dashing off to that night?

Iris evaded her gaze. "They are seeing each other, Isabel. I'm sorry."

"What are you sorry for? It's not your dagger sticking out of my back."

"Calm down. Take a look at this." Iris showed her that day's edition of the *Times*.

Isabel leaned forward to skim the marked article. "It's about us!"

"About you," Iris amended. She read, "'The Honorable Miss Aubrey is a veritable lioness: Defender of the weak, protector of the unfortunate, this fine young lady has appointed herself the champion of war widows, of bereaved mothers, of defenseless sisters, and the godmother of the little boys and girls missing their papas . . .'"

Tears flooded her eyes. Only a simpleton would fail to

recognize the source of the article. Those were Paris's words. He had given the story to the papers. And while it offered an excellent promotion for her cause, she suspected his intent was of a personal nature. "Give it to me."

Clutching the newspaper with trembling hands, Isabel left Iris's office—and ran into Paris. He was on his way out. Swallowing hard, she indicated the article. "You put it there."

"Yes."

"Why?"

He stared at her darkly. "You merit every word."

Her heart pulled toward him in a desperate attempt to tear out of her chest. "Thank you."

"You're welcome." He doffed his hat and marched to the flight of stairs.

"Pa—" His name died on her lips. Resisting the mad impulse to run after him, she watched him disappearing down the stairwell, then sank on the top step and sobbed.

Chapter Twenty-Seven

The ensuing week felt like a nightmare Isabel couldn't awaken from. There was no turning one's head without spotting the Earl of Ashby arm in arm with Mrs. Fairchild. *Sickening*.

The couple attended every social affair Isabel did, spent hours in Sophie's office with the door open—God forbid, anyone happening to walk by might fail to notice they were pleasantly engaged in laughter and conversation—took long luncheons, and basically drove Isabel insane.

A fortnight ago, Paris was her covert project and secret lover. Now he was the talk of the town. Hostesses were bidding against each other for the privilege of his presence at their soirees. The gentlemen were giving him standing ovations at White's, at Alfred Club, and at every other exclusive club he suddenly joined. Women ogled him everywhere. The old Ashby was back.

To make matters worse, additional funds disappeared from the charity box. The one thing both occurrences had in common was the coincidental presence of Lord John in the building at the time of the alleged thefts. Yet unable to fathom why the heir to the Haworth dukedom should result to petty thievery, Isabel deduced that she had misplaced the blunt herself. She had become a scatterbrain of late, to say the least.

She was floundering. *And she was miserable.* Her friend had betrayed her and the man she loved had moved on. No wonder she felt like a madwoman, livid one moment, tearful the next. It was a miracle she dragged her sorry self to work every day.

The sole ray of light in her unhappy existence was a minor crisis at Stilgoe Abbey that had removed her brother from town, thus preventing John from securing her brother's consent on the matter of a possible union between John and Isabel. She made a point of steering clear of John to ensure that his foiled attempt at proposing didn't repeat itself. She absolutely did not want John Hanson. Which made one thing glaringly clear: Spinsterhood beckoned, because the very idea of sharing intimacies with any man who wasn't Paris Nicholas Lancaster repelled her.

Standing at the window overlooking Piccadilly, lost in gloomy thoughts, Isabel jumped at the voice addressing her inside her office. She whipped around, surprised to see a footboy from home. "Yes, Smithy. What is it?"

"Lord Stilgoe is returned, Miss Aubrey. He sent the carriage, requesting your presence at Seven Dover Street. You have guests."

"Guests?" He must have brought her cousins with him, Isabel surmised. Though it was three o'clock in the afternoon, she realized she wanted nothing better than to go home, play with her niece, squabble with her sisters, and chat with her cousins. She collected her bonnet, pelisse, and reticule and headed out. A lovely day welcomed her outside, with the birds chirping and the leaves rustling in the trees, but not lovely enough to pull her out of the doldrums.

As the carriage approached Seven Dover Street, Isabel caught sight of a brand new, shiny, high-perched blue phaeton tied to a matching pair of grays. It was parked in their driveway. In addition, three kennels, prettily designed and carved of wood, lined the stables' wall. Something fishy was afoot at

Seven Dover Street, and she had a solid suspicion *who* it was. "Guests, my foot," she muttered. So now he was invading her home, as well. Well, not for long.

She stomped inside to a rumpus of laughter, chatter, and barks coming from the first floor. "Good afternoon, Norris." She handed the butler her bonnet and pelisse. "Who's our guest?"

"Lord Ashby, Miss Isabel. He is with the family in the drawing room."

Ah-ha! She attributed the fluttering in her belly to the satisfaction derived from possessing stupendous powers of deduction. "Is he staying for dinner?" In the past he always did.

"I believe he is, Miss Isabel. Ugh, we also have dogs in the house," the butler elaborated, on the verge of tears. "They destroyed her ladyship's Persian carpet."

"Mama is not in hysterics?" Suppressing laughter, Isabel studied the pinched-face Norris.

His lips twitched. "Lady Aubrey seems pleased with the canine addition to the household."

"Do not hasten to hand over your resignation, Norris. The dogs may grow on you."

"I highly doubt it, Miss Isabel."

She padded upstairs, wondering what her scheming mother and brother were up to now. Then it hit her—they were setting her after Ashby, believing it to be the desirable conclusion all around. They liked him; she liked him; hence, wedding bells. Pity they were two weeks too late.

Lucy rushed forth to greet her. "Her ladyship requests that you change into your summer blue muslin gown, let your hair down, and join the family in the drawing room."

So she was to preen herself for him, was she? "I look fine as I am."

Lucy hurried beside her. "Please, Miss Isabel. Lady Aubrey said I would be dismissed if you were to make an appearance in a smudged gown and with windblown hair."

"Fine." For Lucy's sake. Poor LJ, she reflected, discarded without a second thought.

Fifteen minutes later, she made her way to the drawing room in a gown that matched her eyes, with a mane of perfect bottle locks cloaking her arms, and suffering of severe palpitations. Her gaze swept the room. Will's trunk lay open at her mother's feet. Her twin sisters sat on the carpet beside it, with black puppies in their laps, and Danielli between them. Charles and Angie occupied the settee. And at the center of this picture of domestic harmony was Paris.

"Oh, Izzy!" Her mother waved her over, the tears in her eyes clashing with her ecstatic smile. "Look who's come to call on us—your favorite person in the entire world, Lord Ashby!"

"Mama!" Isabel sent her mother a murderous look, cursing herself for blushing.

He stood up, sketching a bow. "Miss Isabel. It is a pleasure to see you again."

She forced herself to meet his brilliant gaze squarely. He looked positively heart-stopping in glove-tight buckskin breeches, gleaming Hobys, and a deep blue coat that did the color trick with his stunning blue-green eyes—a quintessence of a wealthy, single nobleman on the town. The significant change, however, was in his air. He seemed . . . happier. *Blast him.* "Lord Ashby." She dipped, a frosty smile playing on her lips. *What are you doing here*, her eyes demanded.

All she got in return was a sphinx-like grin.

"Izzy, look! Ashby brought us puppies!" Freddy jumped to her feet and pranced over with her black pup. So the chit was best friends with him already, Isabel mused sourly. "Isn't he the most adorable thing you've ever seen? I named him Gustavo, and Teddy named hers—"

"Blackberry," Teddy supplied, petting the black bundle in her lap. "Because you're a black little berry, aren't you?" She glanced up at Isabel. "He brought you one, as well."

"And kennels!" Freddy contributed happily. "He made them himself."

"Dogs in the house, Mama?" Isabel scoffed. "How did this miracle come about?"

"Lord Ashby has solicited my permission, and I granted it."

"So long as they are supervised indoors and spend the night in the kennels by the stables," Teddy specified the terms. "It's all been discussed."

"Yes, it's all been discussed," Paris echoed.

"How very kind of you, my lord," Isabel murmured, studying the happy faces around her. They all adored him. Even though he'd decisively stayed away from their home for seven years, and even though it had taken him two years to return Will's belongings, they welcomed him with open arms, grateful for his company. It riled her, knowing she would have reacted likewise.

She lifted Danielli into her arms, inhaling the sweet angel with kisses, and approached the open trunk with pangs in her heart. She longed to explore it with reverence and care, but that she would do later, alone. "I see you've returned Will's belongings to us, my lord, and so promptly. Lancaster House must be a great big depot of moldy old things," she told the room in general but kept her gaze on Paris. "Lost trunks and *antiques*. Indeed, your consideration knows no bounds."

"Izzy, you're coming it much too strong!" Charles shot her a shocked warning look, which she coolly chose to ignore.

"Your sister's complaint is justified," Paris allowed. "I should have returned Will's effects two years ago. It is something I regret keenly." He stared at her, a message in his eyes.

Liar, her eyes returned. *If you had truly regretted it, you would have come two weeks ago.*

"As for my antique collection," he drawled, as she plunked herself down on the carpet and seated Danielli in her lap. "I seem to recall *you* once had a great passion for the antiquity."

Ah, war. Her smile turned bloodthirsty. "Education is very important, wouldn't you say? And what better way to improve one's . . . mind than to learn from the great masters of the past?"

Heat suffused his eyes—and he stepped right into her trap. "Then, I insist you come by and indulge your scholarly appetites. I keep my ancient . . . artifacts polished to a shine."

I'm certain you do. She cursed him silently, smiling. "Thank you, my lord, but the past can only fascinate for so long. At some point one must put his knowledge to good use in the modern world. Quite recently I've developed a passion for golden things, preferably new ones."

"Really?" He raised an eyebrow.

"Yes. Really."

"What a coincidence. I brought you something that answers all of your requirements." He bent down, flipped open a picnic basket similar to the one she'd put Hector in seven years ago, and lifted the golden puppy she'd petted at Ashby Park. He came over to crouch before her. Despite herself, Isabel softened. "Here," he murmured. "New, golden, and . . . beautiful."

As his fingers brushed hers, desire assailed her, and by the look in his eyes, he felt it too. Evading his gaze, she showed Danielli how to stroke the puppy. "She is delightful. Thank you."

"How will you name her, Izzy?" Teddy asked.

"I don't know," Isabel said, struggling to block out Paris's heady scent. It was awful, how he made her want him in spite of his villainous conduct—pursuing her best friend, of all people!

Danielli climbed to her feet, burbling cheerfully, and touched Paris's cheek. "U-cle!"

Charles burst out laughing. "Not yet, he isn't, puppet."

Isabel's face went up in flames. Mortified, she gnashed her teeth, keeping her gaze low.

Chuckling, Paris hoisted the toddler into his arms, and

while doing so, leaned over Isabel's shoulder and murmured, "From the mouth of babes."

Her insides contracted. She looked at him, but aside from humor, she couldn't tell what went on behind those glittering emerald eyes of his.

Norris came to announce dinner, and everyone jumped to their feet.

"It's good to have you over," Charlie told Paris as he claimed his daughter. "I've been the odd man out for too long." He grinned at his wife, standing by his side. "But that may change."

Isabel already knew about that, but when she saw the wistful look in Paris's eyes, her heart skipped a beat. For no good reason.

Throughout dinner, Paris entertained them with stories about Will, and contrary to Isabel's inauspicious forecast, the evening turned out to be as cozy and fun as the ones that had included her dearly missed brother. It seemed the seven years Paris avoided their house were but a day. He slipped back into his former role without ceremony, becoming a natural addition to her nutty family once again. Everyone chatted all at once, forgoing any semblance of decorum.

Isabel was sadly reminded of the reasons she'd become enamored of him years ago. Aside from his physical attributes, he was intelligent, genuine, amusing, and had not a drop of malice in him. Even her mama turned up sweet in his presence, and not just because he was a potential son-in-law. He seemed to possess a certain charm that put everyone in a jolly mood and never attracted hostility. *Like Will.* Strange she hadn't noticed it before.

How could she not love him?

Booming laughter erupted from the end of the table. "You

mad dogs!" Charlie guffawed, hitting the table with both hands. "I can't believe Wellington didn't send you to the brig!"

Ashby chuckled. "He considered it . . . but marching up against Boney without cavalry was unwise under the best of circumstances."

"What are you cackling about? We want to hear the tale!" the twins protested in chorus, followed by similar complaints from Angie and Hyacinth.

All eyes fixed on Ashby. His amused gaze swept the table, briefly colliding with Isabel's.

"Yes, Ashby, we want to hear the tale," she mimicked her sisters' intonation.

"Go on, tell them." Charles exhaled. "I've given up on the brats, and it's just us family."

"Very well," Paris concurred genially. "Ten days before the fighting broke in Quatre Bras, we held cavalry races in a small town near Brussels. We were bored stiff waiting for troops to arrive, and the *ton* was there, having come from England to watch the 'fun.'"

"Are cavalry races the ones in which one has his saber drawn, and if he touches the reins with his right hand during the race, he is disqualified?" Freddy inquired.

"Yes. But there were also matches between ponies and mules, which amused us a lot."

"Is it true that you always took the gold cup?" Freddy smiled coyly.

"Will you stop interrupting and let Ashby tell the tale?" Teddy snapped at her twin.

Paris cast Freddy a kind smile. "I sometimes won the gold cup, but not in mule races."

"He always won," Charlie affirmed. "And you two put a lid on it. Carry on, Ash."

"Halfway through the races, we were assaulted with a violent rainstorm. We took refuge in an old house, where refreshments had been prepared, and sat to a cold dinner, washed down with a lot of champagne. In two hours, the whole party was drunk. Some sot from the 10th Hussars jumped on a table and set out to break all the plates, bottles, and glasses. Then everyone was on the tables, ladies and gentlemen alike, singing and smashing dishes. So Will gets up, crowing, 'Enough with this savagery! Let's get back to the races!' And the maddest rush ensued, men throwing themselves on their horses and going back to the racecourse, half of them falling off on the way, and many of the horses galloping to the stables without their riders."

Chuckling, Isabel noted that even her captious mama was vastly amused.

"We raced headlong to the bell tower—"

"You, too?" Isabel inquired in astonishment. "I always took you for the levelheaded sort."

He raised an eyebrow. "In other words, you think me dull."

"Not dull, precisely." She feigned a frown to disguise the mischief she was up to. "Sensible would be a better word. Will was the rascally sort, knocking up larks, committing follies, making riot and rumpus . . ." She sighed reminiscently. "You were sensible."

Charles gave a shout of laughter. "Sensible, Ashby? How many times did you get rolled-up in a Round-house or were sent down from Cambridge for, eh, indiscretions in your dormitory?"

"Do not put yourself out on my account," Paris drawled. "If your sister says I'm dull . . ."

Isabel smiled sweetly. "Pray do not take me up so literally. Perhaps you weren't always as you are today, but must we hark back to Methuselah's time? I am certain you've outgrown the restiveness of your salad days long before that, my lord."

Paris's lopsided grin broadened. "In those Biblical days, when a woman insulted a man in the guise of flattery, it usually meant something else entirely."

"Izzy, you are ruining the story!" Teddy complained. "You can flirt with him later!"

Reddening, Isabel swallowed her next sweetly disguised verbal abuse and caught Paris's gaze. "I was not flirting, I was heckling," she clarified indignantly. "There is a difference—"

"Whatever you were doing, do it later," Freddy lectured.

"We'll have to do it later." Paris nodded in resignation, a devilish smile lurking in his eyes. "So where was I? Ah, at night, and we were sprinting across the boggy fields, giving the natives a good show of the independence of the English Hussars, and shouting 'Long Live Napoleon!'"

Teddy and Freddy burst out laughing, as did her mother and Angie. Grinning, Isabel cast Paris a surreptitious glance. He was—she thought privately, earnestly—wonderful.

"We accidentally upturned two carriages and gave the ladies inside hysterics as we charged their husbands or protectors in a truly Cossack manner, and discovered the next day that one of the unfortunates was the mayor of the town. Unhappily he declared that he never again wanted to have anything to do with such a gang of English Cossacks. It was, as I said, Will's idea."

More laughter issued from everyone, then a sad silence fell around the table. Dabbing a napkin at her watering eyes, Hyacinth smiled and whispered, "Thank you. You are a dear boy."

"My pleasure, madam."

After dinner Charlie shanghaied Ashby to the library, where he monopolized him for an hour with whiskey and cigars, and the females retired to bed. Jittery and morose, Isabel skulked in the dim hallway, waiting for her brother to quit yammering and retire. She wasn't letting Paris leave without giving him a piece of her mind. She peeped inside. Charlie sat with his back to her, so she leaned in further, trying to catch Paris's notice. Finally, he saw her. He stood and took his leave. "My thanks, Charles, and congratulations on the forthcoming addition to the family." He fondly clapped her brother's shoulder. "If it's the next Viscount Stilgoe, come to Ashby Park. I'll let you choose whichever of my prime cattle catches your eye in the stables."

"Say, that's jolly good of you, Ash!" Her brother shot to his feet. "Come by again soon. It was grand having you over for dinner. You don't need an invitation."

Before her brother walked Paris to the door, Isabel made a faint noise. He was not getting away from the trimming he so well deserved. Paris seemed to catch on. "I'll let myself out, Charlie," he said. "You go on upstairs to your pretty wife."

Finally, Isabel thought. She hid behind the flower arrangement gracing the hallway table, and as soon as she spotted the tall shadow exiting the chamber, she hissed, "Over here."

With a backward glance, Paris approached her. She gripped his hand and pulled him into the adjacent room. A lamp she'd lit beforehand dyed the walls a soft, tawny glow.

"I'm at your disposal," Paris murmured, advancing slowly, his eyes serious.

She took a deep breath. "I don't want you to set foot in this house again," she said firmly.

"You don't?" He took another step. Silky dark hair brushed his white cravat, and a shock of it fell across his forehead, enhancing the brilliance of his emerald eyes. "Why is that?"

For lack of a better response, she blurted, "Save your stories for Sophie and Jerome."

Amusement etched his eyes. "You're jealous."

"Hardly!"

"But you shouldn't be," he went on. "Sophie and I are just friends."

"Do you really expect me to believe that? I hate you!"

He rolled his eyes. "Can't you think of anything else to say to me? Use your imagination, Isabel. Say it pains you to see me with another woman. Say you can't stop thinking about me. Say"—he closed the distance between them but didn't touch her—"you want me back."

She gave a brittle laugh. "I would say you're a victim of an overly developed imagination."

He towered over her, his intense eyes smoldering. "Why don't you stop playing games and tell me the truth?"

"What truth?" She edged back. This was *not* where their conversation was supposed to go. It was her house, and she was setting the rules.

"That you've reconsidered." He smiled benignly. "Have you reconsidered?"

"Stop seeing Sophie and I'll think about it," she challenged archly.

"I won't dangle on a string alongside your male marionettes, my dear. If you want me, you shall have to say it." He tilted his head at her. "Do you want me?"

Yes, her heart cried.

Footsteps sounded in the hallway. "Norris," her brother spoke outside the den. "You've left my bloody office lamp lit again. Do you want to burn the house down around our ears?"

"Apologies, my lord. I shall turn it off immediately."

"I'll do it. Shuttlehead," Charles muttered under his breath as he approached the doorway.

Isabel shoved Paris back against the entrance wall and pulled the door open all the way to conceal them. She met Paris's eyes in the shadows and it dawned on her what a confounded idiot she was. She had just placed herself in a ten times more precarious situation. Being found together in a room was one thing, but being found huddling chest to chest behind a door was quite another. "Spend the day with me tomorrow," Paris suggested very softly.

No, she mouthed back.

He stretched his neck aside. "Eh, Ch—" Isabel clamped a hand over his mouth. He clasped her wrist and tugged. "Yes or no?" he murmured. "The entire day."

Her brother walked in.

"*Yes*," she hissed.

The light went out, and a warm, whiskey-scented mouth found hers. Heat swamped her. His lips plied hers with gentle ease as his tongue swept inside her mouth and tasted her leisurely. *Oh, God.* She melted against him, leaning into his solid frame and sliding her hands beneath his coat and around his waist. She hadn't realized how starved she was for the feel of him, for his kisses. Her mind insisted that this was not an admission of anything, that it was her wanton body taking what she had sworn to forever deprive it of. However she rationalized it, though, what she felt for Paris went so far beyond the proverbial love and desire that it touched the uncanny. She could hate him, rail at him, and still love him to death, for he was a part of her, like her family.

Vaguely she heard Charlie's footsteps receding down the hallway and knew they were in the clear. Loath to bring this incredibly sensual and arousing kiss to a stop, she pretended not to hear.

Paris lifted his mouth from hers and ran his thumb over her swollen lips. "Be ready for me at eleven o'clock and wear a riding habit," he murmured, his voice thicker than usual.

Then he was gone.

Breathing fast and hard, desire pulsing through her veins, she sagged against the wall and slid to the floor. She was becoming one of them, those fallen women he once dangled on a string. *Take care*, a voice inside her head warned. No love confessions and no sexual encounters. So long as he insisted on being friends with Sophie, surrendering to him would surely destroy her.

Chapter Twenty-Eight

"You're early," Isabel exclaimed, as she flew down the stairs, one hand keeping her pretty hat on her head and the other clasping the skirts of her cream-colored riding habit, which was not very practical but had a deep V neck, complimented her figure, and was summery and festive.

"Don't run. There's plenty of time," Paris said from the foot of the staircase.

But Isabel didn't want to waste a minute of it. She'd had a devil of a time falling asleep last night, her body humming with desire and a welter of conflicting thoughts spinning in her head, until she'd finally admitted how terribly excited she was by the prospect of spending a whole day with Paris in the open. Waking up this morning she'd made a pact with herself not to read too much into anything and simply enjoy herself. Nor would she let Sophie's shadow dampen her spirit. Her heart seemed settled on Paris, and she didn't think the poor organ would have further opportunities to indulge in this sort of luxury. One day together, that was all she allowed herself.

He took her hand when she reached him. "Good morning," he murmured, his light sea eyes studying her as he kissed her knuckles. "You look . . . ravishable."

"Stop that," she mumbled, with a glance at her brother, who was lurking unobtrusively at the door.

"I'll expect better from you in private," Paris informed her softly, sending a coil of shivers swirling up her spine. He looked over his shoulder. "I will return your sister in time for dinner."

"If you insist," her brother replied, his blue eyes dancing, and received a glare from Isabel.

Paris wrapped her hand around his warm sleeve and proceeded to the door. She came to a sudden halt, remembering. "We need a chaperone."

"I brought a chaperone," Paris said. "Don't fret. I've been rendered perfectly civilized."

It put her all on end that someone else had been doing any rendering with him when until a fortnight ago he belonged solely to her. *Good Lord, now who was being possessive?*

Norris opened the door, and as they stepped outside to a sunny day, Isabel noticed for the first time that Paris's hair was a rich dark brown rather than black and that it was the exact color of his jacket; that he had a dimple in his right cheek and tiny crinkles at the corners of his eyes from the years he'd spent under a hot Spanish sun; that his smooth shave showed little potential of growing into a bushy beard; that his scars were of a lighter shade than his complexion; and that he was even handsomer in the sunlight than he was by candlelight.

"I have a dozen wrinkles and four white hairs," he drawled, his gaze fixed ahead.

"Just four?" she returned, biting back a chuckle.

He looked at her, humor and concern clashing in his gemlike eyes. A flock of butterflies took wing in her stomach. "I predict you will have trebled the number before the day is over."

Apollo stomped and snorted in the driveway, causing the regal-looking bay beside him to whinny nervously. A liveried groom with a horse of his own—their chaperone—held the reins.

"This is not Luna," Isabel noted, pointing at the beautiful, skittish bay.

"I took the liberty of sending your lovely Arabian back to the stables. I brought you this one." He led her to the tall mare. "She's a sterling hunter, clever and courageous, and has superb stamina, greater than Apollo's. He seems to resent it, I think. Her name"—he ran a loving hand along her shiny neck—"is Milagro. That's Spanish for 'miracle'. And she's yours."

Milagro was by far the finest mare Isabel had ever seen. "What do you mean 'mine'?"

"Yours. A gift. She's young, so you'll have to continue her training, but—"

"I can't accept such a gift from you," she scolded. "We've had this discussion before."

"If Izzy won't take her, I will," Stilgoe announced, coming over to admire the bay.

Ashby sent him an amused look. "You can't afford her, Charlie."

"Go away," Izzy muttered at her brother. This was her day, her horse, and her. . . She did not know how to complete the thought, but it—he—was definitely not Stilgoe's.

"I'm gone." Her brother spun on his heel, his hands in the air. "Have fun!"

"Tell you what." Paris clasped her waist and lifted her effortlessly into the saddle. "If you outrun Apollo and me, we'll say you won her in a fair bet."

"Ha, ha. You'll let me win. Besides, who'd believe I outran you?" She arranged her skirts, grinning at his ridiculous challenge. "Furthermore, racing is prohibited in Hyde Park."

He fluidly swung onto Apollo and met her gaze. "Who says I'm taking you to Hyde Park?"

"Well, I assumed . . ."

"We could go to the park if that is your preference," he conceded, as they walked out of the drive, the groom on their heels. "I . . . eh, was hoping to lure you elsewhere, though."

She glared at him. "That, I believe, is a conversation we've conducted *many* times before. I am not sneaking about with you, Paris," she hissed.

"How is this 'sneaking about,' pray tell? We are out in the open, properly chaperoned, it's not even noon yet, and there are people around us." He doffed his hat at Lady Elington and her daughter and received charmed smiles in return. "It doesn't get to be more respectable than this."

Duly chastised, she asked with a sigh, "Where did you wish to take me?"

"A meadow outside of town, where Apollo and I stretch our bones after midnight."

"Every night?" That explained his lurking outside her house. "Why there?"

"Because it's pretty, with fresh air, and we can race." He sent her a tempting smile.

"Race a centaur?" She made a face. "I'm uncomfortable sitting a horse beside you."

He leaned aside and brushed a fallen leaf off her shoulder. "You are forgetting, love, that I have had the exclusive pleasure of admiring your excellent seat and—"

"Don't—you—dare," she clipped, her complexion turning scarlet. Blast him for putting the picture of a secluded meadow and rampant lovemaking together in her brain.

"I won't, if you come to the meadow with me."

She lifted an eyebrow. "More blackmail? It's turning into a nasty habit, Ashby." *Stop that*, she shouted at herself. *You are ruining my day*. "I'll strike a bargain with you," she relented. "If you promise to behave in a gentlemanlike manner, which excludes blackmails and allusions to . . . certain things, we'll go to the meadow."

"Deal." He threw her a pleased grin. "And you'll race me for the hunter? You'll have a fair chance of winning on an open field, as Milagro was bred for the long days and fast galloping that go with hunting. Apollo could never live up to the rigors of her profession."

Nodding, Isabel wondered whether his choice of mare for

her was coincidental or not. She did hunt him, after all. Did he think her clever, courageous, and full of stamina?

They fell into easy silence as they traversed the streets of London, the groom following a few yards behind. She was amazed at the sharp change Paris had undergone in such a short period of time. Much as it galled her to acknowledge it, Sophie had performed a miracle with him, transforming a brooding, masked recluse into a sterling member of the *ton*. It bothered her that she'd sensed beforehand how well they would suit each other, Sophie and Paris. She never saw them arguing or being anything but pleasant and respectful toward one another in public, whereas her interactions with him were, in a word, volcanic. Even now, while they were being seemingly friendly and civilized, she could feel the tension sizzling between them.

Wanting to alleviate some of it, she asked, "Have you had a chance to look into the missing fifty pounds mystery? By the by, the missing sum has gone up to a hundred and seventy quid."

"Yes, I'm aware of that, and I have my suspicions, but I wouldn't want to implicate anyone without proof."

"It might have been me. I was somewhat addlebrained of late and may have misplaced—"

"I sincerely doubt that. In matters that concern your charity you are as focused as a hawk."

"Paris, please don't accuse anyone without consulting me first. Our housekeeper, Rebecca, is a poor, unfortunate woman. If she or her boys needed the money—"

"Do you trust me?" he asked softly, commanding her gaze.

Though he possessed the power to demolish her heart, she did trust him. "Yes, I do."

"Good." He smiled faintly. "Then let me handle this."

At the city's northern boundaries, they picked up their pace and trotted up a well-traveled road. It was a lovely day, perfect for riding. She could think of no one she would rather spend it with than the man riding beside her. Paris turned left, leaving the road, and led them to an open field. Recognizing the area, Apollo gave an eager snort. Isabel sensed similar vibrations coming from his master. "So"—Paris flashed her an enticing grin—"are you up for a race?"

She answered with a kick to Milagro's ribs. Someone shouted "cheat!" behind her, but she paid him no heed as she loosened the reins and gave Milagro her head, laughing exuberantly. She heard hooves pounding after her, and before long Paris and Apollo caught up—a sight to behold.

For several hundred yards they galloped side by side, her huntress showing well beside the big black. Paris was as magnificent as his thoroughbred stallion, his eyes a brilliant green in the sunlight, his sleek hair whipping at his shoulders, his well-muscled thighs controlling his mount with the same sinuous ease with which he moved and waltzed and made love to her—

She fell behind, but Paris was soon beside her again, grinning. Well, she was not about to be shown up without a fight. Snapping the reins, she lunged forward, ducking beneath the wind. Milagro was a prime runner and an ambitious one at that. Whenever their opponents drew near, she stretched her neck farther, leaving them behind. Her pulse and her spirits high, Isabel glanced back. Paris sent her a devilish grin, gave a shout that sounded like a battle cry, and the ground began roaring. She watched, agape, as he went flying by, heading for the grove beyond. *Oh, my.*

When she reached the woods mere moments later, Apollo was grazing. Paris was sprawled on his back in the tall grass, his eyes shut, pretending to snore. Her cheeks flushed and her pulse brisk, she jumped to the ground and came over to kick his heels. "Very amusing."

His boots tangled with hers, and with a shriek of laughter, she lost her footing and fell into his open arms. He flipped her over, half-covering her with his heavy frame. Choking on giggles, she smiled up into his emerald eyes as she struggled to catch her breath. "You were splendid."

"So were you." He brushed aside the golden tendrils clinging to her brow and cheeks, then removed the ivory clips from her hair. "You lost your hat . . . and your chaperone."

"You were too fast for all three of us."

He pulled off his glove and traced her features with his fingertips. "Adorable, you are."

The warmth in his eyes twisted her into knots. More than anything she wanted to sink her fingers in his hair and kiss him with impunity. But succumbing to lust would lead to heartache. When he lowered his head to kiss her, she turned her head aside. "No, Paris. Please let me up."

"Isabel . . ." His sultry breath fanned her ear. "I can't stand this separation anymore."

"Prove it," she whispered, utterly in turmoil, her eyes on a cricket climbing the tall grass. It was awful, yearning for him when he was involved with a woman who used to be her friend, and when the rest of the female multitude was waiting in the wings for him to tire of *that person*.

"I will . . ." He scattered butterfly kisses along the side of her face down to her neck.

The sound of approaching hooves gave her the strength to put an end to the madness. "Our chaperone is coming." She pushed him aside and sat up.

He stood, drawing her up with him. Her hand in his, he ushered her into the dappled shade of birches and elms, meandering among the trees, crunching leaves and twigs beneath his boots. Abruptly he pulled her aside and pinned her to a tree. His mouth came down on hers, ravening, persuading, seducing. In a moment of insanity, she buried her fingers in his hair and returned his kiss with all the fever in her blood. She caught herself and pushed him back. Whatever he said or did, she was not about to countenance any seductions today.

"You are not behaving as a proper gentleman," she scolded.

Humor sparked his eyes. He leaned into her. "Do you want me to?"

"Isn't it obvious?" she countered, all in a fluster and peeved with herself.

"So, so." He tilted his head from side to side, looking

amused. "Your voice says one thing, and your lips say something else entirely. Last night—"

"Last night meant nothing. You have Sophie."

He gazed at her, his expression reminding her of the little urchins she saw in Spitalfields, their expressive eyes silently begging for affection. "You will give me up without a fight?"

She cocked a quizzical eyebrow. "Are you mine to give?"

His expression sobered. "It's a trick question, Isabel."

"So is yours." What sort of infernal game was he playing? One moment he made her feel she was the only woman he wanted, and the next he had his mask on. *Lud*. He had a mask on!

He twisted his lips, exasperation and humor mingling in his gaze. "An impasse, then."

She regarded him through different, more astute eyes. "So it seems."

"I am by no means deterred." He stepped back and curled her hand around his arm.

"Neither am I." She ambled beside him, plotting the downfall of the *invisible* mask.

As he led her deeper inside the cool grove, she sensed him leaning closer. "I will have you again, repeatedly," he vowed. "And you will be wild for me."

"In your wildest dreams." She smirked archly, though inside she tingled.

"Or in yours." When her gaze shot to his, he chuckled. "Let's stroll to the stream. I'll teach you how to catch fish barehanded." He laced their fingers together, exuding good humor.

"A huntress, a fisherwoman . . . I see you are determined to turn me into a predator."

"Remain a fish, if you like, but be sure to wiggle prettily."

"Is Sophie your gudgeon?" she ventured, and blinked. Was it insight or wishful thinking?

"That remains to be seen," he replied noncommittally.

They came upon a blue stream; it shimmered like diamonds in the sunlight. Captivated by the scenery, Isabel almost stepped onto someone's picnic blanket, heaped with what appeared to be an untouched, elegantly served luncheon. Paris swept the area with a glance. "It seems that someone forgot his luncheon, a pair of lovers, who went for a swim and lost their appetite—for food, that is. I'm starving. How about you, lioness? I say we eat it up before they return."

She gasped when he plunked himself down on the blanket and examined the wine bottle. "What are you, an infant?" she squawked. "Get up before they come back and kill us!"

"Don't be a prude." He found a pair of glasses and uncorked the bottle. "Sit down."

"I'm not a prude! You're mad." She gripped his wrist and tried to drag him to his feet, but he was immovable. A twig snapped behind a tree. "Someone's coming—" Her jaw slackened. The "someone" was Phipps, accompanied by three liveried footmen. She bit her lip on a huge, embarrassed smile and gazed down at her escort. "You arranged this for me."

He offered her a glass of red wine. "Yes, I did. Sit."

She sat, smiling like a dolt, and accepted the wineglass. "It's the nicest surprise anyone has ever prepared for me," she confessed, taking in the opulent fare. "Everything looks wonderful."

"Dotage has made me frivolous, I fear."

"Oh, stuff it." She smiled, then added softly, "This is perfect. Thank you."

He touched his wineglass to hers, perusing her eyes. "You're welcome." His eyes seemed to say something more, but he held his tongue. It suddenly occurred to her that this was precisely what she'd once suggested they do—a horse ride and a picnic. It smacked of a courtship, but considering his recent activities, she didn't know what to make of this, or of him.

The servants remained sentinel at a discreet distance while Isabel and Paris polished off chicken and cucumber sandwiches, along with cheeses and grapes, slicked back with wine.

"I have a question for you," he drawled. "But you must promise not to hack my head off."

"I commit to nothing."

"Very well. I'll brave it." He lowered his voice. "Is there a reason we should marry?"

"What?" She crimsoned, then realized what he was asking and grew warmer. "No." She'd received her monthly flux seven days ago, with a host of mixed emotions.

"I would never put you in a cage, my little sparrow. *Never*."

It sounded like an oblique apology for bullying her with threats to speak to Stilgoe about their night together. His entire approach to the subject of babies baffled her. Most men, even her domesticated brother, trembled at the notion of setting up their nursery. "I have a question for you, too. Why wouldn't you tell me it was Olivia you were engaged to?"

Paris's green eyes turned cold as mossy rocks. "What did she tell you?"

"That you were engaged for three years and that she got tired of waiting for you to return."

A muscle bunched in his jaw. "Is that all she said?"

"She told me you grew up together and that you joined their dinner table during feasts."

"I did. Sometimes. The old duke was . . . kind to me," he ground out the words like nails.

"You never speak about your childhood. You told me you were miserable, but—"

"Elaborate on my misery, what a happy thought." He dug into the basket and took out two slices of raspberry pie, wrapped in napkins. "I believe this is your favorite dessert."

"Thanks. It is." Clearly he was not about to say another word on the subject. She let it go, for now. "It *was* kind of you to bring Will's trunk yesterday. It . . . still carries his scent."

Paris wiped his hands clean, reached inside his breast pocket, and produced a folded piece of paper. "I wanted to give this to you in private. Will wrote it two days before he died. I found it on his person. I didn't read it, but I know it's for you."

Her hands shook as she accepted the stained, wrinkled note. "Oh, Paris—"

"I should have given it to you weeks—*years*—ago, but I . . ."

"Wanted to hold on to his effects for a little while longer?" she guessed with a sad smile.

"You have no idea." He gazed at her. "But perhaps you do."

Misty-eyed, she carefully unfolded the note and read, "'My dearest Izzy—'"

"You don't have to read it aloud," he whispered.

"I want to." She swallowed hard and read aloud:

My dearest Izzy,

I was delighted to receive your letter. I imagine Stilgoe and Mama are still recovering from the fit you gave them when you sent young Lord Milner packing. I applaud your judgment. That muttonhead is not for you, my sweet. Lady Drusberry is a sterling postmistress, so please continue to send your communications to her. I'm eager to learn which poor devil's heart you will have broken next. The weather is horrid. I want home, and I trust I will get my wish, as it appears old Boney left something of himself on his island of Elba. We saw fighting today. The Prussians got a licking but are regrouping. And I am happy to report that both your object of admiration—

She coughed . . .

—and my person remained intact. Please forgive the chicken scratches and the creases. My colonel is hovering and trying to read our secrets, the big snoop.

Her cheeks shining scarlet, she lifted her eyes to Paris.

"I was." He grinned.

Isabel went on:

I offered him my pencil and space on the page. He spent more time debating this than he ever did in the House of Lords and decided to pass, the big coward.

"So now I'm a coward as well as a snoop," Paris observed wryly.

Kiss everyone for me and tell the lazy twins to write separate letters. I love you and miss you and hope to see all of you soon.

Your devoted brother, Will.

When she finished reading, wet blotches covered the sheet. "Thank you." She shut her eyes, clutching the letter to her heart.

Warm lips kissed the tears clinging to her eyelashes and cheeks. "You cannot imagine how many times I wanted to give it to you over the past two years," Paris murmured. "Every day I told myself, 'Go see her.' And every day I lost my nerve. I didn't want you to see me like this."

She opened her eyes and touched his cheek. "I love your face. You seem to be the only one who thinks it's flawed." She smiled sadly. "Every day I prayed that you would come to me."

He swallowed. "I should have. God, I should have . . ." He angled his head to kiss her.

"We are not alone," she reminded him softly and tucked the precious note into her pocket.

"Right." He straightened, his gaze sliding over their liveried audience. He crossed his feet at the ankles and gazed at her fondly. "Change of subject. When is your birthday, Isabel?"

"August tenth. Yours?"

"November thirteenth. You're a Leo, obviously," he drawled. "What were your parents' names?"

"My mother's name was Eve, my father's Jonathan. What was your father's name?"

"Harry. Harold. He was a lot more fun than my mama, and hardly a prig."

He laughed. "Your mama is a dragoness. Fortunately she's always been fond of me."

"Fondness for you is endemic in my bedlamite family," she

returned dryly. "But I imagine that is self-explanatory. Wouldn't you agree?"

"Witch." He tugged on one of her curls, then looped it around his forefinger. His eyes grew dark and heavy; his breathing became shallow. "Do I send the propriety squadron away?"

Her loins melted under his hot gaze. Alone, they would wind up entwined in the nude, their bodies undulating in sexual delirium. Yet painfully tempted though she was, she had to decline—for how could she lie with him now and then encounter him later with Sophie on his arm?

He was watching her intently, waiting for a response. "Shall we play a game, then?"

"What game?" she murmured, her mind conjuring up scorching images.

"Backgammon."

She blinked. "You want to play backgammon?"

"N-o," he breathed slowly. "I want to burn inside your body, but since we can't have that, we may as well play backgammon, or I will have to jump into the cold stream."

She was very hot, herself. "You thought of everything," she commented as he took out the backgammon board from the picnic basket.

"Let's just say I didn't expect your full collaboration, as lamentable as it may be."

He had no idea how lamentably close she was to collaborating. She helped him arrange the tools on the board. "Be warned. I'm a sharp player. I'll lick you."

His eyes shot to hers, vivid and magnetic. "I am beginning to think you will . . ."

And she was beginning to think she might not.

Chapter Twenty-Nine

Propped up on his elbow, his chin in his fist, his legs stretched to the side, Ashby groaned as Isabel trounced him yet again. The chit certainly mastered the game. He was not a poor player, himself, but how the deuce was he supposed to concentrate on backgammon when her pear shaped breasts flirted with his eyes from her deep V neck with every gesture she made?

She looked like a fairy, sitting in the woods in her creamy attire, with her glorious mass of curls spilling about her, and her sky blue eyes shining with feminine mischief. Her vanilla scent made him drool, and he was in agony, trying to ignore the demands of a stone-hard Mr. Jones.

He could not recall an occasion when a female he'd bedded—thoroughly, he might add—held a lingering fascination for him. Lately he discovered that no female held any fascination for him whatsoever. Except this one. Yet if he fell on her, she would think he had planned the day for the sole purpose of seducing her—and she would be right to a certain extent, but it wasn't all he wanted from her. While half his brain plotted and schemed how to render her naked, the other half was perfectly enraptured mooning at her. He wondered what his parents would say about his fairylike goddess if he could introduce her to them, and whether they would agree that she was the loveliest creature on earth. Sure enough, he was biased. He was in love with her.

He sat straight up. *He loved her*. Of course he loved her. He'd known it all along—since the night she had kissed him on the bench. Everything became crystal clear all of a sudden: why he rushed off to propose to the first full-grown female he could think of, why he kept his distance from Seven Dover Street, why Isabel never left his mind, and why when she showed up on his doorstep, no longer a chit in short skirts but a young woman, his world turned upside-down.

"It's getting late. We should be heading home."

He stirred. "Beg pardon?"

She sent him a sympathetic smile. "Don't give me that look. If you stopped woolgathering, you would beat me at least once." She got to her feet and smoothed the wrinkles from her habit.

He consulted his pocket watch—her gift and his most valuable treasure—and blinked. Four hours of eating, chatting, playing, and woolgathering had flown by without his notice.

"Well? Do you plan on spending the night here?" she teased. "I've already confirmed my attendance at Lady Conyngham's soiree this evening, so I am afraid I must leave you."

Reluctantly he stood and was seized by an intense, startling need to hold her. There was no point in prolonging his half-baked charade anymore. The last week had been a hellish test of his endurance, but he had survived it; he toed the line and became a public figure that even the old sticklers, who had once labeled him a scattergood and a rake-shame, now held in high esteem.

He deserved her.

He sent Phipps a look that said, *Leave*, then gathered Isabel into his arms and let his senses savor the moment. With a soft sigh, she put her head on his shoulder, and he knew without doubt that this—embracing her when he no longer disowned his feelings—was the essence of life.

Down on one knee, imbecile, an inner voice commanded. His mouth went dry. Shaking inside, he took her hand and sank to the ground. She almost toppled with him. Lilting laughter filled her throat. She tugged her hand loose and stepped back. "Oh, no, you don't! You are taking me home, Paris." She dashed in the direction of the spot where they'd left the horses.

Poised on his knee alone in the woods, he looked like—and felt like—a cretin. If she did not want him to offer for her and did not want him to seduce her, only one other role remained for him to fill, and he'd be damned if he let her groom him into a puppy-eyed sap who slavered after her! With an oath, he pushed to his feet and followed her to the horses.

"You're being awfully quiet," Isabel observed after they had ridden for almost an hour in absolute silence. They were back in town, taking a shortcut through a dusky, quiet park.

"I've nothing informative to report," he returned, still bristling with indignation. The small box he carried in his pocket was burning a hole in his finest riding jacket. And it was all he could do to keep from tossing it into a flower bush. What the devil had he been thinking?

"I had a very nice time today. Thank you."

"You are welcome."

"Do you attend the Grand Ball of the 18th Hussars at Lord Drogheda's this Friday?"

"I don't wear regimentals."

She glanced at him. "Is it necessary to put them on for the ball?"

"Yes."

"Wouldn't you like to encounter your old—"

"No."

"Oh, for heaven's sake, Ashby—"

"Hand over your purse, guv'nor!" a Cockney-accented voice called out in front of them.

Ashby nudged Apollo forward to stand between Isabel and the two footpads blocking the path; they wielded their pistols too expertly for his peace of mind. "I will, if you let the lady go."

Isabel drew alongside him, whispering, "You are not carrying a weapon, are you?"

"No," he murmured back. "When I tell you to go, kick your heels and sprint home."

"I am not leaving you here alone."

He looked at her. "You are not serious, are you?"

Milagro grew nervous from the close proximity to Apollo, and Isabel had to restrain her. "I care not how many battles you fought," she muttered, struggling to control her mare. "You are a man of peace now, which makes you vulnerable. Together with the groom we are three."

She *was* serious. If he weren't deeply moved by her concern, he would consider throttling her for imperiling herself. But this was absurd. "I'll be fine. Please do as I say."

"No."

"Yes."

"What are ye two whisperin' about?" One of the footpads moved closer to inspect Isabel.

"Let the lady go and I'll make it worth your while," Ashby called out. "Otherwise—"

"The pretty lady stays for the party." The man leered, waving his pistol. "And besides, ye won' give us no trouble with 'er 'round, guv'nor."

Ashby frowned in thought. "Don't I know you from somewhere? You are a soldier."

The man's eyes bulged in recognition. "Colonel Ashby." He staggered backward, crashing into his accomplice. He snapped into attention, saluting. "Rob Folk, sergeant, 3rd Foot Guards. You carried me on your horse off a burning bridge in Orthez, sir. Saved me life, you did!"

"I remember. And who might you be?" Ashby asked Rob's mate.

The second man jumped into a salute. "Ned Miles, sergeant, the 9th East Norfolk Regiment. Mighty honored to meet ye, Colonel!"

"You are war heroes. What the devil are you about, attacking innocent passersby for coin?"

"Times are 'ard, milord," Ned explained apologetically. "Six months we been looking for employment, but we ain't the only hungry blokes back from the friggin' war. Er, begging yer pardon, milady." He yanked the ragged cap off his head and bowed.

"Listen, lads. I'm looking for good men to work on my estate. I'm offering you both well paying positions that will fill your bellies for years, not just for tonight. What do you say, men? Are you up for it? Will you serve me as faithfully as you've served our country?"

The footpads exchanged ecstatic looks and bobbed their heads in unison. "Aye, sir!"

"Mighty kind o' you, milord," Rob added cheerfully.

"Excellent." Ashby gave them directions to Ashby Park and tossed them a few shillings. "That should get you there on a full stomach. Speak to my man, Hamilton. He does the hiring. Be sure to tell him that *I* sent you and that you served with me on the Continent. He will employ you. Now run along, and no more harassing peaceful civilians."

"Aye, milord! Thank you, milord!" They saluted him heartily and went on their merry way.

"You were wonderful!" Isabel exclaimed, clapping her gloved hands together and grinning from ear to ear. "How clever and good of you to offer them employment!"

He tipped his head. "I learned from the best."

Disregarding her mare's skittishness, she sidled closer, curled a hand around his nape, and kissed him. The searing assault of her soft lips dazed him. It was his nature to assume command, to be the aggressor, but when her tongue glided over his, tasting of raspberry and wine, he found himself wanting to lie still and let her have her way with him. He would die loving her.

Isabel drew back, her eyes glittering in the falling darkness. "You felt . . . different," she observed in a breathy voice, a smile of wonderment forming on her lips.

A shot rang in the air, spooking Milagro into whinnying and prancing madly. "You stupid sod!" Ned grumbled in the distance. "You nearly shot me foot off!"

Isabel tried to soothe her mare, when suddenly Milagro reared her forelegs. Ashby watched with impotent terror as Isabel lost her seat and flew backward. His heart froze. "*Isabel!*"

He was beside her in a flash, his mind numb with panic. She lay on the ground, unmoving, her eyes closed. A shout of anguish tore from his chest. *Dear Lord, not her! Not like his mother.*

His groom came galloping toward them. "Mason!" Ashby growled. "Fetch my physician and a carriage at once!"

"Aye, milord!" The groom stormed away.

His heart hammering, Ashby leaned over Isabel's limp form, afraid to touch or move her for fear she might have broken something. "Isabel? Sweetness, open your eyes. Speak to me."

Nothing.

He touched her jugular. Thank God, she had a pulse. "Isabel, can you hear me? Open your eyes," he told her in a firmer tone of voice.

And still nothing.

Irrational dread crept up his spine. His vision misted over; he couldn't breathe. If she had fractured her skull or broken her back . . . The craziest thought darted through his mind: He would rather lose her to another man and live alone in a cave for a hundred years than watch her suffer. His hands shaking, he felt her scalp for blood, careful not to stir her. His fingers came out dry.

All he could do now was pray. "Isabel, please open your eyes, my love. *Please* . . ."

Isabel peeked at Paris from beneath her eyelashes and winced at his petrified expression. *Oh, Lord.* She shouldn't have feigned a faint. The pile of leaves cushioned her fall effectively. But she had been appallingly curious to know if what she had felt in his last kiss was genuine. Plagued with remorse and loath to torment him further, she opened her eyes. "Paris."

"Thank God!" He let out a choked burst of laughter, relief glimmering in his eyes. With a tender smile, he smoothed mussed curls off her forehead. "Are you in pain, my angel?"

"I hit my head, but otherwise I'm fine. I fell into a pile of dry leaves." She tried to get up.

He stayed her with a hand on her shoulder. "You might have shattered bones. Don't move, sweetness. My physician is on his way." He continued stroking her brow and hair. "I'm so happy you opened your eyes. Is my hair all white, as I predicted?"

"Not yet." She chuckled, then lunged again. "Heavens! My habit is ruined. Let me up."

"No." He kept her down. "Lie still."

"I have slithery things crawling all over me," she grumbled. She tried to escape his grip and sank deeper in the leaves. "Let me up, for heaven's sake! My bones are perfectly sound."

"Do you feel pain or discomfort of any kind?" he demanded sternly.

"No. I swear it."

He thrust his arms beneath her back and knees and lifted her up. "I can walk," she told him, but slipped her arms around his neck anyway. He felt so wonderfully strong and attentive that she couldn't help relishing his fussing over her. She was a horrible person. No doubt about it.

He walked to a bench and sat, cuddling her in his arms. "Are you certain nothing hurts?"

Curbing a smile, she outlined his lips with her fingertips. "You were concerned about me."

"Yes, I was. It's my fault. I shouldn't have made you ride a feisty, unfamiliar mare."

"Stuff and nonsense. I've been thrown off a horse many times. Haven't you?"

He extracted dry leaves from her tousled curls and brushed dirt off her habit. "There is a world of difference between being thrown off yourself and watching someone you care for—"

"You care for me?" She searched his gaze hopefully.

He bent his head and caressed her lips with his, whispering, "Madly."

Her heart spilled over. Faking a fainting spell was a nasty ruse, but she had her answer. She hadn't imagined it. He had feelings for her. She closed her eyes and savored his kiss. This wasn't *their* bench, but it was nicely secluded and surrounded by foliage.

"You frightened me, chit," he murmured. "I don't ever want to feel that way again."

"I'm sorry," she whispered, shifting in his lap. She felt his need and became keenly aware of the familiar tingling between her thighs. Their embrace grew hotter, hungrier. His hand slid inside her bodice and cupped her breast, making her moan. Earlier in the grove, when he sent the servants away and tried to drag her to the ground, she wasn't ready to be seduced. She was now.

"How serious *was* the blow to your head? It's possible I'm misreading you, but . . ."

"You are not," she blurted breathily, completely absorbed in the sensations he stirred in her as he fondled her bare breast, rolling her nipple, and devoured her neck. Her bottom wriggled, unable to sit still. "How long before Mason returns with the doctor?"

His lifted his head. He studied her for a long moment. "You lied."

"W-What are you talking about?" she stammered as he removed his hand from her bodice.

"You didn't know Mason's name until I told him to fetch the physician."

Drat. She could argue the point, but the hole she was in seemed deep enough already.

His face furrowed into a mask of fury. "That was a rotten thing to do!" He lifted her off his lap and set her aside. He shot to his feet, stabbing his fingers in his hair. "How could you scare and deceive me so cruelly? How could you let me think you hurt yourself falling from a horse?"

She cringed awkwardly. "I didn't—"

"Yes, you did!" he growled at her. "You set me up! You wanted to see if I'd spill my heart out, believing something terrible had happened to you! How could you be so callous?" He paced before her, cursing under his breath. "Never in a million years would it have occurred to me that *you* had an unkind streak. *Never*! Damn it, Isabel! My mother broke her neck in such a fall!"

Oh, no! She'd forgotten about that. A sinking feeling of guilt assailed her. She was beneath contempt. She was . . . heartless. "I'm so sorry—"

"Thanks to your machinations, I finally know what went on in my father's head when he saw her lying on the ground, lifeless . . . He put a ball through his brains that night!"

Gasping in shock, Isabel vaulted from the bench. "Oh, Paris . . ."

"Sit down!" he ground out angrily. "You asked about my childhood. Well . . . I was shocked into muteness for a year. The servants at Ashby Park called me 'the mute-boy-earl.' I wouldn't come out of my mother's bed chamber, because it carried her scent. I was discouraged from playing with the other children in the area, too lofty and all that rot. So I played with horses."

"Weren't you afraid of horses, considering how your mama died?"

"Horses don't murder humans. They are beautiful, strong, intelligent creatures. My father shot my mother's horse, then shot himself because he was the one who convinced her to jump."

He slumped onto the bench beside her. "The servants were fond of me, but they maintained a respectful distance. No scolding, no touching. They never forgot that their wages came out of my pocket. The only letters I received at Eton were reports from my administrators. I constantly sought reassurance and attention from strangers. I dreaded Christmas. I never got any gifts, for who would buy the wealthiest brat in England anything? I was pathetic."

"You were not. Every child deserves attention and gifts, even fun gifts that don't relate to birthdays or feasts." Tentatively she burrowed against him, threading her hand through his arm.

He leaned his head against hers, took out the watch she'd given him, and held it in his fist. "My most prized possession." He smoothed his thumb over the engraving in a practiced gesture. "The Duke of Haworth learned through gossip that I refused to come down for Easter once. So he came to Eton and took me home with him. I was fourteen-years-old, not very polite. I hated becoming an appendix to their dinner table, but it was preferable to dining alone at Ashby Park. The tradition lasted for three years, until I turned eighteen." He blew out his breath. "Before I left for Cambridge, I discovered that my father hadn't fallen off a horse, as I first told you, but had in fact committed suicide. I was so . . . angry with him. I hated him. After that I . . . stopped caring."

"Stopped caring?" she murmured, aching for him. "About yourself?"

He shrugged dismissively. "I just didn't care anymore. I

immersed myself in indulging my basest appetites. I stopped seeking other people's approval. I reveled in the pandering that ensued around me when the hounds of Society caught a whiff of the power and wealth at my uninitiated self's disposal. I didn't expect their love, and they didn't expect mine. That was before I met Will." He looked at her. "Did he ever tell you how we met?"

She shook her head.

"Your brother lost five hundred quid to me in a game of hazard."

She gaped. "I don't believe it! Will never wagered."

"He did that time, quite recklessly, I should say. He didn't have the blunt to pay his debt."

"So how did you become friends?"

"I made him my tiger for a month. I dragged him from brothels to gaming hells, taught him a few tricks. It was hilarious." He smiled reminiscently. "But I shouldn't be telling you this."

"You corrupted my brother, you evil man." She slapped his arm in jest.

He caught her hand and planted a scorching kiss inside her palm. "And he reformed me."

"You had the best of times together, didn't you?" She smiled, awash with dear memories.

"The very best." He stared into the dusk. "Will was pure of heart."

She put her hand on his cheek, urging him to look at her. "So are you," she whispered.

"No." He shook his head. "After Will died I was back to where I had started."

"You didn't return to your old ways. You became a recluse." As she waited for a response, an explanation, she recalled their very first encounter years ago and what she sensed meeting his gaze: Kindness. Loneliness. Those boyish, sea-colored eyes pulled her right in. "I know why you eschewed Society after Will died. You felt alone among strangers again."

He flinched. "Don't be absurd. I know everybody. Those I didn't encounter at school, or in prize fights, or at the gaming clubs, or in the House of Lord, I came across in regimentals."

"How many of them are your particular friends and allies? How many of them make you feel . . . loved?" Though he remained silent, she knew the answer to that: Just her family. Which explained why he had elected her for a wife. He wanted a home. She couldn't begrudge his *needs* anymore. People married for all sorts of reasons. Wanting to build a home was a legitimate one. "What ultimately made you change your mind about putting an end to your seclusion?"

"The arguments you presented to me sank in, I imagine. The unhealthy living, et cetera."

Their gazes locked. Though she was glad to have been a favorable influence in his life, it saddened her beyond belief that it might be Sophie who would fill the void his parents had left. As though he read her mind, he said, "You told me you never wanted to see me again, Isabel."

She blinked back tears, swallowing the lump in her throat. Was it too late to tell him that she had changed her mind, that she was a fool? He cared for her and desired her, but if he had loved her, truly loved her, as she loved him, he would not have turned to another woman.

Riders pounded up the lane: Mason with the physician and another footman from Lancaster House. It was an awkward reminder of her trickery. Before they drew up, Isabel clasped Paris's hand. "Please forgive my stupidity. I behaved very ill—" She squeezed his hand, searching his obscure gaze. "Please allow me to tell you how much I appreciate your confiding in me, sharing your memories with me. Perhaps if we were more forthright with each other before—"

With a swift glance down the lane Paris leaned in and kissed her. "Let's go home, chit."

Chapter Thirty

Ashby sipped his brandy and tapped his cigar on the balcony railing. Watching ashes drift into Lady Conyngham's jungle-like garden, he pondered Isabel's last words: *If we were more forthright with each other before . . .*

She was right. He had been anything but forthright with her from the start. He concealed his face, the circumstances of her brother's death, his actions in the war, his personal history, the full story of his engagement to Olivia, and he still maintained the charade with Sophie.

And your feelings for her, his conscience interjected. *You conceal them still.*

He had not prevaricated about his reasons for preferring the privacy of his house, though. Those he hid from himself. For two years he felt unworthy of life because of the horrors he had inflicted upon others in the war and for failing Will. And while his self-deprecating sentiments were valid, they also encased a deep-rooted shame, worsened by the scars on his face.

Isabel had read him faithfully. The creature he hid in the cellar at Lancaster House was a pathetic boy starved for affection. His disdain for the boy and for his father's weakness was the driving force behind all of his ill-conceived choices, including his betrothal to a cold bitch.

A gentle hand patted his shoulder. He turned around, and smirked. "Good evening, Olivia."

"Ashby." Smiling coyly, she gave his appearance a comprehensive inspection. "You look very handsome this evening. No stripes, no padding, no fripperies. Some things never change."

"I could say the same about you."

Alarm flashed in her eyes, and she banked it with a practiced queenly smile. "Taking into account that we've known each other for years, I shall take that as a compliment."

"Please do." He put out his cigar and started for the door. "Excuse me."

She blocked his path, resting her gloved hands over his chest. "Can't we bury the hatchet? I've been watching you lately. You are changed. Much as I liked the younger you, I find the mature version . . . irresistible."

"Olivia, we both know that the only thing you find irresistible about me is my wealth."

The coquettish mask lifted from her face. "All right. I admit it. I did welcome your suit for material reasons, but I was young and foolish. How was I to know there was so much more to a marriage than an old title and a generous settlement? The first night Bradford came into my bed chamber, I envisioned you. I still do . . ." She rose on tiptoes, offering her lips to his.

He tugged her hands off his person. "I am sorry."

Resentment etched her eyes. "How can you spurn *me* and dally with that opera singer?"

He smiled. "You ought to know. You've been bandying my sexual preferences for years."

"It was John's idea! I had nothing to do with it! You know how he hates you." She paused, a calculated glint entering her eyes. "What about our darling Miss Aubrey? Does she still warm your bed from time to time? Or have you discarded her, too?"

He lost his humor. "Be careful, Olivia. Even my patience has its limits." He let his words sink in and tipped his head politely. "Enjoy your evening."

He reentered the ballroom but not before hearing her hiss, "You'll pay for this, Ashby!"

Dismissing her from his thoughts, he strolled into the ballroom and let his gaze wander in search of something far more warm and lovable. His quarry had yet to make an appearance, so he continued to the gaming room. He was on his own this evening, Lady Conyngham belonging to the stuffiest matronly circle that would welcome a slow death over polluting its realm with the likes of Sophie Fairchild. He had not planned on attending, until Isabel told him she would be here. It was imperative to his heart condition that he saw her as often as possible, or he would not make it to the next hour. Still, he found himself marveling at the ease with which he tolerated the hypocritical hyenas, unchaperoned. He felt . . . cured. A silly grin twisted his lips at the thought. The cure, of course, was the glow in his heart, instilled there by his love goddess.

Isabel's heart soared when as soon as she entered Lady Conyngham's ballroom, she caught sight of Paris's broad back vanishing into the gaming room. They had parted less than two hours ago, yet she missed him with a keenness bordering on physical pain. "He is all yours tonight," a female voice intimated over her shoulder. "His French hussy was not invited."

Isabel swung around to confront Olivia's icy blue gaze. "Mrs. Fairchild is not a hussy."

"You defend her. Interesting." Olivia smiled. "Considering she stole your lover . . ."

An alarm knell pealed in Isabel's head. "Beg pardon?" she returned quietly.

"You love him. Don't bother denying it. You all but shouted it to the world when you ran out of the theatre in crying hysterics last week."

Isabel drew herself up. "I left because your brother assaulted me."

"Poppycock. I know precisely what you were going through. Ashby did the same thing to me four years ago. Shall we go into the library? This conversation is best conducted in private."

Wary but curious, Isabel followed Olivia out of the ballroom and into Lord Conyngham's well-appointed library.

"You must have thought me deprived of all proper feelings for breaking my engagement over a mere lack of patience," Olivia began. "I have my faults, but I am not daft. Nothing less than the worst possible circumstances could have persuaded me to trade Ashby for Bradford. I cried off after catching Ashby *en flagrant* with a French opera singer. I'm certain you understand why I was taciturn about the true particulars of the unhappy affair."

Shocked, bewildered, skeptical, dismayed, Isabel didn't know what to think. It must have shown on her face, for Olivia thereupon supplied the details. "After the Treaty of Fontainebleau was ratified, I convinced John to accompany me on a visit to Ashby in Paris. Imagine my distress when I discovered him with . . . with that French tart! John was appalled. He wanted to call Ashby out, but I begged him not to. Ashby is a crack shot and a professional soldier. I could not bear the thought of losing a cherished brother over a faithless, undeserving fiancé. My grandfather used all his power to hush the affair, and I was married to Bradford within three months."

Isabel was in turmoil, her acrimony toward Sophie resurfacing with violent nausea.

"A week before my wedding to Bradford, I received a letter from Ashby, full of romantic utterances and false regret. He begged me to reconsider and tried to coax me into an elopement. He can be very persuasive when he chooses to be, but I was not deceived," Olivia clipped.

Isabel needed to sit down. Her head was spinning with fractured sentences all too similar to what Olivia described. "What induced you to unburden the truth to me?" she asked when she finally found her voice. "It has not escaped my notice that you do not bear me much affection."

"True, but my brother does. I thought you should be better informed about your 'sponsor's' character before you dismiss John's suit out of hand. But I will not be sorry if you do. You don't deserve John." She whirled on her high heels and stalked back into the ballroom.

Isabel's head felt feverish. She was going to be sick. She sank into a chair and caught her head between her hands. The details Olivia had provided left no doubt as to her veracity, but what she hadn't expressed was the logical conclusion: That if Olivia had eloped with Paris, she would have landed herself an unfaithful scoundrel for a husband. Evidently a consummate rake could no more change his wicked ways than the leopard his spots.

"Hiding from me?"

Isabel's head shot up. Paris stood in the doorway, casually leaning against its frame. He stirred, frowning. "You look ill. Perhaps the blow to your head was severe, after all." He closed the door softly and ambled inside. He halted before her, framing her face with both hands.

"Don't." She knocked his hands aside and stood. "We can't be caught alone here."

He gripped her arm as she headed for the door. "What's wrong?"

She couldn't look at him. "Nothing. I had a dizzy spell. Now it's gone. I want to return to the ballroom."

He wrapped his free arm around her waist and pinned her back to his chest. "Don't lie to me," he murmured in her hair. "Let's be totally forthright with each other from now on."

"You don't understand the meaning of the word!" Isabel retorted harshly.

"Stilgoe saw you leave the ballroom with Olivia. What did the nasty cobra tell you now?"

She stepped out of his embrace and faced him. "The truth about your broken engagement!"

"I see." He folded his arms across his chest. "Regale me with her tale, why don't you?"

"She caught you *en flagrant* with an opera singer in Paris. You lied to me! You said that you and Sophie were just friends, but you are using her, aren't you? As you used me!"

"My sins, as derived from your investigation, are grave indeed—infidelity, manipulation, abuse, treachery. Did I leave something out?"

"Then you don't deny any of it?" she cried in shock.

"This is not the issue. The material point is—do you believe it? I could tell you a different version, but would you accept it as true? If I'm deceitful, it stands to reason that whatever I say will be false. Therefore, before we go on, you must make up your mind whether you deem me an honorable person or a dishonorable one. Otherwise, I'll be wasting my breath."

"Don't play 'semantics' with me. There is a difference between being honorable and being forthright. I wouldn't doubt your sincerity if you didn't conceal the truth about your fiancée."

"*Ex*-fiancée. And yes, I should have told you the truth, but I felt uncomfortable with it." He regarded her. "According to Olivia, when did she discover me *en flagrant* with an opera singer?"

"Four years ago." Suddenly it hit her. "You were wounded at that time, weren't you?"

"A little over four years ago a French cannonball hit the ground mere inches in front of me. The explosion ripped my face apart. I underwent surgery and was bedridden for six months. My darling *ex*-fiancée, having received contradictory reports concerning my health, trotted to Spain with her charming brother. She found me in a field hospital and was quite attentive, until the day my surgeon removed the bandages. Alas he unveiled a gargoyle, slashed, stitched, and ghastly inflamed. Olivia's delicate constitution didn't survive the ordeal, and she cast the accounts of her stomach in my presence. Her dear brother wasted no time in rushing her back to England, where she became Lady Bradford three months later. When I got wind of the joyous affair, it came as a double surprise, since she never bothered to inform me of the change in our status."

Olivia was a snake. Isabel should have known better than to believe anything the malicious iceberg said, especially when Will deemed Ashby's character beyond reproach. "I believe you. I shouldn't have doubted you—but it's your fault! If you were forthright with me . . ."

"Even so, you were quick to assume the worst about me, knowing me as well as you do."

"Olivia's tale had several grains of truth to it."

"Such as?"

"For one, the letter you wrote her, begging her to reconsider and suggesting an elopement. It sounded plausible, and very like you."

"Why shouldn't it sound like me? She has known me for years, well enough to know better than to invent a letter, since the only correspondences I ever exchanged were with men of affairs. But don't take my word for it. Ask her to produce this incriminating letter, or any letter from me. Ten quid say she cannot."

"There is one other thing." Which she was dying to know but was loath to discuss.

"By all means, bring it on." He slumped on a couch, stretching and crossing his long legs.

She paced, fidgeting. "Why would Olivia specifically claim to have found you with a . . ."

"An opera singer? Ask your friend Hanson. He's the one who came up with the lurid tale and bandied it about. I certainly didn't mind. My reputation was already a shambles. 'A black-hearted scoundrel' has a better ring to it than a 'jilted gargoyle,' wouldn't you agree?"

She stopped pacing and looked at him. "You are so cynical about it," she whispered, "but I know it must have hurt you deeply. Did you love her?"

"No, and it is ancient history. What else? I'm game."

"That's it."

"Then why the dour face?"

"Because . . . because . . ." *There is still Sophie!* "Nothing."

"Good. Come here."

Uh-oh. She backed away, feeling much too warm all of a sudden. She knew that dark look, that low, seductive drawl; they would lead directly to being caught *en flagrant* with him. "As I said this morning—you have Sophie." She went to the door and turned the knob.

A white-gloved hand flew over her shoulder and shut the door. Paris's large frame leaned into her; his brandy spiced breath fanned her cheek. "There is no Sophie. It was a ploy, a charade, a fake courtship. I was desperate to get you back."

Joy spread in her breast. She spun around to gauge his sincerity. His solemn eyes reflected the glitter of the sapphire pin stuck through his snowy cravat—and guilt. Her heart sank. "How gullible do you think I am? I saw you kissing her hand at Covent Garden. I see how she looks at you, how well you deal with each other. You are lovers, admit it."

"She wore gloves, for God's sake! And no, we are not lovers. It was a subterfuge. Nothing more. What you saw in the theatre was an intentional gesture to get your attention."

"It certainly did."

"Isabel, I swear to you on my mother's grave, I never touched her in any way that could be construed as remotely intimate or sexual. How could I, when you are constantly on my mind?" When she still looked unconvinced, he said, "Do you think me so low that of all the women in town I would pounce on your friend? Give me some credit. I am not completely insensitive." He shoved his hand through his hair. "Look, my dealings with her were all straightforward. I would pick her up, we would attend together whichever rout you did, then I would return her home and drive off. Nothing of a personal nature was taking place."

"You claimed to be friends with her."

"Your friend Sophie is a kind and clever lady. She understood my contrariness at returning to Polite Society and knew precisely how to convey advice and support without making me feel like a gawky village idiot. She cares deeply for you, despite your deplorable treatment of her this past week. She expected it. She was fully prepared to endure your disregard and disdain, your cut direct, because she believes, as I do, that you and I belong together."

"You depict her as a veritable saint," Isabel mumbled. "Perhaps you belong with her."

He exhaled haggardly. "You don't believe me."

She wanted to kill him. "To be honest, I am not sure what is worse—your embarking on an affair with my friend a few days after our beautiful night together, or your pretending to do so."

"Must I remind you how our beautiful night together ended? You spurned me, scorned me, told me to stay away from you, and fled my offensive presence, never to return. You compelled me to do something drastic! You would not have come back to me without inducement."

"I did," she confessed earnestly. "I came back three nights later and saw you climbing into your fine carriage in your fine eveningwear . . . Was it then that you and Sophie 'hatched your scheme' by the light of the moon?"

The beautiful Spartan plains of his face softened with a smile. "You came back to me?"

"I don't understand you. Once you made the decision to end your seclusion, there was no reason for us to continue being at odds with each other. What you did . . . seeing the two of you together . . . and you accused me of cruelty! You deliberately set out to hurt and humiliate me, to injure my feelings. It was diabolical. I would never hurt you like this."

He looked pained. "It was *never* my intention to hurt and humiliate you."

"Oh, please! You *wanted* to punish me—to make me rue 'spurning and scorning you,' as you put it. You were settling an account with me. Deny it if you dare!"

His jaw tightened. "I could ask you the same. Why did you persist in encouraging Hanson? Didn't I make my hopes and wishes clear to you early on? You were kissing me in the morning and waltzing with him in the evening. Which of us was—or still is—the substitute?"

Beset with sudden bleakness, she said, "Before Charlie met Angie he fell in love with one Miss Lane. She was sweet and amiable. She liked Charlie a great deal, but they never managed to get along. He would say something she would take offense to; she would do something that displeased him. The courtship was doomed to failure from the very beginning. Yet Charlie was so smitten with her, he refused to accept it, until Will told him something that stuck with me. He said, 'When it takes a hammer to screw in a bolt, one should look for a different hole.'"

Paris smiled. "He said that in front of you?"

"I was eavesdropping. It means that—"

"I know what it means. Do you?" His eyes twinkled wickedly. The sexual innuendo finally dawned on her. She turned scarlet. "You shouldn't eavesdrop to men's conversations, Izzy."

"Don't change the subject. My point is very clear. When something is supposed to go smoothly and doesn't, one should let go."

His caressed her cheek. "We are not incompatible, sweetness, tool-wise or otherwise."

She swatted his hand. "Aren't you smug? Desire can't fix everything. If you had it in you to intentionally hurt me once, what will stop you from doing it again?"

"I was wrong to do what I did. I apologize."

She scrutinized him thoughtfully. "I wish you would remove your mask in my presence."

His lips curved in a sensual smile. "As I recall, you did that for me."

"I meant your invisible mask."

"Now you've lost me."

"You are a dissembler, Paris. You constantly walk the thin line between truth and lie. You measure words. You check your conduct. Everything is calculated to hide your real thoughts and feelings, or to give the wrong idea of them. So introverted, you are. So secretive as regards your inner self."

He seemed shaken by her observation. "I tell you everything. I answer all your questions."

"In delay. Weeks of delay. Your eyes, they sparkle and shine, sometimes green, sometimes blue, and tell me nothing. But I can see the battle raging inside of you, the things you want to say and cannot. Do they come out into the open only in that cellar of yours? Is that where you live?"

His Adam's apple moved as he swallowed. "You want me to strip down bare before you."

"It is only then that I truly see the man I love," she whispered.

"The one no one else loved?" he uttered cynically.

"The one Will loved."

They stared into each other's eyes, unmoving.

The door opened behind her. She jumped, quickly putting some distance between them.

Stilgoe appeared in the doorway. His gaze bounced between them. "Angie is tired," he said matter-of-factly. "Danielli woke her up at dawn."

Isabel nodded, casting furtive glances at Paris. Her brother held the door open for her, his gaze on Ashby. "Wait for me outside, Izzy. I'll be with you in a moment."

With another look at Paris, she sauntered outside.

Charles closed the door. "What are you doing with her, Ash? You've been dancing 'round each other from day one. Don't you think it's time to end the sport? Isabel is of age."

"I know," Paris returned softly.

"Do you want her?"

"Yes."

Smiling crookedly, Charles opened the door. "Then take her already! She's regularly blue-deviled these days, driving us all scatty."

Chapter Thirty-One

"Good morning."

Recognizing Sophie's voice, Isabel halted before her office door. She dithered for several heartbeats, then turned around. "Good morning."

Hope and wariness clashed in Sophie's deep brown eyes. "You are speaking to me. Are we friends again . . . or just being polite to one another?" she trawled in a conciliatory tone of voice.

"I haven't made up my mind yet," Isabel replied truthfully. "Last evening Paris told me—"

"Paris?" Sophie scowled in puzzlement.

That was something, at least, Isabel thought. "I meant Ashby. He mentioned a charade . . . ?"

Sophie clamped her hands together. "*Grace à Dieu*! He finally told you!"

"Then . . . it is true." Isabel lowered her voice. "You are not . . ."

"What? Oh, no, no!" Sophie shuddered. "Absolutely not! He did it for you."

A tight knot of tension unraveled in Isabel's belly. "What is your excuse?"

"Do you prefer to have this conversation out in the hallway or inside your office?"

"Come in." Isabel unlocked the door and stepped inside. She hung her pelisse, bonnet, and reticule, and went to open the shutters and let the sunlight in. "I'm listening."

Sophie closed the door. "He came to see me five days after the masquerade ball."

"Five? Not three?"

"The day I got the urgent note and rushed home. You saw us later at the theatre."

Isabel remembered Iris mentioning a mysterious note. But if it wasn't Sophie he had gone to see the night she took a hack to his house, what had he been up to? "Go on."

"He wanted you back and knew he would have to change his way of life. He asked me to become his companion about town, someone who would stand up with him in public."

"You should have sent him to me and stayed out of it, Sophie!" The mere picture of Paris talking with Sophie and waltzing with Sophie was enough to get her dander up again.

"Be reasonable, Izzy. Ashby is a proud man. He wanted to impress you, to lure you back to him, not lean on you. It wasn't easy for him. He was a fish out of water."

"You are *my* friend. You should have told me in confidence what he asked you to do. We would have discussed it together. Instead, you chose to upset me. Did you enjoy the charade?"

"Goodness, no! But you were so stubborn. You would not listen to reason. Forgive me if I erred. I had the best intentions at heart. I wanted to see the two of you together."

"It was a nasty ruse, a thoughtless, hurtful pretense. Which makes me wonder . . . You find him stupendously attractive, do you not? Perhaps you—"

"Don't be a goose! There are men aplenty, and I only have two dear friends who care not about my checkered past and embrace me as an equal. I would never throw that away over

a man, even if he is the Regent himself. Never! *Jamais*!"
Sophie vowed heatedly.

Isabel's umbrage mellowed. "Good, for it would be a great
pity, for both of us."

A tearful smile relaxed Sophie's countenance. "Am I forgiven?"

Isabel mulled it over. "I'm still angry with you, but yes,
you are forgiven."

Sophie rushed forward, startling Isabel with a bear hug.
"How I missed my sweet friend!"

"Me, too," Isabel returned in a strangled, amused voice. A
knock separated them. "Yes?"

The Golden Angel strolled in, holding out a red rose. Isabel
moaned inwardly. *Not again.*

"Good morning, ladies." He sketched a bow.

"Lord John." Sophie curtseyed. She leaned over to whisper
in Isabel's ear. "Get rid of him. Enough with the games." She
cast John a pained smile. "Excuse me. I have an appointment." She walked outside, wisely leaving the door half open.

"This is for you." John offered Isabel the red rose.

"Thank you." She gazed at the rose and then at John. She
decided to take Sophie's advice and do something she had not
done before. In the past she used evasion and flippancy to put
off suitors for as long as she could. That way she still maintained the appearance of a normal female eager to matri-
monify, while in reality she was biding her time, hoping . . .
waiting . . . for Ashby.

She didn't know when it had become a way of life: Toler-
ating men's attentions and then refusing them at the last possible moment. It was the tool she applied to mollify her
pestering mother and brother. Last night, while tossing and
turning in bed, it dawned on her that she was doing the same
thing with the one man she had been waiting for: *She was
pushing Paris away.*

Well, no more. She set the rose aside. "I'm sorry, John. I

cannot marry you. My feelings, my heart belong to someone else. Please forgive me. I wish you very happy."

His smile chilled her. "No coy flattery, no flowery explanations. I appreciate that. But we will marry, my lovely. I devoted too much time and effort to let go of my investment. Besides, you attract me, and for that you must pay. You see, I know your naughty little secret. I followed you the night of the masquerade ball. You spread your legs for Ashby, and you will for me, in the marriage bed—or I will destroy you, your agency, and your French friend at one fell swoop."

Isabel stared at him in shock.

"No objections? Splendid. Tell your brother to expect me at eight o'clock this evening."

"I will never marry you!" a voice from inside of her shouted. "I am not without friends."

"You speak of Ashby. Maybe he'll wed you, maybe he won't, but who'll save the French hussy? He cannot marry both of you. Her blemished reputation will not survive a campaign of defamation. No respectable hostess will have her in her house. She will receive the cut direct wherever she goes. She will be ostracized publicly and effectively . . . Your charity establishment will become known as a very different sort of operation. Two whores in one charity. Tsk-tsk."

The blood drained from her face.

"How many respectable households will want to hire workers through your agency? What will befall these poor women you champion? Perhaps brothels—"

She slapped him. "You are contemptible! I will never give in to your blackmail!"

He yanked her to him. "Desperate times call for desperate measures." His mouth slammed down on hers, lusty and forceful. She shoved at his chest with all her might, struggling to be free, but he clutched her chignon, trapping her. "You will be mine, Isabel. No escape possible."

"Think again." The office door crashed against the wall.

John lifted his head and caught a punch of steel that sent him flying to the floor. Paris marched forward, gripped him by the collar, and shoved him up against the wall, pressing his forearm against John's windpipe. "If you ever lay a hand on her again, I'll kill you," he rasped in a dark, angry voice Isabel didn't recognize.

"No, Ashby, don't!" she implored. "He's not worth breaking your . . . promise over."

Releasing John, Paris's gaze veered to hers. "He's not . . . but you are."

John's fist connected with Paris's jaw, sending him staggering. "I've wanted to do that for years," John snarled, dancing as a pugilist in a prize fight. "Courtesy of Gentleman Jack's." He threw a second punch and a third, but Paris kept his head well back. "Fight me, coward!"

Firm on his feet, every line in his body rigid, Paris flexed his fingers, balling them into fists . . . Then, he loosened his posture, rejecting the challenge. "I won't fight you. Get out."

"And leave Isabel alone with you to scheme behind my back?" John spat snidely. "It's time I delivered the lesson you so well deserve." His arm shot out with a fist aimed at Paris's head.

Paris caught it in his palm. "Not the eyes. Isabel likes my eyes." He twisted John's arm and buried an iron fist in John's abdomen. *Once. Twice.* John doubled over and dropped to his knees, gasping for air. "Had enough?" Paris demanded. "Or would you like to deliver another lesson?"

With a savage growl, John lunged to his feet and hurled himself at Paris. Isabel winced as John took a punishing from hell: an elbow to the neck, a sharp blow to a kidney, and a flat hit to the nose that cracked the bone, bringing forth a spurt of blood. John reeled, sweaty, panting, bruised. He wiped the blood off his mouth with the back of his hand, his eyes glinting. "You may be a damned earl, but you brawl like a scrub and are no better than a rubbishing commoner! Lord knows why my grandfather brought you into our home, or what he saw in you that gained his admiration. You ruined my sister's life! You think I'll let you ruin mine, too?"

"You and your sister accomplish that all on your own. What will Prinny say when he hears the next Duke of Haworth is a petty thief who steals from charity? He'll cancel Oscar's bequest."

"You have no proof. It will be your word against mine."

Isabel was stunned. John didn't bother refuting the allegation. Paris set his jaw. "If you ever come near Miss Aubrey again, I swear I'll bring the dunners down on your entire family."

"We both know you respect my grandfather too much to send him to debtors' prison."

"Oscar won't live forever."

"My grandfather is seventy years old and grows younger every day," John announced. "My father, unfortunately, is dying of a liver disease. So supposing you do convince Prinny to cancel the transference of the Haworth title directly to me, I will inherit my grandfather nonetheless."

"We are not in a competition, John. We never were."

"Oh, yes, we are, and I won. Isabel and I are engaged. Tell him, my dear."

Paris's complexion turned ashen. "Isabel? Is this true?" he asked her very quietly.

She swallowed. "He's threatened to ruin all of us—Sophie, the charity, myself. He knows."

Moving like the wind, Paris stalked up to John and punched him lightning fast. When John hit the floor, he was already out cold.

"Oh, Paris," Isabel whispered, horror-struck. "What have you done? You killed him."

"I didn't kill him." Paris knelt beside John's limp form and checked his pulse. "He is still breathing, the bastard." He dragged him by the scruff of the neck and dumped him in a chair. He wiped his blood-smeared fist on John's crumpled cravat, then came over to embrace her. Isabel wrapped her arms around his waist, rested her head on his comforting shoulder, and could almost pretend that all was good in her world. "I'm sorry I was too late to prevent his pouncing on you," he murmured against her hair. "Did I understand you correctly? He knows about us?"

Anxiety choked her. "He followed me to your house the night of the masquerade ball. He threatened to use this as well as malicious, prejudicial slander against Sophie to . . . to destroy the agency. Dear Lord! All those poor women and their children! A scandal of this magnitude—"

"Hush. Don't worry, sweetness. I'll deal with Hanson. You may depend upon it. After I am finished with him, the blond shark will never trouble you again. I promise."

She looked up at him. "What will you do? How did you know he stole the money?"

"An educated guess. The whole family is penniless and deep in debt. Oscar, fond as I am of him, was a great wastrel in his day. So was John's father, until his liver collapsed after years of hard drinking and fast living. I tried to help them. All their properties were mortgaged. So I bought the lands surrounding Haworth Castle at twice their worth and annexed it to Ashby Park. The profit Oscar made from the sale went to repossess his houses. I would have done more, but Olivia . . ." He exhaled. "She killed my benevolence. Anyway, John is more judicious than them. But he loves his clothes and his women and makes his living on the hazard tables."

"Fancy women? But every chit in Mayfair is hard-set on dragging him to the altar."

"That's business, the ladybirds are fun. He's desperate to salvage his family's money woes by marrying a fortune. I didn't tell you this before out of respect for Oscar. The old man—"

"Took you under his wing." His kind, loyal, generous nature made her heart smile.

"Besides, it's bad form to besmirch a rival. I wanted to win you on my own merit."

She smiled up at him. "Sometimes, Ashby, when you are not trying to undress me, you can be quite the gentleman."

His expression turned glum. "A gentleman who breaks his vows is not a gentleman."

She kissed him. "You were dashed heroic, defending my honor. I'm duly grateful."

"You are not mad at me anymore?"

"It's all forgotten now. I made peace with Sophie. No more grudges."

His eyes filled with tenderness. "Pure of heart." He lifted her up against him, capturing her mouth in a dizzying kiss that went on and on until every fiber in her body fizzed with pleasure.

Someone coughed. Isabel jumped backward to find Iris and Sophie grinning at them. Paris materialized beside her and laced his fingers with hers.

"What happened to him?" Iris indicated the golden pulp in the chair.

By the time Isabel finished explaining, Sophie was terribly pale. "I will disassociate myself from the agency . . . and leave England for a while. I could take Jerome to Paris—"

"You will do nothing of the sort. This is my fault." Isabel glanced at Paris. "I should have put a stop to Hanson's courtship a while ago. No one will pay for my stupidity but me."

His eyes bright with emotion, Paris brought her fingers to his lips. "I won't let him hurt either one of you. Nor will I allow him to destroy our agency. You have my word on it."

"Thank you." Sophie sagged with relief. "I would hate to quit my work here."

"I want you to go home and stay home," Paris told Isabel. "He may show up at your house, so you must let everyone in your household know that he's taken your rejection unsportsmanlike and that he is not to be admitted under any circumstances. Make certain Stilgoe realizes how dangerous and irrational Hanson is. Tell him that I'm on top of it, but say as little as possible. We don't want him rushing off to kill Hanson. We want to keep the entire affair quiet."

"What if John . . . starts spreading gossip?"

"He won't. He would lose all his power over you. Instead he'll try to corner you again. So you must stay home for the next few days, until I will have dealt with him. Make a list of people you trust, and tell the servants to send away anyone who isn't on it. Hanson is desperate. He may try anything, including abducting you. Be very careful, sweetness," he implored softly.

"I will," she promised, apprehension gnawing at her. "How will you deal with him?"

"I'll drop him off at his town house. Then I'll look into a number of options." He glanced at her friends. "Would you please see her home?"

"We'll take good care of her, Lord Ashby." Iris smiled. "Rest your mind at ease."

"My thanks." He returned his gaze to Isabel. Emerald eyes studied her for a long moment, as though he wanted to say more. He stirred. "I'd better haul him home before he awakes."

Isabel grasped his lapels, noting that even his cravat remained as crisp and immaculate as the rest of him, unlike the rumpled heap in the chair. "When will I see you again?"

"Soon."

"How soon?"

A wicked gleam entered his eyes. "Soon enough."

Making a face, she tugged him closer and pressed her lips to his. "Make it sooner."

Chapter Thirty-Two

Come back to me in dreams, that I may give
Pulse for pulse, breath for breath:
Speak low, lean low,
As long ago, my love, how long ago.
　　　　　—Christina Rossetti

The feel of soft lips molding hers seeped into her dream. A dark, seductive scent engulfed her, awakening her body to deep, raw desire. Submerged in warmth and darkness, she looped her arms about the silky head leaning into her and asked sleepily, "Are you a dream?"

"God, I hope not," Paris murmured. He scooped her soft body into his embrace, deepening his kiss. Her eyes closed, her mind not fully aware, she absorbed herself in the taste of his mouth, in the pleasure of his sensuous kiss, and in the feel of his arms around her, keeping her safe from harm, crushing her to his solid chest. His hands moved in circles over her thinly clad back; his tongue explored hers in lingering strokes. The heat pooling in her belly melted the secret place between her thighs until her entire self yearned to be touched, appeased, pleasured . . .

She sighed, intoxicated by him. "Paris . . ."

"Yes, my love?"

"How did you get in here? The house is practically barri-caded."

"I climbed the oak tree into the guest bedchamber."

She'd forgotten he knew her home as well as she did. "What did you do with John?"

"I dropped him off at his house. Literally."

The image made her giggle. "It explains why he didn't come by this evening, after all."

"Isabel," he whispered, his warm mouth devouring her neck and making her feel tingly all over. "I didn't come here to discuss your former suitor. I missed you. I want to be with you."

"I want to be with you." She shoved his coat past his shoulders and tugged on his cravat. She needed to feel his skin against hers, satisfy the desire clawing at her body and the yearning clawing at her heart. She needed to hold him in her arms. Without him, she felt bereft.

"Then let's renew our acquaintance." He shrugged out of his coat, then made hasty work of his cravat, waistcoat, and shirt. Sitting at the edge of the bed, he bent over to yank his boots off.

She rose to her knees and smoothed her hands up his broad back, kissing his velvety skin. He stood up to dispense with his trousers and drawers, then faced her. "Lift your arms." When she did, he swept the shift off her body and tossed it to the floor. Her back was to the window; she stared up at his tall, moonlit form in thrilled anticipation. He flung her mane of curls past her shoulders and cupped her face in his large palms. "Isabel," he whispered, leaning forward to kiss her. His fingers glided to her breasts and outlined her nipples with electrifying sensitivity. As her nipples puckered and tingled, he squeezed her gently, possessively, shooting fire to her loins.

She gripped his muscular waist, not wanting him to stop. "I love it when you touch me," she whispered. He made her feel so beautiful and desirable and cherished.

"I love touching you," he returned huskily. "You are a blaze masquerading as fine art." He lowered his head and drew one breast into his sultry mouth, sucking hungrily.

A soft cry left her lips. The sinfully pleasurable things he did to her with his tongue and lips and teeth increased the flow of moisture between her thighs until she could barely stand the urgency building inside of her.

Her hands roamed his back and chest, sensing muscles jump to attention. He was warm and lean and hard. She reveled in the thought that soon she would be lying beneath his strong body, subject to the force of his desire, becoming one with him, burning together in a storm of passion.

Her hands slid along his narrow hips, over hair-sprinkled thighs, and clasped his aroused member. He jerked upright, his eyes a pair of glittering gemstones in the dark. "If you stroke me, I'll explode," he warned gruffly, as her fists wrung the length of him. Undaunted, she repeated the motion. A powerful shudder wracked him. "*Christ*, Isabel. Do you want to kill me?"

"I want to pleasure you." She skimmed her hands up his abdomen, over bunching muscles shaped as cubes. She strained up against him, rubbing her breasts over his torso, growing hotter.

"Don't you understand? If I desired you more than I do now, I'd burn to a cinder." With a haggard sigh, he laid her back on the bed and came down atop her, reclining intimately between her thighs. She wrapped her limbs around him, relishing the squishing weight of his large body, the tantalizing caress and scent of his smooth skin. She loved this man to distraction.

"Hello," he said.

"Hello." She smiled up at his shadowed face. "You feel intriguingly familiar, my lord."

"You feel deliciously unforgettable." He reintroduced himself with a sensual, purposeful kiss, shifting his hips between her thighs, teasing himself against her liquid heat. "I, eh, brought someone with me. He is embarrassingly eager to meet you. I hope you'll like him."

"Is he a gentleman?" she asked, swallowing down a giggle.

"Not really. He is a bang-up fellow, though. I'm positive he'll endeavor to please you."

"Then, he is welcome," she returned throatily. Her hands coasted down the sinuous stretch of his back and cupped his firm buttocks. She raised her hips, beckoning him to enter her body.

Paris groaned. "Before you drive me insane, I've been fantasizing of sampling one luscious raspberry again." He pushed southward, kissed one taut nipple, then another, scorched her belly with kisses, and braced his hands on her thighs. She shut her eyes tightly, her body tensing.

He tongued the hidden nub, and still she held, relishing the shocks of pleasure bringing her closer but not close enough to ecstasy. She grasped the bedclothes, immersed in pure sensation, as the strokes of his raspy tongue pushed her to the edge of reason. A tidal wave of need swelled within her. Her heart pounded like a thoroughbred at a dead run. She tossed her head back, her moans begging for release. He suckled the sensitized kernel into his mouth, and she shot off the bed in a perfect arc, thrashing and bucking, panting strenuously, gripped by mad convulsions.

He pushed up to gulp her cries of release with open-mouthed kisses and embedded himself deeply inside her. Her mind had not yet drifted back to earth, and she was riding the storm again, clutching at his shoulders to anchor his rocking body against her, saturated with pleasure. They made love in a trance, perfectly intertwined, fluently undulating, soaring and crashing as surf.

She lost herself in the scent and heat of his skin, in the strength of his thrusting motion, and in the profound contentment she experienced when his body completed hers, as only Paris could. She became a quivering, blazing, liquid mass on the verge of explosion. "Oh, my . . . *Oh, Paris!*"

He ground his teeth, his moonlit skin glistening with sweat. "Yes . . . *yes.*" He increased his rhythm, pumping his hips furiously against her. "Yes . . . yes, oh, God—*Isabel!*" He stiffened in her arms. As his climax overtook him, shockwave after shockwave of sweet oblivion washed her, as richly satisfying as his. He filled her with his warm passion and collapsed on her, damp and spent, his harsh breathing filling her ear. Isabel felt drained, lax, and . . . utterly happy.

Paris raised his head, strands of hair falling over his brow. Now that her vision adapted to the dimness, she perceived his sated smile and the adoring look in his eyes. He dropped a tender kiss on her lips and smoothed damp curls off her face. "Do you still think us incompatible?"

She cradled his head on her shoulder, hugging him to her heart, lovingly stroking his back. "I didn't, but you made me so angry."

"Forgive me, my roaring lioness. I will never conceive of hurting you again. Nor will I let anyone else hurt you," he added in a hard, resolute tone that rekindled her fears and anxieties.

"How do I stop him, Paris? Those poor women . . . How will I look them in the eye and say it was my stupidity that stole their last hope? When I think of their small, starving children—"

"*I* will stop him."

She threaded her fingers through his silken tresses. "You shouldn't enmesh yourself in this ordeal. You've just returned into the fold of your peers. My scandal will reflect poorly on you."

He went rigid in her arms. "You won't get rid of me this time, Isabel."

"I don't want to be rid of you. But I shouldn't impose—"

"Then it's settled. I'll take care of him. I may need your assistance, though."

"You have it, naturally, but how does one stop a man from spreading gossip? Do you recall Shakespeare's *Titus Andronicus*, how Demetrius and Chiron cut off Lavinia's hands and tongue after ravishing her to prevent her from implicating them? There is no remedy for blackmail."

"Cutting off his tongue and hands is a sterling remedy," he drawled.

"That is my point. There is no solution. I will have to marry him." More than she trembled at the idea of marrying John, she was in agony over the possibility she might never be with Paris.

"Over my dead body!" he growled bleakly, adamantly. He rolled to his back and glowered at the shadowy white canopy. "Your faith in my competence is heartwarming, Isabel."

Shivering from the loss of his heat, she threw the blanket around them and snuggled close to him. "I have every faith in you, but what can you do? There is nothing to be done."

"I will have to discredit him somehow, so that whatever he says will be construed as false."

"That is an excellent idea. How will you accomplish it?"

"I haven't figured it out yet. I'm working on it, though. It will come to me. It always does. In the meantime continue to stay indoors. Hanson will surmise that you are afraid of him and that will increase his confidence in his imminent victory. He knows you can't hide forever."

"My brother senses that I'm withholding something. You may expect his visit tomorrow."

"He already paid me a visit." He gazed at her. "He intimated that if you and I were to wed, Hanson would cease to be a problem."

Nothing enticed her more than the concept of becoming his wife. Nevertheless, she would never ask him to wed her for the sole purpose of rescuing her from social ruin. "We both know it won't solve the problem. Sophie and the agency's reputes are at stake here. I'll simply have to contrive a way to render myself unappealing to him."

"An unappealing you is an oxymoron." He curved an arm around her waist and tucked her against him. "I would marry you in a heartbeat if you wanted me to," he whispered.

Her heart jolted. Yet his phrasing left no doubt as to what her answer should be. "Thank you for offering, but I think it is something we should *both* want, for the right reasons."

He brooded in silence.

"Where did you go that night I saw you climbing into your carriage?" she asked, drawing imaginary circles on his chest.

"To Macalister's club. I couldn't stand being inside my house for another minute."

She chuckled.

"What is so funny?"

"I think we've unwittingly swapped our phobias. You can't stand to stay indoors anymore, and I dread going out. It's funny."

"I assigned three men to shadow Hanson at all hours of the day, so you mustn't be afraid."

"Thank you. It's very reassuring, but I was referring to something else. Today I understood for the first time the need to hide oneself from the world. What an awful thing it is, becoming a curio, the target of vicious rumors and speculations. I owe you an apology. I was too harsh on you in this matter, when I should have practiced sympathy and patience. Forgive me."

"It is I who owes you an apology. You were right, as I'm beginning to fear you always are. I didn't want to dwell on the real reason I closeted myself. So I lashed out at you and frightened you into a fit. The sight of you leaning out the window, crying . . . I'm so sorry, sweetness."

She wrapped her hand around the side of his neck, tipped his head to hers, and kissed him. "Whatever happens, I will always be your friend, and you will always be welcome in our house."

"Just a friend?" he asked very quietly.

Suddenly the enormity of her predicament came crashing down on her. If John Hanson had his way, if neither Paris nor she came up with a plan to stop him from destroying her agency and Sophie's life, she would never be with Paris. They would never have another night like this. She might not even be allowed to speak with him again. Desperation gripped her. She buried her face in the crook of his neck and clung tightly to him. *Memorize this moment*, her heart wept.

He caressed her back and spoke soothingly, "This is not all your fault, angel. I am much to blame for the vulnerable situation in which you find yourself. I shouldn't have compromised you. I should have kept my hands off you. I—"

She lifted her head. "But how could you prevent me from putting my hands all over you?" Kissing his neck, she sailed her hand down his smooth, sculpted torso all the way to his groins.

He sucked in a breath, growing stiff and rampant in her hand. "I'd be absolutely powerless against such an occurrence," he returned gruffly.

"You? Powerless?" She smiled in the darkness while continuing to stroke him firmly.

His chest rose and fell with his rumbling breaths. "Putty in your hands."

She chuckled. "I should hope not." She shifted atop him, about to impale herself on him.

"Wait. I want to see you this time. Where do you keep a lamp?"

"On the dresser." Her gaze followed his strong, beautiful,

moonlit body as he crossed the room, marveling at his graceful movement, at the poise he exuded. He struck a light and turned up the lamp, silting the room with soft radiance. Her admiration ripened into pure carnal hunger.

"The last time I was in this chamber, there were dolls on the bed and a dog underneath it."

"I remember."

He flung back the dark shocks of hair obscuring his emerald eyes and grinned knowingly at her. "If you keep looking at me like that, I may be forced to abduct you, myself."

It sounded like an excellent idea at the moment. "Come here," she said, patting the bed.

"At your service." He approached her in his confident swagger, enjoying her eyes on him. His tall, virile frame rippled with muscle; Mr. Jones manifested an acute state of arousal. But it was the dark promise in his brilliant eyes that made her pulse leap and her belly tighten. She lay back at the center of the bed, excited and restless and welcoming. He planted his hands on either side of her head and sank down slowly, covering her body with his. "Where were we?"

"You were on your back, putty in my hands."

"Yes, well, we'll get there." He pressed his lips to her collarbone and moved lower. "First I must feast on this pert, rosy, tempting confection . . ." He lapped up her nipple, sensitizing it into a pebble, firing her up with intense desire. She pushed a hand between them and guided him into her fluid tunnel. His starved gaze met hers as he moved inside her, leisurely, provocatively.

Entranced by the heat and need in his eyes, she flowed with him once again toward bliss.

"Paris." She caressed his chest with her fingertips, her head resting on his shoulder. "I want to make you feel as you make me feel. You know every inch of me. I hardly know you."

He turned his head. "You know me very well, sweetness. Better than anyone ever did."

"I meant your body. I want to learn your secrets. I want to be bold and natural with you . . ." *As I would never be with anyone else*, she finished gloomily.

"Uninhibited." The expression on his Spartan face was arrestingly sensual and male.

"Yes," she breathed resolutely, searching his bright green eyes. "I want to pleasure you."

His grin took her breath away. "You never cease to amaze me. Do with me as you please."

She threw him a naughty smile and rolled onto her stomach. She kissed his smooth, round shoulder. She could tell he'd bathed before coming to see her, for the scent of soap still clung to his skin. Utterly captivated, she made love to his chest with her mouth and hands. She licked his flat, dark nipple, then bit it gently, wringing pleased groans from her lover. She navigated by his low grunts of approval, traveling downward, lingering over slabs of muscle. "You are beautiful," she said, kissing the hilly grid of his stomach. "Like the Greek marbles in the museum."

He sent her a sheepish smile. "I felt rather off-putting in the past several years."

"You are off-putting," she taunted him sweetly. "But not physically."

"Witch."

Grinning, she continued to rove him freely. The lower she journeyed, the tenser he grew. He groaned when she bit his taut waist, caught and held his breath when she tongued his navel, and tossed his head back with a growl when she kissed the tip of his penis.

"Shh!" she scolded. "You'll rouse the neighbors. Be quiet, for heaven's sake!"

"You're the vocalist. I can be as quiet as a mouse." He sent her a smarmy grin, tucking his hands behind his head.

"Oh, really?" Commanding his gaze, she moistened her lips and closed them around him. His hips jerked up, a low roar breaking from his throat as he thrust between her lips. Deciding to rib him a bit, she stopped and regarded his taut features with concern. "Quiet as a mouse, eh? You are not enjoying this. I should stop."

"*No.*" He swallowed. "That is . . . Do whatever you wish. I'm your subject tonight."

"I'll remember you said that." She clasped him in her hand and explored the length of him with slow strokes, but when she touched him with the tip of her tongue, she was yanked upward.

"This is not a good idea," Paris said. "If you take me into your sweet mouth again, they'll hear me in the Colonies. You want to please me? Sit on my stomach and let me look at you."

"Very well." Bemused, she straddled his stomach and sat still while his eyes caressed her face, hair, breasts, every visible inch of her, while his warm hands caressed her thighs.

"I love looking at you. I love the fact that you don't try to hide yourself from me. You are so lovely to look at, Isabel. I would sculpt you as you are right now."

"And what do I do in the meantime? Embroider?" she suggested wryly.

Fire leapt in his eyes. "Put your hands on your breasts."

"I thought you wanted to look."

"I do." A sensuous smile curved his lips. "I thought you wanted to learn secrets, become bold and uninhibited."

Heat rose in her cheeks when understanding dawned. Sustaining his rapt gaze, she put her hands on her breasts and rubbed them slowly. His emerald eyes smoldered, sending a sharp stab of thrill to her loins that made her hips jerk. Oh, this was wicked, she thought, unable to sit still. Sparks of awareness flew between them; it was electrifying.

"You are wet and hot for me."

"Yes," she breathed, splaying her hands on his chest. "Your lesson is . . . very interesting."

"Do you want me inside you, or do you wish to continue the lesson?"

A subtle beat of blood rushed to her slick flesh. She slid lower, teasing herself against his jutting penis. "I want both. What do you want?"

"I want you to sit on my face and let me devour your honeypot."

"Paris!" she exclaimed, astonished at his language—and even more amazed at her body's intense reaction to the image he instilled in her brain. Her female parts virtually melted.

"That will be an advanced lesson, then, for our next class." His chest heaved beneath her. His voice grew thicker as he restrained himself from thrusting into her. "Tell me what you feel."

She closed her eyes and concentrated. "I feel tingly, tight, terribly excited . . . needful."

He lunged up, catching her about the waist. "The lesson is over, as your teacher is about to embarrass himself in front of the class." He lifted her in his arms and impaled her slowly on him. Groaning with him, she clung to his broad shoulders as he strongly pumped her hips atop him.

They couldn't seem to get enough of one another tonight. His handsome face expressed the agony and the ecstasy of their fierce, wild coupling, mirroring her passionate turmoil. His swift, harsh breaths fanned her cheek. "Is this not the best sensation . . . being together . . . making love?"

"Yes . . . oh, yes—*Paris*." She needed him so much that she feared she might die if she lost him. *My love, my love*, her heart called to him. She gripped him tightly, vowing to never let go.

He captured her mouth in an all-consuming kiss as he continued to thrust hard and steadily into her. She spun out of control; her inner muscles tightened spasmodically as she shuddered upon her release. Her climax was the sweetest ever. He followed her with bursting alacrity, and as he caught her limp frame against his thumping heart, she felt . . . loved.

Isabel hid a yawn. Paris stirred. "I should go and let you sleep."

"*No* . . . Stay with me, sleep with me," she implored. "You can depart at dawn."

He regarded her angelic, sleepy face, perched on his out-flung arm. He'd grown accustomed to the low flutter in his gut that her presence always engendered, but that he should still crave her after lingering over her for hours was a scientific marvel. Their lessons had progressed rapidly after she had overcome some of her remaining inhibitions, and he couldn't wait to begin the next. However, it would have to take place at a future date, as his sated fairy was yawning.

Looking at her now, no one would suspect there was an ul-trasensual lioness dozing within. He was still in awe over the fact that she let him discover her, have her, be with her.

He would stop at nothing to make her his wife.

She stretched like a purring cat, thrusting her perfect breasts up, spreading her golden curls on the bedclothes. The temptation to cuddle her spoon-like and fall asleep together staggered him—but he couldn't. "I don't think it is a sound idea, sweetness."

"Why?" Sky blue eyes blinked drowsily at him. "Is it be-cause of the nightmares?"

His heart missed a beat. "How do you know about that?"

"Will's letters." She smiled. "Information travels both ways, Ashby." She shimmied closer to him. "Tell me your most recurring one."

"Are you a dream-interpreter?"

"Cynic, cynic," she scoffed. "For your information, when I started having those infernal fits, I also had nightmares. Will used to rush to my bedside in the middle of the night, hold me, make me describe the dream, and then he would invent a good ending. In time my nightmares cured themselves into positive dreams, in which I was saved. Then they stopped altogether. We dream of what we know, Paris. You need a new ending."

"So what you are saying is that if we slept together and I happened to have one, you would hold me and listen to me babble about it and then cure my ending?"

She turned beet red and buried her face in the sheet. "Go away. I hate you."

He embraced the little porcupine to his heart, whispering, "I'll stay, but I may never leave."

At dawn, before the household stirred, she escorted him to the kitchen entrance. They stood kissing in the nippy drizzle for long moments, loath to part. "I won't return today," Paris said. "I need to track down someone who could help us with our situation."

"May I come with you?" she asked hopefully.

"I'm afraid not. I'll be doing most of my hunting at the gentlemen's clubs."

"I could dress up in gentlemen's clothing. Will's should fit me quite nicely."

"That is a sure road to ruination, Isabel."

He looked so handsome when he was exasperated with her that she couldn't help ribbing him some more. "I promise not to kiss you in public. Perhaps a discreet pat here and there—"

He silenced her with a rough kiss, pressing her slender, nightshift-clad body to his. "Are you hell bent on turning my hair all white, or do you simply enjoy bamming me to death?"

She sighed. "It's just that I realized I actually do enjoy sneaking about with you."

"I'll remember you said that." He gazed at her. "I should go before someone sees us here."

There were so many things she wanted to tell him, and she sensed that he did too, but as if in a taciturn agreement, they decided to wait till after the crisis was resolved. *If it were resolved.*

"Will you miss me and think about me all the time?" she asked sweetly.

"It's become a way of life by now." He put his lips to her ear. "Don't continue the lessons without me." He kissed her possessively one last time and left.

Sighing dreamily, Isabel dragged herself back to bed, where they had slept entwined till the crack of dawn, when he had awakened her to slow, heavy-eyed, tender lovemaking. He was not a prig when he was the one imperiling her reputation. She giggled at the picture of her walking up to the Earl of Ashby at White's, disguised as a man, and kissing him full on the mouth.

Good God. She had just solved her problem.

Chapter Thirty-Three

"Did I lose a wager or something?" Major Ryan Macalister studied the three anxious faces crammed in the shadowy coach with him and stayed on the third. "Gads, I hardly recognize you in these clothes. You look like a lad, a very pretty lad, but a lad nonetheless."

"That is the whole point," Isabel said. Her nerves were strung so tightly she could barely speak. Yet the rush coursing through her veins kept her sharp and alert despite her lack of sleep.

Immediately after Paris left her that morning, she summoned Iris and Sophie to help work out the details of her risky plan. She assigned Jackson, the discreet, dependable coachman, to garner information about Hanson: his address, the clubs he frequented, his schedule for the day, and any other pertinent detail that could prove useful. She called upon dear Mary to make the necessary alterations to a set of Will's evening clothes and fit her out as a regular buck. Sophie supplied the short brown wig and matching mustache Isabel wore to disguise her features.

Iris proved the most difficult to bring round; her cautious friend kept harping on the perils involved and even threatened to clue Ashby in. But once Iris realized how serious and desperate Isabel was, she threw herself into the scheme and came up with the brilliant solution to their major problem: How to get inside the clubs.

Isabel studied Ryan. He was somewhat of a mystery. On the one hand, Will had considered him a reliable fellow and a friend, as Paris did now, but on the other hand, he had betrayed Iris. And yet it was Iris who vouched for his dependability and practically ordered him to collaborate.

"Would you care to run the plan by me again?" he asked Isabel.

She took a deep breath, ignoring the thumping, the sharp pangs, and the tightening that was eating away at her internal organs. "We'll follow him to wherever he goes and—"

"It could be anywhere: a ball, a mistress, a gaming hell, a bawdy house . . ."

"I happen to know he is not attending any social function this evening, and that he depends on gambling for finances. If he decides to indulge with a woman tonight, we will be in trouble."

Ryan grinned. "Let us hope he is more hard for currency than—"

"Ryan!" Iris shot him a glower. "Do not let Izzy's apparel and no-nonsense speech deceive you into thinking she is one of your crude army friends."

Ryan's slow gaze went to Iris. "One of my crude army friends was her brother and another is the man she loves. Which of us is the insensitive blabbermouth, do you think?"

"Do you mind deferring your bloodthirsty flirtations for some other time?" Sophie asked.

"Regarding the plan," Isabel continued. "We'll follow him, hopefully, to a posh club. Ryan and I will go inside. Ryan, you must stay out of the way, since John knows you to be Ashby's friend, and it might rouse his suspicion. I will walk up to him with a greeting and then embarrass him in front of his peers with a . . . an improper overture."

"Do you have the stomach for it?" Sophie asked. "If you have any reservations—"

"I have a mountain of reservations," Isabel returned, "but I won't let it stop me. Everything depends on my being focused, hardy, and successful—your life, my life, other women's lives. I think I can manage one swift kiss, disgusting as it may be."

Ryan made a choking sound. "That's your plan? To give the impression that Hanson is . . ."

"By tomorrow it will be all over town that he was seen kissing a man. I'm sure that before long he'll have everyone believing him a victim of a tasteless prank. But for the next few days, it will discredit him as a reliable source of gossip. Whatever he may bandy about us, everyone will think he is making up stories to remove the beehive attention from himself."

"I hope you know what you are doing, Isabel," Ryan said quietly. "Be sure to be quick and out the door as soon as possible, or one of my crude army friends will have my head for this."

"I will."

"Here he comes." Sophie pointed at the house across the street. She rapped on the vehicle's ceiling and called out softly to her driver, "Follow that man."

Isabel grew equally relieved and panicky when their destination proved to be St. James's Street, where some of the finest gentlemen's clubs were located. The coach stopped, and she saw John striding into the oldest club in London. "Let's go," she prompted Ryan before she lost her nerve. Her cold hands shook; her head and heart were pounding. *Oh, God. Not a fit, not now.*

Ryan didn't budge. "I can't get us in there. I don't have a membership and . . . I'm sorry."

Isabel caught the flitting glance between Ryan and Iris. "Perhaps it's for the best," she said, losing some of the tension fizzing along her nerves. "Ashby sent me a note this evening, letting me know that in case of an emergency he could be reached at White's."

"Ashby is in there right now?" Ryan repeated slowly. He stared out the window.

"What do we do?" Sophie asked.

Isabel was not about to abort the mission just because she'd been on the point of collapsing a moment ago. "We wait. With a bit of luck he might decide to take himself elsewhere later on."

So they waited. On tenterhooks. For two hours.

"How did you explain your absence to Chilton?" Ryan broke the laden silence.

"My husband is away. Not that it's any of your business," Iris replied snappishly.

"Away from London?" Ryan prodded.

"This is pointless," Sophie interjected. "He is not coming out. It's almost midnight . . ."

Isabel's heart felt heavy in her chest. Giving up now would be giving in, unless Paris could save her, and more importantly—her charity agency. Sudden, black anger assailed her, aimed not at John, but at herself. How could she have jeopardized their cause? How could she let herself be governed by desire? She had known in advance what could happen if she were found out, and yet she had rushed off to Paris without a moment's hesitation, brushing aside all sense of prudence and responsibility, because the only thing that mattered to her at that moment was not losing him.

He meant more to her than the agency, more than her reputation, more than life itself.

And that made her selfish.

She studied the tired faces around her. Iris and Sophie had been with her all day, and Ryan had his own affairs to pursue. She couldn't ask for better friends. And it was time to get off her high horse and bear the consequences of her mistakes. "Very well," she conceded. "Let's go."

"No, wait. Here he comes." Ryan alerted their driver to the man leaving the premises. They were fast on his tracks, tailing him 'round town. He stopped at Alfred Club on Albermarle Street, but only to converse with someone outside. Then they were off again, meandering through the misty streets of London. "After this, I'm selling my commission and applying for a position with the Foreign Office," Ryan joked. "Do you suppose they are still in the market for spies?"

"Spying is for shrewd, capable, serious men. Not for cocky, empty-headed bounders."

Ryan's gaze clashed with Iris's. "I'll pretend I didn't hear that."

"That's another thing," Iris dogged, amusement creeping into her tone. "Spies pay attention to everything. They do not discard information merely because it displeases them to hear it."

He sent her a knowing smile. "When is your husband due back in town?"

Iris lowered her gaze, a telltale sign that she was blushing. Isabel winked at Sophie.

"There he goes again," Ryan announced, when they arrived at a third destination. "And this time we're in luck. I am not a member at this club, but I know the porter. He was a corporal in my regiment. Let me have a word with him. He might let us in for a few moments."

Isabel went numb. She waited, tensely frozen, while Ryan talked to the man. Since it was taking him a nerve-raking amount of time, she closed her eyes and performed her slow breathing exercises. He returned and opened the door. "I've arranged it. Are you ready, Isabel?"

Her earlier symptoms returned with frightful alacrity and force: crazy heart rate, quivering, nausea, cold hands, warm face, throbbing head, staccato breathing . . . "A moment," she gasped, cupping her burning cheeks. Her manly garments were heavy and awfully warm, but they also afforded her a certain degree of protection—and anonymity. *Walk up to him, say hello, give a kiss, and go*, her mind drummed out the planned course of action. It was now or never. "Ready."

The chilly night air was a reviving shock to her senses, as was movement, after the long hours in the coach. She walked stiffly beside the tall, swaggering, decorated war hero, restraining the urge to grip his hand. Ryan exchanged a few jokes with the porter, and they were let inside.

Gentlemen of myriad ages milled about heavy oak furniture, thick carpets, and smoke.

"Remove your hat," Ryan murmured. "Remember, we are regular patrons here to have a good time. Look casual, but not too obvious. The instant you want to bolt, we're out the door."

"Thank you," she whispered back. Her legs seemed to operate with a mind of their own.

"I don't see him. Let's find a table and sit for a moment. You look ill."

"I could very much use a drop of whiskey right now, but I don't care to sit."

"Certainly. Wait here." He left her near a table, where three young bucks sat drinking and bragging about their fast contraptions. One of them locked gazes with her for a moment. But then he returned his attention to his cronies as though he'd seen nothing out of the ordinary.

She exhaled. At least her disguise was effective. Then she saw John, and her heart stopped.

His handsome face bruised, he strolled past her and didn't give her a second glance. Ryan returned with a glass of whiskey. She gripped it with both hands and gulped it down.

"Not so fast, old chap," he pronounced in a normal tone of voice. "You'll fall on your face before the night is over." He took the glass from her and gave it to a passing footman.

"I saw him," she gasped. "He didn't notice me."

"Good. Take a moment to resume your normal breathing."

"I'm afraid that is impossible." Abruptly it occurred to her that he might be stalling.

"Think about something else. How was last summer at Stilgoe Abby? Did it rain?"

His ploy worked to calm her down. She went along with it, answering his questions, taking slow, deep breaths. Then her tension returned. "Let's do it. I want it to be over already."

Together they crossed the main room toward the one John had disappeared into. It turned out to be the gaming room. At the doorway, Ryan stopped. "Who pounded him? Ashby?" Her nod elicited a chuckle. "I thought I recognized the fist imprint. I'll stay out of sight now."

"But not too far." Her eyes were on the blond head sitting across from them at the table.

"Not too far." He touched her elbow. "You have your brother's courage. Good luck."

Moving as if in a dream, she entered the room at a strolling pace, her hands gripped behind her back; the only sound she heard was the thudding in her ears. She circled the table, stepping back when one of the gamblers left the table. Three more chairs and she would reach him.

Finally she stopped behind *his* chair. She shut her eyes. *One. Two. Three.* She patted his shoulder. He looked up at her. "Hanson, you devil," she enunciated in a deep voice.

"Who the—"

She leaned down, kissed his mouth, then jerked upright and hastened toward the door. The resulting uproar was deafening. Chairs scraped back. John was shouting vulgar disclaimers.

As soon as she crossed the threshold into the main room, she picked up her pace until she was almost running. Without warning, steely fingers seized her arm and whipped her backward.

"I'll murder you, filthy bugger!" the Golden Angel, livid as she had never seen him before, barked in her face. His complexion was red; his icy blue eyes glinted murderously. Men gathered around them, rumbling rowdily. *Where the devil was Ryan?* She struggled to escape but couldn't.

"Wait a minute!" John bellowed. "You are not a man—you're a woman!" He reached out to snatch the wig from her head.

Something very large and black rammed itself in between them. A greatcoat flew over her head, trapping her like a fish in a net. "Don't—say—a—word!" a low, angry voice that sounded like Paris's ground out harshly. "Remember my warning, Hanson. If you open your mouth about *this*, I'll bury you so deep it would take you a lifetime to crawl out of your pit! Best to keep your mouth stuffed about a harmless lark while you're still holding the winning hand."

"Tell whomever should be told to expect me tomorrow after the morning session in the House," Hanson bit out. "Or I won't lack for female company in that pit. Understood?"

Imprisoned in the thick, black material, Isabel was dragged away by the unyielding arm wrapped around her shoulders. She knew they were outside when her boots hit the pavement.

"My thanks, Macalister," Paris called out. "I'm in your debt."

She was shoved into a closed carriage like so much baggage, her cloaked face bashing into the squabs. The door slammed shut behind her, and the carriage rocked into motion.

Swaying with the carriage, Isabel pushed to a sitting position and at the same time flung off the shroud she was trapped in. Her wig was tipped aside, so she yanked it off and shook out her hair. She was intensely aware of the man sitting across from her, fighting to control his temper.

With a *woosh* she relaxed back against the squabs and leveled her gaze at Paris's hard face. It wasn't the first time she'd roused his ire, but she had never seen him this *enraged* before.

He leaned forward and ripped her mustache off. She pressed a hand to her mouth, covering a giggle. Unmoved, his voice was deep and terse. "Do you realize what you've done?"

There he went, assuming the role of a big brother again. Well, he was not her brother. They were not married. And she did not owe him a single blasted explanation. "How did you find out? Did Ryan merely pretend to play along?"

"If he did, you'd be locked inside your bedchamber right now."

"He alerted you, then. Sent a message to you at White's."

"Yes."

She cringed at his hostile tone. It seemed a year had passed since they parted that morning. "Go ahead," she snapped. "Ring your dreadful peal over me. Let's get it over and done with."

"To be perfectly honest, I don't know where to begin." His jaw was set in a hard line; his glittering gaze pierced the shadows. "How many times did I ask you to leave Hanson to me? Do you think I enjoy gamboling about town, importuning individuals who have important things on their minds to help me extract a certain chit from the hole she is in—a hole that has just grown much deeper? Has it not occurred to you that a man who tries to force himself on a female and at the same time blackmail her is extremely dangerous and not to be trifled with?"

"It is my problem, Paris," she replied curtly. "Don't expect me to sit back and do nothing."

"You did enough."

She narrowed her eyes. "What is that supposed to mean?"

"You are an impetuous, reckless, irresponsible brat, who's been permitted to run wild all her life and has not learned to check her impulses."

"Stop the carriage," she said, as tears rushed to her eyes and she blinked them back.

"You have guts, I'll give you that, but you stepped so far outside your purview tonight—"

If she had to sit there for one more word . . . "Stop—the—coach!"

"I'm taking you home. We'll be there in a minute."

Last night he had encouraged her and taught her how to let go of her inhibitions, and now he was reproaching her for being such a person? Mustering all her powers of restraint, she said in a tight voice, "As there are two sides to every coin, so there are different facets to every character trait. I may be impetuous and reckless, but if I didn't possess these traits, if I let cool rationality have the reins of me, you would still be wearing a mask behind the walls of Lancaster House, and we would not be sitting here together, having this unpleasant conversation."

"Tomorrow after the morning session, Lord John Hanson will come to ask your brother for your hand in marriage. If you say 'no,' he will leave your house, pay a visit to the worst gossiper in London, and regale her with stories of seductions, indiscretions, and lewd behavior, involving two, maybe three people. Sophie's life in England will be over. Your agency will cease to—"

"You think I don't know that?" she shouted at him.

"I could have prevented it, Isabel!" he growled back. "If only you hadn't cut short the already restricted timeframe in which I had to operate!"

The carriage drew to a halt outside her house. Clutching the door handle before he reached for it, she fixed him with a hard, painful, unforgiving look. "Congratulations, my lord. You have just made a most successful escape from leg-shackling yourself to a stupid, thoughtless, childlike chit, who by noon tomorrow will be known as a lightskirt and a hoyden!"

She pushed the door open and jumped outside. Blinded by tears, her heart sinking, she ran toward the front steps, wishing for something to come down from the sky and strike her dead.

Feet pounded after her. Paris caught her around the waist and dragged her aside toward the bench near the rose garden. He pulled her down beside him, keeping a firm grip on her arms.

"Do you know what happened to me on this bench seven years ago?" he breathed harshly. "I fell in love with a beautiful, sweet, clever girl with the purest, largest heart in the world. How can I describe the feeling? Thunderbolt and lightning.

With a single kiss she pulled me out of an abyss of darkness and despair and set my heart aglow for the first time in my life. But you see, this girl, this angel of light and love and warmth was forbidden to me because I was a man and she was still a child. So I did the stupidest, most impetuous thing possible. I rode out to another woman and asked her to be my wife. I couldn't stand pining for something I believed I could never have and was probably no more than a passing fancy on this girl's part. As it happened, someone above took pity on me, deciding to save me from my own reckless, gutless, stupid self. He sent a ball of fire that freed me from the witch I was to make the mother of my unfortunate offspring. There was a price attached to my salvation. I paid my dues secretly, waiting, praying, not daring to hope . . . until one day my miracle arrived. My beautiful angel came looking for me, all grown up, lovelier than sunshine, sweeter than a dream, and she claimed she loved me still—"

His voice broke; his eyes glistened. "Having told you my sad story, do you still presume to think that I will let *my* angel fall into the hands of a cold-blooded bastard, or into the hands of any man who isn't me? I would rip the sun from the sky before I let that happen."

Isabel could no more have dammed her silly tears than she could have quenched her bright, adoring smile. *He loved her.*

"Now you tell me how my story ends," Paris implored. "You invent my ending. Do I get to keep my angel, this woman who is the love of my life, my light, my adored goddess of desire and beauty, and make her my eternal companion? Or do I fall back into the abyss and wade through life 'like a phantom, huddled in dreams, the perplexed story of his days confounded'?"

She wrapped her hands around his neck and pressed her lips to his. "You get to keep her."

Paris crushed her in his arms with sufficient force to choke the life out of her. She never felt better, held against his heart, her cheek pressed to his.

"I take back everything I said in the carriage," he apologized gruffly. "I'm the villain. I'm the fool in tonight's production. What you said is true. Every character trait has its diverse facets. Everything you do comes from the heart, your very large, very brave heart. I will be the luckiest fellow alive if you could find a place there for a rambling idiot like me."

Isabel tilted her head back. "I am terribly sorry, sir, but the entire space was robbed a long time ago by this hussar fellow I pounced upon on this very bench."

He scowled fiercely. "Who was that damnably fortunate devil?"

She caressed his dear face, combing back his hair with her fingers. Huskily she said, "Why, that man was you, my love. I *am* wild and irresponsible. I made a shambles of my life to be with you. I pray you would still think me loveable after I have made a shambles of yours as well."

He burst out laughing, richly, deeply, his head thrown back. It was the most beautiful thing to watch. "What's so funny?" she inquired.

His laughter abated to chuckles. "Could my life be any more a shambles than it was till you started meddling in it? Good luck in trying." He pulled her onto his lap and kissed her deeply.

"Take heed, Ashby," Isabel murmured in between blood-heating, toe-curling, overlapping kisses, her smile unquenchable. "People may drive by and see you kissing a man."

"Their impression would be far worse than that." His fingers opened her squashed sunset curls, draping the burnished stuff past her greatcoat-clad shoulders, so that it cascaded in waves to her waist. "They'll see me kissing a lion-like hoyden in men's clothing."

Chapter Thirty-Four

Isabel found Ashby pacing in her mother's drawing room, where she had stashed him upon Hanson's arrival. Wearing an expression of subdued curiosity and confusion, her mama sat on the couch, Angie cradling Danielli beside her. The twins sat side by side on the settee, not daring to utter a sound. Seven Dover Street seemed to be holding its breath, ever since Paris had arrived early that morning to confer with Stilgoe and Isabel in private.

The moment Paris saw Isabel, he stopped pacing. "Is he gone?"

"Yes." The extreme amplitude of her emotions frustrated every attempt on her part to make sense of her situation. She was engaged to John Hanson, while the man she loved, the man claiming to love her in return, was the one who convinced her to accept John's suit. Whatever Paris was plotting, if he failed or changed his mind about her, she would become Hanson's bride.

Paris strode to her and gripped her cold hands. "I wouldn't ask you to do this if there was another way to be rid of him. Trust me, sweetness," he murmured softly. "I won't let him win."

Stilgoe materialized in the doorway. He took in Isabel and

Paris's laced hands and decided to address the room in general. "I've just had a visit from Lord John Hanson. He asked for Izzy's hand in marriage, and she accepted him. They are engaged."

"Engaged to Lord John?" Freddy exclaimed in horror, the look in her wide eyes reflecting her female relatives' disappointment. "But . . . but . . ." Her gaze darted between Isabel and Paris.

"Izzy, have you gone completely bonkers?" Teddy demanded, bolting to her feet.

"You can't marry that man!" Freddy protested. "You love—" she trailed off.

All eyes settled on Paris. His eyes were on Isabel. Quietly he said, "And I love her, but this man threatened to embroil Izzy's charity in a fallacious scandal if she refused him. So until I set it to rights, she cannot be mine." He squeezed her hands. "But she will be."

The sincerity in his eyes and words sent a wave of warmth through Isabel. "I love you."

The twins were in an uproar, disparaging LJ and rooting for Ashby. Their mother came to her feet. "Come along, girls. Your brother needs to confer with Lord Ashby in private."

"Hanson will accompany us to the 18th grand ball tonight," Stilgoe informed his mother.

She huffed scornfully. "Charles Harold Aubrey, I am always pleasant, even to toads!"

Everyone but Paris, Isabel, and Stilgoe shuffled to the door. Angie halted beside Paris. "Welcome to the family, my lord. You come highly recommended." She smiled as the bundle in her arms, in raptures at recognizing her playmate, attempted to transfer herself into his embrace.

"Thank you." He gave Danielli's cheek a light caress, the worry not leaving his eyes.

Stilgoe escorted his wife and daughter to the hallway, then

returned inside and closed the door. "I hope you know what you are doing, Ash."

Paris turned businesslike. "What did you offer him?"

"Twice her initial dowry, as you told me to. I made a big fuss over keeping things quiet."

Paris nodded stiffly, his jaw clenched. "I hope it pacifies him into keeping his mouth shut."

"He seemed cheerful enough when he left," Stilgoe remarked. "I heard him whistling."

Paris looked the opposite of cheerful. "Did you remember to insist upon a specific sum of pin money to be put in the official marriage agreement and how much of it goes to the charity?"

"I expressed everything you had dictated to me before breakfast. I put 'funds' and 'charity' in the same sentence at least fifty times. Hanson must think us the oddest clan in Christendom—materialistic humanitarians. As you predicted, he didn't offer to donate anything, himself."

Looking rather grave, Paris stared at Isabel. "Did you explain how important your work at the agency is to you and begged his consideration in allowing you to continue—?"

"Yes, yes," she assured him. "I said everything we'd agreed upon."

"And what did he say?"

"He didn't seem to mind. He said it would benefit his political standing and ambitions."

"Excellent."

She bit her lip. "Actually . . . in view of his positive response, I took the liberty of soliciting his endorsement in Parliament. I asked him to promote our bill proposal."

He looked crestfallen. "I am doing that. I told you I was putting together a committee."

"I know, my love." She touched his face, grateful for Olivia's providential stupidity. "It seemed the logical thing to do, though, considering that he is to be my husband."

A look of amused disbelief attacked his face. "I'll thrash you, Isabel."

"*Supposedly,*" she amended sweetly, praying she wasn't wrong.

"Much better." His eyes slid toward her brother. "Charlie, might I have a moment . . ?"

"Yes, yes . . . You may have as many as you wish. I'll be in my office. Next door," Stilgoe emphasized firmly. He gave Isabel a kiss on the cheek. "Snagged yourself the best of the lot, my dear Izzy. I wish you very happy. You, too, Ash."

"Thank you," they replied. As soon as the door closed, they were in each other's arms, kissing urgently, seeking love, abandon, and reassurance in their passionate embrace. Her heart was in palpitations since the audience with John and growing more frantic as thoughts of the pending evening flitted in her mind. The number of variables impinging on her happiness was alarmingly large and abysmal. Yet in all the chaos, Paris remained a rock of strength and affection, a balm to her distress.

"I'm sorry I had to ask you to let him tag along with your family this evening. He needs to believe and to demonstrate to the world that you are to be wed and that he has been accepted into the Aubrey family fold. Your invitation will allay his suspicions. I couldn't think of anything—"

"I'll be fine, and you'll be there, too." She smiled. "In your blue regimentals."

He grimaced. "That's what's on your mind at a time like this, seeing me in regimentals?"

"Since you refuse to impart your plan, it will give me something to look forward to."

"It is imperative that you look genuinely surprised. Whatever transpires at the ball must come as a shock, or Hanson will sniff a trap. You have to be attentive with him and ignore me."

"There's the rub." She kissed his warm, soap-scented neck

up to his ear. "All those nights I lay in bed, imagining us waltzing together, you always wore regimentals."

"That's odd. In my dreams you don't wear anything." He nudged her against the door and resumed kissing her and pressing into her until they were both panting with need. "Can you feel how much I desire you? You've had this damnable effect on me since our forbidden kiss."

"You've had this damnable effect on me since I saw you shirtless in the cellar."

"That was the whole idea," he drawled. "I figured I shouldn't be the only one suffering."

Her lips twitched in a smile. "Now you're bamming me, but thanks for taking my mind off having an apoplexy." *And the cold dread twisting her insides*. He kissed her again, roughly, hotly, until she moaned low in her throat. The knot of ice began thawing as her body responded to the call of his. "I want you," she gasped. "I wish we could make love standing up."

"Actually, we could, but I advise against it, as Stilgoe has his ear to the wall. Nevertheless"—he nibbled softly on her lips with the patience and relish of an addict—"as we mustn't neglect your education, I promise to come by tonight."

"And sleep with me till dawn . . ."

Chapter Thirty-Five

I will be Paris, and for love of thee,
Instead of Troy, shall Wertenberg be sacked;
And I will combat with weak Menelaus,
And wear thy colors on my pluméd crest;
Yea, I will wound Achilles in the heel,
And then return to Helen for a kiss.
—Christopher Marlowe:
The Tragical History Of Doctor Faustus

Lord Drogheda's well-lit ballroom resembled a parade. Officers sporting the 18th Hussars's royal blue, silver, and white uniform swaggered in packs, drinking, joking, and eyeballing pretty ladies. The first moments were a bit of a shock to the four members of the Aubrey Pride. The last time they attended the regiment's annual ball was with Will. They exchanged sad glances among themselves, sharing the heart-wrenching longing they all felt. *Will was gone for good.*

To Isabel his loss felt more final and real than ever before. Her brother—her soul mate—was gone. She would never speak to him again, never hug him, never hear his laughter; what she had left of Will was his effects, her memories, and . . . Paris, in a way. He shared her grief and filled her heart with so much love that she began to feel as half a person without him—she, the independent hoyden!

"Hanson," Stilgoe ventured genially, "let's fetch the ladies a glass of punch."

"Certainly." John removed Isabel's gloved hand from his sleeve and kissed it. "Do not give away the first waltz of the evening. I should like to perform it with my bride-to-be."

He truly seemed to be partial to her—and that troubled her far more than his greed. She put a smile on her face. "Of course."

"What a nasty fellow," her mother remarked once John disappeared with her brother.

"I recall a time when you declared him a pattern of rectitude and good breeding, Mama."

"Never!" her mother vowed heatedly. "It has always been my fondest wish that you unite with dear Ashby. What a splendid fellow! Everything that is good and amiable. He cares deeply for you, Izzy, but a man of his sort won't put up with your rascally ways and ungoverned tongue. If you wish to become the Countess of Ashby, you must be on your best behavior with him."

"Yes, Mama." Isabel hid a smile. She would have to ask Paris whether he classified lessons in lovemaking under "rascally behavior" or "best behavior."

"I do not see Lord Ashby anywhere," Angie observed with a slight frown.

Isabel felt a jolt of anxiety. "He will be here," she said quietly.

Sophie and Iris emerged from the crowd. "Izzy, you look lovely!" Iris remarked, perusing Isabel's décolleté gown of silvery gauze and dark blue ribbon. "A hussaress!"

"What are you doing here?" Isabel exclaimed, grateful for their company. She clasped their hands, stirring them aside. "I had no idea you were invited. I am so happy to see you."

Her friends looked baffled. "Ashby sent us invitations," Sophie explained in a low voice.

"The invitations arrived with a note begging us to attend, for you might need us," Iris said.

Isabel's throat constricted. His thoughtfulness in inviting her friends to support her turned her insides to mush. "He loves me," she whispered, a smile of wonder bursting from her heart.

"Of course he does, silly goose!" Sophie laughed and squeezed her hand.

"Everyone is talking about the female rogue who pounced on the Golden Angel last night," Iris put in, curiosity and concern mingling in her eyes. "What happened inside the club?"

"Everything went according to plan, until John recognized me," Isabel explained. "Before he unmasked me in front of everyone, Ashby showed up and covered me in his greatcoat. He rattled me off something awful on the way home. He worried about me."

"You should have seen his face when he arrived at the club," Iris said. "The poor man was as pale as a ghost. He told us to go home and stormed inside like a black blizzard."

"People are saying that he defended this unfortunate female because he felt sorry for her," Sophie contributed. "They say she had a mustache, so everyone thinks it was Louisa Talbot."

"Nonsense," Isabel disputed. "My mustache was much finer than Louisa's."

"They say she tried trapping him into matrimony, as she's violently in love with him. Let's hope she is more successful in the future." Iris winked. "Perhaps we should offer her advice."

Isabel's angst returned in full force. "At the moment, the honor is mine. We are engaged." Noting their apprehension, she described everything that had occurred from the moment she entered the club till now and how wonderfully supportive

Paris was. "He told Charlie what to say to John and held my hand throughout the ordeal, but he wouldn't tell me what he planned to do. All he said was that the trap is set. Whether I'm the cheese or the mouse remains to be seen."

Iris's response was drowned in the sound of raging applause. The crowd split before them, and Isabel's heart stilled. Colonel Lord Ashby, Commander of the 18th Hussars, strolled into the ballroom with the Duke of Wellington, Lord Castlereagh, several MPs, and a mixed entourage of high ranking officers trailing behind. She knew how much he despised war and the hypocrisy surrounding it—and yet he did this for her: To save her charity and her friend; to free her from Hanson; and to claim her for his own. His grand entrance made her smile. A powerful earl and a decorated war hero, he certainly had a knack for doing things grandly.

Her eyes caressed him from head to toe: A royal blue dolman trimmed with bars of silver and adorned with medals stretched across the muscular expanse of his chest; snug white breeches molded his thighs down to shiny black jackboots; and a matching blue and silver pelisse, secure to his chest with a diagonal silver thread, slung rakishly from one shoulder. His dark brown hair was neatly cut to his nape; his eyes glittered with confidence and pride. *He was stunning*.

His eyes swiftly scanned the stately room and found her. Their gazes touched. The strength of his love lifted her angst and imbued her with courage and faith. *He is mine*, her heart affirmed. She was no longer forbidden to the dashing hussar who'd stolen her heart so long ago. Together they would prevail over John the Pest one way or the other, because their bond was unbreakable.

Overcome with emotion, tears sprang in her eyes. She had loved him for years, had grown into womanhood loving him, and that he should reciprocate her love with such intensity . . . humbled her. *I love you*, she mouthed.

I love you, he replied, his bluish-green eyes burning with longing.

"Here come Hanson and your brother," Iris alerted. "I suggest you tear your adoring gaze away from the god in regimentals and play your role of dutiful betrothed."

"Here you are, my dear." John handed her a glass of punch. "Ladies."

"Lady Chilton and Mrs. Fairchild should like to tender their congratulations on the happy occasion of our betrothal." Subtly Isabel elbowed Sophie. All at once her friends stammered out their best wishes, to which John replied in a most convincing display of affability. Isabel found it extremely difficult to concentrate on the commonplaces when her eyes kept sliding elsewhere.

Abruptly John's color rose; his eyes darted in every direction; he began fidgeting. He gave the impression of a man keen on bolting toward the privy.

"John, is something the matter?" Isabel inquired, wondering if Ashby had simply poisoned the rat.

"I . . . Excuse me." He took a step back and stumbled into Stilgoe, who wouldn't budge.

"Hanson!" a voice boomed behind her.

Isabel, Iris, and Sophie turned around to find Wellington standing a pace away, surrounded by several of his cronies. The ladies curtseyed; the gentlemen bowed.

"I hear congratulations are in order," the duke rumbled genially, grabbing John's hand and shaking it. He appraised the women. "And which of you ladies is the fortunate bride-to-be?"

"That would be me, your grace." Isabel dipped, stifling her annoyance. She had hoped to keep this farce of an engagement secret until its termination. *Blast it all.*

"Your grace." John's smile was tenuous; his countenance one of consternation.

"I am waiting to be properly introduced to this vision of loveliness, you rascal."

John tugged at his intricately knotted neckcloth. "Isabel, this is the legendary Duke of Wellington. My lord, I present my fiancée, Miss Isabel Aubrey."

A gleam of approval entered the duke's eyes as he took her hand. "Miss Aubrey, you've become a legend in your own right. 'Champion of war widows, defender of bereaved mothers, sisters, and little boys,'" he quoted the line in the *Times*. "You do your country a great service."

Isabel blushed. "Thank you, my lord. I've had tremendous support from one of your—"

"Have you found my wife a new cook yet?" Wellington interrupted her. "Won't have any peace until she has one." He winked at his uniformed gaggle, who cackled as if on cue.

Oh, dear. "I'm sorry, your grace, I didn't receive any such request." She turned aside. "Iris, Sophie, did any of you happen to . . . ?" They shook their heads. She was mortified. Of all their applicants, to misplace a request from the Duchess of Wellington was . . . an unmitigated disaster!

"Hanson, you dog!" Wellington grumbled lightheartedly. "Where is your head, m'boy?"

"I . . . I . . ." John stuttered in panic.

"Miss Aubrey, search this young man's pockets. You will find my two thousand pounds donation and a note from Lady Wellington specifying her persnickety request for a cook."

John was on the verge of having a fatal apoplexy. The one person he could never gainsay was the Duke of Wellington, the hero who'd trounced Napoleon and saved the world from ruin.

The noise in the ballroom diminished quickly into absolute silence.

"John?" Isabel prodded, while inside she was jumping with joy! John was ruined, unless he could come up with two thousand pounds, which he obviously couldn't. It was too large a sum to produce on such short notice when one spent it on the hazard tables. *Paris had pulled it off!* They were off the hook—Sophie, their charity, and . . . *She and Paris!* They would be together! How well Paris knew his nemesis! How clever and *generous* he was to set this brilliant trap!

Her gaze sought him everywhere; he was not to be found. The air stirred on her nape, and a comforting, familiar hand touched the small of her back. "Hanson," Paris's deep voice spoke behind her. "I believe you owe Miss Aubrey's charity the exact sum of two thousand pounds."

Boxed into a tight corner, Lord John Hanson did the only thing possible: He fled.

Harsh exclamations such as "He pocketed the Duke of Wellington's donation!", "He stole from charity!", and "The petty thief!" swelled uproariously. Stilgoe was telling everyone how the engagement was a ruse to expose Hanson's thievery. Isabel, Sophie, and Iris clasped hands.

"How did it come about?" her friends demanded to know all at once.

"Don't you see? It was all Ashby's doing." Isabel laughed, sending Paris a bright, adoring smile over her shoulder. "He put Wellington up to this. He gave the duke the blunt and the note."

"Last night, at White's," he confirmed, "when the three of you went out on your escapade."

"How could you know Hanson wouldn't hand over the bait to Isabel?" Sophie asked him.

He exhaled explosively. "I gambled."

"He's brilliant, that's all." Isabel faced Paris. Ignoring the crowd, she slid her hands up his chest, smiling at him. "What have I done to deserve you?" she whispered.

His face glowed with emotion as he wrapped his arms around her. "All my life I've been ashamed of my hunger for love. You gave me yours without my doing anything to deserve it and never took it back, no matter what I did or said or how undeserving I was of it. My Pure of Heart, I beg you now, love me always, for your love is more precious to me than life itself."

"*Mon Cœur de Lion* . . . You think I chose you? We don't choose the people we fall in love with. You stole my heart the day Will brought you into our home and never gave it back. I love you because I do. It is your loving me in return that makes me the most fortunate woman alive."

He kissed her, smiling, his eyes sparkling. "Will was our matchmaker. He ordered me to go read your letters. He said, 'If you ever find yourself alone and in need of family, go to Isabel.'"

"Good for Will." She laughed. "He must be very pleased with himself right now."

"Stealing another man's bride, Ashby?" Wellington's amused voice made them suddenly aware of the crowd of delighted snoops—her family and his hussars—converging around them.

Paris's warm smile enveloped her with love. "Actually, this one has always belonged to me." He removed a small object from his pocket, took Isabel's hand, and pulled off her glove. Nonplussed, she watched him sliding an obscenely huge, heart-shaped diamond onto her finger.

"Gads, Ashby," Stilgoe said. "She'll need personal guards to go about town with this ring."

"The woman who possesses the largest heart on earth deserves the largest heart of diamond the earth has yielded." He kissed her hand. "Twice you said 'no.' I am not asking this time."

"Twice?" She blinked, mystified. "Did I miss the second time?"

"At the picnic. You dashed away."

"I dashed away when you tried to . . ." *Seduce me*. Obviously she'd misconstrued his intent.

Understanding dawned in his eyes. "I think I've corrupted you, too," he murmured softly.

She examined her ring with awe. "Good education separates the man from the beast."

He put his lips to her ear. "Or brings the woman and the beast together."

"Now, now, Ashby, decorum!" Wellington rebuked with a twinkle in his eye. "Your ardors for this beauty are understandable, but bear in mind you set the standard for the entire regiment."

"I do?" Paris blinked innocently. "Well, in that case . . ." He embraced Isabel's waist, lifted her feet off the ground, and whirled her about, kissing her hard and openmouthed.

His hussars cheered boisterously. A cry went out, "He flies like lightning and strikes like a thunderbolt!" It was the most candid, heartwarming standing ovation any soldier ever received.

Paris set Isabel down and shook Wellington's hand. "Thanks for your assistance."

"I was repaying my debt of honor for what you did to Napoleon's Imperial Guard."

"What did he do?" Isabel asked the duke, leaning against Paris's broad shoulder.

"Demolished them at Waterloo," the duke replied, eyeing Paris fondly.

"Your secret stash of red-coated fellows made my task a lot easier," Paris acknowledged.

"You've snagged yourself the best of the lot, my dear," Wellington told Isabel.

"That's what everyone keeps telling me." She smiled up at Paris, squeezing the hand laced with hers. "But I knew that long before anyone else did."

"I wish you both very happy." The duke clapped Paris's back. "You are dismissed."

"Thank you." Paris exhaled. Isabel sensed his relief as though his soul was an extension of hers. "He let me go," he explained hauntingly. "I can now sell my commission and begin my life, with you, sweetness. Together we will put this war behind us."

"We can begin our life together tonight," she suggested

huskily, her heart thudding, her body tingling in anticipation. "Take me to Gretna Green, Colonel Lord Ashby."

He shook his head, mimicking her insulted pout. "Haven't I earned a church wedding with flowers and a champagne reception with family and friends around us, wishing us very happy?"

"Tell you what," she imitated him in return, running her hands over the silver bars of his blue dolman jacket. "I'll let you waltz with me and convince me why I should endure months of tedious courtship before I can spend every night making love with the man I adore . . ."

A bedroom look darkened his eyes. "When you put it this way . . ."

> *If thou must love me, let it be for naught*
> *Except for love's sake only. Do not say,*
> *'I love her for her smile—her look—her way*
> *Of speaking gently,—for a trick of thought*
> *That falls in well with mine, and certes brought*
> *A sense of pleasant ease on such a day'—*
> *For these things in themselves, Beloved, may*
> *Be changed, or change for thee—*
> *and love, so wrought,*
> *May be unwrought so. Neither love me for*
> *Thine own dear pity's wiping my cheeks dry:*
> *A creature might forget to weep, who bore*
> *Thy comfort long, and lose thy love thereby!*
> *But love me for love's sake, that evermore*
> *Thou mayst love on, through love's eternity.*
> *—Elizabeth Barrett Browning*